MISJUDGED

MISJUDGED

A NOVEL BY

GAIL TUSAN WASHINGTON

authorHOUSE®

AuthorHouse™
1663 Liberty Drive, Suite 200
Bloomington, IN 47403
www.authorhouse.com
Phone: 1-800-839-8640

*This book is a work of fiction. People, places, events, and situations
are the product of the author's imagination. Any resemblance to actual
persons, living or dead, or historical events, is purely coincidental.*

First published by AuthorHouse 12/19/2007

ISBN: 978-1-4343-5020-6 (sc)

*Printed in the United States of America
Bloomington, Indiana*

This book is printed on acid-free paper.

For Momo and Mama Tu,
Grandmas Lois, Helen and Dorothy,
and Grandmargaret,
the grandmothers who have blessed my family
with their abundant love.

ACKNOWLEDGMENT

The creation of Suzanne's story began a couple of years ago in a very special place in South Georgia called Sapelo Island. On a warm October afternoon, a small group of women boarded a ferryboat headed for the Sea Island Writers' Retreat. We spent the next few days talking, sharing, writing and most importantly, learning the tools for refining our craft from two incredible women, Tina McElroy Ansa and Blanche Richardson. I must thank Tina in particular for her invaluable feedback and encouragement empowering me to birth *Misjudged*.

Many individuals helped me with this project. I extend my heartfelt appreciation to the following individuals for their research and technical assistance: Bahiyya Amh-Shere, Annette Anderson, Cassandre Galette, Nicole Golson, Karlisle Grier, Jannifer Hill Keyes and Kara Walker. Joe Beck and Sheryl Morgan, thanks for checking-in on me throughout the process. Several others adjusted their busy schedules to read the manuscript. For their time and constructive criticism, I am deeply grateful to: Constance Curry, Kevin Franks, Wilma Jenkins, Angelique Jordan, Monica McCullough, Jennifer Monroe, Monica Parker, Makila Sands, Denise Speigl, Gary Spencer, Ike Umunnah and Mark Winne.

Without the loving support of my family, I would not have been able to put in the time required to give life to Suzanne's story. Ashley, Shannon, Lauren, Colin and Brian, thank you for encouraging me from beginning to end. Mom, thanks for believing in me and saving that cherished spot in your library for *Misjudged*. Dad and CV, thanks for your fatherly perspective on certain details of the story. I will forever treasure the thesaurus and dictionary my mother-in-law gave me prior to her passing. Theresa, thanks for your sisterly love and positive vibe. And finally, Carl, without your unwavering support *Misjudged* would still be just an idea floating around in my head. You, above everyone else, know what it is like to live with a writer: the countless requests to read my pages, and the time spent away from you while I was writing in my cave or on my sojourns to New Orleans and Cape Cod. Thank you, my love, for never complaining and always inspiring.

PROLOGUE

S uzanne tried to focus on her last Spanish exam question: **Why would Florentino, a self proclaimed virgin, bury himself in mindless sex as a weapon against the pain of separation from his true love, Fermina?** Five hundred Spanish words and her tenure at Wayne County Community College would be history. Still, her mind was empty and overflowing simultaneously. Her four years of high school Spanish were of no use. Neither were the three times she had read the Spanish novel, *Love in the Time of Cholera,* by Gabriel Garcia-Marquez. *Este impossible! No puedo pensar ahora!* She couldn't formulate anything to write down. *I might as well add my teacher to the growing list of people I've let down this miserable year.* Only fifty minutes remained before Professor Carlos Mora would collect the exam booklets.

The atmosphere was all wrong. Instead of pulling an all-nighter cramming for the exam with her UCLA roommate, Tammy, the one who spoke fluent Spanish and had aced her high school AP World Literature test, Suzanne had stayed up past midnight by herself. Alone, in her grandparents' guest room three thousand miles away, she had sat paralyzed with pain from the sharp kicks by the restless fetus nestled inside of her womb.

She'd selected the Spanish course to give her something to do during the final trimester of the pregnancy. The class had been challenging, yet interesting. Suzanne loved the story and its premise of unrequited love. She rubbed the curve of her very round stomach in a useless attempt to calm the baby. *Will any guy ever love me as deeply as Florentino loved Fermina? I wonder when Keith did it for the first time. No way was I his first, not the way he kept telling me he'd be gentle and not to worry.*

Suzanne looked at the clock on the wall of the classroom. Twenty-two minutes remained. Suzanne opened her notebook and started to write. She only got ten words down on the page when she felt the long anticipated warm fluid gush down her pant leg and form an embarrassing puddle under her chair. Suzanne didn't move anything other than her yellow Converse sneakers to keep them from getting wet. She waited until the bell sounded and the last student handed in his exam booklet before budging.

Professor Mora looked inquisitively over the top of his glasses at his star student and in a rare moment, spoke English. "Suzanne, time is up. Even my best students have to abide by the rules."

She stood up with all of her might, stuck her pencil in her book bag and walked slowly toward his desk, squeezing her sticky thighs together, trying to keep everything in place until she could call her grandmother to come save her from the nightmare unfolding. Suzanne really wanted her mother, but she wasn't due to arrive into Detroit until the next day. There was no way the pregnant teenager would be able to take the bus home as planned. Suzanne handed Professor Mora her exam.

"Suzanne, you're perspiring. Are you not feeling well, muchacha?"

She looked blankly at her professor. She'd misjudged her ability to pretend any longer. Nothing about the previous nine months was okay. Not Keith or his reaction to learning she'd gotten pregnant, nor her mother shooing her out of Southern California until she had to come home. In fact, if anyone cared to know, as far as Suzanne was concerned, the entire situation sucked. The sad thing was if anyone did care, nobody bothered to ask.

All of a sudden, everything was blurry. The exam questions written in Spanish on the chalkboard behind his desk began to shift. And so did Suzanne. Before she could answer him, all went dark in Suzanne's world. She passed out. When the quiet girl from California came to, her life as she once knew it might well have been a misplaced black and white photograph.

♥

The distinctive smell of childbirth hung in the air. With one final bloody push it was over. All eyes and attention shifted from between Suzanne's legs to the squirming neonate in Dr. Silas' firm hands. Suzanne's body was hers once again. The shy, eighteen-year-old college student closed her quivering thighs and gingerly lowered them on the damp, soiled hospital sheet. She was a smart, young woman paying a high price for trying to fit in. The messy display of body fluids at the end of the delivery table painted a sobering backdrop for Suzanne's sacrifice.

"Dr. Silas, would you please make an exception and let me hold him for a few moments," Suzanne said in a husky, leaden voice.

At least there were no more foreign objects violating private places. For that Suzanne was grateful. Not a happy gratitude. Something more akin to a dull relief, camouflaging deep remorse for having screwed up big time. She watched the obstetrical nurse wash and wrap her son.

"Dear, I don't think that's a very good idea," Mrs. Vincent said, frowning as she studied her daughter. "You've been through a lot. Holding him will only upset you." After a long nine months, it was time to return to normal. And normal didn't include cuddling a bastard child.

"All I want to do is tell my baby goodbye," Suzanne pressed. She avoided making eye contact with her mother. "That's all, Dr. Silas."

Suzanne glanced over at the door where the adoptive parents anxiously hovered outside of the delivery room like buzzards contemplating their kill. Their muffled cheer and a cold draft of air filtered in through the opening below the door. *How dare you be happy. Go away and leave us alone.* Her son would become theirs soon enough.

Dr. Silas smiled at his patient and nodded assent. Suzanne wasn't the typical teenage mother. She'd grown up an only child, cradled in upper middle class suburbia.

"Mrs. Vincent, won't you give us a moment?" He motioned to the door.

Suzanne shifted on the table seeking out a dry spot before reaching up to receive her son from Dr. Silas. She carefully took her baby, holding him close for a few uninterrupted moments, smelling and fingering his newness. Looking directly into his alert, dark brown eyes, Suzanne spoke softly to her son. "Riley, I'll make this up to you. Somehow. No matter what, I'll never forget you, baby boy. Love you."

She kissed him lightly on his forehead, whispered goodbye and handed him back to Dr. Silas. The nurse took the baby from the physician and headed outside to show him to his soon-to-be-parents. Dr. Silas remained in the room with Suzanne. He pulled up a chair and sat down, facing his patient.

"You're a brave young woman, Suzanne," Dr. Silas said, smiling at her.

"I don't feel brave." She frowned. "Nobody told me giving him up would be so hard."

"In time, living with your decision will become easier. Not to worry. They'll take good care of him." Suzanne made an effort to smile. Dr. Silas patted her shoulder lightly. "But right now, young lady, we need to get you moved to a more comfortable room. Don't try to do too much too soon. Get some rest. And, Suzanne—

"Yes, Dr. Silas?"

"Promise me you won't use this experience as a lifelong excuse."

"I promise, Dr. Silas."

One promise to her son, the other to the grandfatherly physician. Through both promises, Suzanne claimed a better place.

ONE

"Here's to Affirmative Action!" The cocky, boyish looking prosecutor sealed his toast with a messy final swallow of beer. He wiped his mouth with the back of his hand and confidently grinned at Sam Haskell. The older man returned the salute with his raised bottle.

"Here, here. I'll drink to that any damn day. We're gonna affirmatively kick the Pantyhose Brigade the hell outta my courthouse."

Chance Rotherman was pumped, sitting at a table toward the back of Headlamps with the chief judge of the Atlanta District Court. Only two more weeks and he would officially qualify as a candidate for the judicial seat that should've been his in the first place. His time had finally come.

The judge's cousin, Lou, owned the establishment. Free beer, free counsel, pretty women. An ambitious senior assistant district attorney couldn't ask for much more. It was late afternoon, not yet time for happy hour or the feature act. Rotherman looked around, over his shoulder. Relieved, he saw no sign of Escobar Secret. They'd met at the gym and after a few discreet lunchtime trysts, she'd invited him there to see her dance. Perhaps she had the day off. Rotherman turned back to Haskell.

"I'm sorry, Chief. What were you saying?"

"Relax, son. We'll be long gone before the place fills up." Haskell laughed with a wink. "Unless, of course, you wanna sneak a peek before you hit the campaign trail."

The judge had no idea that his protégé knew one of the Headlamp's most popular dancers a little too well. Rotherman laughed off the invitation.

"Hmmm. No thanks, Chief. I promised the little wife I'd pick up the kids from daycare today." Rotherman checked his watch.

"Good answer, good answer. Your public expects family values. If you're gonna wear a black robe, you gotta know when to keep your nose clean and your fly zipped. You get my meaning, Rotherman?"

"Now, Chief, have I ever given you reason to question my judgment, legal or otherwise?"

"Absolutely not. That's why I'm backing you over Suzanne Vincent. I warned the governor not to appoint her, but she wouldn't listen."

"Has Suzy Q fucked up any more?"

"You'll be the first to know if I catch a whiff of anything," Haskell said. "You should get a lot of mileage out of that adoption fiasco in her courtroom earlier this spring."

"That's what I was hoping, but that's sort of old news, isn't it?"

"Nothing is old news during a political campaign. All you need is the right spin doctor and a few choice opportunities to highlight your opponent's liabilities. Talk about opportunities, you do appreciate why I appointed Vincent to head up next week's Adoption Day, don't you?"

Rotherman quickly nodded his head, although when he'd heard, he began to doubt Haskell's allegiance. Suddenly, it came to him what needed to be done.

"I'm on it."

"That's my boy!"

"'Scuse me, gentlemen." They looked up from their conversation at the waitress. "Lou sent me over to see if you want another round." Bethany Lovejoy was pretty in an unassuming way. No extensions, tattooed eyebrows or synthetic boobs like the other girls who entertained at Headlamps.

"Nah. Thanks, hon. I think we're about to wrap things up," Haskell said.

Rotherman didn't recognize the girl from any of his previous visits. She lingered beside the table.

"Lou told me I could ask you somethin'. He said you were a judge." She looked at Haskell.

Haskell tried not to scowl. His cousin should've known better. "What's that, little lady?"

"I have a case with my kid's daddy. We go to court next week."

"Is that so?"

"Yeah. I can't afford a lawyer and I'm worried."

"You'll do fine, I'm sure," Haskell lied. Pro se litigants almost never fared well in court. There was a reason God created lawyers.

"My judge's name is Judge Vincent. Is he okay?"

"Sure." Haskell chuckled. "Hey Rotherman, what've you heard about Judge Vincent?"

"About the same, I guess. By the way, Judge Vincent is a she."

"Really? Cool. A lady judge."

"Yes, she's quite a trailblazer," Haskell said. He pulled out his wallet and tipped Bethany with a ten dollar bill. Over his career, he'd been called a lot of things. Cheap was not one of them.

"Thanks a lot, Mister." Bethany collected their empty bottles and left.

"Might not be a bad idea to have someone poke around a bit; maybe even sit in on a few of Vincent's hearings. You never know."

"Chief, I appreciate your support. I really want this." Rotherman reached across the table and offered a firm hand.

Sam Haskell returned his handshake, looking Rotherman straight in the eye. "You won't win if you try to play nice."

TWO

Oliver Mason, Suzanne's mentor and the newly announced managing partner at her former law firm, McKinney & Lasley, had called late that afternoon to ask that she stop by after work to discuss a possible television appearance on the *AM Atlanta Show*. In his world, even judges rearranged their schedules to be where he commanded them to be. Oliver was chairing Suzanne's 2006 re-election campaign committee. He'd been dialing up folks asking for contributions and plotting for months.

Wow! It's hard to believe I've been gone for almost five years. Memories from her days as a medical malpractice defense lawyer rushed back as Suzanne parked. Billable hours and clients' emergencies commanded her full attention. Now, as a trial judge, she did the commanding. The beautiful, brilliant bold woman in the black robe preferred plans going her way. Suzanne thrived on calling the shots. She loved being a judge. The intellectual challenge of a civil case got her out of bed long before dawn reviewing the files and reading the briefs to make sure she hadn't missed anything. The heart wrenching complexities of a domestic case and the dull eyes of the abused and neglected children kept her held up in her chambers late at night dining on microwaved Ramen noodles. Despite the pressure of her job, as far as the public and her mother were concerned, she had little to complain about. Professional acclaim and success came early for Suzanne and for that reason she made a point of playing the part of judge as others expected her to. The role required her to keep her personal issues to herself.

She loved her job. No question. Every once in a while, though, she yearned to be back in front of a jury arguing her case. The challenge always boiled down to keeping the jury's sympathy for the plaintiff from driving the verdict in the wrong direction.

"Ladies and Gentlemen of the Jury, let me remind you that the issue for you to decide is whether or not my client's treatment of the plaintiff met the requisite standard of care. Once you have carefully considered the evidence, I am confident that all twelve of you will agree that it most definitely did."

She stuck it out for eight years, putting in the long hours and making the personal sacrifices required. Her clients and the firm came before everything. After racking up a string of defense verdicts exonerating the reputations of many of Atlanta's finest physicians, McKinney & Lasley made Suzanne a partner. The firm's founding partner, then retired, was first in line to congratulate her. It was the least he could do after mistaking her for a secretary the first time he met her. *I bet Ole' Man McKinney would roll over in his grave at the thought of a black woman dispensing justice.*

Not long after she joined the partnership, a vacancy opened up on the Atlanta District Court. Oliver insisted that she apply for the position. Suzanne obliged, fully aware that Chance Rotherman was the buzz. *"You know I've paid my dues and this seat is mine,"* Rotherman reminded her as they sat in the governor's reception area waiting for their interviews, his politician's fake smile as sharp as a shard of glass. *"Your turn will come."* She expected simply to test the waters, float her name as a prospective judicial candidate in the inner circles of the legal community and return to practicing law. Much to her surprise and that of the heir apparent, she got the governor's nod.

Suzanne checked her reflection in the polished brass plated elevator doors before they opened. *You got it going on, girl. Let's hope the voters agree.* The receptionist recognized her immediately and phoned to let Oliver know she had arrived. Suzanne took a seat in one of the overstuffed tapestry armchairs in the firm's lobby on the forty-ninth story of the Crickman Consortium Building. It was the first time since very early that morning she had a chance to be still and catch her breath. Suzanne gazed out the picture windows framing the waiting area toward the tall state-of-the-art skyscrapers and the new Georgia Aquarium standing out on Atlanta's horizon. Urban sprawl leaped out in every direction.

Behind her, a large original oil canvas of the firm's founders hung on the wall. Suzanne turned back from the window, hearing her former partner's wing-tipped shoes stepping across the waxed white marble foyer past the receptionist desk in her direction.

Oliver Mason was a robust man in his late fifties, with sharp facial features and jet black wavy hair. He was known throughout the city's finest dining establishments and business clubs for his imported collection of handmade bowties and gregarious personality.

"Suzanne, it's so good to see you. You look fabulous!" He leaned down to pull her up out of the chair and planted a kiss on her cheek. Suzanne's shoulder length bob was pulled back into an elegant chignon. She wore a cherry-red silk wool blend suit, with a tailored jacket and a pencil skirt with kick pleats, cherry fishnets and black suede heels. "Let's go back to my office where we can talk."

She walked beside him past her old office through the highly appointed hallways where much of McKinney & Lasley's southern folk art was displayed. The small space now housed some other young associate. *I remember how thrilled I was to hang my diplomas and that black and white photograph of the Grandma Vincent's family house in New Orleans' Historic Garden District.* The firm had the largest private collection in the Southeast. *As much as the firm has invested in the art, it's a shame no one has time to appreciate it.*

As they breezed through the office, Suzanne noticed the firm was still bustling with activity as harried attorneys, paralegals and secretaries remained at their desks eking out a few more billable hours, trying to keep clients happy and supervisors off their backs. She caught the eye of a few of the lawyers who looked up from their work to be acknowledged by Oliver. The creased foreheads, quick nods and tight smiles said it all. To make it at the firm, laboring past sundown and missing dinner and bedtime stories with spouses and children was a given. They wanted the managing partner to take note of who was still there slaving away and, just as importantly, who was not.

Suzanne and her mentor turned one last corner to reach his ornate, corner double office – a rainmaker's haven with all of the accoutrements that impressed clients. As he closed the leather-paneled door, the judge noticed a platter of gourmet sandwiches, condiments, chips and freshly baked molasses cookies was set out on a buffet near a sitting area under the elaborate, imported wood inlaid tray ceiling.

"Please, help yourself. I figured you wouldn't have time to grab anything to eat, so I ordered us a little something from Edible Briefs downstairs," Oliver said.

"How thoughtful, Oliver," Suzanne said. At the mention of the delicatessen, Suzanne fondly remembered the countless times she and her boyfriend, John English, had met there to grab a quick late lunch during those busy work weeks when their schedules left no time for a leisurely dinner together.

Oliver waited until Suzanne had fixed herself a small plate. She picked up a black linen M & L gold monogrammed napkin and spread it over her lap.

"What would you like to drink?" Oliver asked.

"I would love a glass of wine."

Oliver shot her one of his infamous scolding looks. *Well, why did you ask, then?* He opened a cabinet under the bookshelves and selected a bottle of wine.

Suzanne needed something to take the edge off. Something told her this meeting was going to take awhile.

THREE

Oliver poured two glasses of wine and set them on an end table between their chairs. Suzanne frowned. His glass was full. Hers contained little more than a tasting. *Okay, Oliver, you've made your point.*

"You know you can't drink alcohol on the campaign trail," he said. "Everything you do will be open to discussion. Hear me when I say, image is everything. But later for your crash course in Campaign Etiquette 101, there're more pressing issues to discuss."

"Like?"

"Like your cantankerous chief judge and his boy, Chance Rotherman."

"No possibility he's going to change his mind and sit out the race, eh?"

"Suzanne, I'd hoped as much as you that at the end of this month, we'd slap down your qualifying check and go on vacation. That's not likely to happen. Rotherman plans to oppose you."

"Lucky me."

"Haskell outsmarted himself by putting you in charge of Adoption Day. Don't think for a moment that he's forgiven you for that little tragedy in the courthouse."

I'm not sure I'd call a deranged mother barging into my courtroom to block the adoption of her newborn child and then jumping out of the open window, plummeting to her instant death, a little tragedy.

"It's been a lot of work getting ready for it, Oliver. My office has reviewed all of the adoption files three times to make sure everything is in order. There will be no mistakes this time."

"What do you mean, this time? You didn't make any mistakes the last time. Hell, Suzanne, are you planning to give your job away?"

"No."

"As a candidate, you're gonna have to talk the way you write your judicial opinions: with deliberate precision, each and every word. Understand?"

"Understood."

"I'm sure it has been taxing organizing the event, but Haskell isn't trying to punish you. He appointed you so there would be a public event to rehash what happened. Prepare for it just as you would for a public flogging."

"Oh, Oliver, aren't you being just a tad melodramatic."

Oliver pressed on, determined to fine tune his candidate's mindset. She might be more difficult to manage than he'd thought.

"I know Haskell. Trust me when I say he's out to get you. I wouldn't put anything past him. He wants blood. Rotherman is still his candidate."

"But I'm the incumbent, his colleague, after all. Doesn't that count for anything?"

"Are you kidding? This is politics, Suzanne. Get ready to play dirty."

Suzanne nodded as she listened to Oliver, and took a sip of her wine. Voting and writing a few contribution checks were the extent of her political involvement. Public service was one thing. Running a campaign was another. The judge knew how lucky she was to have Oliver run her campaign.

"I ran into a reporter friend of mine. She's going to try and squeeze in a story about you and Adoption Day in the next day or so."

"How nice."

"I gave her your private line in chambers in case they decide to go with the story. This kind of publicity is priceless, Suzanne."

"Oh, I know." Suzanne tried to look as excited as Oliver did.

"Once the campaign is officially underway, we'll have to pay big bucks for airtime and the press will have to give Rotherman equal access. We want everybody to know you and the great job you're doing on the bench."

Suzanne set her plate down. The governor had appointed her to a newly created seat on the Atlanta District Court. Judges in her district served six year terms. She needed fifty-one percent of the electorate's votes to hang onto her black robe.

"Did you bring the sound bite I asked you to prepare?"

"Yes, here, take a look." Suzanne pulled out the short spiel and handed it to Oliver. He frowned as he perused what she'd written.

"What's wrong, you don't like it?"

He did some quick editing and handed it back to her.

"That's a good start. It sounds like you're trying to educate viewers about foster kid adoptions."

"And I'm not? What's the point then?"

"To get folks fired up about justice a la Suzanne Vincent. In fact, you know what? I think we should consider making adoption reform a central part of your re-election platform."

No, Oliver, please; anything but adoptions.

Oliver drilled Suzanne on her answers to the television host's likely questions. She would take control of the interview so the viewers would hear what she, the candidate, needed them to know. He made Suzanne practice how to sit, gesture, and mesmerize the television audience. Oliver paused to jot something on his legal pad.

"Okay you, I recognize that 'I'm on to something look'," Suzanne probed. They had worked closely at the firm. "Whattaya got going there on the pad?"

"Hold on for a minute." Still writing, he held up his other hand. "How do you like this for a campaign slogan: Don't take a chance, vote for a sure thing. Re-elect Judge Suzanne Vincent?"

She flashed him her winner's smile. "I like it!"

"Good. We can play with it for a few days, but I think the spin on Rotherman's name will work."

"What do you think his angle will be?"

"We'll know soon enough. But it doesn't matter. You're the one with the judicial experience and proven track record. You're doing the job, he merely wants it. Every opportunity, you've got to hit home with these bullets."

"Yikes, Oliver. Bullets? You make it sound like urban warfare."

"That's exactly what it is," he replied, dark eyes gleaming. "And my job is to get you ready for it."

FOUR

Oliver's latest bride called, interrupting his meeting with Suzanne.

Suzanne finished off her wine and food while Oliver spoke in hushed tones over by his desk, his back to her. "Yes, Sugarlump. Yes, yes, I know. I miss you too. I'll be home soon."

He hung up and walked back to sit adjacent to her. He laid a folder on the couch next to him. *I do believe Oliver is blushing.*

"Sorry about that interruption. Now where were we?"

"Oliver, you've been so generous with your time. I know how busy you are and –

"Never too busy to help a friend. Let me ask you something before we call it quits for tonight. Is there anything you're not prepared to deal with publicly, Suzanne?" Oliver asked, looking across at her intently.

"I'm not sure I'm following you, Oliver." Suzanne's grip on the edge of her seat cushion tightened hearing his question.

"You're very important to me, Suzanne. The firm has invested a lot in you and is very proud of you," he said. "I've watched you develop from a baby lawyer to a trial judge, a very fine one in the making, if I may add." He broke into a broad grin. "That is, once you remembered that in order to act the part, you actually have to wear your robe."

They both laughed, remembering how she was in such a hurry for her first time to take the bench that she had walked out of her chambers, head high, file under her arm, leaving her new robe on the back of the chair in her chambers.

"Now you had to go and bring that up again. Talk about embarrassing," Suzanne murmured, her mind still on his last question.

"However, you know me. Nobody is going to catch me with my pants down." *As I recall your last wife did, right here in this fabulous office of yours.* "Rotherman is arrogant enough to think he can do your job better than you. Contested elections aren't pretty and with the new rules and all, your record, background, all of it will be fair game." He cleared his throat. "Once you step out on that campaign trail, you can say goodbye to your privacy. They'll start with the 3-H's—

"What do you mean, the 3-H's?" *Why don't I already know this stuff?*

"Your hairdo, your hemline and your husband, or in your case, the lack of one. They'll pounce on your cases taken up to the Supremes, your sentencing patterns. And if you're not careful, when you least expect it, your deepest secret could end up as the front page news."

"You're scaring me, Oliver."

"Mission accomplished. If there's anything you'd rather folks not know, promise me, you'll tell me first. I want to know before Rotherman does. Haskell is watching and will be digging for anything to use against you."

All of a sudden, Suzanne felt flushed and exposed under Oliver's scrutiny. His pointed questions bore into her like a carpenter bee. *Why is he zeroing in on me like this? What a fool I've been. I bet he already knows.* Suzanne stalled for a long moment, uncrossed her legs and reached down into her purse fumbling to find a mint. When she applied for her judgeship, her mouth fell open at the extensiveness of the application. Twenty pages long, replete with personal questions reaching as far back to college. She cleared the personal background check and extensive vetting without anyone stumbling upon that one piece of information. *You won't be the first political candidate to have her promising career destroyed by raw truth and youthful indiscretion. You better tell him.*

"Nothing comes to mind," Suzanne said. Conflicted, she avoided Oliver's eye. "No disgruntled spouse, offshore accounts, unpaid taxes, nothing. Really."

Suzanne was ready to change the subject. She nervously reached for her wine glass, and then sat back, remembering it was empty. Out of the corner of her eye, she saw Oliver staring at her.

"You're saying you have no regretted decisions?" Oliver pressed to see if Suzanne would do as he asked and confide in him.

"Well, there have been a couple of reversals I wasn't too happy about," she conceded.

Oliver sat back against the sofa and cracked his broad knuckles.

"Suzanne, that goes with the territory. This is me, kid. Stop bullshitting. Let's cut to the chase." The attorney looked the judge squarely in the eye. "How will you respond if someone asks you point blank to explain what happened? Forget that the law says the record is sealed. I have the file right here."

Oliver patted the brown folder resting next to him. *Did I just hear him correctly? How did Oliver find out? Who else knows?*

"I-I-I'm not sure," she stammered. "Where did you get that—

"Now maybe you'll believe me. It's human nature to cover up things about which we feel vulnerable. Disarm the opposition by disclosing those things yourself. Better to be proactive, than put on the defensive. Remember, Suzanne, just like you used to do when we tried cases together. Take the sting out of cross examination by dealing with it on direct."

Oliver stood, signally the end of their meeting. He handed her the unmarked file. Suzanne opened it, her heart pounding and her legs feeling weak. The folder was empty.

"I strongly suggest you go home, and bring closure to whatever it is you're not telling me, Suzanne. Life is a series of decisions and lessons. There are no mistakes. Got that, Your Honor?"

"Got it."

Maybe my campaign brochure could lead off with this personal quote: "I got pregnant in college. My son's name is Riley. Funny thing, there's a good probability that he's living here in Atlanta. Just not with me." Can't be more direct than that, now can I?

FIVE

No one else was yet in the office when Suzanne arrived Wednesday morning. Her meeting with Oliver kept her from sleeping well. It was long before her staff was due. The judge liked her chambers best when she had the entire office to herself. Her sergeant didn't like her to be there alone, unprotected, but she actually found the quiet comforting. As she sat at her desk sipping her favorite caffeine concoction, a low-fat caramel macchiato, the judge felt much better than she had in quite a while.

Her chambers stood out in the stately turn-of-the-century courthouse. Inspired by the legal cases she was charged to resolve, the judge's personal working space was accented with tones of black, white and gray. She worked from a large black contemporary desk, always in order. At the very front of her desk rested her nameplate retired from McKinney & Lasley. A few special items were carefully arranged to her left on the desktop – a handmade doll made by a group of girls she mentored, the crystal butterfly her parents gave her when she graduated from law school, and a framed picture of a Turks and Caicos sunset she had shared with John. *I miss you, Muffin. Our talks, your firm body, everything...*

Two black and grey upholstered chairs stood in front of her desk for attorneys, their clients or whoever might need a moment of her time. White embroidered pillows rested in the chairs and on the long black couch against the wall. A mounting stack of files awaiting written orders were stacked on the conference table. Opposite the couch was an entire wall of bookcases holding the tan and red case reporters the judge preferred using for research instead of her online legal library.

Out of habit she picked up the phone to dial John, and then slammed down the phone, as she looked at her clock, remembering they now were in different time zones and that he was probably still asleep. *"A change of scenery will do you a world of good. Suzanne, you're not Mother Theresa. You need to take a break from the dysfunction those families and their lawyers constantly dump in your lap, put your hectic routine on hold, and take care of yourself for a change. Or better yet, let me take care of you. I'm really concerned about you, baby."*

On Valentine's Day, John had served her a candlelit dinner. They'd eaten his English Pea Risotto and a Shitake Mushroom Soufflé fireside in his newly renovated loft in the Historic Old Fourth Ward. She'd spotted the signature turquoise ring box tied with the white satin ribbon tucked behind the antique pewter candelabra on the mantle over the fireplace. The conversation turned to their tenuous relationship, and how little quality time they spent together. He suggested a getaway cruise. Suzanne put him off claiming it was not a convenient time to be away from court. He pressed her on when would be a better time. She was embarrassed by the lameness of her response. They finished the evening with cordials and had each other for dessert. When dawn came, it was time for her to get dressed for work. The turquoise box remained unopened and out of plain view.

She sat at the desk with her back to the sunrise and forced herself to concentrate on her notes taken the previous day in the custody hearing underway in the *Lovejoy v. Wainwright case.* As was often the case, the demands of her job required the judge to table her personal troubles. What started as an uncomplicated paternity petition seeking child support had mushroomed into a full-blown custody action. At the moment, the most pressing issue before her was procuring a parenting plan for the two young people who had stumbled into parenthood and would be returning to her courtroom in little over an hour.

The day before, Suzanne heard testimony from everyone who had a stake in the custody decision with the exception of the child at issue, a two year old boy named Damien, and his mother,

Bethany Lovejoy. Because of the legal posture of the cross-claims, the mother was scheduled to be the last witness. It didn't take Suzanne long to pick up on the unhealthy dynamic in the case. Damien Lovejoy's young mother coped by simplifying her son's best interests. One plus for the mother was that she, at least, was trying. The father, Quentin Wainwright, came off as oblivious that the judge would expect him to care about his child's welfare. Quentin's mother was still babying him and he seemed to fully expect that she should do the same for his progeny.

Damien's basic physical needs could be met at either parent's address. Regardless of whether his clothes were designer boutique treasures purchased by his paternal grandmother, hand laundered daily by the dowager's hired help, or thrift shop bargains snatched up by his tired cocktail waitress mom that she washed at the corner laundromat, he was well clothed. Suzanne's much greater concern was the child's mental well being. She wanted to protect his precious psyche from being singed by the predictable sparks set off whenever his mother's pistol pride clashed with his grandmother's arrogance or challenged his father's indifference.

By the time Suzanne had drained the last drop of cold coffee, she had finished reviewing her notes and could hear the front office coming to life for another day of courthouse drama. Her staff's voices and the ringing telephone trailed into her office. It was a few minutes before nine and the beginning of court.

She had just enough time to run into her "inner chambers" to make sure she had on her judge's face. Locked inside her bathroom, Suzanne stared into the mirror for a long moment. *Where is Riley at this very moment, and what is he doing?* Her face's stoic reflection willed her to put on her robe and set about the task of putting others' lives in order. There were families whose happily ever after waited to be crafted at her hand.

Six

Judge Vincent slipped on her black robe, picked up the file and headed out for the courtroom. Her judicial assistant, Andi, handed her a fresh cup of coffee and a smile — a good start for the day. Sergeant Quarles was waiting for her in the private hall behind the courtroom. He greeted her, opened the door to the courtroom and called court to order.

"All rise," the bailiff commanded.

The judge settled into her tall blue leather chair behind the massive bench at the front of her courtroom. Everyone remained standing, waiting for her to tell them to take their seats as she had the day before. But Judge Vincent was preoccupied with personal matters and forgot to do so. She set her cup down and logged onto her laptop. Judge Vincent signed onto the instant messenger she and Andi used to communicate during the day when the judge was conducting hearings. Recognizing that the judge was distracted and had forgotten that the parties and the attorney were still on their feet, Sergeant Quarles motioned to everyone to have a seat.

It was a beautiful, austere courtroom consisting of a sea of warm teak paneled walls, sturdy desks, turquoise chair cushions and matching pew pads to make the long stints of sitting more comfortable for the jurors, lawyers, litigants and the audience. The white-haired attorney and his clients had seized one table for their camp and the pro se petitioner sat at the other. The attorney couldn't tell if he should wait for the judge to say something or not, so he spoke up.

"Your Honor, for our final witness, we call Bethany Lovejoy."

The attorney's announcement brought Judge Vincent's attention back to where it needed to be. She recovered and nodded from her bench at Paul Yates, the seasoned, family law attorney who specialized in representing fathers seeking custody of their children. Then the judge glanced over at the second table where her dark brown eyes locked with those of the single young mother seated there. From the moment the hearing had started the day before, Bethany Lovejoy had been at the petitioner's table, alone. No lawyer. No family. No friends. *She's just a kid herself. What a shame to be going through this all alone.*

"Ms. Lovejoy, please come take the witness stand," Judge Vincent directed, pointing to the seat positioned between her bench and the jury box. The judge took a quick sip of her coffee.

After listening to Quentin, his mother and the guardian *ad litem* she had appointed to investigate the case, Judge Vincent was ready to hear from Damien's mother. Bethany rose from her seat slowly. The girl appeared flustered as she clumsily gathered the few sheets of notebook paper she had been writing on during the previous day. She wore her hair in a short, low maintenance do. There was no way Quentin's lawyer could argue that Bethany squandered money on herself at the expense of the child.

Bethany walked toward the witness stand located to the left of the judge's bench. It was clear that the teenage mother had made an effort to dress for court. Yet, her attire was no match for the knitted, jeweled, heavily perfumed ensemble across the room. Perhaps fearing Quentin's mother would use the skimpiness of her only good dress against her, the cocktail waitress clutched the front of her white denim, fur trimmed jacket as her baby's grandmother glared at her behind. Bethany's black jersey dress was tight and bore slits on both sides, exposing much more of the young woman's thighs than anyone present needed to see. The run in her black grocery store hose was far less noticeable than the squeaking emanating from her bargain basement pumps.

Bethany watched anxiously as the bailiff, Sgt. Quarles, approached her and set the customary "this is to help you relax" cup of water several inches before her on the witness stand. When the muscular deputy spoke to administer the oath, Bethany jumped, knocking over the paper cup. Water splashed everywhere, some of it ruining her notepaper. The deputy quickly came to Bethany's aid. He blotted the wasted water with paper towels, and tossed the clump of used towels and cup in the trashcan. Judge Vincent smiled sympathetically at Bethany and patiently waited for the girl to collect herself.

"Please raise your right hand," Sgt Quarles said, when Bethany appeared ready to proceed. "Do you swear to tell the truth, the whole truth and nothing but the truth?"

"Uh-huh." Judge Vincent shook her head at the witness. "I mean, yes," Bethany said.

"Bethany, you're our last witness," Judge Vincent spoke in her firm, but gentle tone. "Quentin's lawyer, Mr. Yates here, is going to ask you some questions. I need you to answer them, please. Okay?"

Bethany nodded. The young mother had no idea what was getting ready to happen. Folks hired Paul Yates when money was not an issue and the stakes were high. The more he got paid, the fiercer he became with his cross-examination. In this case, the father, Quentin Wainwright, was only nineteen. The blond spike-haired, blue-eyed kid sat slouched down in his chair at the petitioner's table — a nominal party at best. Owning up to fatherhood was the least of his concerns.

The true instigator behind the custody case was his mother, Desiree Wainwright, who sat directly behind Quentin. She had money, and she meant to win. Not because she was eager to take on the toilet training of her grandson, however. The arrogant matriarch simply had no intentions of bankrolling her son's child support obligations created by some unprotected sex.

"Very well. You may begin now, counsel."

"Thank you, Your Honor." Paul Yates stood, fastening the middle button of his black, pinstriped, hand tailored suit. He stepped up to the podium centered between his table and where Bethany had been sitting, ready to begin what he had been paid to do.

"Ms. Lovejoy, you're contesting my client's petition for custody of Damien, true?

"Yes."

"You believe that you're able to provide Damien with a better lifestyle than Quentin and his mother?"

"Yes. Well no, I mean yes," Bethany sputtered, not sure how to answer the lawyer's compound question.

"And what basis could you possibly have for claiming you can do better by this child than the Wainwrights?" Paul Yates scoffed.

"Because I'm his mother, and he needs to be with me."

"And Quentin is his father. So, what other reasons do you have?" The attorney responded with a sneer.

"Mr. Yates, let's not go there!"

"As you wish, Your Honor," Paul Yates responded through clenched teeth, visibly annoyed that the judge had interrupted him. He paused to regroup and took a sip of the cup of water he had placed on the right edge of the podium where he stood. The judge suspected that the attorney was not accustomed to being chastised when doing what he got paid to do.

Bolstered by the judge's admonition of the lawyer, Bethany sat up a little bit in the witness chair.

"Now Ms. Lovejoy, you heard Quentin testify yesterday, didn't you, that he's tried many times to visit with Damien and you won't make him available?"

The mother leaned forward toward the microphone as she gained the strength to say what needed to be said.

"Your client doesn't want Damien."

Judge Vincent noticed Bethany's chair was positioned dangerously close to the edge of the platform. It was too late to warn her. Before anyone could do anything to prevent the fall, Bethany's chair slid off the platform, throwing the girl onto the floor. She struggled to pull down her dress which had risen to around her waist, exposing her tattered underwear. Sgt. Quarles rushed to help her up. Desiree Wainwright feigned scolding her son, who was doubled over in laughter, and signaled to him to straighten up and pour her a cup of water. Everyone waited for Bethany to pull herself back together.

"You were saying, Bethany..." Judge Vincent interceded, trying to level the playing field.

Bethany took a deep breath. "Quentin never comes by to see him or offers to help with him. This is all about what she wants." Everyone knew Bethany was referring to Quentin's mother.

"In fact, you don't think Damien really needs any one but you, do you?"

"That's not true."

"Well, let's see here..." The lawyer turned to take a note from Mrs. Wainwright who was perched on the edge of her seat. "Have you ever taken him to visit his father?"

"Quentin is the one with all the free time and the car. I keep too busy with school and stuff. Besides, I take the bus, and it doesn't run out where Quentin stays."

"I see. Well, what about Quentin coming to visit you and Damien in the evening?"

Quentin cracked his knuckles. His attorney glared at him, shaking his head for him to stop.

"I work at night," Bethany said.

"Yes, that's what the guardian *ad litem* told us. What's the name of the place again – uh, Headlights?" Paul Yates was on a roll. He confidently leaned against the side of the podium as he continued with his questioning.

"It's Headlamps, sir."

"I stand corrected. Now—

"And it's not the kind of place you making it out to be. Lots of our customers look and talk just like you."

Suzanne looked over at her bailiff, who winked.

"Ms. Lovejoy, back to *my* questions. You used to be a dancer, am I correct?"

"Yes."

"And just so we're clear, not a tap dancer or a ballerina, but the kind that uses poles and tables to feel the rhythm, correct?"

"As I said, I don't dance anymore. I wait tables now."

"Where?"

"I already told you, Headlamps!"

"Which is my point, Bethany. You are working in the same environment—

"Really, Mr. Yates, you're getting bogged down." Judge Vincent was disappointed in the attorney. He had checked his lawyerly intuition at the door and had taken on Desiree Wainwright's persona as his own. "Move on, please!"

"If you wish." Judge Vincent caught his smirk. "What are your work hours?"

"Eight to two on Thursdays and I stay till four on the weekend. My boss, Lou, lets me have Sundays off."

Desiree Wainwright rolled her eyes, and then began sneezing uncontrollably.

"One moment please, Your Honor," the attorney said.

He turned to confer with Desiree Wainwright, who was pointing at the bouquet of fresh azaleas sitting in the plastic vase on the court reporter's desk.

"Excuse, me, Judge Vincent, I've never had this come up before. They're certainly lovely, but it's been my observation that most courtrooms aren't furnished with fresh flowers. Would it be possible to remove them?" he asked, smugly. "Mrs. Wainwright believes she may be allergic to them."

How about if we just eject Desiree Wainwright from the courtroom. The judge motioned to Sgt. Quarles to step up from the back of the courtroom into the well to remove them.

"Shall we continue, now?" Judge Vincent asked the attorney, ignoring his red-faced client whose sneezing had subsided.

"Yes, of course. Judge, my client appreciates your accommodation."

The Wainwrights' attorney returned to his appointed job of skillfully chiseling away at Bethany, exposing the inadequacies of her circumstances.

"Now, Bethany, who keeps Damien while you're at work?"

"My landlady, Mrs. Evans, keeps him until I get him."

"I see." The attorney picked up a photograph from his table. "Your Honor, permission to approach the witness to show her this picture which I've marked as Exhibit 3." He paused for the judge's response.

"Permission granted," Judge Vincent replied.

Paul Yates walked up to the side of the witness stand and handed Bethany the picture.

"Thank you. Now, Ms Lovejoy, is this picture an accurate depiction of your room? I mean, home?"

"Yes."

"Would you please point out where Damien sleeps?"

"He and I, we sleep in the same bed," Bethany glumly admitted.

"Now, I don't mean to be rude, but your living quarters are a bit cramped, is that fair to say?" the attorney asked.

Bethany gave no verbal response. She simply glared at him. With that point made, the attorney returned to the subject of the mother's working hours.

"Do I correctly understand the guardian *ad litem's* report to indicate that several nights out of the week you wake up your son in the wee hours of the morning only to put him to bed?" The attorney sneered.

"No sir, I get him in the mornings around 8:00 a.m. after he's awake."

"You see a distinction there, do you?" Paul Yates started to walk back to his seat, but then stopped. "Ms. Lovejoy, forgive me. Please disregard that last question. There's one last thing I need to ask you and then I'm through." Bethany braced herself for what she knew by now wouldn't be a friendly question.

"Unlike Quentin here, you can't tell the Court that you'll have the support of your family to help with Damien, now can you?"

Bethany shook her head in response to the attorney's hard hitting question. Smugness had restored the normal color to Desiree Wainwright's face. The young mother's lower lip trembled as she fought hard to deprive the Wainwrights the pleasure of witnessing a tearful end to her testimony. The old dame patted the shoulder of her son's attorney as he took his seat.

That last question was completely unnecessary. Or was it? Am I losing my impartiality in trying to keep things fair? Why is this case affecting me so differently than most?

Paul Yates was finished. He had over tried his client's case. Like the attorney, she had read the guardian *ad litem's* report. But unlike the attorney who seized on the girl's tragic upbringing as ammunition to accomplish his client's objective, the judge had read the report with great sadness. The guardian *ad litem* had reported that Bethany and her eight siblings had grown up in foster care after their parents' rights were terminated. Bethany's father tried to hang onto his family by selling drugs, guns and homemade liquor in the projects where they lived, while her white crack addict mother turned tricks to support her habit and help with the rent. Both parents were believed to be dead. Bethany had been completely on her own since her 16th birthday. Judge Vincent was not surprised that the girl had become pregnant and had her own child within a few years of her emancipation. There were hundreds like Bethany in the world. But as far as the judge was concerned, this one was different. Bethany Lovejoy needed her help.

"Bethany, we can take a break if you need one," Judge Vincent said, regretting that was all she could offer the girl. In truth, the judge wanted a break as badly as she thought Bethany Lovejoy should be in need of one.

"No, ma'am," Bethany replied, surprising the judge. "I just want to get through this. What now?"

"Nothing else, Bethany," Judge Vincent assured her. "You may step down. Please watch your step." Despite the girl's willingness to stick it out, Judge Vincent elected to recess anyway. "This is a good time to take a short lunch break. Report back in forty-five minutes. At that time, I will hear closing remarks from both sides."

SEVEN

After lunch, the parties reconvened for closing arguments – a time for the two sides to argue to the judge as to why she should rule in their respective favor. Paul Yates said about what Judge Vincent had expected. He emphasized the case was not simply a matter of financial comparisons. However, according to his view the little boy deserved all that the Wainwright family could offer. He was entitled to a more nurturing environment than the struggling mother was providing. She didn't have a support base to help her with caring for the boy. Desiree Wainwright would be there day and night to assist with the child's care. They were not opposed to Bethany being granted visitation, but the totality of the circumstances demanded that the father be awarded sole legal and physical custody. As the attorney earned his fee, Judge Vincent listened and took notes.

When he was finished, Bethany stood, pressing her hands into the table to steady herself. The young woman had to grow up earlier than most teenagers, but she had matured even more over the past two days. She was there to fight for her right to raise her son who she loved dearly. Bethany Lovejoy took a long look at Quentin and his mother, before she turned her attention to Judge Vincent. When she finally spoke, her words came out in a rush.

"Your Honor, I love my baby. He's all I got. I know I can't do for him like Quentin's mama, but if you let me keep him I'll do my best. I don't just work at Headlamps like the rest of them girls there. I'm going to school so I can get a better job, one with benefits. When I finish and get my dental hygienist's license, I'll be able to get a nicer place for Dami and me. It won't be much longer. If you give Dami to them, they won't let me be his mother. You see how she be lookin' at me. That's 'cause she don't consider me to be her kind. When I got pregnant, Quentin said to get rid of it. I told him no, 'cause I'm not okay with that stuff. He kept goin' on 'bout me not havin' my baby. He don't give a fu-----, I mean he don't want this baby. Your Honor, I know it's jus' me, but don't it matter that I'm his mama?"

"Thank you, Bethany," Judge Vincent said gently. "You may take your seat. No matter what I decide, Bethany and Quentin, I want you to promise yourselves that you'll do your best in parenting him. He is a fine little boy and will need love and support from both of you as he grows up. This is not a contest." She looked hard in the direction of Desiree Wainwright, before turning back to the teenagers before her. "Rather this is an opportunity for everyone to work together in the best interest of Damien. I plan to take this case under advisement. You'll have my decision before the end of the week."

Judge Vincent could tell from their faces that they were expecting her to rule from the bench. Father's Day was the following week and both sides wanted to know where Damien would be spending it. But the judge had been on the bench long enough to know she needed time to absorb all she had heard before opining what would be in the best interest of Damien. She dismissed the disappointed parties and Sgt. Quarles escorted them out of the courtroom.

EIGHT

S uzanne leaned back in her tall, leather chair and sighed as she glanced out over the empty, silent courtroom. She was mentally exhausted from the contentiousness of the Damien Lovejoy case. The courtroom clock on the wood paneled wall read 1:30. Sgt. Quarles was sitting in his chair at the rear of the courtroom completing his daily paperwork. He had partially raised the window near him to get some air. Every time Suzanne looked in the direction of the window, the security bars subsequently installed over the opening served as a grim reminder of the young woman's horrific decision to end her life rather than try to live it without her baby. The judge could hear the shrill sirens of the escort vehicles stopping traffic as the long white Sheriff's buses backed out from under the courthouse to return the morning's load of prisoners back to the jail.

"Say Quarles," Suzanne called out to her deputy.

"Yes, Your Honor," Sgt. Quarles rose to his feet.

"Ever wonder how many young men might not be defendants if their mothers had fought for them as hard as Bethany Lovejoy is fighting for her son?"

"You got a good point there, Judge." The sergeant returned to his seat. He rarely tried to answer her questions because there never seemed to be a good answer.

Suzanne wanted to be still and think. Her pressing schedule kept her from doing so. The high case volume kept everyone moving fast and somewhat on edge to keep case counts on the decline. Occasionally after a proceeding concluded and she wanted to think about the evidence and weigh in on the attorneys' arguments, the judge would step down from her bench and sit in one of the jury chairs – a view of justice from the people's side. Her television interview and mid-afternoon appointment with her therapist, Dr. Nan Peters, made that impossible. She pushed back her chair and stood.

"Judge, need any help?" Sgt. Quarles always kept his distance, but was close enough if she needed him. Sgt. Quarles had been with the judge since her first day in Atlanta District Court.

"No Sergeant, I'm good. Thanks for waiting on me. I'm going to check in with Andi and then I'm leaving early today for an appointment. See you in the morning."

"Take care then, Judge."

Department policy required him to remain with her whenever she was on the bench. He had a good way with people, and she could never recall not feeling safe in his presence. The bailiff, court reporter, case manager, judicial assistant and staff attorney all served at her exclusive pleasure. The care taken in assembling her judicial team had paid off. She was confident she had assembled the best staff in the courthouse. Suzanne quickly gathered the case file and her notes, closed out her email and headed out of her private courtroom door into her chambers.

NINE

Judge Vincent's voluptuous judicial assistant, Andi – Sgt. Quarles liked to call her Queen Andi – was sitting at her desk in the front office, sorting through the afternoon mail when the judge came in from the courtroom. Andi's hair was her crown, and she loved changing its color, often to match the earth tones of her notorious clinging leather outfits.

"How'd it go, Judge?" Andi gave her boss an empathetic smile. They had been through a lot together. Suzanne had consoled Andi when the woman had a false positive on a breast biopsy. In turn, Andi was there for Suzanne when her grandmother died.

"Man, that attorney is relentless, and talk about nerve," Suzanne said. She lingered by Andi's desk and unzipped her robe, feeling warm. She bent over to smell the flowers Sgt. Quarles had brought in from the courtroom.

"Judge, you should have seen your face when he made that comment about your flowers." Andi laughed. She could monitor the proceedings from a closed circuit television mounted on the wall by her desk. "I heard you promise them a decision by Friday. Should I cancel my plans for this afternoon after work?"

Wednesday was Andi's day to join several other judicial assistants for happy hour at Courtside, a nearby pub. The judge sighed.

"No, I'll have to start on it tomorrow. The AM Atlanta folks are expecting me in a few, and then I have my other appointment today."

"Well, there's nothing here that can't wait till tomorrow, Judge. You look like you could use an afternoon off. Don't worry, we'll get everything done before Saturday."

The judge smiled appreciatively at her judicial assistant and headed back to her office. When Suzanne first read the court-wide memorandum from her chief judge, Sam Haskell, delegating to her the responsibility for the court's observance of County Adoption Day, she was floored. As far as she was concerned, the fewer adoptions she had to handle the better. After that traumatic adoption earlier in the year, she hadn't received any other petitions. She had assumed that Judge Haskell intentionally was diverting the adoptions to the other judges. Apparently, she was mistaken, or at least her quarantine was over, since now she had an entire day long parade of giddy new parents, gushing grandparents, and kids galore to look forward to.

The more she thought about the public aspects of the event and the inevitable media interest, the more anxious she became. Eventually, she convinced herself something terrible was going to happen again. She kept imagining irrational scenarios playing out before her in the courtroom with cameras rolling and there would be nothing she could do about it. *Why couldn't he have picked someone else? Someone who hasn't been on the painful end of an adoption? Someone less likely to spoil such a worthwhile endeavor.*

Even though her apprehension over publicly handling a multitude of adoptions compounded the ill-defined stress already brewing inside, Suzanne stayed close enough on task in her daily routine to conceal her lack of confidence. She would never forget Oliver pulling her aside at her swearing-in at the State Capitol and telling her, "Suzanne, you'll do well in this new position. But never forget the bar for you as a black woman is higher," Oliver stressed, "and no matter what, you have to stay the course. By election time we'll want those voters to know that you've got what it takes and then some."

No one needed to remind her that there were those anxious for her to fail. Pride and anxiety kept the judge from discussing her personal crisis with anyone. What was she supposed to say when Oliver had grilled her in his office the previous evening on whether or not her personal affairs were in order. *"Well, Oliver, so glad you asked. There actually is something that you should know that may change your plans for making me the 'poster judge' for adoption awareness."*

During her time on the bench, Suzanne had grown accustomed to the pace in the Atlanta courthouse slowing as summer approached. When assigned to the Criminal Docket, trying to find attorneys and jurors willing to suspend vacation plans long enough to squeeze in a gruesome murder or rape trial proved difficult. But this June bore little resemblance to previous ones. Attorneys seeking the judge's intervention had inundated her case manager, Tina, with *rule nisis* requesting a time in court for their clients. Because Suzanne found especially distressing the prospect of children being unable to spend time with both parents during school breaks, Tina had booked their summer calendar much heavier than normal. She simply did not know how she was going to give her cases the attention they deserved and start campaigning at the same time.

Divorcing couples with children were particularly disagreeable when it came to dividing up summer vacation, and if one spouse or the other couldn't manipulate matters to their own advantage, they were more than happy to spend time in court messing up things for each other. Judge Haskell had warned Suzanne that custody decisions would be emotionally exhausting, and that the many couples would litigate away the hot fun of the summertime.

"You'll think your visitation order couldn't have been clearer," he had bemoaned, *"and that you've anticipated even the least likely contingency so that all they have to do is follow the order. But, the term reasonable simply isn't in their vocabularies."*

In her chambers, Suzanne set the Damien Lovejoy file on her conference table and hung up her robe. She picked up her tan Coach briefcase, checking to make sure her keys were in the front pouch, turned out the ceiling light on the way out the door, and waved goodbye to Andi, who was speaking to someone on the telephone.

TEN

"Hallelujah!" Suzanne was free of the courthouse, sorry to leave behind only the building's air conditioning on the thick, humid June afternoon. She pulled her midnight blue Mercedes convertible roadster out of the underground parking structure. Suzanne had to pause due to the steady one-way traffic traveling past the exit from the judges' garage. As she reached for the button to retract her roof, she suddenly stopped. Across the street, she saw Bethany Lovejoy standing in a line of people boarding a MARTA bus. The young mother's slumped shoulders in the white denim jacket with the matted fur collar interrupted Suzanne's escape. The girl deserved a break from the stale smells and compressed bodies on the public bus. But Suzanne dared not offer her a ride. Catching a break in the traffic, she slipped on her dark shades and turned left, no longer in the mood for a ride with the top down.

Suzanne drove to Dr. Nan Peters' office in silence. No smooth jazz. No cell phone. No to-do lists created with a free hand. Two months before, it would have been a different ride. She might have used the lull in her hectic day to catch John between meetings. Instead, the void was packed with thoughts of a precocious little boy named Thomas who she recently met during an in camera interview.

Such interviews where she talked privately with children of all ages were a new experience for her. There was little reason for her to interact at all with kids outside of the courthouse. Since her transition to the Family Docket, she often met with older children to discuss their elections, if any, regarding custodial arrangements once their parents were divorced. By law, she was bound to abide by the wishes of children who were fourteen years old or older, unless the parent selected was deemed unfit. Younger children were only permitted to express preferences, and judges were not obliged to act on such desires.

Thomas' parents were divorcing two short years after his adoption was finalized. The basis for the couple's irreconcilable differences was not evident. Suzanne's hunch was that the adoption had been their last ditch effort to salvage the marriage. She felt badly for the child as she listened to him. Thomas' piercing words of confusion and despair over his own crumbling world took her by surprise and refused to let go.

"Miss Judge, please make my parents stay together. I think they forgot, but I remember what the judge said when I got adopted. He promised we'd be a family forever. They can't change their mind now, can they?"

Until faced with the child's predicament, the reality that an adoptive family's world might collapse just like any other family hadn't occurred to her. Thomas' situation left her feeling uneasy and within minutes of Sergeant Quarles escorting him away from her chambers, Suzanne dialed Nan Peter's office to make the appointment John had urged her to make weeks before. There were simply too many unresolved issues colliding in her life, and she was ready for help in tackling them one by one.

Fortunately, the analyst's office was in-town, not far from the courthouse. Shortly before her appointment time, she eased her roadster into a parking space right in front of Dr. Peters' lavender brick, two story house. She pulled her visor down for a quick look in the small mirror, ran a comb through her softly curled, shoulder length, auburn brown hair and touched up her sienna spice lipstick. She waited and watched as the preceding appointment paused at the end of the walkway to allow a woman pushing a baby carriage to pass in front of him, lit a cigarette and then strode off up the street after the mother. Suzanne stepped out of her car, locked her briefcase in the trunk, and exhaled, heading toward the front door.

Suzanne's focus was getting inside as quickly as possible without being noticed, not on the mother with the carriage who had turned around, pulled out a camera and shot several frames of her. No front view, but enough to suggest the judge had a problem.

ELEVEN

D r. Peters lived on the second floor of the house and facilitated others' lives on the first. Her clients didn't have to wait in a reception area. Troubled souls arrived promptly and left on the hour. One appointment rarely encountered another.

Suzanne pressed the buzzer. "Dr. Peters, it's Suzanne Vincent." The magenta door clicked open and Suzanne went inside. The house's original interior walls had been knocked out to convert the entire downstairs into one large, comfortable room. It was painted mauve and tastefully decorated with African artifacts and a wall-length water garden.

The tall, bespectacled psychologist with salt and pepper twists was seated at a wooden mahogany table. The table's polished surface was clear except for her notepad and a black and white soapstone tea set on a matching tray. Behind her were floor-to-ceiling shelves filled with books, glowing candles and several photographs of faraway places.

Dr. Peters gestured to Suzanne to choose one of the two chairs in front of the table. Her attractive patient's silk pantsuit hung limply belying the judge's strenuous day.

"Hello, Suzanne. Would you care for some tea?"

"Not just now, but thanks."

The psychologist was concerned about the weariness she saw in the judge's face, more obdurate than the previous week. The dark circles under Suzanne's eyes confirmed the acuteness of the stress seeping from within. She was not yet sure exactly what had the judge most worried: her work or her love life.

"Last week, we talked some about John and work." She glanced down at her notes. "You also mentioned your upcoming election."

"Yes, I met yesterday with my campaign chairman. Looks like I'm definitely going to draw opposition this time."

"When will your campaigning start?"

"Soon, the end of this month. After Labor Day, things will really pick up."

"Do you know the person running against you?"

"Not very well. More so by rep, he's one of our prosecutors."

"I'm sure there's nothing to worry about."

"I hope you're right."

"Suzanne, last time you appeared worried about a custody hearing scheduled this week. Did you have it?"

Suzanne nodded, turning slightly in her chair to get more comfortable and ease the tension in her lower back.

"How did it go?"

Suzanne let out a deep sigh and shuddered, remembering Desiree Wainwright's condescending tone while testifying the day before. Bethany Lovejoy didn't stand a chance with her son's grandmother.

"Another hard case."

"I suspect it was the tough cases Governor Moss had in mind when she appointed you to the bench." Dr. Peters smiled, peering over her tortoise-shelled reading glasses held together on one side with scotch tape. She studied Suzanne who was staring off into space. "What makes this case so difficult for you?"

The judge cleared her throat. "Well, as you know, I'm supposed to determine what's in the best interest—

"Suzanne, save the legalese for your courtroom," Dr. Peters said as she stood and came around the table and sat in the chair next to Suzanne. "Share with me what you're feeling."

"To put it simply, I guess I just don't want timing and circumstances to cause this young mother to miss out on the precious opportunity to raise her son." *Like I have with Riley.* "The child's grandmother is fighting hard for custody."

"Is the girl a good mother?"

"From what I can tell."

"The child's healthy, developing normally?"

"Yes."

"Then, it's a matter of standard of living?"

"The grandmother feels it is."

"Suzanne, you strike me as being a very thoughtful, compassionate person. I'm sure that you'll make the best decision you can.

Dr. Peters sat silently, twirling a pencil with her fingers, studying her patient's tense face and allowed a few moments to pass before prodding a little further.

"Do you and John talk much about your work?"

"We used to. When I was still at the firm, I had a case down in South Georgia. John helped me a lot in dealing with the stares and presumptions of folks who'd never seen a lawyer like...me."

"Is John also a lawyer?"

"No, he's in advertising. But he grew up in the south, and has a good sense of people."

"Then, John is a good listener?"

"He is or let's say, was."

"When my grandmother was murdered last year, John was there for me. And then, the incident with the woman committing suicide in my courtroom, he tried to get me past that."

"You said 'was.' What happened between you and John?"

"Things just got so complicated."

"In what way?"

"John says I started to withdraw, wouldn't let him help me sort through stuff."

"Is he right?"

"Yeah, for the most part."

"Grieving the loss of your grandmother, coping with a stressful job, the life of public figure – that's a lot to deal with, Suzanne."

"You're right, and I tried to explain all of that to John."

"Sometimes those who care about us don't know how to help us wade through times of crisis."

"I know. I'm here in part because John said I needed to talk to someone...a professional. Lately, we haven't talked much about anything. Things kind of blew up back in May when I canceled our plans to take a cruise."

"Why did you cancel?"

"I'm not sure. I panicked. I wasn't ready to confront John."

"Were there strings attached to the cruise?"

"Not really. John stressed it was just a little sanity getaway, but I felt, oh, I don't know..."

"You felt what, Suzanne?"

Suzanne took a deep breath, wishing that she was talking to a girlfriend instead of a therapist.

"Conflicted, I guess. He told me he's tired of living out of an overnight bag and alternating nights between our two places."

"You are content with the way things are?"

"I love John and we both want our future to be together. There's just so much going on. Too many unresolved issues."

"Has he ever been married?"

"No."

"Any kids?"

"None. What's wrong with me? You'd think, at thirty-six, I'd be thrilled to settle down with a wonderful man like John, and exchange my two-seater convertible for a more practical vehicle capable of accommodating baby seats and full cartloads of groceries."

"If you're not ready, then so be it. How long have you two been seeing each other?"

"Close to five years."

"Let's commit to working on some of this together." Dr. Peters smiled. "We've made good progress today. And I think we can look forward to continuing to move forward."

And we haven't even gotten to the matter of Riley.

Dr. Peters noted the time out of the corner of her eye. Suzanne glanced at her watch.

"Our time today is just about up. I have you down for meeting with me again on next Wednesday."

Suzanne paused before confirming. The session had done her some good.

"I don't know, Dr. Peters. I'm flying home for a long Father's Day weekend. You know how crazy things can get when you're trying to get out of town."

"Suzanne, I understand, but we don't want to lose our momentum. I really would urge you not to cancel next week's appointment. You've uncovered a lot today. I would like to talk with you once again, especially if there is a chance you might see John while you're in California."

"Wednesday, it is, then," Suzanne said.

Both women stood and Dr. Peters followed Suzanne to the door.

"Good luck with the case involving the young mother, Suzanne. Don't rush back to the courthouse. Give yourself a break this afternoon."

"You sound like John." Dr. Peters reached over and gently patted her shoulder. Suzanne smiled at her new confidant, soothed by the casual gesture and time well spent. "Goodbye, Dr. Peters."

TWELVE

The midweek chitchat and gossip passing between the customers in Maree's packed hair salon was nonstop. Everybody in the salon had a story to tell. Suzanne always appreciated hearing every day folk telling their stories and sharing the woes and occasional triumphs the women had in common. Tight plastic shower caps, rinse dripping down your cheeks and hot as hell hair dryers will humble even the proudest diva.

"Girl, I sure appreciate your squeezing me in."

Suzanne sat down in Maree's chair. The stylist spread out the leopard printed drape and tied it around her neck.

"You know I'll do what I can. Can't have nobody talkin' about your hair, your Judgeness, not with me bein' your stylist and all."

They both laughed. A few customers stole a glance at Suzanne.

"My boy won't listen to a word I say, Suzanne," Maree said in a low voice, as she combed out her hair.

"Maybe he needs to talk to someone," Suzanne said. "I know a few male counselors who work well with young men."

"I'm open to almost anything. Now you know how I feel about George W. and his war, right?" Suzanne nodded slightly, to keep Maree from burning her ear with the flat iron. "I'm getting desperate. I actually considered taking him down to that Army Recruiting Office on Tara Boulevard in Jonesboro."

They spoke in low voices about Maree's son, the weed she found in his room, his anger and rebellion. Maree finished Suzanne's hair and offered her a hand mirror to admire how her hair fell in the back. *I guess she was right about my needing a trim.* Suzanne swung around in the chair to take a look at the front.

"Thanks, Maree. You hooked me up like always. I'll leave those names for you on your voice mail on Monday."

THIRTEEN

Rotherman was home early. His wife was out running an errand, leaving him at home, sprawled out in front of the television, switching channels, and taking advantage of an uncensored scratch. Everything had been great until he answered the phone and Escobar Secret was on the other end complicating his life.

"Is this the Rotherman residence?"

"Who wants to know?"

The call was off to a funky start. The Rothermans' telephone number was not listed purposely to protect against harassing phone calls from defendants or their families calling about cases he had prosecuted. After the 2005 courthouse shootings, everyone who worked on the square block between Pryor Street, Central Avenue and MLK Jr. Boulevard took extra precautions in the name of safety.

"Chance, this is Escobar."

"Escobar," Chance replied, playing it safe for a married man recovering from a recent affair.

"There's something you need to know. Can you meet me at Headlamps later this evening?"

"No. We agreed that it's over. Besides, I'm babysitting."

"You didn't tell me you have kids."

"So now you know."

"Has any one told you recently what a fuck face you are?"

"Noted."

"Chance, sounds as if you might be tied up tonight. How about us hooking up tomorrow during lunchtime like we used to?"

Her persistent invitation was tempting. He'd been trying to untangle himself from the lingering effect of Escobar's long sensuous legs and naturally full lips. Every time his wife reached for him, his shame over betraying his high school sweetheart and confusion between lust and love filled their conjugal nest. His wife's predictable pillow talk was no match for that of the Nubian goddess. The Rothermans' bi-weekly routine barely kept him sane, but he was a family man who wanted to be on the bench so he'd sent Escobar and her sex toys packing. He needed to get Escobar off of the phone before his scratching segued into a more meaningful manual maneuver.

"Between work and my campaign, all of my…uh…spare time is gone."

"What campaign?"

"I'm running for Judge on the Atlanta District Court."

"You, a judge?" Escobar snorted. "What a joke!"

"Excuse me?"

"I'm just surprised, that's all. Most guys I know would've avoided any extracurricular conduct so close to a bid for public office. Man, are you sure you're ready for Washington?"

"Nobody said anything about Washington. My campaign will be strictly local. This is a state judgeship, here in Atlanta."

"Good then, we can continue to see each other."

"Escobar, you're not listening to me. We're over. I'm moving on. I have a campaign to run."

"Do you think I give a fuck about you and your campaign?"

The excitement of Escobar's sultry voice had worn off. Rotherman needed to sort through things. He'd thought a good bit about their comings and goings over the past year and was confident that no one had seen them. There hadn't been any reason to worry until now. Rotherman never dreamed that the woman would track him down. It had been almost six months since he'd last seen or talked with her.

"Escobar, you need to go wash your mouth out and I need to go. The evening news is about to come on. Don't call my house again."

"Is that a threat?"

"Call it whatever you like. Call here again and I'll have you prosecuted for harassment, Escobar."

"You're really not going to meet me?"

"No."

"Then, you'll have to find out over the phone."

"Find out what?"

"I'm pregnant."

Prosecutors are trained to not to visibly react to surprises. Rotherman was well trained to mask his shock over unexpected information. He looked into the playroom where his kids were getting antsy and held up five fingers.

"Ms. Secret, I have no idea why you chose to call my house with such news. Your predicament, shall we call it, has absolutely nothing to do with me or the District Attorney's Office. I simply must hang up now."

"You prick. Hang up on me and you'll be sorry! You'll be the evening news, just you watch and see!"

Chance clicked the receiver, took the phone off of the hook, reached over for the remote and released the mute button. He never should have answered the phone. On her way out of the door, his wife had urged him to ignore the telephone if it rung and to keep the television off. *"Chance, play with the kids while I'm gone. Don't just vegetate on the couch, channel surfing. Spend some time with your kids. They'll be grown before you know it."*

"Judge Vincent, tell us why you are spearheading Atlanta District Court's County Adoption Day this Saturday."

"What the hell!" He sat up and raised the volume on the flat screen television his kids had given him recently as a combination birthday/Father's Day gift. The television camera zoomed in on Suzanne Vincent.

"Thank you, Amanda. It's been such an honor for me to serve on the Atlanta District Court for the past several years. Every year we open the doors of the courthouse for this special event. Many of our families want to adopt, but don't know enough about the

process. Information will be available and the public is invited to witness several adoptions taking place in my courtroom."

"*Judge, let me ask you this...*

Rotherman watched the brief interview, clenching his teeth. Even he had to admit she was good in front of the camera. He flicked off the television to make the call. It had taken a while, but his investigator had tracked down the mother of the girl who had killed herself by jumping out of Suzanne Vincent's courtroom window. With any luck, maybe she had just seen the interview. He needed the lady to be mad as hell to do what he wanted.

FOURTEEN

"Mrs. Fury, please accept my condolences and I apologize for this intrusion."

"Augusta was my only child. Just a baby herself."

"I can't imagine how you're coping with such a tragedy."

Rotherman detected his telephone call may have interrupted Gladys Fury's early evening cocktail. The grieving woman's slurred speech alerted him to be quick and to the point. She was already primed for some payback.

"It's been tough," she said. "Funny thing is nobody seems to care. The county offered me a goddamned pine box to bury her in and that was it. What kinda justice is that?"

"Ma'am, I agree with you. But you can't wait on the government to make things right, sometimes you have to take action first."

"Whatcha mean go public?"

"I mean put on your "I am somebody, listen to me or else" clothes, go downtown and speak your mind face to face."

"Nah, that won't do any good. She's gone. Grandbaby's gone."

She was fading on him. He quickly told her about his plan for Adoption Day. She was silent while he talked.

"That's all you have to do," Rotherman said when he had finished. "Leave the rest to me."

"I'm not sure. Saturday is my only off day. After a nice breakfast, I usually go down to the Auburn Avenue Market and pick out some fresh vegetables."

"Ma'am, how about I'll send my investigator out Saturday morning to pick you up and after you're done at the courthouse, he'll take you by the market, give you a chance to shop and then bring you home when you're done."

"Humph, now that might work. I never had a car come and fetch me before."

"He'll be at your door right at nine o'clock, okay?"

"I guess that'll be okay."

Rotherman hung up, smiling. Saturday couldn't get there soon enough.

FIFTEEN

Thursday morning, Suzanne was back at her desk, long before the sun rose from behind the gold dome of the State Capitol looming in the background of her window. She made an effort whenever she could to be in her office early enough to embrace the sunrise. Each morning when she made it in time, Suzanne gazed out of her picture window across Capitol Square to the white painted copper statute of the Goddess of Liberty standing with a torch – perpetually lit – atop the gold dome. Inside, on the credenza along the window, she would light a candle, say a prayer for her son and recite her daily affirmation.

Suzanne reached back onto her desk for the caramel macchiato she had picked up on the way into work, but then accidentally knocked the cup into her lap. "Ouch," she exclaimed, as the scalding drink bled through her crème wool skirt, burning her thigh. She did her best to clean the large spot in the middle of her skirt, but not much could be done – the skirt was ruined and her calm threatened. Back at her desk, Suzanne unclipped the Polaroid photograph of Bethany and her son, Damien, from the front of the file. She took another look at the single bed Bethany shared with her two year old son in the tidy, spartan room they barely managed to keep from week to week at Mrs. Evan's boarding house. For a couple of hours, Suzanne agonized over the decision. Unable to think of a better temporary outcome, she reluctantly granted Desiree Wainwright's wish and awarded Quentin temporary primary custody of the little boy. Suzanne could only pray that she had read Bethany correctly and that the mother would seize the temporary custody arrangement as the opportunity the judge intended for it to be. She drafted and then, redrafted the order, word by word, to fertilize, not abort Bethany's maternal efforts. *Prove that woman wrong, Bethany.*

Suzanne read the order one last time before attaching it to an email to Andi and instructing her to finalize it and print it out for her signature. Everyone should receive her decision by Friday as she had promised. The judge stood and stretched, relieved to be done. *One more family on its way,* she thought. Her skirt was still damp and had drawn up in the middle from the hot liquid spill. She pulled at the skirt to straighten it out, but to no avail.

"Good Morning, Andi," she said, speaking to her judicial assistant over the telephone intercom. "I just sent you an email with the Lovejoy custody order attached.   Can you get it ready before the morning mail run?"

"No problem, Judge. I know you're happy to have it done. I'll get right on it."

Suzanne closed out the document and proceeded to check her email messages while she waited for Andi to bring her the original of the order to sign. She clicked on an email from her colleague, Rebecca Fitzgerald. Two years after her own appointment to Atlanta District Court, the governor selected Judge Fitzgerald to join the bench. Suzanne welcomed her, and went out of her way to show her colleague the inner workings of wielding the gavel. As the only women and the two most junior judges on their bench, Suzanne and Rebecca had bonded quickly. Suzanne called Rebecca the time she needed to vent her extreme embarrassment after an attorney had asked to approach the bench to point out she had forgotten to remove a hair roller. Rebecca, in turn, called her to vent when Judge Haskell had summoned Rebecca to his office when he learned of her impending divorce. He intimated that she might find her newfound freedom distracting from her judicial responsibilities. Their workloads didn't give them much opportunity to see each other during the day, so they kept up with each other online and broke away for an occasional lunch.

"What's the word on Rotherman? Call me when you get a moment," Rebecca emailed. Just as she was about to pick up

the phone to call Rebecca, her red leather clad judicial assistant walked into her office.

"Judge, I think we have a problem. I can't seem to open the attachment," Andi said. "Why don't you just store it for me on a disk and I'll take it from there."

While she waited for the disk, Andi began pulling dead leaves from the planters bordering Suzanne's desk, a habit she had acquired over their five years together. Andi didn't offer her any assistance with the document because she knew her judge was fiercely independent, prone to impatience and didn't take kindly to unsolicited help. As a result, she drafted most of her orders without any formal word processing training and managed to produce documents that were almost as polished as those typed by Andi.

Suzanne turned around from her desk to transfer the order from the hard drive to a disk and then she remembered she had converted the document to an email attachment without saving it. It was that kind of morning – the kind when coming into work while it was still pitch black outside didn't pay off. Andi slipped out of the office. It was that kind of moment.

As Suzanne began to recreate the order, it occurred to her the document snafu had been fortuitous. *What was I thinking granting custody to Quentin Wainwright? If I don't stand up for Bethany, who will?*

The Wainwrights had failed to show how uprooting Damien from the only home he had ever known would be in his best interest. Bethany Lovejoy was a good mother and deserved everyone's support. Suzanne stored the order on the hard drive and on a disk, and took it out to Andi, confident that justice had prevailed.

She kept the new decision simple:

IN THE ATLANTA DISTRICT COURT
STATE OF GEORGIA
FAMILY DOCKET

BETHANY LOVEJOY,	)
Petitioner,	)
	)
v.	) CIVIL ACTION FILE
QUENTIN WAINWRIGHT,	) NO. 06FD021336
Respondent.	)

ORDER DETERMINING PATERNITY
AND AWARDING CUSTODY

Having carefully considered all the evidence and argument presented by the parties, Petitioner appearing pro se and Respondent, represented by counsel, as well as the applicable standard of what is in the best interest of the parties' minor child, Damien Lovejoy, the Court hereby declares Respondent to be the legal father of said child, with the attendant rights and responsibilities of paying child support and exercising visitation.

Additionally, the Court awards the parties joint legal custody of Damien, meaning that each parent shall have the right to voice opinions and participate in making decisions which affect the health and welfare of this child, to confer with health care providers and teachers and the like regarding the child's development. Should the parties be unable to reach an agreement regarding any material issue affecting Damien, Petitioner will have the final decision making authority.

The primary issue in this case has been the physical custody of Damien. Although Petitioner has been and continues to be the child's sole physical custodian, Respondent argues that he and Damien's paternal grandmother are better suited to serve as the child's primary custodian going forward. The evidence does not support this conclusion. Damien's best interest will be served by his continuing to benefit from his mother's care and attention.

Respondent and his family are urged to support Petitioner and to supplement her humble means with their own love and resources.

Therefore, Petitioner is hereby awarded primary physical custody of Damien. Respondent shall have parenting time (traditionally referred to as visitation) as follows....

Sixteen

"Judge, the courtroom is beginning to fill up."

"Thank you, Quarles." Suzanne looked up at her sergeant who was standing in the doorway of her chambers. Her staff had been in the courtroom setting up and checking in the adopting families, their guests and other spectators. "I want to start the program promptly at ten, so I'll be out shortly." They had already discussed Oliver's plan that she work the crowd before her formal remarks.

"I'll wait for you outside your door."

"Great, spotted any press?"

"FOX-5 has their camera in place. And I believe there's a reporter from the Atlanta Journal Constitution."

"Only silent shutters on the still cameras, right?"

"It's all under control, Judge."

"Okay, then give me a moment and I'll be ready."

The last adoption she handled produced enough drama to last for her entire career. Fortunately, the Judicial Qualifications Commission investigated the matter and concluded that the judge hadn't committed any malfeasance. Yet, the adoption had left her shaken. *Exhale. Inhale. It's show time.*

Suzanne picked up the file Andi had prepared for her. Everything was there: her remarks, the adoption checklist, fact sheets for the scheduled adoptions, and Oliver's list of gratuitous campaign plugs. She put Oliver's list at the bottom and closed the folder, replenished her lipstick and smoothed out the skirt of her powder pink St. John suit. Her public was waiting.

Suzanne tapped the microphone at the podium in the well, turned from the bench to face the audience. Oliver had suggested speaking off of the bench would be better. The result would be an accessible judge who cared, a judge who took time for families and foster children.

"Ladies and Gentlemen, I am Judge Suzanne Vincent and on behalf of the judges of the Atlanta District Court, I'd like to welcome each of you to the Fulton County Judicial Center Complex. Through this annual event, we strive to raise the public's awareness of the thousands of foster children who rarely get adopted. Additionally, we hope to provide the community with a better understanding of the adoption process." Andi caught Suzanne's eye and mouthed to her to slow down a bit. "Adoptions are typically closed proceedings held in the judge's private chambers. But today, several families have agreed to share this special moment in their lives with you. You will witness a relative adoption, step-parent adoption and a variety of third party adoptions."

Community activists, court volunteers, a local chapter of the Alpha Phi Alpha fraternity who donated Father's Day dinner baskets, the Chair of Suzanne's Services to Youth Committee from her Links chapter, adoptive families, court personnel and Freda the Clown all were present and excited about their hand in extending grace to a few deserving foster children.

"Our first speaker is a young man in the fifth grade at M. Agnes Jones Elementary School. He's on the Principal's Honor Roll and participates in the Academic Cadre program. But today he is here to share with us his personal essay entitled *Starting Over*. Let's welcome Jonathan Little as he comes to share with us."

The soon to be adopted boy delighted everyone with his wit, intellect and charming smile. He couldn't take his eyes off of his new parents and literally ran back to take his seat between them, when done. Suzanne paused, hearing a commotion at the public entrance to her courtroom. Trouble had arrived. The audience turned toward the noise. A group of women wearing all black and plenty of attitude were coming through the door.

"I've never heard of such a thing. You must not be from the South." A very short woman pulling a small black suitcase on rollers was yelling at Quarles. "How dare you ask a lady to remove her hat!"

Suzanne signaled to Quarles to bend their "no hats, caps or do-rags" rule. The ladies were there to attend a community event on a Saturday, court was not in session, and she was anxious to continue with the program.

The latecomers pushed past Quarles and filed down the center aisle to the very first row. The woman with the suitcase sat directly in front of Suzanne's podium. Each of them was wearing a photo button of a young woman who looked vaguely familiar to Suzanne. She smiled at them, hoping to improve their mood. It didn't.

"As each adoption is taking place, out of respect for the families and children involved, we're going to ask you to refrain from doing two things please: no talking and no pictures. Before, after and in between the adoptions, I will be happy to answer your questions." Suzanne pointed to the three floor microphones. "Please use the microphones and that way everyone can hear your questions. Are there any questions?" Nobody moved toward a microphone. "Very well, then, let's proceed with the first adoption."

Suzanne's case manager, Tina, handed her the file and Quarles directed the family's attorney, the petitioning grandmother and her six grandchildren, soon to become her exclusive charges to take seats at the table in front of Suzanne. The children's fathers were unknown and their mother was a crackhead. Suzanne explained to the audience that the parental rights of the natural parents had been previously terminated. She made the pertinent inquiries and signed off on the adoption. Andi ushered them off to get their picture taken by the court photographer.

"Any questions?" Suzanne scanned over the crowd. She ignored Rotherman who had come in right after the ladies in black. He was seated near the rear, trying to hide behind the cameraman. Tina passed her the next file. "Alright then, our next adoption is a third party private adoption, meaning the adopting parents are not related to the child, and the mother surrendered her baby to a private, licensed adoption agency and did not revoke her surrender within ten days."

A younger white couple with their rosy cheeked baby boy came around the wooden railing with their attorney.

"Now, you watch what happens," said the woman with the suitcase, whispering loudly to her friends seated next to her. "You see that Gerber baby there, I bet if his mama showed up to take him home, they'd hand him right over. You know what I'm sayin'."

"Mmmhmm. Ain't that the truth." The woman's cohorts nodded, feeling her pain.

Suzanne peered out at the agitated woman to give her an opportunity to ask a question. The lady stared back, silent for the moment. *Oh, dear!* Suzanne figured out why the photograph each of the women in the group was wearing on her chest looked familiar. Oliver had warned her something like this might happen. *"Keep your cool. Stick to the script."* Suzanne stepped back and spoke to the couple's attorney, "You may swear in your petitioners."

Their adoption pleading was all in order. Suzanne signed the final order presented by the couple's attorney and was about to send them on their way. When she looked up, the woman with the suitcase was standing at the microphone.

"All you're doing here is showing out for the cameras and papers. This whole thing is nothing but a publicity charade."

Murmurs rumbled over the courtroom, a wooden gavel moment for sure. Suzanne retreated behind the podium, silently counting to ten as she pulled out Oliver's cheat sheet. Her hand was shaking, the sound bites on the paper a blur. *"If attacked or criticized, remember it's not what you say but how you respond that counts."*

"Ma'am, this is a very special day for several families. They've been patiently waiting for their adoption."

"And what? I'm interrupting – is that it?" The woman's agitation mushroomed into visible anger. "You brushed aside my baby girl when she came to assert her rights, like she was nobody." She stooped over to unzip her suitcase and began to pull out a small metal urn, holding it high with her right hand for everyone to see.

There wasn't anything on Oliver's list about a heartbroken mother showing up with her daughter's ashes. Suzanne went off script. "Ma'am, I deeply regret your loss. However, this isn't the place—

Quarles sprung into action. He approached the woman and firmly took hold of her left arm. "Okay, Miss, let's put that away. You need to take your seat," he said.

"This is all I have left of my baby," the woman said, clutching the urn, her anger lapsing into great sadness, "and you up there, acting all high and mighty, like she's never been on this earth."

"I will never *ever* forget your daughter," Suzanne said, her own eyes threatening to take over. "Her name was Augusta, correct?" The grieving mother nodded. "She was very pretty, very polite. I just couldn't help her. She asked for help a little too late."

Quarles nudged the woman toward her seat. "Don't you touch me!" She pulled away from the sergeant and lost her grip on the urn. The airborne container landed at Suzanne's feet, its lid flew off and a spray of ashes dusted Suzanne's knit suit.

Rotherman caught Suzanne's eye before ducking out. His work was done. He'd set the stage for the confrontation. The drama, the special effects were the creative license of a pitiful woman who'd had one too many cocktails.

SEVENTEEN

J udge Vincent was working in her office on Monday morning preparing a memorandum for Judge Haskell regarding Saturday's activities. Rotherman would report on the woman's outburst. Everyone agreed she'd handled the situation well. Her memo focused on the positive. Suzanne was both relieved and pleased at having survived County Adoption Day. It was all about making a child's life complete. The advance publicity that Oliver had helped arrange paid off. The press covered the event fairly and an article featuring Suzanne appeared in the *Metro* section of the Sunday paper. Forty foster children including a couple of sets of siblings were adopted into loving families and by the end of the day, everyone agreed that the tremendous work they had put forth resulted in making a positive difference in the community they served.

Commotion in her front reception area commanded her attention. *Now what!* She stuck the pointed toe of her boot under the metal box beneath her desk to trip the emergency alert button. Just last week during their office staff meeting, her sergeant had implored her to call on him first before she tried to handle the emotionally charged traffic coming in and out of their office. Moments later, Judge Vincent heard her bailiff's powerful voice rising above Andi's and that of another female.

Andi slipped back to her boss' office to explain to her what was going on. The judicial assistant pulled on the front of her tan suede bolero jacket as she spoke in excited ebbs and flows.

"Ooh, Judge, Desiree Wainwright is out there, demanding that you talk with her. She's really upset about the order. What should we do?"

The judicial assistant's usual low-keyed voice was now frantic and her hands were talking as fast as her tongue. Judge Vincent sighed, bracing for an unpleasant exchange. *Now I could understand Bethany showing up unannounced. Desiree Wainwright should know better.* She had tried her best to remain objective and not let the parties' personalities cloud her judgment. The judge couldn't help it, though. It had been quite a while since she had taken such a disliking to anyone involved in a case.

"Have Sgt. Quarles bring her back," Judge Vincent said. Andi paused, as if to make sure that was really what her judge wanted. The judge normally only permitted attorneys back in her chambers. "It's okay, Andi."

"Judge, Mrs. Wainwright is here to speak to you," Sgt. Quarles announced at her doorway.

Quarles motioned to the woman to take a seat in one of the two upholstered black chairs in front of the judge's desk. He hung back by the doorway assessing Desiree Wainwright's ability to practice self control. When he was satisfied the woman planned to behave, he left them alone.

Once Sgt. Quarles was out of sight, the woman wasted no time in explaining why she was there.

"When our attorney informed us you were the judge, I told him to get you thrown off of our case. I couldn't afford to have you screw up my grandchild's future the way you did that poor girl's, the one who killed herself in your very own courtroom."

"I beg your pardon. You're way out of line, Mrs. Wainwright. I agreed to speak to you in an effort to be courteous. However, if your sole purpose in coming here is attack me, do us both a favor and leave at once."

"I will leave after I've said what I came here to say. Don't you forget that as a tax paying citizen, I pay your salary and have a right to register any complaint I may have with your judgment." Judge Vincent did her best to keep her cool as the haughty woman spoke. "Paul Yates assured me that there was no way in hell you'd see fit to rule in that little tramp's favor. He said even you couldn't mess up a case like ours. I can't believe you bought her testimony about loving Damien. All she wants is to get her sorry hands on some of my money."

"We obviously have differing opinions about Bethany Lovejoy," Judge Vincent replied coolly. "My order speaks for itself. If you don't like my decision, feel free to appeal it." *Stop, before she makes you say something you'll regret.* "But before you waste any more of your precious money, keep in mind that in custody decisions appellate courts afford the trial judge broad discretion to do what she believes to be in the best interest of the child."

"You haven't seen the last of me. This election season, you can bet your discretion that I will be out there campaigning hard to unseat you. Clearly, you're too young and inexperienced for this job."

"As a citizen you do have the right to vote for and support whoever you believe will do the best job. Judging isn't easy. It takes temperance, grace, patience and a good understanding of people. I have all of those things and am confident that my record and reputation will prevail come election time. Your son had a child with Bethany and then failed to support him as he is legally obligated to do. Bethany did the right thing by asking the legal system to hold your son accountable for his actions. Instead of forcing your son to be responsible and be a man, you have chosen to retaliate against your grandson's mother for no good reason other than that you can. I remained objective and open minded until I heard the entire case. When it was all over it was clear that there's absolutely no reason why Bethany can't or shouldn't raise your grandson. You need to wake up and get over yourself. Now if you don't mind, I've work to do!"

Desiree Wainwright stood up without saying another word and stormed out of Judge Vincent's office. She barely avoided colliding with Andi on her way out of the office. Andi stepped back to check on her boss. Suzanne looked up from her desk.

"Things sounded like they were getting out of hand. Is everything okay, Judge?" Andi asked.

"Everything's peachy," Judge Vincent answered as she massaged her throbbing temples.

At least for the moment, that is. I suppose time will tell if my standing up to that witch proves to be a career buster.

EIGHTEEN

When her realtor first introduced her to the area several years ago, she instantly fell in love with the neighborhood – its close proximity to work, the shaded biking trails, the sidewalk cafes, ethnic restaurants and trendy boutiques. The only downside to her complex was the daily potential for parking rage. There were no covered or assigned parking spaces, strictly park-as-you can.

The phone was ringing as she unlocked the door.

"Hey, Mom, what's up?"

"I won't keep you, Dear. I can hear that judicial edge in your voice."

"Sorry, Mom, I just walked in. It's been a long day, that's all."

"I meant to ask you this earlier when we talked, have you spoken to John lately?"

Here we go! I'll say this and then no more, I promise." *You mean until next time, don't you, Mom?* "He's such a wonderful man, Suzanne. You really need to patch things up with him before someone else snatches him up."

"Now why didn't I think of that?" Suzanne hadn't meant to snap at her mother. *If only you'd stop treating me like a passed over debutante. Don't ask me when or how but somehow John and I will work things out.* As much as her mother's needling annoyed her, she really couldn't argue with her. John was special, unlike any of the other guys she had dated in Atlanta. She had only herself to blame for John taking the special job assignment in California. She hadn't given him any reason not to.

"No, Mom, I haven't and I don't want to talk about him right now," Suzanne replied. "But since you called, let me give you my flight info."

"Thanks, dear, I've written it down."

"How's Dad?"

"He's fine, working too hard as usual. We're looking forward to your Father's Day visit."

"Me, too."

They said goodbye. Suzanne went into the kitchen to prepare a salad and pour herself a glass of wine before she headed upstairs to shower and change clothes. As she was setting her tray down in the den, the phone rang again.

"Hey girl." It was her closest girlfriend, Cacey. They met shortly after Suzanne moved to Atlanta. Cacey was the real estate agent who found Suzanne's condominium.

"Hey, Cacey." Suzanne looked over at her food. As much as she loved Cacey, she wanted to get comfortable and enjoy some quiet time. *Make it quick, Cacey.*

"Suzanne, I need your advice on something."

"Sure, what's up?"

"It's my sister, Candace. Girl, her sorry husband is making her life a living hell. I don't think he's done anything physical yet, but it's just a matter of time. He's a bodybuilder and insists on wrestling with Candace. And talk about a control freak. If she's not on the air where he can keep his eye on her, she better be at home waiting for his ass."

Suzanne had never met Candace. She felt as though she knew her anyway. Candace Maxwell was a newscaster on CNN. This was not the first time Cacey had intimated that her sister's life was not as glamorous as it appeared.

"I've told her she needs to sue the bastard for all the crap she's had to put up with during their marriage. Fortunately, they don't have any kids. Candace isn't ready to file for divorce. Isn't there something she can do to get some peace from his abuse? If she doesn't do something soon, I may have go over there and duke him out myself."

"Sure, your sister can seek out a TPO."

"What's that?"

"T-P-O stands for temporary protective order. We have an office at the courthouse where victims of domestic violence can come get help with filing for one."

"What's the chance a judge will believe her? You know who her husband is, right?"

Brady Maxwell was a prominent member of the Georgia and District of Columbia bars.

"All she needs to do is tell the truth. Maybe you can come down with her. Domestic violence victims need lots of support. I'll email you the phone number of the office tomorrow, okay?"

"Thanks, Suzanne. Candace needs to make a move before it's too late. She's got to do something. If he hurts her, I swear—

"Cacey, let the judicial system do its job."

Cacey's line clicked.

"You're right, girl. Hey, that's her calling me. I better switch over and see what's going on. Thanks for the advice. I'll talk to you later. Goodnight, Suzanne."

"Goodnight."

NINETEEN

"How did Adoption Day go?"

"I got through it." Suzanne was happy to be back in the therapist's colorful cocoon. Suzanne took off her jacket and set it on the chair beside her. "My intuition that something would happen turned out to be right on."

Suzanne told her about the woman with the suitcase containing the urn. Dr. Peters shook her head. "I hope she's seeing someone. Clearly, she needs help."

"Dr. Peters, today, I think I'd like to talk less about work, more about me."

"Whatever you'd like."

"My visit to California won't be long, but I'm ready to talk with my mother about something we've avoided discussing."

Suzanne had the therapist's undivided attention. "You talk. I'll listen."

"I was a virgin when I began college. I attended UCLA, like you, correct?" Dr. Peters didn't reply, just nodded. "You don't have much of a social life as the only black girl attending an all-female private high school. When I revealed that to my roommate, my chastity became her independent study." Suzanne smiled, thinking of the wasted energy Tammy Odom had put into getting her laid.

"The boys all loved Tammy. My brains and little boobs couldn't compete with her size C cups."

"Winter semester my freshman year Tammy invited me to go with her and a group of other girls to Cancun for spring break."

Dr. Peters reached in her lap drawer for a pen and started twirling it.

"My first semester grades made the case with my parents, and they agreed to let me go."

Suzanne rose, talking while she walked over to look at some of the therapist's travel photos.

"To make a very long story not so long—

"Suzanne, you don't need to rush or edit your memories. Just tell me what happened."

"I thought it was going to be a group of girls going to Cancun. But when we got to the airport, Tammy told me some of her sorority sisters cancelled because of the cost and a few guys were going in their place."

"Did you know the boys?"

Suzanne returned to her chair and slipped her shoes off.

"I knew one of them – well sort of, anyway. When we got on the plane, a boy from my first semester African American Studies class, Keith Grayson, and his friend, Lance Dillard, sat across the aisle from Tammy and me. Lance was a freshman like us. And oh, did Tammy have the hots for Lance. Without even asking Keith or me, she jumped up and suggested that she and Keith switch seats. He was about six foot four, so I let him sit on the outside. Keith had the prettiest eyes."

The therapist smiled.

"Sorry, Dr. Peters, I guess you don't need all those details. Memories of that school girl crush are taking over."

"I'd never spoken to him before spring break. Keith was a junior, a member of the football team and a bevy of giggling co-eds constantly buzzed around him like queen bees."

Suzanne finally took a sip of the water Dr. Peters had placed in front of her.

"By the time we landed in Cancun, I had forgotten all about my mother's rules and my shyness. Spring break in Cancun was a week-long party. I tried not to let on, but I couldn't believe how all the kids drank."

Dr. Peters wrote down a note on her pad.

"Our third night there, at one of the clubs, Keith asked me to dance....I loved to dance, still do. He stayed close by all evening.

The more attention Keith paid me, the bolder I became. The next afternoon, he came over to where I was lying out by the pool and suggested we go out to dinner that night, just the two of us."

"This would be your first date?"

"With him, you mean?"

"Him or anyone else."

"Yes."

The therapist motioned for her to continue. Dr. Peters jotted another note, while Suzanne paused to reflect.

"The resort where we were staying was an all-inclusive, a feature whose value was important to our parents who were footing the bill but completely wasted on all of us college kids. Keith suggested we eat at one of the dining spots onsite. It didn't cost him anything, but he acted as though it should be a big deal that he let me select the restaurant. I picked one located in a gazebo-like open air setting out by the water."

"Dinner went well enough. He told me about being the oldest of five kids, growing up with a single mother who caught the bus every day in southeast L.A. to head across town to cook for an elementary school. I tried hard to downplay my sheltered South Pasadena existence. By the time we finished dinner, it was almost 11:00. Neither one of us was thinking about trying to catch up with our friends."

"He kissed my hand on our walk back to our rooms. My first instinct was to break away."

"But you didn't?"

"No. Right there on that starlit beach, I could hear my mother telling me all the things good girls didn't do. But looking up into Keith's face, I knew being with him simply couldn't be one of them. And if it were, I didn't care."

"Everything after that's a blur, all I remember is us in the elevator. The next thing I knew we were stepping out on his floor, headed for his room."

"Did you discuss going to this room?"

Suzanne shook her head. "Although, I can't say he did anything I didn't want him to do. He unlocked the door to his room and we went inside. Keith turned on some music and then led me to the couch in the dark living room. He began kissing me so hard

I thought I was going to gag on his tongue. To catch my breath, I asked him for something to drink. While he was in the kitchen, I considered leaving, but I didn't."

"Do you think you should have left?"

Suzanne silently winced, pondering the question. Through the years, she had gone over and over in her mind, the events of that evening and why she had stayed.

"Probably," she said, "but by the time he returned with our drinks, I had lost all my inhibition. When he sat back down next to me on the couch, he said just what you'd expect from a testosterone driven nineteen-year-old boy. I actually believed Keith's pitiful palaver. When he started kissing me the second time, I kissed him back. The next thing I knew—

Dr. Peters stood and stretched her back, and glanced at the clock behind Suzanne.

"Suzanne, what were you thinking, afterwards?"

"I remember wondering where the magic of the evening went so quickly. And yeah, maybe it was my first time, but even I knew we should be talking more than we were. Then it occurred to me that if Keith had been the right guy, neither of us would have been at a loss for what to say."

"Panic set in the minute he left me, locked inside my room. I wasn't even sure if he'd used a condom. Not knowing what else to do, I took a long shower, as if the water would make a difference. I tried to stay up until Tammy got back, but I fell asleep. She woke me up when she came in, wanting to hear all about my date or so I thought. But I quickly realized that she wasn't interested in the details of our dinner or walk along the beach – the things I just told you – she wanted to know if anything physical had happened. So for her benefit, I abbreviated my account of what transpired, tucking away the minutia and shame. I must have had a strange dazed expression on my face because all of a sudden she was screaming at me and asking had he raped me."

"Did he, Suzanne?"

The judge took her time answering. She had asked herself the same question during one of her first trials on the bench when the jury's not guilty verdict had thrust a rape victim into a post traumatic episode right on the courtroom floor.

"No," she said in a low voice.

"My period was due a couple of weeks after spring break. It didn't come. By the middle of April, Tammy agreed that my nerves weren't the problem. We skipped classes one day and headed off campus to buy a home pregnancy test. Tammy urged me to do the test right there in the drugstore's restroom since our dorm facilities were communal. I reluctantly agreed. It was so hard to do what was needed in the dim light of that damp, dirty stall. But even in the bad lighting, I could see the strip was showing positive."

"Tammy thought Keith should know. I hadn't seen him since we got back from Cancun. She tracked down his number and sat right next to me while I called him. My conversation with Keith didn't last as long as it took for the pregnancy strip to turn blue."

"Days later, I found myself waiting to dispose of my problem, behind this ugly, torn, blue plastic curtain in a rundown Van Nuys abortion clinic Tammy had located. I remember being cold and shivering in a green paper-thin surgery gown they gave me. I sat there staring at the chipped walls and surgical instruments. We didn't belong on that table."

"We?"

"We, meaning me and my baby. Somehow I found the strength to get down and redress. I just left, forgetting about my cashed savings bonds and discounting, I guess, the consequences of having changed my mind."

"Suzanne, I'm proud of you for getting that out, in the open. Now, let's turn to your mother. How does she relate to what you've shared with me?"

"You know, Dr. Peters, even though I don't think Tammy understood my change of mind, she accepted my decision. To this day, I don't think my mother has tried to do either."

"Although getting through finals was difficult, my bigger challenge was going home and facing my parents, especially my mother. Tammy and I didn't talk about it, but as we piled stuff into our suitcases, taking with us the memories of all we had gone through together as roommates that first year, the very real possibility that I might not return rested right near the top of everything. We parted, playing lip service to staying in touch, but our freshman year bond had unraveled by the end of the summer."

"I decided to wait until after Mother's Day to break the news to my mom. But by mid-May, I still hadn't said anything. Once I did, our house wasn't big enough for my mother and her disappointment in me."

"What about your father? How did he react?"

Suzanne's face fell as she recalled her father's reaction.

"My dad was waiting for us when we got home from my appointment. I could tell he was hurt. Mom did most of the talking. My choices were simple and she made her expectations painfully clear. She told me keeping the baby was not an option. When I told them about my trip to the Van Nuys clinic, my dad made it clear to my mother that an abortion was also not an option. So we turned to the only remaining alternative – having the baby and giving it up for adoption."

"Our family meeting ended with the decision that I would go stay with my paternal grandparents in Detroit. While I knew my mom was upset, I kept waiting for her to change her mind and tell me how we would work everything out – there, at home in California."

Suzanne had held up as long as she could, but reliving it all again had taken more out of her than she had expected. She walked over to the leopard skin chaise by the water garden and wept softly. Dr. Peters left her alone, sitting quietly at her desk and making some critical notes on Suzanne's breakthrough. Everything the judge needed was within reach – tissue, water and expiation.

After several minutes, Suzanne sat up on the chaise, dabbing at her moist dark brown eyes, and spoke up so Dr. Peters could hear her from across the room.

"It was a miserable summer. The fact that I had come pretty darn close to being a perfect daughter while growing up, never rebelling or wavering, only seemed to exacerbate her inability to accept my situation. She acted as though something had been done to her, not that it was happening to me."

"I overheard her whispering and discussing 'the problem' with my dad and my grandmother, Momo, but she wouldn't discuss anything with me. Once I even heard her telling someone over the telephone that I would be away during the fall participating in some type of semester abroad program. My gosh, talk about denial. By mid-summer, I was beginning to show, prompting my mom to start making the arrangements for me to leave for Detroit."

"When I arrived back East in early August, my grandparents did their best to make me feel welcome and comfortable. But despite their efforts and genuine concern, I missed my parents. I needed to be able to draw on the comfort of my yellow and orange room as I made my way through the wave of nausea and backache."

"Sounds like you were feeling very hurt and rejected," Dr. Peters said.

Suzanne walked slowly back and sat in the chair by the desk.

"I really got to know my dad's parents during that time. They're good people. Fortunately, Grandma Vincent had no intentions of holding me hostage inside their house for the next four months. She decided I needed something constructive to do. Grandma Vincent's church was located in downtown Detroit near the Charles H. Wright Museum of African American History and the Detroit Institute of Art. Her church ministered to the surrounding community which was suffering from urban blight. A few months before I arrived, my grandmother's church had established a day shelter for homeless women and their children. She served on the shelter's board and asked me if I would be interested in working as a volunteer with the children."

"I agreed, so happy to be able to focus on something other than my protruding stomach. She took me down to the shelter to introduce me to the other church ladies." Suzanne smiled. "I will never forget how she quickly put an end to their rude haughty stares by telling them quite matter-of-factly that I was her granddaughter from California and I would be staying with them until my baby was born in December." The judge chuckled, "Grandma Vincent had one of those looks, you know? Before too long, they only seemed to care about the extra pair of hands I contributed to their mission, not the extra weight I was accumulating."

"It may sound silly, but I felt almost invisible during those last few weeks," Suzanne admitted.

"Tell me what you mean by invisible," Dr. Peters said, leaning forward, folding her hands in front of her on the desk.

Suzanne pushed back in the chair and sat up, wanting her explanation to make sense.

"Long before I turned him over to the nurse and signed away all that was mine in the world, I felt like I had lost control of my destiny," Suzanne said. "That I may have had feelings for him never seemed to occur to my mother. I wasn't ready to give him up. My mother took control of the entire situation doing just about everything except cutting the umbilical cord herself."

"A long time has passed, and I gather a lot of feelings. I'm curious about why you haven't broached with your parents or at least, your mother, the subject regarding your feelings about your pregnancy, son and adoption."

Suzanne was stumped. She shrugged her shoulders, silently processing the therapist's questions. *Why haven't I talked to them? Especially Dad, who's better at listening than Mom.* After confiding in Dr. Peters, Suzanne now wondered if it really was her, not her parents, who she had conveniently blamed all this time, who didn't want to openly embrace the fact that she was an unwed mother.

"She won't want to talk about this," Suzanne murmured. "The topic would be too volatile."

"After all you shared with me today it seems you want to talk to your mother. What's your fear? You'll know when the right opportunity presents itself for the two of you to talk. When it does, take charge just like you would in your courtroom. That is, without the gavel, of course," Dr. Peters laughed and Suzanne joined in. The judge needed something to laugh about.

"Dr. Peters, I definitely want to talk with my mother."

"You're ready, Suzanne. It's time."

TWENTY

Suzanne arrived at the airport two hours early to creep through a security line winding back almost to the expressway. She had even stood in her $30 designer hose on the grungy terminal floor while a humorless inspector scanned her breasts and crotch because of the alleged security risk posed by the under wire of her bra. Yet, the airline still screwed up the only thing she expected in return: her bulkhead aisle seat. When Suzanne arrived at the check-in counter, she was informed by the gate agent that her seat had been reassigned and she now was expected to endure a four and one-half hour flight to LAX in Seat 36D – way in the back, in the middle of the center section of the Boeing 767.

Suzanne was pissed. *So much for supporting the hometown airline, and booking the ticket online. After all of this hassle I'm in no mood to finish those custody orders I brought with me.* Fuming, she stored her laptop in the compartment above and climbed over a mother with a screaming baby squirming to get down from her lap. Settling into her seat, Suzanne inhaled just enough so she wouldn't touch the hairy arms of the fully dressed sumo wrestler wearing a sleeveless muscle shirt that read: Want to Go a Round? *He should have purchased two seats, to keep me from having to share mine*, she thought, as she noted his arm misappropriating her right arm rest. A glass of wine and a transcontinental nap was the only way she would get through this flight. She put on her shades to block out the light and sat with her arms crossed, waiting for the beverage cart. *Am I missing the part where it shows how much you love to fly?*

Suzanne fell asleep without getting her wine. She woke up to the sound of the high pitched beeps signaling the plane's initial descent into Los Angeles, and let up the back of her seat. The sumo wrestler was snoring big time. She leaned forward and strained to get a glimpse through a tiny sliver of the right portal window visible past her hairy neighbor's heaving potbelly.

Suzanne turned to her left to try her chances out of the other window where the familiar, dense Los Angeles landscape was coming into view just below the yellow gray cotton-like layer of smog. She set her watch back three hours to reflect the correct time, and then realized in all the commotion over the mix-up with her seat that she had forgotten to call her mother. There was no need to worry since her mother always arrived early.

The traveling young mother seated next to her was feeding the baby out of a jar of strained beets. Going back to the restroom to freshen up wasn't going to happen. Her row was too jammed with bodies and activity anyway to justify the effort, so she reached down for her purse to get her compact and lipstick. Just then, the baby grabbed the spoon out of his mother's hand, flinging a spoonful of beets over on Suzanne. Profusely apologetic, the mother quickly recapped the jar of baby food and whipped out a blue case of baby wipes, offering one to Suzanne. *Will I ever experience such joys of motherhood?* She gave the woman her most gracious judicial smile assuring her that she understood accidents happen and there was no problem or damage done. The plane touched ground, and several minutes later Suzanne was free of the stale plane air, baby beets and beefy, hairy arm pits.

Suzanne spotted Velda Vincent as she rode down the escalator. Her mother was standing one floor below, in the crowd awaiting arriving passengers assembled outside of the baggage area. The judge was a couple of inches shorter than her mother, but there was a striking resemblance between the two women. Her mother's platinum gray hair was swept up in a French twist, and she was wearing the pearl earrings and expensive flats which were her mother's trademarks. Suzanne waved from the escalator trying to catch her eye without making a scene. Her mother saw her and waved back, as she made her way to the front of the crowd.

"Hi Mom! I love your hair." They embraced.

"Hello, dear. Thank you, I thought I would try something new for the summer. It's so good to see you!" Suzanne was visibly thinner than when her mother saw her last, but she didn't comment. "How was your flight?" her mother asked, as they walked over to the carousel to wait for Suzanne's luggage.

"I've been on better," Suzanne said, telling her mother about her seat from hell. "I thought you said Dad was coming with you. Where is he?"

"He went into work early today in hopes of being able to come home before closing so he could spend some of the evening with you."

"I hope so. I've missed you guys." Suzanne reached for her luggage.

"It'll be just us girls for most of the day."

"Well, you know two stops I want to make first, right?"

Suzanne's visits home always included a trip to Winky's to pick up a couple of her favorite cherry and maple iced cake donuts and Ernesto's, a family owned Mexican restaurant. The Vincents had patronized both establishments for as long as she could remember.

"You're talking to your mother, girl. Of course, I do!" Her mother smiled as they headed for the car.

Outside of the terminal, Suzanne put on her shades to temper the bright California sun beaming down. She immediately removed them to rub off one remaining dried splatter of beet juice. Her mother merged into an eastbound exit lane leading out of the airport down Century Boulevard.

"Is that Winky's a few blocks from here still in business?"

"You mean the one with the gigantic plaster donut on the roof?" her mother asked. Suzanne nodded. "It sure is."

They chatted easily, each woman clinging closely to their comfortable conversation. Her mother pulled into Winky's parking lot and watched her daughter as she dashed in to get the donuts. Velda's motherly intuition told her that deep down beneath her daughter's cheerful exterior, something was amiss.

The city's landscape – the people, buildings, traffic – had changed radically since Suzanne had moved away. Lately on her visits home, there always seem to be more brown everywhere than she remembered growing up – smoggy air, plywood sealing up storefronts that no longer were in business, dirt patches and tree stumps where lush trees once grew abundantly. The plentiful tall brown palm trees that once marshaled tourists throughout the city boulevards and neighborhood streets were now rare, succumbing to decay and too expensive to replace on the average taxpayer's tab. Suzanne found the scenery depressing as "Cash for car title" businesses, liquor stores, strip clubs and homes now in a state of decay with barred windows appeared one after the other. The closer they got to the northbound entrance to the Harbor Freeway, the more she looked forward to getting home.

TWENTY-ONE

The midday traffic clogging the freeway didn't ease until they passed the Los Angeles Dodgers Stadium and cleared the Figueroa Street tunnels carved out of the bottom of the foothills marking the beginning of the Pasadena freeway. As the congestion eased, the expansive San Gabriel Mountains came into view. Way up at the top of the mountain range, Suzanne could see several RF antennas which broadcast the majority of Los Angeles city's radio and television transmissions.

Suzanne reached up, taking hold of the safety strap as her mother's CRV hugged the treacherous curves in the fast lane of the narrow Pasadena freeway. The freeway was the first one built in the area, and very little earth was moved to accommodate it.

The familiar sights lulled Suzanne into a quiet spell. Her mother drove in silence allowing her to stare out of the window. When they passed by the elementary school up on the hill right next to the freeway, where her mother had first taught, it was as if she was back in Mrs. Puglasia's first grade class all over again.

Suzanne's classmates were dirt poor and lived in the trailer parks, crowded apartments and small houses which abutted the freeway and cement canal. When her mother first started at the school, the community was in transition – Spanish speaking families were replacing the white families who had originally settled there. Suzanne attended kindergarten, first and second grades at the school. She would never forget the day she was sick in the girls' bathroom, and wanted her mother, but all she could hear were a couple of little girls laughing and gossiping in

Spanish about the *"la muchacha negra con su piel fea."* Suzanne knew enough Spanish to know they were gossiping about her being black.

The girls never really warmed up to her, so despite the convenience to her mother of having Suzanne attending the same school where she taught, her parents pulled her out after the second grade and placed her in an all-white Lutheran school located in South Pasadena, which she attended until high school. The whispering, stares and pointing continued at her new school, making being "the only one" all the more painful because the occasional hateful words her classmates spat out were in plain English.

She received invitations from kids whose mothers believed everyone in the class should be invited. But her excitement over attending the slumber parties waned when her thick hair and silk scarf for tying down her hair became the center of attention just before lights out. To fit in, she left off the scarf and fell asleep trying to look like Goldilocks. She paid for it the next morning as she endured sitting with her wild, tangled hair at the table eating breakfast with her pale classmates. She began to accept fewer and fewer invitations, and retreated into a world that centered around her family, piano lessons and a Camp Fire group led by her mother. When Suzanne shared these early experiences with Dr. Peters, it became clear why Suzanne came across as reserved and was reticent to open up to others as an adult.

"Almost home," Suzanne's mother announced as she always did the moment they passed the stone cutters spelling S-O-U-T-H P-A-S-A-D-E-N-A set in the grassy embankment adjacent to the Orange Grove/Rose Bowl exit off of the freeway. Suzanne set her memories aside.

"Suzanne, do you want to stop now for lunch at Ernesto's?"

"Mom, I'm sorry, but those yummy donuts spoiled my appetite. If it's okay with you, I'd like to wait a bit."

"Sure dear. The last thing I want is for you to feel rushed during your time away from court."

The Vincents lived on a quiet street in South Pasadena – an exclusive area featuring custom homes and lush, well manicured yards. Beckham Vincent – known to his friends and customers as

"Beck" – had remodeled their home in keeping with the historic Garden District homes he fell in love with as a child visiting New Orleans, the home of his mother's family. The home was a two-story, terra cotta stucco, with a Spanish clay slate roof with white wrought iron railings bordering the terrace on the second level, tall white plantation style shutters on the first floor and a courtyard in front. In the center of the courtyard was a fountain with a statute of a jazz man playing the saxophone – just like Beck and his father both played. Suzanne's father had planted a rose garden inside the courtyard in tribute to the three ladies in his life – his mother, his wife and his daughter. Each had her own breed of rose. Suzanne's mother loved flowers and kept vases of freshly cut roses and sunflowers throughout the house.

The Spanish tile roof of the Vincents' South Pasadena residence appeared over the tall bottlebrush bushes bordering the property. They pulled up in the circular cobblestone drive her father had installed himself years before. Suzanne opened the handcrafted wrought iron gate with the large "V" leading inside from the driveway through the courtyard. The wrought iron detailing throughout the design of the outside of the house made the home distinctive, even among the other custom homes in the neighborhood, especially since Beck Vincent made sure everyone who complimented the house went away knowing that wrought iron was a craft refined by free people of color from New Orleans. Their closest family friends had heard him say it so often they usually rattled off that bit of trivia themselves as they came and went.

Suzanne and her mother walked through the open, breezy foyer.

"Welcome home, dear."

"Thanks. I think I'll go ahead and unpack. I'll be back down in a little while," Suzanne said, heading upstairs with her bag.

"If you need me, I'll be out reading on the patio by the pool. Now don't be shocked when you see your old room. Remember I told you I've done some redecorating up there."

TWENTY-TWO

S uzanne started up the stairs with her bag, pausing to
straighten one of the several framed family photographs
lining the wall leading to the top level. It was a picture of her the
day she learned to roller skate, about age seven, with her hair
pulled back in that horrible "can't do much else with it" hairdo
her mother often resorted to back in the day.

Suzanne turned on the light in her former room and set down
her bag. Her room as she once had lived in it was no more. The
juvenile hues were replaced with more versatile, subdued tones,
the worn traditional furniture with new, contemporary pieces,
framed art hung where music posters once were tacked up in
excited haste. Suzanne was glad her mother had finally gotten
around to redecorating the space. The painful memories from the
summer of 1988 overshadowed the joy of the now gone bold, funky
psychedelic colored walls. She picked up a note her father had
left on the nightstand next to a tall vase of beaming sunflowers,
suggesting they spend the following morning together. It was
nice to be home.

The house was perfectly quiet. She hoisted her bag up onto
the bed, and unzipped it. As always, she tried not to over pack.
Her shift toward Lycra blends and fine knits made packing much
easier. Still, she had brought along much more than she could
possibly wear in the short time she would be at home. Walking
back and forth from the bed to the closet, Suzanne remembered
the summer in 1988 when the walls served as her fortress between
her mother and her future. Suddenly it occurred to her that just

as Dr. Peters had predicted, the right time to talk with her mother had arrived. She left the bag open, turned off the light, and went to get some answers.

"Mom, you did a great job on the room. I really like it." The porch swing pushed back slightly as Suzanne sat down next to her mother. The Vincents' pool had reminded Suzanne of a large, turquoise kidney bean ever since she was a little girl. "The yard looks nice. Is Felipe still doing it?" she asked.

"Yes, he still comes by. I don't know what we'll do the day he decides to retire." Her mother smiled.

"By the way, Mom, that picture of me in the hallway with that tired hairdo has got to go!"

"Oh, I like that picture – it shows your determination, a judge in the making," her mother replied. "I'm so glad you liked the room, dear. It was long overdue for a face lift. Just like me, I'm afraid."

"Don't you dare, Velda! You look fabulous," Suzanne told her. And she did. Suzanne's mother would be sixty-one on her next birthday and didn't look a day over forty.

"I tried not to go overboard, just in case we need the room for a nursery one day," her mother said.

Suzanne bit her lip. The grandchild on Suzanne's mind was too big for a crib.

"Mom, there's something I'd like to talk with you about," Suzanne said.

"I knew something was wrong, you've seemed a little distracted ever since I picked you up from the airport. Is it one of your cases? You know, I've been worried about you ever since your new assignment –

Suzanne reached out and patted her mother's arm. "Mom, please…In order for me to get out all I need to say, I've got to ask you to do something that's going to be very hard for you."

"Dear, this sounds serious – what's wrong?"

"I need you to let me talk, without you asking any questions, please."

Her mother nodded, and silently turned over to her daughter the one thing Suzanne wielded in the courtroom, but rarely at home – control.

"Do you know what two things I dread every year?" Her mother, obedient, shook her head. "The first days of December and my annual pap smear. And it's for the same reason."

The swing moved as her mother shifted on the cushion to look at her more directly.

"They both remind me of when I gave him – my son, your grandson – away."

Her mother stopped rocking. "Darling, what's brought all of this on? Your room? The changes must've upset you."

Suzanne shook her head, blinking back tears. "Oh gosh, Mom. This has absolutely nothing to do with new paint and furniture."

"Then what—

"I've begun working with a therapist. She encouraged me to talk to you about what happened."

"A therapist?"

"Yes, a wonderful woman named Nan Peters."

"Suzanne, tell me what this is all about?"

"I'm actually glad you changed the room. The old way, it was filled with sad memories. Each morning, I'd wake up regretting that I hadn't told you the day before. When you came in with the dorm registration card from UCLA, asking about my plans to room with Tammy again, I just blurted it out. Remember that?"

"Yes."

"Do you remember how you reacted?"

"Not specifically, no."

"You fired off a bunch of who dunnit questions. Then you tore up the dorm card, threw the pieces at me and left me alone in my room."

"I'm sorry, Suzanne. Surely, you can understand I was shocked."

"Yes, but I kept waiting for you to get over the shock and come back and talk to me. The next day when you drove me to the doctor, you said virtually nothing to me. You said plenty to the doctor, to Dad. Me, I got the silent treatment for practically the entire summer."

"Dear, that's not how I recall things. I remember us doing our best to get through it."

"That's just it. It didn't feel much like we or us."

"How can you say that?"

"Mom, I don't think you have any idea how difficult that time was for me. It was as though you sent me to Detroit because you couldn't stand the sight of me. Why else would you send me thousands of miles away at a time when I needed you more than ever before in my life?"

Suzanne began crying.

"Oh, my dear Suzanne. I was simply trying to do what needed to be done. I see my mistake was focusing on your life afterwards, rather than helping get through the pregnancy itself. Sure I was hurt by what happened, but I never sent you away because I was ashamed of you. I love you. Your father loves you."

"During those first few weeks back in Detroit, I kept thinking, Mom will show up any day now and take me back home. But you never did, Mom!"

"I see now I might have made a big mistake. Knowing now that you're still carrying this pain with you, I can't imagine why it didn't occur to me you needed to talk. I'm just sorry I haven't been where you needed me to be."

Her mother leaned over and tried to put her arm around Suzanne, but she pulled away, needing to get everything out.

"Doesn't it strike you as odd that you and I have never talked about any of this since?

Her mother got up from the swing, and walked over to a patch of blooming Bird of Paradise and broke off a dead leaf. She came back and sat down in a garden chair adjacent to the swing where Suzanne was sitting waiting for her mother's reaction.

"Surely, you must know how proud we are of you. What happened back then was so long ago, your father and I don't even think about it any more."

"Well I have off and on ever since he was born. I worry about him. I'm embarrassed that it happened. I'm not satisfied with my decision. I think I've disappointed you by not marrying like your other friends' daughters and providing you with a grandchild you can hold and show off and love."

"You have no reason to be embarrassed and I'm certainly not disappointed. I don't know where to start." Her mother gazed into her daughter's dark brown eyes.

Suzanne put her finger up to her lips, shushing her, begging her to listen.

"From that January after Riley was born until this very day I've done everything that I could to forget him, but nothing works. I graduated from UCLA magna cum laude, made Law Review, passed the bar exam in two states, became the first female partner at McKinney & Lasley, and I was appointed to the Atlanta District Court. Yet ..."

Suzanne's voice broke.

"Take your time, Suzanne."

"Every day since we gave him away, Mom, I get down on my knees and pray that he's okay, happy, you know?" Suzanne studied her mother to see if any of what she was saying made sense. "I've lit a candle and made a wish that he has joy in his life, on each and every last one of his seventeen birthdays." Suzanne sighed.

"Mothers worry about their children. I've certainly done my share. Riley has had a good life. The Caines were good people."

"Yet, I feel so damn guilty. The guilt oozes into places I don't want it to be, like my work, undercutting my confidence in making decisions. Who am I to judge some other woman's fitness to parent when I forfeited my own rights and responsibility?"

Her mother came over and knelt down in front of her daughter and buried her face in Suzanne's lap, letting her own tears flow.

"Baby, I had no idea," her mother said, looking up at her. "Why didn't you tell me?" There was so much she wanted to ask her daughter, to say, to explain. "Claim your life experiences. They make you imminently qualified to wear your robe."

"Why did we name him Riley?"

Her mother wiped away her own tears; her carefully applied make-up had begun to run.

"We didn't have much time to think of a name, so when the nurse came to me to get the information needed for the birth certificate, your father suggested Riley."

"Wasn't that your father's name?" Suzanne remembered pulling out her grandfather's obituary from the back of a family photo album.

"Yes, it sure was – a family name from way back."

"Mom, when you drop your hints about wanting grandchildren, do you ever think about Riley?"

"No, Suzanne, I don't. You might fault me for that," her mother said. "But keep in mind we didn't just leave him in a basket covered with a blanket at the door of a convent. We carefully selected a loving family who wanted a child of their own. I suspect his adoptive grandparents have showered him with lots of love over the years. Surely there can be nothing wrong with my wanting to have that same experience with my own grandchildren in the future."

"I liked the couple that adopted Riley. If it wasn't for them, I don't know what I would've done all these years."

"You're right. They were a blessing sent our way."

"I've taken some comfort in knowing that he was growing up as part of a family that loved him and was providing him with many of the things you and Dad gave me growing up. The home I couldn't provide for him myself... under the circumstances."

"You're such a good girl, a kind and loving woman. I love you so much." Velda took her daughter's hands in hers. "Whatever, whenever you need me, I'm here. Okay?"

"I love you too."

Suzanne reached out and gave her mother a long hug. For a long time, they sat by the pool holding hands in reconciliatory silence. Their conversation wasn't finished. They'd pick up where they'd left off another time. She'd never felt as close to her mother as she did on that afternoon. Velda Vincent was first and foremost her mother. But Suzanne now also felt the security of knowing she could count on her mother to be her friend.

After several minutes of saying nothing, a loud growl erupted from Suzanne's stomach and broke their solitude. Both women chuckled.

"Don't you think we've earned ourselves a couple of Ernesto's signature margaritas," her mother asked. "Let's go get some lunch!"

"Absolutely," Suzanne laughed. "I'll be right back. I'm going to go get my purse."

At that moment, she could think of nothing better than sipping a tangerine margarita across the table from her mother.

TWENTY-THREE

S uzanne and her mother had the restaurant all to themselves. The afternoon had passed them by as they talked out by the pool, so they arrived in between the lunch and dinner crowds. Ernesto greeted them warmly, recognizing the two women, and offered them their choice of table. Suzanne chose her favorite booth in the back of the restaurant because of its window's picturesque view of the San Gabriel foothills, the custom homes on the cliff and the huge boulder shaped like the head of an eagle. The elderly waiter handed them two menus and turned away, prepared to allow them a few minutes to consider the selections. Hunger and habit quickly intervened. Suzanne's mother stopped him and placed the only order they had ever placed in their fifteen years of patronage – tangerine margaritas and the chicken verde enchilada special.

It was a lovely Southern California autumn afternoon. Drained by their earlier conversation, they quietly waited for the waiter to return with their orders. Outside the restaurant adjacent to their booth was a beautiful Japanese elm tree. Suzanne reminded her mother of the multi-colored ceramic cockatoo the restaurant owner had put on one of the tree branches when the restaurant first opened. She had first discovered the ornamental bird one day when she was there with her grandmother celebrating her first perm and piano recital – all in the same day.

"I'm afraid I have very sad news about the Floodys."

Mamie Floody was her mother's oldest friend and had been the maid of honor at her parents' wedding. Joe Floody and her father were golf buddies.

"Why? What's wrong?"

"They're getting a divorce," her mother said.

"A divorce? At their age? They've been married forever, what reason could they possibly have at this point in their lives to separate?"

"It's a long story. Suffice it to say that Mamie found a box of cancelled child support checks Joe had written to some woman from his past tucked away in their basement. When she confronted him about them, he confessed to getting a girl pregnant back before they got married. I tried to convince her to change her mind and let bygones be bygones. She won't listen to me. She's devastated that Joe kept something this important from her all of these years. Poor Joe, he's a wreck. The whole thing is a disaster. It just doesn't pay to try to keep a secret from your mate. Sooner or later, he or she will find out and whatever you were trying to hide will mushroom into something even bigger."

"Has she filed yet, Mom?"

"No, this is all new. She was downstairs last week doing some spring cleaning when she found the box of checks."

"Well, maybe I can talk to her before I leave. At the very least, they shouldn't rush and get a divorce. They need to take some time to reflect. Divorcing isn't the only answer. Sometimes older couples facing irreconcilable differences will file for what's called a legal separation, and then ultimately get back together."

Some of Suzanne's saddest cases involved couples who have been married for thirty, forty or more years and then appear in court to finalize a divorce neither spouse truly wants. Pride and stubbornness prevents them from admitting they've made a mistake. Suzanne always made sure the parties coming before her knew it's never too late to change their minds.

"Oh, would you, dear? I can't bear the thought of either of them living out the rest of their time alone, apart from the other."

"I'd be happy to. The Floodys are like family to me."

Warm rays from the westerly sun massaged the back of Suzanne's shoulders as she sipped her margarita and dipped the freshly made tortilla chips in the chunky guacamole dip. Suzanne was content, eating and listening to her mother catch her up on the faculty room drama at her school and the private lives of her bridge club's grown children. They commiserated about how to get their sorors from their respective chapters to talk less about doing for the community and actually rolling up the sleeves of their knit suits to execute projects that had a meaningful impact on the less fortunate. When the waiter returned to check on them, mother and daughter each happily ordered a second margarita and continued to bask in the joy of each other's company.

TWENTY-FOUR

T he telephone was ringing as Suzanne and her mother were coming into the kitchen from the garage.

"Suzanne, would you grab that please?"

She reached for the phone which stood out amongst the high tech electronics and ultra modern kitchen appliances in the Vincents' kitchen. For some reason which Suzanne never understood, her mother was still hanging onto the quaint rotary phone.

Piano bar music was playing in the background. "Oh, Hi, Dad."

"Hi Babe. Welcome, home," her dad replied. "I called the house a little earlier but nobody answered."

"Mom and I just got back from having lunch at Ernesto's."

He laughed. "What do you mean, lunch? It's after six!"

"Well, we got off to a late start –

"Say no more, I bet you and your mother got to talking. Look Babe, unfortunately, I'm not going to be able to get home early tonight like I'd hoped. My night manager had to drop everything and take his wife to the hospital. They're expecting their first baby and I just can't –

"Don't worry about it, Dad." Suzanne was disappointed, but understood how hectic her father's schedule at the club usually was. As she talked, she smelled the large basket of yellow and orange nasturtiums her mother had set out at the bend in the kitchen counter. "We'll have plenty of time to catch up. It's almost

9:30 Atlanta time, so I'll probably head up for bed before too long, anyway."

"Did you see my note?" He asked.

"I sure did."

"So you're available to hang out tomorrow morning with your ole' man?"

"Of course. I'm looking forward to it."

"As am I. But I gotta run, now. Give your mom a kiss for me. Sleep tight, Babe."

"Sure thing. Good night, Dad."

She replaced the receiver in the antique gold cradle, touched that her father was still so open with his love for her mother. Just maybe, if she were lucky, she might enjoy forty years of marriage like her parents. Suzanne dimmed the track lighting so it wouldn't be totally dark when her father came home.

On her way upstairs to deliver her father's kiss, her cell phone went off.

"Hello."

"Suzanne, it's Oliver."

"Hey, Oliver, it's me. Everything okay?"

"Actually, it's not. There's an article in today's *Courthouse Review* about Saturday. They got a hold of that angry grandmother and encouraged her to spill her guts. Rotherman is quoted extensively."

"And what gems of wisdom does he dispel?"

"Listen to this crap. Quote: Adoption is a sacred ritual, the beginning of a family, the cornerstones of our communities. When I'm elected, I will respect the sanctity of adoptions and the families created thereby without the Jerry Springer drama which personifies the incumbent. Close quote."

"What a jerk!"

"I hate to say I told you so. I won't keep you. We'll talk more about this when you return. Give my regards to your parents."

"Thanks, Oliver, I will. Have a great weekend."

"I will. Oh, I've got some good news."

"Do share!"

"Next year you'll be able to wish me Happy Father's Day. Jaxie and I found out yesterday that we're expecting."

"Congratulations. I know you've always wanted a namesake."

"Indeed, we're already decided on the baby's name. Oliver the third, if it's a boy and Olivia, if it's a girl."

I guess you can't keep a virile man down.

Suzanne poked her head in her parents' room. Velda was sitting at her dressing table taking off her jewelry. The white dressing table had been an anniversary gift from Suzanne's father. He had found it in an antique shop in the romantic seaside town of Carmel along Highway 101.

"Special delivery," Suzanne said, planting a kiss on her mother's smooth cheek. "That's from your adoring husband."

"Oh?" The sixty year old woman blushed. "That must mean he's been detained," she said.

"You know your Beck well. He said Luther had to cut out to take his wife to the hospital – time for the baby."

"I'm sorry dear. Hopefully, you're not too disappointed. I confess, though, I wouldn't trade having you all to myself today for anything." She smiled up at Suzanne.

Her mother unpinned her hair. Suzanne reached for the gold plated cloisonné brush. It was a family heirloom, having belonged to her great grandmother, then her grandmother and now it belonged to her mother.

"I agree, today has been special," Suzanne said softly. Velda closed her eyes as Suzanne began to brush her mother's hair, each gentle stroke a loving assurance that all was forgiven. She kissed her mother again, this time for herself, and said good night.

TWENTY-FIVE

A strong waft from her father's coffee brewing downstairs roused Suzanne from a deep, peaceful sleep. She put on the pink and green quilted silk kimono and slippers her mother had left at the foot of her bed. *Mom never overlooks a detail.* Beckham Vincent was right where he was every morning – sitting at the table in the bright breakfast nook, drinking a cup of coffee. Suzanne's father looked up from reading the morning edition of the *Valley News*, as she walked in.

"Good morning, Daddy," Suzanne missed a step as the toe of her right slipper folded backwards.

"Careful, Babe. Good morning to you!" He folded the section he was reading twice, laid it down and got up to give her a big hug.

"Mmmm, that coffee smells good." She fixed herself a cup and sat down with him at the table. The nook was chilly. Her dad liked to sit there with the window raised slightly to let in the crisp Southern California morning air. She pulled up the collar of her robe. "What time is it anyway?"

"A little past eight," her father said.

"How long have you been up?" Suzanne asked him.

"Just for about a half an hour. You know me. I wanted to get the paper read before it got too busy around here."

"Mom's still sleep, eh?"

"Yep, she waited up for me last night and then we talked for quite awhile about a certain someone and things."

He knows. That was how it used to be growing up when she had something really important to tell her parents. Suzanne would confide in her mother, who in turn would tell her father to pave the way for further discussion. Then when she was ready to discuss things with her father he would already know. She had missed their three-way means of communicating and was relieved to know her mother had reinstituted it last night. It hadn't been as hard as she anticipated telling her mother, after first sharing what had happened with Dr. Peters. But she wasn't looking forward to repeating everything for a third time to her dad.

"Dad, I was wondering—

"Yeah, Babe?"

"Would you mind taking me by the cemetery this morning to visit Momo?"

"Not at all," Her father smiled at Suzanne, as he got up to fix his standard breakfast of a slice of cracked oat wheat toast with a smear of peanut butter.

"How's the club?" she asked.

"I can't complain. Business is good. There's a steady stream of regulars with a good amount of new folks."

"Anything new on stage?"

"As a matter of fact, about a month ago, I decided to try an open mic night on Tuesdays."

"That's great, Dad. All the hot spots in Atlanta have open mic nights."

Beck came by his love of jazz naturally. His father was a real jazz man who honed the harmony of his horn down in the bayou. It was not until after Suzanne's college graduation that her father retired from the South Pasadena Police Department and opened his supper club, Mr. V's Jazz Cellar. Located on a vista overlooking the Rose Bowl near the corner of Orange Grove and Colorado boulevards, the club was one of the few things Suzanne remembered her mother ever complaining about. Velda wanted her husband at home at night. Suzanne's father prided himself on featuring the full range of jazz onstage, and occasionally would pick up his saxophone and join the band, treating his customers to a rift or two.

"Which reminds me, a woman came into the club last night with a group of folks to hear our new act," Suzanne's dad said. "She asked me if I was your father. I didn't recognize her at first. I thought she might be some private investigator hired by some hot shot attorney with a case before you trying to get the goods on you." Her dad winked at her. "But she said you two went to UCLA together."

"Oh, Dad, don't you know anybody can go online – do a Google search and get the goods on me and you, for that matter." Suzanne and her dad laughed. "What was her name?"

"Tamara something. Here, I wrote it down so I wouldn't forget."

He walked over to the kitchen counter and pulled a card out of his wallet. Suzanne glanced at the name, Tamara Odom, and number jotted down on the back of her father's business card.

"Oh my God, Dad, this is my freshman roommate, Tammy. I can't believe it! I haven't seen or talked to her since college."

Of all times for Tammy to resurface!

"She said she would be around this week and made me promise to have you call her," her father said, sitting back down at the table with his toast.

"Oh, I definitely will. If it weren't so early, I'd call her right now."

Through the years Tammy had crossed her mind. The firecracker co-ed had taught Suzanne more about her self than any of her college professors. *Will we be able to just pick up where we left off?*

"You look great, Dad. Are you still exercising regularly?"

"At least a couple of days during the week, I try to walk or cycle a few miles. I go a little longer on the weekend."

"Yes, a worried mama bird has told me," Suzanne teased.

She had to smile. Her father had a proclivity toward long walks and rides. Velda often called her daughter on Saturday mornings, worried because her dad hadn't yet returned from his extended weekend jaunts. He refused to comply with his wife's request that he wear a watch because he said trying to keep track of time while exercising made him feel like a hamster on its exercise wheel.

Suzanne's father reached behind her to pull a couple of bananas out of the hanging copper wire basket.

"Here have one," he said, handing Suzanne one of the bananas.

"What do you want to do this morning, Dad?" she asked, as she peeled the banana.

"Well, I've an idea," he replied. "Did you bring any exercise clothes?"

"Maybe." she smiled. "My answer will definitely depend on what you have up your sleeve, Daddy Beck."

Prior experience taught her not to head out with her father, without first being clear on the destination.

"What do you say we leave the car at home, and pump over to Pine Glory to pay our respects?"

"Isn't that pretty ambitious, Dad?"

"Come on, it's not that far. I'd have to map it out, but my guess is that the cemetery is probably only about five miles or so from here."

Oh, Lord. Five miles there and five more back! I can't remember the last time I've been on a bicycle, but then again, these thirty-something thighs of mine could always use a work out. What the heck, a little spontaneity might be fun.

"Okay, you're on! Let me run upstairs and throw something on."

"That's my girl. Meet me outside in the garage."

A few minutes later she joined him. His helmet was on and he was leaning over a map spread out over the hood of his car. She peered around his shoulder.

"Did you come up with our route?"

"Yep, sure did," he said.

He showed her on the map, then folded it and put it back in the glove compartment of his truck.

"I guess that looks doable," Suzanne said.

If I dance every week, I should be able to pull this off.

She walked toward the 5-speed bicycle her father had set out for her, picking up the helmet hanging on the handle bars.

"I don't suppose I can talk you out of making me wear this awful thing, now can I?"

"Nonnegotiable, as you lawyers like to say," he chuckled, watching her fuss with folding her hair into the helmet and frown as she adjusted the strap. "Oh come on, now, you women and your hair."

"Easy for you to say, you didn't just get yours done," she said with a pout.

Her father led the way out of the driveway and she fell in behind as they pedaled through the neighborhood to make their way to the main thoroughfare. The homes were older, well built, showplaces with thick green lawns and carefully tended rose gardens. The sun was trying to break through the light fog. Suzanne released her worry about the helmet and dampness ruining her hair and focused on peddling faster to keep up with her almost 70 year old father. By the time they reached Pine Glory Memorial Park, her aching legs were talking to her – a painful reminder that it had been awhile since she had mounted the elliptical machine at her neighborhood "Y."

Her grandmother's grave was located in a newer section of the cemetery, around a couple of bends, not far beyond the massive gates at the entrance. Families paid premium prices to secure one of the shaded spots for their loved ones. They braked at the foot of a grassy incline.

"I'll wait down here with the bikes, so you can have some time alone," her father said.

She paused. *Am I ready for this?* Her father nodded at her, urging her to go on up.

"Thanks, Dad. I won't be long."

"It's near a large fig tree. Take your time, Babe."

Twenty-Six

S he walked up the slight hill, taking care on top not to slip or step on the neighboring graves. It was her first visit to the cemetery since the funeral. The previous December, the shock of her grandmother's murder numbed her to the core, leaving her dazed throughout the interment, remembering very little except the entanglement of extended hands and well meaning hugs and the smell of freshly plowed earth. When she found the shaded marker, she knelt down on the moist grass, tracing the bronze lettering with her fingers.

Helen Thomas Carrington
Beloved Wife, Mother, Grandmother
1926 - 2006

"Momo, it's me. Suzanne. You may not recognize me with this stupid helmet on my head – you know, Dad, him and his safety thing. I miss you so much – do you hear me when I talk to your picture on my piano. Mom and I finally talked about Riley. She listened, just like you used to."

Cause of death: homicide by asphyxiation. Suzanne had a copy of her grandmother's death certificate and the retiring homicide detective's preliminary and only report which speculated that the home invasion and theft was motivated by a need for drug money. A year later the authorities had uncovered no leads on the murder suspects. They had tied her up with her own bed sheet, suffocated her with a pillowcase and left her to be discovered by her daughter. There were signs of a struggle, as much as an eighty year old woman could put up.

"They were such cowards, running around somewhere still pretending as though what they did made them men and worthy of membership in the some gang. You were so brave to try to defend yourself, your home, your honor. When under attack, you fought back. The courthouse mafia's coming after me, Momo. I'm going to do my best to fend them off, just like you fought off your attackers. That's the least I can do to honor you."

As Suzanne stood up, she noticed another grave. It didn't have the characteristics of a new grave. The grass grew long and thick out of hard dirt. What stood out about the grave was its size: not more than a few feet in length, a sure sign that the grave's occupant had graced the earth for only a short period before reaching her destination of baby heaven. She studied the words carefully, trying to place the name of the deceased:

One of God's Littlest Angels
Patience Thomas
Beloved Daughter
1944 - 1945

How come I never knew? Maybe she had misjudged the comparative magnitude of her own grief in giving up Riley. Surely, nothing could be more tragic than to lose a child of such tender years to the hand of death.

On the way back home Suzanne and Beck spotted a curbside bagel shop with a bike rack. They stopped to grab something to eat. Suzanne ordered her favorite – pumpernickel toasted with light butter.

Waiting for her dad to come out with their orders, she sat at an outside table near their bikes, knowing their conversation would ultimately turn to Riley.

"Dad, I guess everyone but me knows about Patience?"

"Yes, Babe, your grandmother didn't like to talk about it. My understanding from your mother is that before your grandmother met Popo, she was a school teacher in a small town in Mississippi and the white principal took a fancy to her and the next thing she knew she came up pregnant. She moved back to California and had the baby. The baby caught pneumonia and died before her first birthday. Momo never quite got over the baby's death."

"How sad. Now I understand why Momo doted on Mother so." *Or tried to intervene when you and Mother sent me back to your folks in Detroit.*

"The minister who married us warned me never to try to come between your mother and grandmother. Trust me, I never did. That was one recipe for living I tried to follow to the letter."

"Speaking of recipes, are you making your famous Motown macaroni and pepper jack cheese casserole for dinner tonight?"

"That's the plan, unless your mother bans me from the kitchen. She said something last night about running over this afternoon to that Lake Avenue boutique she loves to get something festive to wear for dinner." He laughed. "Any excuse for something new. Maybe I can sneak into the kitchen and make it while she's gone. You'd think Sidney Poitier was coming to dinner."

Suzanne let out a hearty laugh. She felt good sitting with her father. "Well, maybe I'll join you. Help me choose. I can't decide between making crab bisque or butternut squash soup."

"Either would be nice. Suzanne, I hesitate to bring this up, but there will be four of us for dinner."

"Four?"

"Yes, has your mother said anything to you about John?"

"Like three times yesterday." Suzanne rolled her eyes. "Please tell me she didn't..."

"You know your mother. She's convinced you two belong together."

Suzanne sighed. "And what do you think?"

"You know I'm very fond of John. He's a father's dream of a son-in-law. By that I mean he seemed to care for you and treat you the way you deserve to be treated. But, as I told your mother, we should respect your judgment about him."

"Was he invited for dinner or just dessert?"

"The last I heard, he'll be joining us – for all four courses."

"Is that a problem, Suzanne? Because if it is..."

She really didn't know. The longer she put off calling, the harder it became to convince herself it was the right thing to do.

"I'm not sure, Dad. We speak only infrequently now. Actually, I'm surprised he accepted."

"And pass up my macaroni and cheese?" Her father smiled.

"You've got a point there. The main reason why John is out here is because I haven't been myself for several months, and I can't explain to him why."

Her father shook his head. "You women are always whining about us men – how we aren't sensitive enough, how we don't listen to you when we come home, how we don't understand the pressure you're under, blah, blah, blah. Then when you have something we might really be able to help you with, you withdraw."

"What do you mean, help how?"

"I worry about you being all alone in Atlanta. You've got a high pressure job, maybe a campaign around the corner and from what your mother shared with me last evening some other issues."

"John doesn't know anything about Riley. He wants to settle down and start a family... a family of his own."

A family of his own, some babies to bounce on his knee and show off to his friends, not my almost grown abandoned son and whatever baggage might come with him!

"A single guy with no kids and eyes only for you, and you send him packing?"

"Come on, Dad, I didn't send him anywhere. He took an assignment out here. We needed some space, that's all."

"So you're one of these 21st century women who pretend they prefer early morning power breakfasts to making French toast for their children?"

"No. Yes. I don't know, Dad. Until I work through my issues, as you call them, I'm not sure what I want."

"Babe, I'm going to say this, and then I'm through. I've already exceeded my fatherly advice. Since the day I laid eyes on your mother in that smoky, juke joint down in New Orleans, I've always been honest with her. At times, to be true to that ideal, I risked disappointing or hurting her, and honesty may boomerang. But we got through whatever the issue might have been, together."

"Hey Jazz Man, you're a pretty wise dude. You may be right about John. We'll see what happens tonight."

"That's a good start." He glanced at his watch. "Can you believe it's almost noon? We'd better head back home before your mother sends out her truancy posse."

TWENTY-SEVEN

As six o'clock drew near, Suzanne hovered in front of her bedroom mirror. She could feel the warmth of her breath as she closely examined her perfect make-up. *How about if I stay up here for the rest of the evening and let them do dinner without me.* Her mother had assured her at least three times that her white capri pantsuit was flattering and didn't make her look bloated. *"Are you kidding? If you were any thinner, you'd blow over."* Sensing her daughter's nervousness, Velda eventually left Suzanne alone to fret about nothing in particular. A million thoughts swirled around in her head as she put off facing John for as long as she could. *Has he met someone else? Did he accept the dinner invitation simply to be polite? Or does he miss me as much as I miss him?*

Their time apart over the past few months had given Suzanne a chance to reflect on their relationship and forced her to acknowledge what a significant part of her life he had become. He meant a great deal and she was ready to let him know how much. All she needed was an opportunity to talk to John and if he indicated a willingness to give her another chance, she would accept it and never take him or his love for granted again. She didn't know many women whose men offered to cook on days when they arrived home from work dead tired, or sent flowers regularly for no reason at all, or listened attentively to whatever they wanted to gripe about, with the television turned off. John did all of that and so much more. And all he wanted in return was for them to plan a future together. *How many more people*

do you need to tell you the same thing: fix things with your man,
Suzanne!

John arrived right on time. Suzanne could hear her parents
greeting John downstairs at the front door. She joined them in the
foyer. As hard as she tried, she couldn't help but beam when she
saw him. Suzanne felt like an excited school girl, having a boy over
for the first time. John arrived with an expensive chardonnay for
dinner and an exquisite chocolate creation for dessert. He also
brought Velda a bouquet of white and purple orchids and pink
stargazer lilies. Her mother took the flowers to put them in water.
Suzanne excused herself and followed her with the wine and
dessert box to the kitchen. John and her father wasted no time
catching up and comparing golf scores while the women attended
to the last minute details.

Once seated, the dinner conversation flowed easily amongst
the four of them, as so many others had before. John had flown
out with her to visit her parents on several occasions. Suzanne
was struck by how comfortable things felt throughout the meal
with her parents on each side of her and John sitting across the
table.

While sitting there, Suzanne began telling them about some
of her cases since her transition from the Criminal Docket to the
Family Docket.

"I bet you don't miss having to sentence the defendants,"
Velda said.

"You're right about that, Mom."

"In Atlanta I'd imagine most of the defendants are black?" her
father asked.

"Yes," Suzanne replied. "Sadly, that's true, and very young."

"We're never going to reduce crime in our communities if we
don't reach back and lend some support to these kids coming up,"
Suzanne's mother said. "The schools can't do it alone and it's too
late for most when they enter the criminal justice system.

"Mrs. Vincent, you're absolutely correct," John said. "I've
actually been considering recently how I can do my part. At least
while I'm still single, I'd like to make some time for mentoring a
kid."

Suzanne avoided her father's *'I told you so'* stare.

"It has to be tough growing up without a support system." John turned his attention away from Suzanne's mom to look at her. "What I'm not as sure about is whether I should get involved in a mentoring program out here or wait until I return to Atlanta."

"That's an important question, John. Kids can form attachments pretty quickly. Nothing would be worse than making that kind of commitment and then having to pull out of the program." Suzanne's mother glanced over at her daughter as if to say *'chime in any time.'*

"Well, something to think about.... Mrs. Vincent, everything was delicious."

"Why thank you, John. We are so pleased you were able to join us."

Velda Vincent was in great spirits. "But I can't take credit for the entire meal, Suzanne and her dad helped a great deal. In fact, can you believe they kicked me out of my own kitchen this afternoon?" Everyone laughed.

Suzanne's mother turned to her husband. "Dear, would you help me clear away some of these dishes so we can make room for the wonderful dessert John brought us?"

Her parents filed out of the dining room, carrying dishes and left Suzanne alone with John for the first time all afternoon.

"You look well, Suzanne," John said.

She returned the gaze of the man who had won her heart and had become her best friend in the process. They had met through mutual friends – her first and only blind date. A bold sky dive together sealed their fate.

John was wearing the blue, Italian silk pullover she had given him for Christmas the year before. It hung perfectly over his broad defined shoulders exactly as she knew it would when she spotted it in the window of a small shop back in Atlanta.

"Thank you. So do you."

"When do you leave?"

"I'm flying home Sunday after brunch with my dad."

"Then would you have dinner with me tomorrow?"

Man, he looks good.

"I was hoping you'd ask," she said as she played with her linen napkin.

"Great."

"Where would you like to meet?" Suzanne smiled.

"I'll pick you up at seven."

Her parents rejoined them. John rose to leave shortly after they finished with the dessert and coffee. After he said goodbye to her parents, Suzanne followed him to the door. He reached down and kissed her gently on the forehead, then whispered in her ear, "I've missed you."

"Me too," she mouthed back to him. "See you tomorrow."

She closed the glass door behind John, her heart beating rapidly. *Pushing him out of my life was the second biggest mistake I've ever made.*

TWENTY-EIGHT

H er trip home had taken one unexpected turn after another. A reunion with her college roommate after eighteen years was the last thing Suzanne would have expected. Tammy was thrilled to hear from her when she called the previous day. *Tamara Odom, a minister's wife – one just never knew.*

Tammy suggested they meet at her husband's church. The church was located in Altadena, a community nestled at the base of the foothills, only a short distance directly north from where the Vincents lived. Tammy had given Suzanne two landmarks to watch for. Straight ahead on her right was the first, a cluster of public housing apartments. Suzanne slowed down when she saw the second, the strip plaza containing the liquor store, a laundromat and a Korean owned grocery store. According to Tammy's directions, the church should be coming up soon. Suzanne glanced at the address she had jotted down, then proceeded to park her mother's CRV in front of the modest edifice. The magnetic letters posted on the portable sign stationed in front of the church read:

Mountain View Community Church
"The Empty Chair at the Table"
11:00 a.m. Sunday
Rev. Lance Dillard, Pastor

She walked around to the side door Tammy told her would be unlocked. Taped on the door was a handwritten sign: *"Boys Night In"* Volunteers, See Sister Dillard.

"Oh, Sister Dillard!" Suzanne couldn't resist. "God sent you some help."

Tammy looked back over her shoulder from the table across the room where she was busy setting out drinks and other snacks. Dressed in overalls and her hair pulled up with a scrunchie, she broke into a broad grin and hurried across the floor to greet Suzanne. Time stopped for hugs and squeals.

"Girrrl, it's been too long, now hasn't it?" Suzanne smiled at the familiar homegirl timbre in Tammy's high pitched voice.

"It sure has," Suzanne said. "And look at you, Mrs. Preacher's Wife! You're all grown-up and . . ."

Tammy broke in to spare Suzanne having to find the right words. Tammy was no longer the hot little mama from UCLA. For each of the years since their school days, her former roommate had gained a pound or two.

"You're the one. God damn, you've gotten so sophisticated! Am I still allowed to call you, Suze?"

"Sure. But excuse me, I know you didn't just curse," Suzanne said, chuckling. "See, I knew you weren't really a minister's wife."

"Oh hush, girl. I know one thing, though, you're right on time. As you can see, my volunteers are late as usual."

"Well, you are competing with Tax Free Weekend," Suzanne said.

"Humph. Tax free nothing, this is for their boys, not mine."

"Look, I'm not in a rush. Put me to work, girlfriend."

"If nobody shows up soon, I may take you up on that. But for now, I do believe we have some major catching up to do!"

Suzanne surveyed the large room. At one end of the room was a pile of sleeping bags. They walked down to the other end and sat down on some folding chairs set up in a circle.

"I'm not sure where to start. But you go first," Suzanne said, looking around the large room, opening her arms up in a 'V'. "Tell me about you, Lance and God's work."

"There's not much to tell. You remember Lance from school, don't you?"

"Yes, but don't get mad – I only recall him as one of many guys you hung out with."

Tammy laughed. "No offense intended, none taken, girlfriend. I was generous with my love and affection, that's all."

"So when did you two get serious?" Suzanne asked.

"Toward the end of junior year. Lance and I got married the summer following graduation. The wedding was very small, that's why—

Suzanne raised her hand to spare Tammy's awkwardness. She understood. They both regretted losing contact with each other. Tammy was not to blame for anything. Suzanne sat out the fall semester to have the baby and then commuted thirty-four miles each way from home for the remainder of her time at UCLA. Life had taken its toll on their relationship.

"Anyway, I got pregnant right away with the twins, Bryan and Jason. They'll be fourteen in February. Our daughter, Alexis, is twelve."

"Sounds like you have your hands full."

"You got that right. Lance has the twins with him now running some errands for this lock-in he's planned for tonight. I can't even begin to imagine raising kids alone, especially boys. Women our age who choose to be single mothers are crazy in my book."

Suzanne wanted to challenge Tammy on her last point, but didn't.

"And what about Miss Alexis?"

"She begged us not to make her hang around here all day. Since it's a boys-only event, we let her off the hook. She's spending the day with a friend."

"I'm sorry I won't get to meet them."

"So am I. Although, there's a chance you might get to see the boys. They should be back before too long."

"Wow, I don't think I've spoken to Lance since—

"Freshman spring break?"

Suzanne nodded. "When did he get interested in the ministry?"

"It just sort of happened. But you know, I think more than anything else, it was his passion about working with inner city kids, especially the boys that called him to Mountain View."

"How so?"

"We joined this church about ten years ago after Lance accepted a job coaching high school football at a school not far from here. Many of his players lived in the public housing across the street. Every day, he'd come home talking about the life skills the boys were lacking."

"Sounds like the defendants that come through my court."

"I bet it does. There's so much he wanted to help them with, more than he could during the limited time he had them for football practice. And then a youth minister position was created here. Lance had all of these ideas for how he could build the youth program for the church. I think he started out thinking it would be a way for him to spend more time with the boys from the school – you know, keep them out of trouble."

"You must be very proud of him," Suzanne said.

Tammy broke out in her broad smile.

"Oh, I am. He served as our youth minister for a few years and then, stunned me one day by announcing he wanted to go to seminary school. He did and four years ago, after the senior minister retired, Lance was called to pastor the church."

"What's it like to be the first lady of the church?"

"That's kind of hard to explain. I'm Lance's partner in this ministry. Every day is different." Tammy smiled, looping her fingers through her overall straps. "As you can see, I do a helluva lot more than wear those big hats TV preachers' wives have on."

"Does he ever preview his sermons for you?"

"Funny you should ask. Not usually. But I did actually help him with the title for this week."

"I noticed it when I drove up. Catchy title: *The Empty Table.*"

"Thanks. Tonight's lock-in, Sunday's sermon, Lance's boyhood, they're all related."

"How so?"

"For our congregation, doting on fathers at jazz brunches or barbecues in the park only happens on Cosby show reruns or a Hallmark E-card."

"Lance didn't grow up with a father?"

"Nope. I think that's why he connects with these boys, their anger, sadness, he's been there. The purpose of the lock-in is to give the boys a safe place to talk about their feelings."

"We need more Lances," Suzanne said.

"When he told me what he wanted to focus on this week, the concept of the empty chair came to me, you know, the emptiness filling the voids caused by unresolved relationships or the nagging issues lurking in everyone's life."

"Now that's a sermon I need to hear," Suzanne said, not meaning to.

"Trust me, we all do. But now it's your turn. What's going on with you?"

Tammy had talked for almost an hour, practically non-stop. It was no accident that Suzanne had urged her former roommate to bridge their eighteen year hiatus before she did.

"Well let's see... After UCLA, I headed up north to attend Stanford's law school."

"I've been to San Francisco, but never Palo Alto. I hear it's simply beautiful." Tammy said.

"Yes, it is. From there, I moved to Georgia to practice law in the Atlanta office of a national firm I clerked with during law school."

"What kind of law did you practice?"

"I was a trial lawyer, primarily representing physicians sued by their patients for medical malpractice."

"You defended doctors?"

"Yes. Doctors often get a bad rap. Medicine isn't a perfect science. Once I represented a young obstetrician. He did nothing wrong. His patient died during childbirth."

"Her family sued him?"

"The patient's husband brought a wrongful death action accusing my client of committing medical malpractice."

"You won?"

"I did. It wasn't easy, though."

"Why? I'm assuming he was black, right?"

"No, Tammy. He wasn't. Most of my clients were not African American."

"Well you're being black probably didn't help his cause."

"My being black may have factored in some, but there was a heap in the mix. He was a newcomer to a small town. She was from a very prominent family there—

"Old plantation money, I bet."

"I was from Atlanta which can actually be a liability when you're in a rural part of Georgia. The jury probably had just as many issues with me being a female attorney as being black."

"Then why did your firm send you down there in the first place?"

She'd wondered the same thing herself at the time. Ignoring the skeptical stares and gawks from folks who had never seen a lawyer like her, she tried the hell out of the case. To everyone's surprise except Oliver, the jury sided with Suzanne and her client and returned a defense verdict in the wrongful death case.

"My supervising partner felt I was ready and the attorney originally slated to handle the case suffered a heart attack a few days before he was scheduled to begin the trial."

"Well alright then, Ms. Johnnie Cochran! Your pops said you're a judge now, when did that happen?"

"Shortly after I made partner at McKinney & Lasley, a seat opened up on the Atlanta District Court. I thought it would be a long shot, so I applied merely to test my chances and to put my name in circulation."

"What was the selection process like?"

"At the time I applied, there weren't any women on the Atlanta District Court.

"I thought Hotlanta was supposed to be Mecca, you know, progressive. How could there be no women on your court in the twenty-first century?"

"Oh, the former governor had appointed a couple of women. One of them was confirmed to sit on the federal trial bench and the other was selected to serve as a state appellate judge."

Tammy giggled. "Leaving you – the drop of coffee – in a big cup of cream. Go on, Suze, forgive me for interrupting."

"Girl, the things that come out of your mouth." Suzanne smiled.

"Yeah, I know, I have to be really careful around the elder sisters of our church."

"The N.A.A.C.P. and the Georgia chapter of the Sandra Day O'Connor National Women's Bar Association lobbied hard for me. Attorneys who knew my reputation as a trial lawyer wrote endorsement letters. I made lots of phone calls soliciting support. You have to fill out a very long application. Then, you go and interview in front of a statewide selection panel. They come up with a short list – four men and me to interview with the governor. I interviewed with her first."

"I bet after your interview they cancelled the others."

Suzanne smiled. "Well, not quite."

"Girl, I'm so proud of you. All that studying you did while I was out partying paid off."

"I guess so. Except nothing's guaranteed; I'm up for reelection this year. And Tammy, I admit, I'm scared."

"Dang, you mean you got to get out and press the flesh, kiss some babies and stuff?"

"Yep. Speak at forums, raise money. Can you believe I've even got someone building me a website?"

"Get out of here. Don't worry, you'll win by a landslide."

"Let's hope so."

"Do they give you your due respect in court?"

"I have to bite my tongue every once in a while in the courtroom when some male lawyer who's only dealt with a black nanny or cook doesn't take kindly to my rebuking him from the bench, but there's a certain decorum that exists in the courtroom that holds stuff in check. Off the bench, most of the white folks I come into contact with act as though they're too busy to hate.'"

"Good. Now, what I really want to know is who's getting up under that black robe of yours."

"Oh, here we go. You haven't changed a bit."

"Then, spill it, girl. Is there a Mr. Judge Vincent? Or is the female-male ratio out of whack in Atlanta like it is everywhere else."

"Women are bumping heads and behinds over guys there just like here, DC, anywhere these days. But, yes, there's a wonderful guy in my life. Sort of."

"Is it serious?"

"Quite. He wants to get married."

"Then, what's the sort of?"

"I told him I wasn't ready."

"Why?"

Which empty chair should I start with? "Because I didn't know how to tell him about the pregnancy."

"I always wondered since you took fall semester off. Suze, did you go ahead and have it?" Suzanne nodded her head. "What's your guy's name?"

"John. John English."

"Does John need to know? For whatever it's worth, I certainly haven't told Lance everything about my past."

"This is different."

"In what way?"

"Whatever mistakes you've made you've been able to put them behind you and move on."

"For the most part," Tammy said.

"Back then, you never asked me why I didn't go through with the abortion."

"There was no need to ask. You made your decision. I thought it was courageous to walk out of the clinic and respected you for doing so."

"In the end, I gave him up. I didn't carry through on that courage."

"Suzanne, you weren't in any position to raise him, were you? And I bet your parents weren't exactly thrilled about smelly diapers and nuking baby bottles late at night, now am I right?"

"True, but, I still feel like I've failed him. Putting my life before his was so selfish."

"Okay, timeout," Tammy said. "What does this have to do with you and your guy?"

"Don't you see? John's concept of our future together didn't contemplate my already having a seventeen year old son."

"Come on, if this man loves you enough to want to marry you, it seems pretty far fetched that he would dump you merely because of a teenage pregnancy."

"It's not that simple." Sitting there, talking with Tammy, Suzanne realized how much she'd missed her friend over the years, her laugh, her unwavering support, her perspective on life – but mostly, she missed their talks. Her time with Dr. Peters had been invaluable in opening her up. Nobody could take that from her. "For the last couple of months, I've had this compelling need to find my son, and make sure he's happy."

Tammy laughed. "Now there's a thought – a happy teenager."

"Oh, well, anyway, you know what I mean. All I'm seeking is peace of mind as to his well-being."

"Then why haven't you done something by now?"

There's nothing keeping me from taking action. Nothing except some lame excuses.

"Just chicken, I suppose."

"May I give you some advice on both fronts?" Tammy asked.

"Of course."

"The first chance you get to tell John about all of this, take it!" Tammy said.

"And on the other—

"Act on your intuition."

"So, I guess you see why our black robes are so roomy – I've kept a good bit of crap swept up under mine." Suzanne said.

"That's what girlfriends are for, to help with the sweeping. You know my number, use it."

Tammy checked her watch, then glanced toward the door. Two hours later and still none of her volunteers had arrived. Suzanne helped Tammy unpack several boxes containing soft drinks, snacks and sleeping bags donated to the church. A couple of ladies finally showed up to help. Satisfied her friend had things under control, Suzanne prepared to leave. They walked out together to her mother's car.

"Suzanne, there's something I think you should know."

"What's that?"

"Keith Grayson was killed last year. You know he and Lance were real tight. Keith's family asked him to perform the eulogy."

"Oh, that's terrible. What happened?"

"He had a sporting goods store over in South Central Los Angeles. A bunch of kids broke into the store after-hours, surprised Keith who was in the back working on inventory and shot him. The police said they used an AK47."

"I appreciate your letting me know."

"Suzanne, I'm so glad we had this chance to catch up on things."

"So am I. Here's my card," Suzanne said. "My home number's on the back. I'll be in touch. You should come visit, give me a chance to show you why I love Atlanta."

The two embraced and promised, as busy women are prone to do, to keep in touch.

TWENTY-NINE

John had insisted Suzanne shut her eyes once they neared the end of the Santa Monica Freeway. It curved straight into the scenic Pacific Coast Highway. Once they came off the freeway, John kept his windows up and the heater blowing low, but let the convertible top down on his chocolate brown Porsche. The mix of the cool air above with the warm air swirling inside the car teased Suzanne who periodically suffered extreme wanderlust for the Pacific Ocean.

"Okay, you can open your eyes...in a moment...just a few.... now!" He pulled into the valet landing. The attendant opened the passenger door for Suzanne. She stood adjusting the drape of her dress. Recognizing the name of the restaurant, she let out a squeal. Splash Bar Bistro had been reviewed by all of the leading fine dining guides. It had a six month waiting list. John pulled on one of the alabaster shell door handles, and guided Suzanne into the intimate restaurant.

"After you," he said. They had a reservation for the 7:45 seating, one of only eight tables. They followed the maître d through the dimly lit restaurant anchored on stilts over the sand to a quiet corner table with a spectacular view overlooking the ocean – not much further than a wave's splash. The tables were covered with crème linen table cloths and the chair backs were carved fish. A lovely Japanese woman was bent over the black, glossy piano keys playing a soft jazz tune near the bar.

"Oh, John, this place is lovely! That woman on the piano looks familiar. I'm almost positive she lives in Atlanta."

John asked about the pianist. The maître d confirmed she was the recording artist, Takana Miyamoto, and remarked how excited the management was to have their establishment included on her West Coast tour.

Suzanne watched the waves break against the rocks while John studied the wine list. She had never noticed how the receding sea water left behind miniature rivers in the sand. She waited until he had given the sommelier their wine selections. After their first several dates, it became apparent that John was quite knowledgeable about wines and he always liked her choice of appetizer better than his own. What started as a flirtatious challenge for each to impress the other evolved into an understood custom of John choosing a short bottle of their wine to go with her selection of appetizers, and then his ordering another bottle for dinner. With their initial ordering out of the way, John settled back into his chair and gazed over at Suzanne.

"You look beautiful tonight," John said.

"Thanks." Suzanne smiled back at him, enjoying his attention. She was wearing a strapless black silk dress with a fitted bodice and full skirt exquisitely draped on a bias. Her mother had insisted she borrow a beautiful pair of drop diamond and onyx earrings and a matching necklace, which set off her bronze neckline. "This place couldn't be more perfect."

He feigned a butler's bow. "I knew you'd love it. Can a brother get his props?"

She laughed, having missed his antics.

"Maybe I should be doing the bowing!"

"Are you still playing to the night whispers in the wee hours?"

Suzanne nodded. A few years before, her paternal grandparents sold their home in Detroit and gave her the baby grand. Many nights when unable to sleep, Suzanne retreated to what John called her musical cave to play the piano. She'd leave him asleep upstairs and tiptoed to her basement where she drew on the ivory keys to restore a comforting balance in her life. Suzanne looked over at the pianist, who was deeply engrossed in an improv piece inspired, no doubt, by the restless pacific waves outside the bar window. Neither of them spoke for a few moments as they enjoyed the view.

"Hey you, I brought you up to date on the happenings back in Atlanta on the way here," Suzanne said. "It's your turn now. How do you like your new position?"

"Things are going well. I like the people I'm working with. The projects are challenging. They're keeping me busy."

"Sounds like things are working out, then."

Don't be a poor sport. Be happy for him.

A full white moon radiated down on the sand, as darkness fell.

"We never got around to our moon-lit rendezvous, did we, baby," John murmured softly, looking at her and then out at the ocean.

Suzanne was spared answering by the arrival of their waiter who placed their wine glasses on the table. John had selected a Pouilly-Fuisse. They gently touched their glasses.

"Here's to –

"Candor," she said, seizing his salute to begin the conversation she finally was ready to have.

John's eyebrows rose as he swirled his glass around to release the bouquet from the wine.

"You've got my attention. But first, do you like the wine?"

She took another sip and felt the wine in her mouth. "Yes, I do. As always, you made a great selection."

The waiter interrupted their conversation again to place their appetizers on the table.

"So, baby, what's on your mind?" John asked, looking at her intently. Suzanne absently reached up and pulled on her mother's necklace.

"John, I need to tell you about someone. His name is Riley."

The familiar crease appeared on John's forehead.

"Look Suzanne, maybe I misunderstood the reason for your accepting my dinner invitation. Let's do ourselves a favor and keep things light. If you've moved on and met someone, I'm happy for you. But for tonight, how about we just keep things simple and enjoy....the view."

He turned to look out toward the ocean.

"John, look at me." Suzanne reached for his hand. "It's nothing like that, not in the least. I love you with all of my heart and if you're still willing to put up with me, nothing would make me happier than to pick things up and move forward, as a couple."

He turned back to look at her. Suzanne had never seen him look so puzzled.

"I'm sorry. I didn't mean to jump you." *Oh, baby, but I wish you would.* "Then, who is this Riley?"

"Riley's my son." Suzanne didn't take her eyes off of John because she wanted to see his initial reaction.

John's eyes widened. He pulled his hand away from hers. "A son? You've never once mentioned having a son."

"It's a long story, but one I'm finally prepared to share with you. Please hear me out."

Most of their appetizers remained untouched in front of them. Suzanne noticed the waiter who was standing by, not sure whether he should give them more time to finish or move the meal along. She nodded to the waiter and he approached them to clear away their first course. He lifted the dishes and returned with John's choice for their dinner wine. Intuitively, the waiter picked up on the intensity of their conversation. He showed John the label, filled their glasses with their dinner wine, and after bringing them their dinner, left them to their suspended discussion.

Pretending she was talking to Tammy or Dr. Peters, Suzanne pushed forward, while John ate. She took a bite of one of the seared Dover sole she had ordered and a sip of her wine. Once she started to relate to him what had transpired back in 1988 and what she felt compelled to do, the disclosure turned out to be much less difficult than she had expected. As John listened patiently, his face softened and loving concern replaced the initial anger. There was no contempt in his eyes as she once feared. *I should have told you years ago.* She spared her best friend and lover no detail – not even her sessions with her therapist. When she had finished, he leaned over with the unused portion of his napkin and gently dabbed at the tears gathered at the corner of her eye.

"Baby, no more secrets, okay?" John said.

"Agreed. I guess I didn't want any of this to change... us."

"Give me some credit. Have I ever given you a reason to doubt my feelings for you?" John asked.

She shook her head. It was true, he never had. Suzanne lifted her glass to finish her wine, but only took a sip. She was beginning to feel a little light-headed.

"No. It's just the longer I waited to tell you, the harder it was to tell you."

John nodded, then reached across the table and gave her hand a little squeeze. He gazed into her eyes.

"You will always be the most important person in this world to me," he said. "I may not always respond with the words you'd choose for me to use, but I'm never too busy to listen."

Suzanne smiled back at John. There was no reason to doubt what he was telling her. She knew he was genuine and that she was lucky that he still cared about her. She suddenly felt very self conscious as the two of them were the only patrons left. The other tables had emptied and the restaurant was getting ready for its second seating that evening.

Their waiter approached them warily. He gestured toward her plate. "Miss, you've barely touched your dinner. Would you like me to take it back to the kitchen to warm it for you?"

Suzanne felt badly that John had taken her to such a lovely restaurant and she hadn't been able to enjoy it as he had planned.

"Actually, if you don't mind, would you wrap my entrée for me and I'll take it with me," Suzanne said.

"Yes, of course," the waiter said, looking slightly relieved that they didn't accept his offer to extend the length of dinner.

She excused herself to go to the ladies' room. When she returned, the dinner was wrapped in a foil swan and John was stirring his cup of cappuccino as he waited for her. He stood, as she took her seat.

"Here I'd hoped you were de-stressing your life, and instead, you've added another complication—

"Not adding, John, that's what I want you to understand. The Riley factor has always been a part of my existence, sort of like an undiagnosed bleeding ulcer, growing with time."

"You sound like one of your former clients."

"Do I?"

"Just a little. Anyway, what will you do when you find him?"

"I'm really not sure. I guess it'll all depend on what exactly I find."

"Baby, you need to prepare yourself for the fact that Riley is practically a grown man. He's not likely to embrace you with the affection and openness of a young kid. For every ounce of guilt you have over your separation from him, he's going to have a pound of hurt and anger."

She sighed. "I know... I know."

"Qualifying comes up pretty soon, doesn't it?"

"Week after next."

"It might be wise to wait until after the election before you go looking for him."

"John, I'm not sure I can wait any longer."

THIRTY

John and Suzanne finished their coffee and left the restaurant. They rode with the car top down for several minutes enjoying the night and each other's company.

"Do you have this one yet?" John turned up the volume.

"Is that Kem's latest project?"

"Yes, listen, this is a slightly different sound." John turned up the music so Suzanne could enjoy the sexy, smooth crooning vocalist.

John reached in her lap for her hand with his strong fingers. She turned and looked at John's profile. He shaved off his mustache since she'd last seen him and she loved his new look. The open sky overhead was covered with a brilliant spray of stars. An occasional airplane banked for a landing at LAX.

Suzanne leaned forward to turn down the heater. She was not sure if it was the temperature in the car or her anxiety over John's expectations of her for the rest of the evening that was making her warm.

Do I want to see his place? I could simply suggest that he take me back to my parents. But that would be rude, especially after I ruined our wonderful dinner. How does life stay so complicated?

John turned off of the Santa Monica Freeway, and headed north on the Harbor Freeway, getting off at Orange Grove Boulevard instead of taking the 210 west in the direction of his place. Suzanne sighed. John had given her a pass. Not that she really wanted one. With all of her distractions lately, she had managed to do without. But she was ready to make up for all those nights she had fallen asleep alone, pretending it was John touching her, and not herself.

They turned into her parents' driveway shortly before ten o'clock. Neither was ready to say goodbye, so they lingered outside. John came around, opened her door, took her hand and led her into an alcove located away from the front entrance, adjacent to the garage wall. An overhead trellis, covered with wandering vines of ivy and wisteria shielded them from the full moon illuminating the remainder of the courtyard. John took her into his arms and pulled her close to his chest. She was close enough that she could hear his heart beating and feel the warmth rising through the open neck of his shirt. She could smell his cologne mixed with traces of soap and him.

"I've missed my California girl," John whispered in a low husky voice. He kissed her long and deeply. A slow hot pulsating started midway down her body and spread south, growing stronger with his caresses. He slid his hand under the full skirt of her dress, and let out a low whistle upon feeling her red French lace thong.

"Are you wearing my favorite color?"

As he pressed against her, she could feel his growing erection beneath his pants. She gingerly unzipped them to free his bulge. John sat down on the stone bench beside them in the corner of the courtyard. Suzanne stood facing him, between his legs. He pulled her up on his lap, her legs straddling his and her full skirt draped around her waist. John unhooked the back of her dress, and the corseted bodice fell down. When he unfastened her bra, Suzanne trembled as the air danced against her nipples. He pushed her back and lightly tickled her soft skin with the tips of his fingers and his tongue, before kissing her full breasts.

Suzanne didn't know how she had endured their separation for as long as she had, but it didn't matter anymore. She was ready to give in, take what John was offering in exchange for all she had saved for him. He grabbed her hips, launching her up gently toward heaven and then eased her down on his lap. As he entered her, they found their rhythm and lost themselves in the consequence.

THIRTY-ONE

Just before dawn Monday morning, Suzanne was heading home from the Hartsfield Jackson International Airport for a quick shower and change before her 10 a.m. child support calendar, after her red eye flight from California, when Sgt. Quarles called on her cell phone. He rarely called her unless there was an emergency.

"Hello, Quarles. Your timing is good. I landed only a little while ago."

"Good morning, Judge. Disregard the message I left you at home. Good visit?"

"Very much so. I hope you had a great Father's Day as well."

"Oh, you know I did. Look, Judge, I'm sorry to call you so early but something's come up."

"What's going on?"

"I got a call from a Detective Zeller with APD. She has Bethany Lovejoy with her at police headquarters."

"Why?" Suzanne pulled right to the emergency lane to give the sergeant her full attention. "Is she in some kind of trouble?"

"I'm not sure exactly, but from what I could make out, Bethany isn't the perp, she's the victim."

"That poor girl! Do you know why they called you?"

"Judge, when she left court last week, she was pretty bummed. I gave her my card and told her to call me if she needed anything."

One of her deputy's special qualities was his willingness to help folks, often without their even asking. It was one of the things about him Suzanne most appreciated.

"Did you get a chance to speak with Bethany directly?"

"No," Sgt. Quarles said.

"The detective said Bethany was refusing to cooperate unless you were present."

Suzanne was sorry to hear about Bethany's mishap, but the young woman's request of the judge was highly unusual. Her job was not to befriend or personally aid the parties coming before her no matter how desperate or sympathetic their predicament might be. Doing so could undermine the very impartiality the judge depended upon to make her decisions. One of the more difficult aspects of her job was holding back in a situation when she knew she could best make a difference in a party's life off the bench. Bethany's situation threatened to be such a case. Judges weren't social workers, yet Bethany's unorthodox outcry pulled at her. The torn judge knew the girl had no one else to call.

"Do you know anymore about her situation?"

"Not really, Judge. Where are you right now?"

"I'm on the downtown connector, just south of Turner Field."

"Do you want me to meet you at the station?"

"No, that's not necessary." Suzanne sighed, processing what to do. "Would you call Detective Zeller back for me and tell her I'm on my way? It shouldn't take me more than fifteen minutes to get there."

"Sure thing, Judge. Page me when you find out something."

"Thanks, Quarles. I will." The judge pulled back onto the expressway, her mind on Bethany. She'd have to freshen up and change at her office, and find time for a spur of the moment ex parte encounter.

THIRTY-TWO

A matronly receptionist pointed for Judge Vincent to have a seat, her tone conveying an attitude of "I've heard it all, save it for someone who cares." As far as the receptionist was concerned, everyone got the same treatment, judges included. The hard wooden bench creaked as she took her seat. She sat up to avoid touching the wall behind her which was covered with brown stains and black streaks left by the countless heads who had waited on the same bench for news of friends or loved ones who had fallen into the hands of the law.

Directly in front of Judge Vincent, beyond the long counter where the receptionist sat, at a small desk over in the corner, an overweight, burly cop was leaning over the shoulder of a younger one. From what she could tell, it was the end of their shift and he was helping the new officer fill out an incident report. The rookie wanted to make sure the report was accurate and that he got the charges correct. The veteran wanted out of the station and a cold beer.

"Kid, what's the problem?" The older officer's booming, raspy voice bellowed. "You searched him, found a dub of coke stuck up his butt. Where I come from, that's called possession – O.C.G.A. § 16-13-30," the officer barked. "Book him so we can get the hell out of here!"

A freckled female with short wavy red hair, wearing a tailored navy pantsuit with a City of Atlanta Police Department badge clipped on her lapel approached the judge and extended her hand.

"Judge Vincent?"

"Yes." The judge stood up to greet the detective.

"Thank you for coming," she said. "I'm Detective Rhonda Zeller."

"Pleased to meet you." Judge Vincent shook her hand. "What's going on with Ms. Lovejoy?"

"Well, I'm afraid I haven't been very successful in getting to the bottom of what's happened. At this point, all I can really tell you is how things appear. It's clear Bethany's been roughed up, but we're not sure if she's been sexually assaulted, Judge. How well do you know her?"

"Not all that well. That's why I was surprised when my sergeant called to tell me Bethany had requested that I come down here. I'm only familiar with Bethany from a custody case assigned to me."

"It did seem out of the ordinary when she asked me to contact you. I just assumed you knew her personally, you know?"

Detective Zeller asked Judge Vincent to follow her down the dismal corridor. A few detectives were standing around a coffee station. The women walked past the officers.

The detective paused outside a frosted glass door marked Interrogation Room.

"Can you tell me a bit about the custody matter?" Detective Zeller asked, pulling out her notepad.

"She filed a paternity action seeking child support and her baby's father's mother retaliated with a petition for a change of custody."

"Working nights at a place like Headlamps probably doesn't bode well for her case for fitness, I would imagine."

"Custody fight aside, Bethany's doing the best she can to provide for her son," Judge Vincent replied, with a touch of irritation in her voice.

"Has anything come out in court that might shed some light on who did this to her? A boyfriend, an estranged husband, perhaps?"

"There's no husband or significant other, just her son's father, and they don't appear to have much of a relationship. Nothing surfaced during the custody hearing to suggest him as a likely suspect."

"How old is the little boy?" The detective asked.

"Two," Judge Vincent said.

"Have you established any sort of rapport with her?"

"Not to speak of, Detective. Other than what I observe of the parties during hearings, I don't typically interact with them one on one."

"Well, maybe you can help me. She's been reluctant to say who assaulted her or exactly what happened."

"Has she divulged anything?"

"No. Bethany hasn't said very much, although it's clear something happened," Detective Zeller said. "Basically all she's volunteered is that she worked her regular shift last night, got off about 4 a.m. and something happened to her on the way home."

"How did the police get involved?"

"A MARTA bus driver picked her up on one of his routes early this morning. He radioed MARTA police and they met her at one of the bus stops and took her off the bus to question her. After asking her a few questions and determining that nothing had happened on MARTA property, they brought her down to APD headquarters for further investigation. That's how I got involved. I work female assault detail."

"Since I'm here, I'll be happy to see what I can find out."

"That would be great, Judge. I'll wait outside. Any assistance you can provide would be appreciated."

THIRTY-THREE

They agreed the detective would wait outside to give her a chance to talk to Bethany alone. The glass door rattled as Judge Vincent knocked. The judge opened the door leading into the small cramped witness room where Bethany was sitting at a black metal table facing away from the entrance. The notepad in front of her was blank.

"Hello, Bethany." She announced herself so as not to startle the girl from behind.

She looked up as Judge Vincent stepped from behind to take a seat across from her at the table. The right side of her face was discolored and swollen. A couple of drops of dried blood had stained Bethany's white denim jacket. Her blouse was missing buttons and a paperclip held the front together. Judge Vincent found it hard not to show a reaction to the girl's disheveled appearance.

"Do I look that jacked up?" Bethany asked.

"No, although you do look like there's something we need to talk about," Judge Vincent said.

"That detective lady keeps asking me all these questions. I just wanna go home and get Dami from Miz Evans." Bethany scratched her head.

"We need to know what happened, Bethany," Judge Vincent said. "The sooner you tell us, the sooner you'll get to go home."

"The cop's been going on and on about how I should press charges like I don't know how things will go down if I listen to her. It'll be my word against his, and I'll be back in court with folks making me out to be something I'm not. Plus, he's already warned me that he'll mess up things for me big time if I make trouble." Bethany crossed her arms. "There's nothing to talk about."

"Bethany who are you speaking about? Who assaulted you?"

"See that's what I'm talking about. I ain't said nothing 'bout no assault."

"Bethany, this isn't a game, come clean or I'm leaving," Judge Vincent said.

"I ain't playin' no game. You were the only person I could think of that could make her let me go. She refuses to accept what I keep tellin' her."

"Bethany, it's your call about whether to take any action. But it's not reasonable to call me down here and then refuse to tell me what happened."

"Judge Vincent, you gotta promise not to tell 'em about this, okay?" Bethany looked at the judge in earnest.

"By them, I assume you're referring to Quentin and his lawyer?"

"Yep, them," Bethany said.

"Bethany, the only communication I've ever had with the Wainwrights has been in my courtroom in your presence. That's how it'll always be. I didn't come here to talk to you about the custody case or to gather any evidence."

Nothing would be gained by telling the frantic girl that the judge's involvement with the assault investigation might result in Judge Vincent's disqualification from presiding over her custody case. After hanging up with Sgt. Quarles, the judge had weighed the legal ramifications of her becoming involved against leaving the girl to deal with this crisis on her own. Judge Vincent came because she knew it was the right thing to do.

"I don't know what I'm going to do now," Bethany said.

"About what?"

"Money. You know how the order said you were giving them long weekends with Dami so I could work faster on getting my dental hygienist certificate in the next few months and get things right for me and Damien?"

Judge Vincent nodded. *Maybe I'm beginning to get through to her.* Bethany's eyes revealed to the judge all of the worry and burdens her diminutive shoulders carried.

"How's I supposed to get ahead if shit like this happens. This all started because I stood up to my boss and insisted I had to have my paycheck. I should've known better with him drinking and stuff. Now I've lost my job on top of everything else."

"Are you telling me your boss at Headlamps did this to you?"

Bethany nodded and continued, "We get paid on Saturdays. By the time I was ready to go home after work this morning, my boss, Lou, hadn't given me my check yet. I'd seen him passing them out earlier so I asked him for mine. He said mine was missing so I'd have to wait until I came in on Monday night to get it. I told him I had to pay my rent today and couldn't wait. He looked at me like that wasn't his problem. I think he thought I would let it go. But I didn't. I asked him why he couldn't just this once pay me out of the cash drawer. He gave me some line about his tax man wouldn't allow him to pay folks in cash. He finally agreed to run me by his place to get a check. So, I waited for him to close up the club and rode with him to get my money."

"What time was this?"

"Right after we closed, about 4:30."

"Just the two of you?" The judge cringed at the thought of Bethany in a car alone with her drunken boss.

"Yeah. I know it was stupid to go with him. But I knew from overhearing him talking with some of his friends that hang out at the club that he didn't live far from there and I needed my money."

"Go on," Judge Vincent said, "What happened next?"

"We pull up in front of his place and get out. While we're walking to the door, he reaches behind me and starts feeling on my butt. I didn't say anything because I knew he'd been drinking and I didn't wanna make him mad. Once we're inside I stood as close to the front door as I could, hoping he'd go write my check and give it to me. Then I would be out of there."

"I take it your boss had other plans."

"Yeah, right. The next thing I knew, he'd pinned me up against the back of his door, breathing his bad ass breath all over me and started trying to kiss me and shit. He tore open my blouse and started pulling at my pants. I pushed him away screaming at him to leave me the hell alone. He told me to shut up and knocked me to the floor. Before I could stand up, he sat on top of me pinning down my legs with his and holding down my arms. Then he pulled a knife out of his pocket and pressed the tip up under my chin. He leaned over me telling me he wasn't playing games and if I wanted my pay I better make it worth his while. I didn't know what else to do to try to get him off of me so I spit up into his eyes. That really made him mad and he punched hard right here."

Bethany touched the side of her face and turned to give Judge Vincent a better view.

"I can still feel the sting from his ring. Shit, that motherfucker hurt! That's when I ran out of his apartment."

As she listened, Judge Vincent silently listed the various charges she knew Detective Zeller would be prepared to place on Bethany's boss. Aggravated assault with intent to rape. Sexual Battery. False Imprisonment. Yet as she looked at the shaken, but determined single mother sitting across from her, she knew the man would escape responsibility. Bethany was the perfect victim. A young woman struggling to achieve a better life by waiting tables in a strip club owned by Sam Haskell's cousin.

Taking the stand was not going to happen. Judge Vincent knew without asking Bethany, that she would elect not to prosecute. If the State insisted on bringing charges as they sometimes did despite a reluctant victim, chances were they would lose the case. She couldn't blame the girl for her cynicism. What would she have to gain from another demeaning encounter with the legal system? That was not the kind of help Bethany needed.

"I'm glad you fought back. You were lucky, Bethany."

Bethany scoffed. "Lucky don't feel too good right now."

"You've got much more going for you than luck, you're very bright and you've got your whole life ahead of you. Are you ready to speak to Detective Zeller now?"

"You mean I have to go through all that again?"

"Not everything. You just need to tell her what happened so she can complete her report and if you still don't want to prosecute, explain why not."

"You think I should press charges, don't you."

"What I think isn't important, Bethany," Judge Vincent said.

"It is to me," the girl said softly. The judge smiled at her.

"Then here's what I think. Your boss' conduct is criminal. He should be held accountable. That can only happen if you help the prosecution prove what he did. Your testimony will make the difference between a so-so case and proof beyond a reasonable doubt. On the other hand, I think you should do whatever will move you forward to a better place. I'd be willing to accept your decision not to prosecute provided you make something positive come from last night."

"Such as?"

"Such as quitting Headlamps immediately."

"I was only working there 'cuz the pay was good and they give us girls our uniforms... for free."

"How generous."

"I guess I won't miss wearing the uniform."

"From what I remember from your financial affidavit, you manage your money well," Judge Vincent said. She had been impressed by the girl's financial acumen – unlike Bethany's baby's daddy who had never worked much less put on anyone's uniform.

"What little I got, I do okay with. I make enough to cover my rent, pay Miz Evans to keep Dami, and our food. We eat a lot of grits and animal crackers. I pick up clothes for Dami at the Open Closet and I wear mainly throwaway T-shirts – you know the extra-large ones with companies' names and stuff on 'em."

Judge Vincent nodded. She had never met a teenager as self sufficient as Bethany. "Bethany, I'm pretty sure you must qualify for some kind of public assistance." The proud mother scowled. "Don't think of it as welfare," Judge Vincent said. "In your case, it would only be temporary assistance – simply a way to help you get on your feet. Honey, you've earned it. I'm going to do some checking around and will have someone from my office let you know in a couple of days what you need to do. In the meantime, the pay your boss owes you, how far will that take you?"

"One whole whopping week," Bethany said.

"Don't worry Bethany, things will look better soon."

They called in the detective and Bethany told her what happened. The girl was adamant that she didn't want to press charges. All she wanted was her pay. Judge Vincent wanted to make sure she got her check, without any problems from her assailant.

"Detective Zeller, would you be able to go with Bethany tomorrow evening to pick up her check?"

"Certainly," Detective Zeller said. "I'll stop by her place and will make sure that happens. When your boss sees that the police are involved, Bethany, I'm sure that we can get your money and you won't hear from him again."

"That'll be great," Judge Vincent said. "Thanks so much. Is there anything else you need from us?"

Detective Zeller glanced over her notes and shook her head.

"No, I have what I need to do my report. Young lady, you're free to go."

"Okay then. Bethany, I'll be happy to give you a ride home," Judge Vincent said.

Bethany hesitated, "Uh, Judge Vincent, no thanks. I need to catch the bus over to the Open Closet to get Dami some more clothes. The ones he's got are getting tight. I want him to look good when they come to get him."

Detective Zeller glanced at Judge Vincent, but the judge saw no reason to explain about the transfer of custody scheduled to begin in a few days. She simply nodded at Bethany. The detective stepped in. "Bethany, why don't I give you a lift. We can run by and get the clothes, and then I'll take you home. That way, I'll know exactly where to come tomorrow evening."

Judge Vincent smiled at the detective. The woman was good at her job, very professional, yet sensitive. The judge shook the detective's hand and said goodbye to Bethany. She whispered a prayer asking God to keep Bethany strong.

THIRTY-FOUR

"Chief Judge Haskell is here to see you." Andi looked worried. Chief judges rarely made office calls.

"Send him in, I'm expecting him." He had sent Suzanne an email telling her he needed to speak with her immediately about one of her cases.

"Yes, Judge."

Moments later, Haskell knocked loudly on Suzanne's open door. He closed it, without asking.

"Please have a seat, Sam," Suzanne said.

"I'll get right to the point," Haskell said. "Folks are waiting for me."

"What's going on?"

"I've received some more complaints about you, Suzanne. If I might give you some unsolicited advice, with your re-election around the corner, you really need to tighten up."

You bastard! Finally getting around to raking me over about Pamela's mother outburst the other day, are you?

"Sam, you're being pretty vague, don't you think?"

"You know what I'm talking about."

"No, I'm not sure that I do."

"Based on what I've heard—

"When you want to know what's going on in my courtroom, don't send Rotherman to spy for you, show up yourself!"

"I don't need spies. I run this courthouse and make it my business to know what's going on in every courtroom."

"Seeing how you have people waiting on you, go ahead and tell me why you're really here, Sam. I'm busy as well, and don't have time for this go cry to the chief crap."

"I thought you could use this extra copy of the Code of Judicial Conduct." He slid the booklet across her desk. Furious, she stood and handed it back to him.

"That wasn't necessary. I'm quite familiar with it."

"Very well then, I suggest you re-read Canon Three regarding your obligation to perform the duties of this office impartially and diligently. You should know better than to meet privately with a party appearing before you and providing legal advice at that."

Haskell was not there about adoptions and spilled remains. A very different family matter brought him to her office.

"I've done no such thing! How dare you come in here accusing me of violating my oath of office."

Haskell stood up and pointed a fat finger at her.

"She's out of her league and so are you."

"Your cousin tried to rape the girl!"

"Says who? There's not a judge in Atlanta who will believe a word out of her mouth."

"There's an official incident report with an assigned detective ready to charge."

"If she brings charges and tries to smear the Haskell family's reputation, rest assured Rotherman will be the least of your concerns."

THIRTY-FIVE

No one got to speak to Judge Vincent without first clearing it through her judicial assistant. Andi screened visitors as religiously as the numbers she played in the "Big Game" on the weekend. Wednesday morning she buzzed her boss, letting her know Carey Nelson, the Court's Community Resources Officer, was heading back to her office to report on what he had found out regarding Bethany Lovejoy.

Judge Vincent had called Carey the day before about Bethany. She wanted to get some help for the girl. The girl's financial affidavit disclosed that her weekly budget just about depleted the $200.00 she made at Headlamps each week. She was stretching her meager earnings as far as she could. Not a cent was being wasted.

At the police headquarters, Bethany had explained that after paying for her room, Damien's babysitter and their other expenses, she had barely scraped together the cost of tuition for the minimum required credits in working towards obtaining her dental hygienist license. Quitting her job at Headlamps might force Bethany to withdraw altogether because she hadn't been able to put aside anything for the upcoming winter quarter registration. There had to be an easier way for the young mother to complete her training and get on her feet. Bethany was so close to obtaining her dental hygienist certificate.

Carey asked the judge to give him the rest of the day to make some inquiries, before reporting back. Judge Vincent wanted the best for Bethany and her little boy. Looking up at the handsome man appearing in her doorway, the judge smiled, and beckoned to him to come in and have a seat. Carey's enthusiasm about life always warmed those in his company. Judge Vincent liked working with him. Tackling challenges and helping people were his passion. His job was to identify the community resources litigants needed when making the difficult transitions in their lives which brought them through the Family Docket, and to facilitate the folks accessing them.

"Hey, Judge, how goes it?" Carey always sat in the chair in front of her desk on the right.

"Things are good, Carey. How about with you?"

"Oh, you know me, Judge. Today's the best day of my life. You won't hear any complaints from me, now."

"Were you able to find out anything?"

He cocked his head to one side, patting himself on the shoulder.

"Now, Judge, have I ever let you down? Not only have I found housing for Ms. Lovejoy, but she qualifies for free childcare and a tuition waiver. Here, I downloaded this from their website."

She took the printed information from him.

"You truly are a miracle worker. I'm all ears. Tell me the details."

"Sometimes, our tax dollars are put to good use. As a long term foster care dependent, Bethany is entitled to transitional assistance to help her achieve self sufficiency. You said she was nineteen, right?"

"Yes, that's correct," Judge Vincent said.

"Good, as long as she's going to school fulltime, the State will pick up the tab for the majority of her living and educational expenses."

"Oh, Carey, I'm so encouraged. She's determined, but really struggling. All she needs is a little boost. What happens next?"

"She'll need to fill out an application and schedule an interview. I'll contact her this afternoon to come in and meet with me first, then we'll go from there."

"Excellent. How soon can all of this be done?" Judge Vincent asked.

"I'll do my best to get her in to see someone this week. Realistically, though, it may take several weeks for them to assign her housing. The school part should take less time," Carey said.

"Did I mention she's carrying the minimum credits this quarter? I want her to be able to register for the maximum load over the next two sessions. The goal is to have her certificate by June."

"I understand, Judge. There's one potential problem."

"And what's that?"

Carey never oversold what he could deliver for the people he was assigned to help. He and the judge worked well together because he kept her apprised as he went about his work. Often, he would check in to discuss the best strategies to break through anticipated bureaucratic bumps in the road.

"Technically, once a teen Bethany's age leaves the foster care system, the State is not supposed to take them back."

"But, Carey," she said, glancing over what he have given her, "this says the purpose is to help kids who have aged out of foster care, yet aren't ready to be completely on their own. That certainly sounds like Bethany's situation to me. Why should she or any other young person, for that matter, be penalized because of first trying to tackle life alone." She read back over the relevant section, making sure she had read it correctly.

"Judge, as usual, you've got a point there. Looks like you've really taken a liking to this girl. Don't worry. Actually, I don't anticipate there'll be much of an issue. You always tell me to give you the good and the bad of a case, though."

"Will you be able to go with her, as her advocate?"

"You know we're busy trying to make these parents do right for the summer. But, I'll make the time. Sometimes these bureaucrats can be a pain in the butt. That's where having me along will come in handy." He flashed her another smile. "If this is what you want, we'll make this work."

"It is. Thanks again, Carey. Here's the file. Everything you need to contact Bethany should be in there."

"I'm on it. Don't give her another thought."

In cases like Bethany's, Carey could make such a difference. His work enabled the Family Docket judge to focus on the legal aspect of the cases, while he performed the social services. She felt better knowing things were about to change for the young mother. After he left, Judge Vincent slipped out of her private exit to mail an envelope she had addressed to the girl with the dingy white, denim jacket. The judge didn't include a note or a return address. Bethany didn't need to repay her and Sam Haskell certainly didn't need to know. She hoped the four $300.00 money orders enclosed would grant the girl some temporary reprieve from her daily worry about how to make ends meet.

THIRTY-SIX

S uzanne's re-election campaign was not off to a good start. She was late, and no doubt, Oliver wasn't. Their plan had been to grab some whole wheat pancakes at Thumbs Up Diner and then be first in line at the Secretary of State's Office to claim a second term.

She disregarded the yellow light and slick asphalt, pressed the gas pedal and cleared the intersection, only to catch another red signal not even a half a block away. *Dammit!* Atlanta traffic lights never gave her a break. As Suzanne pulled to a stop at the corner, a couple of homeless men dashed up from opposite sides of her car. *Give me a break, it just finished raining for God's sake. Go get a real job. And don't you dare touch my car!* An ambush by some street peddlers toting bootleg cleaning fluid and dirty rags wasn't on her morning's packed itinerary.

She waved her hands in a frantic, futile effort to keep the guys from attacking her windshield. They ignored her. The taller of the two sprayed the glass and whipped out a soiled rag to wipe off the driver's side. Then he tossed the cloth to his partner, who rubbed away on the right. The light turned green overhead and the cars began blowing their horns. Despite the small traffic jam caused by their busywork, the urban slickers didn't intend to donate their toil. The shorter man stood directly in front of her car, posing as if to admire their handiwork. His cohort knocked on the driver window, smudging it in the process, and held out his palm.

Okay, enough already. A marked patrol car pulled up behind her and activated its blue lights. "PROCEED STRAIGHT,

YOU'RE BLOCKING TRAFFIC," the patrolman commanded over his bullhorn. *Now what!* Startled by the police, the window cleaners forfeited their tip and took off running down the narrow one-way street. Prior experience with traffic cops cautioned her to do as directed. She drove through the intersection with the patrol car on her tail.

There was no place to pull over. Reluctantly, Suzanne turned left into the parking lot of an extended stay motel, a place that prostitutes, homeless families and drug deals kept in the news. Recently, a homeless man returned to his room there to find his child stabbed to death and his wife missing. Authorities located the mother wandering nude through the streets a few hours later. The woman confessed that motherhood had driven her to free the boy's body of its demons.

Suzanne retrieved her insurance card, car registration and driver's license from her purse, but decided to hold off on pulling out her judge's badge. She would resort to that only if necessary. She lowered her window.

"Two red lights. Obstructing traffic. Failure to obey an officer's command. What's the problem, lady?"

"Excuse me?" Suzanne felt her voice rising. *Be nice. You don't need any bad press on Qualifying Monday.* "I'm sorry, officer. I'm late for an important appointment."

"Ma'am, for officer safety, I need you to step out of your car. Slowly, please."

Get out into that mist and turn this into a bad hair day as well? She placed her trusty badge right on top.

"Officer, here's my identification. I can assure you I'm not a safety risk. Please look at all of this and then if you still need me to get out, I will."

"Judge Vincent, is it? This isn't your courtroom. I'm in charge." Suzanne stayed put. He walked back to his vehicle.

"Okay, Judge," he said, back at her window. "Here's your ID. Slow down and watch the lights. Without that black robe, you're no different than anybody else."

THIRTY-SEVEN

Not anxious about another round with the press, Suzanne nixed Oliver's suggestion that they hold a press conference at the State Capitol to kick off her campaign. Instead they quietly filled out the paperwork and tendered her qualifying check. By close of business on Thursday, the 2006 Georgia Election Division website revealed no other takers for her job.

"Judge?"

"Yes, Andi?" Suzanne was in her office, trying to forget her title was on the auction block.

"He did it."

"He, who? Did what?"

"Rotherman." Andi made a face. "According to the website, he qualified first thing this morning."

"I see. Oliver told me last night not to get excited, that Rotherman probably would go for the suspense factor."

"What now, Judge?"

"For you and the rest of the staff, nothing." Savvy judges shield their staffs from their campaigns. "Mostly business as usual. Juggling campaign stumps with my court docket will be the challenge."

"Do you want us to cancel anything?"

"No, Andi, I've got to do my job."

"Doesn't seem right."

"What's that?"

"Sitting judges having to go out and campaign and all."

"I'm an elected official. We knew going into this, that a campaign was possible."

"Yea, I guess you're right."

"The election isn't for four months. My schedule shouldn't get too bad until after Labor Day."

"Oh, I almost forgot." Andi handed Suzanne a slip of paper. "Here's his website."

"Thanks. I'll check it out in a little bit, maybe send him a fan email." Suzanne winked at Andi.

THIRTY-EIGHT

Suzanne typed **www.chancerothermanforjudge.com**. The homepage opened up before her. Rotherman's website was on the mark. All the critical components for a successful campaign website were prominently featured: digital images showcasing the candidate, a platform punch list, a string of endorsements by notables and common citizens. Desiree Wainwright and Gladys Fury were at the top of the list of supporters. Testimonials, a critique of the opponent and most importantly, a link for online contributions all enticed the voter. She didn't know where to start clicking.

Suzanne studied Rotherman's family photo. It screamed Buckhead Atlanta and all of its treasured traditions. His family was standing in front of their traditional Atlanta red brick two story home. A robust wife. Three small kids. A golden retriever sporting a red, white and blue bandana. Everyone was smiling, even the dog.

Curious, Suzanne clicked onto his platform page. It didn't set forth much about his race for judge. Instead it was all about her. "SURELY THE VOTERS DESERVE BETTER THAN THIS." There for everyone to see, right below the page's header, in high resolution was Judge Suzanne Vincent, standing on the steps of her therapist's office, ringing the buzzer. *How could the bastard?* The image included a sign identifying the pink building as the office of Nan Peters, Psychotherapist.

Rotherman was just getting started. At the bottom of the page was a photo of Suzanne shaking her behind on stage during her weekly dance class. Jumping out beneath it, *"Perhaps the incumbent should spend more time contemplating the life altering decisions she's been charged to make, and less time engaging in behavior unbefitting of a judge."*

The webpage highlighted her 'problem' cases with slanderous parenthetical slants spun by a pro. <u>*In re Adoption of Boy Doe*</u> *(Judge Vincent's decision leads to mother's suicide and wasted ashes).* An Adoption Day photo was posted for those who had missed the local paper's account. *"Judge Vincent dismisses child molestation charges forcing distraught mother to take matters into her own hands, blinding child in the process.*

She clicked on another photo. Rotherman was ruthless. *"Your judges are duty bound to avoid the appearance of impropriety or scandal. The recent murder of Suzanne Vincent's grandmother leaves many unanswered questions."*

Suzanne spun around in her chair and dialed Oliver Mason. It was time to turn up the heat a few degrees.

THIRTY-NINE

"Hold up!"

Riley and his associate, Isaiah, turned around to see who was yelling. Beaming flashlights partially blocked their view. Cops! They stopped as commanded.

"Shit, where did they come from? Mothafucka, youz 'pose to be keepin' an eye out," Isaiah said.

"I did," Riley said. "You said you'd be in and out. What took so long, nigga?"

"Don't worry 'bout it. Keep your fuckin' mouth shut, let me do the talkin' and if they ask your name, make up somethin'."

Two officers, one black, one white, rushed them from behind.

"Hands up!" Officer Blanco had his hand on his holster. "Higher, where I can see them."

They pushed the kids down against the hood of a car parked alongside the street, and patted them down. Blanco jammed his hand down Isaiah's pocket and pulled out a thick wad of $20 bills.

"What's this?"

Riley, having no clue, kept silent, while Isaiah smarted off.

"I don't got to tell you jack—

"No you don't, but if you want to get on your way any time soon, I suggest you do your best to convince us not to take your sorry asses down to the station."

"That's my grandmother's rent money. She give it to me to pay the man."

"Is that so?" His bushy eyebrow raised, Blanco glanced over at his partner. "Exactly where does your grandmother live?"

Riley did as Isaiah had told him and said nothing. But Isaiah's talking was only making matters worse. Isaiah had told Riley his grandmother was hard of hearing, often unable to hear the doorbell. She kept his money for him because there were too many break-ins over where he stayed. He'd left Riley in front of the house, while he slipped through the back window to get his money. Riley's job was to watch for cops in case a nosy neighbor took neighborhood watch patrol seriously.

"You're lying, kid," Officer Black said. "'Fess up, you're out here again selling dope, aren't you?"

"Hey Blanco, let's split them up, maybe they'll become a bit more cooperative with our investigative stop here."

Black placed a hand on Riley's shoulder and turned him around. "You're awfully quiet. Maybe you'd like to tell me what's going on."

"I got nuthin' to add."

"You're sure? It's the quiet ones we have to watch out for."

"What's your name?"

"Uh, Vincent Riley. Sir," he added, praying some politeness would catch him a break.

"Got something with your name on it?"

Riley shook his head.

"Didn't think so. You live around here?"

"No."

"Then what are you doing in this neighborhood?"

"I attend South Fulton Alternative Campus."

"Cut the bullcrap, kid. School's out for the summer and it's almost nine o'clock. My hunch is your friend over there is the ringleader and you're just along for the stroll. Tell me which house his grandmother lives in and this could be your lucky day."

Riley looked over at Isaiah who no longer was within ear's reach. He was on his own. Isaiah's reason for stopping by the house seemed a little far fetched, but then again his associate hadn't really given him any reason to suspect foul play. All Riley had done was to wait outside. He pointed toward the small white wood frame house.

"Thatta boy, Vincent. You did the right thing." Black radioed Blanco to advise that his one-on-one had been fruitful. He walked Riley over to Blanco and Isaiah. "I'm going to check out the house. "Boys, if Isaiah's story pans out, you'll be on your way in no time."

Black walked around the dark house. Everything appeared to be in order. He rang the doorbell and waited. No one answered. Black returned to the back yard and noticed that the rear window was slightly ajar. He jiggled the doorknob, but it was locked. Black raised the window and entered the same way Isaiah had. The house had been ransacked. A low muffled moan was coming from the bathroom down the hall. Black pushed open the door and found an elderly woman stripped down to her undergarments sitting in the bathtub with her mouth gagged and her hands tied behind her back. Her robe was on the floor.

"Did he hurt you?" She shook her head. Black untied the gag and freed her hands, and helped her get out of the tub. He handed the poor woman her robe.

"God bless you! If you hadn't come to my rescue I don't know what I would've done." She led him out of the small bathroom into the kitchen. "I hadn't been home long from Bible Study when I heard him come inside."

"I checked outside. He came through your back window."

"Officer, I don't know what I'm going to do. He took my rent money. I told him it's due the first of the month, but he just laughed."

Black looked at the date on his watch. The first of August was only a week away. He'd talk to the Complaint Room and see if they'd make an exception to the rule requiring him to inventory property found on the perpetrator and let him return her money.

"He said you're his grandmother? Is that true?"

Black hoped not, family on family crime had risen since he'd joined the force. In his book, anybody who dared to violate an old woman didn't deserve her forgiveness.

"Oh, no. I have two grandsons and they haven't been in trouble a day of their lives."

"Do you know him?"

"It's possible, but I don't think so. A lot of kids travel through here on their way to the high school. I like to sit out on my porch and watch them come and go. I guess you already know he was wearing a red mask."

Black hid his disappointment. Without her identification, it would be harder to make the case.

"I'm glad you weren't hurt. I'll send over one of our female officers to check on you, okay, ma'am?"

"That'll be fine. Thank you, officer."

"Book 'em!" Black hollered, as he approached the patrol car. Blanco and Black cuffed Riley and Isaiah and placed them in the back seat of their patrol unit.

Blanco drove, while Black advised the boys that they were being arrested for aggravated assault, burglary and a bunch of other charges Riley had never heard of. The one thing he did know was he wasn't walking back up the street like Black promised.

"You have the right to remain silent. Anything you say..." Having advised the boys of their Miranda rights, Black turned away from them, pretending to give his partner his undivided attention.

"Punk, I told you to keep a lid on it," Isaiah hissed at Riley.

"I didn't say anything. I just pointed," Riley said. "What did you do, man?"

"Nothin' you want to know. Besides, the old lady couldn't see shit."

"So now you're an eye doctor on top of being Little Red Riding Hood? You better hope she pulls through, or else you'll be looking at murder charges as well," Black said, overhearing Isaiah. He turned around. "By the way, did you lose something?" Black pressed a red knit ski mask against the mesh partition separating the front and black seat.

Riley's eyes widened. "What's he talkin' about?"

"Aw, don't listen to him, man. He's just tryin' to fuck with us, doin' they thang, plantin' evidence. When we get to the station, just ask to call your folks."

"Folks? Man you know I don't have any folks."

Riley stared out of the window as they pulled into the dock of Atlanta Pre-Trial Detention. There was only one person who might accept his call. And that was a long shot. The elderly woman turned off her hearing aid at night.

FORTY

The familiar frame appeared through the booth from the jail pod below. He nodded at his attorney and sat down, picking up the telephone for privacy. Montante was glad to see him. It had only taken an extra hour for the jail personnel to find him. They'd tried to convince him that his own client had already been released.

"Kid, I'm sorry about the bond hearing yesterday. We gave it our best shot."

No different from most young black male defendants in the county's jail, Riley's presumption of innocence wasn't buying freedom. Unable to make bond, he'd be forced to serve some DA time while awaiting disposition of his case.

"Yeah, whatever."

The South Central County Jail terrified Riley, but he didn't let on. What was the point, he was stuck there. Stuck and misplaced, just as he'd been his entire life. If there's a family for every child, he'd never known it. Riley was accustomed to being the oldest, not one of the county's youngest charges. His cellmate was larger, older and meaner than he was. Every day since he'd been there, he did his best not to get on the guy's bad side. To think he'd ever complained about the noise level at the YRC. The decibels were off the chart practically 24/7 at the jail.

"Some of the guys say my charges are wrong. Like kidnapping, what's that about?"

"Isaiah tied her up and forced her into her bathtub."

"But he didn't take her anywhere, so how's that kidnapping?"

"Under Georgia law, it doesn't matter as long as she was forced from one spot to another against her will for an illegal purpose."

"How much I can get for that one?"

"The statutory minimum for kidnapping is ten, the range for aggravated assault is one to twenty, criminal trespass is a misdemeanor."

"Man, you need to get me out of here."

"The only way is to file what's called a speedy trial demand."

Riley had heard some of the men in the jail talking about speedy demands during free time. "That means they have to bring me to court, right?"

"Sooner rather than later." The public defender slipped Riley a thin manila envelope, with the attorney's name crossed out and Riley's written on it, through the narrow slit in the divider between them in the locked consultation booth. Riley was still trying to get used to his alias. "Here's a copy of what I've filed yesterday in your case. A discovery motion, a motion to suppress, a speedy trial demand. You can read them later, when you need something constructive to do."

"What's discovery?"

Montante looked at his client through the clear window. When he first started practicing with the Public Defender's Office, you couldn't even see your client during a jail visit. The clear window was dark mesh, making it virtually impossible to recognize the person talking to you.

"Facts, evidence, things about your case in the State's possession."

"And whattaya mean suppress?"

"If there is anything we don't want the jury to know about, we can try to suppress it – keep it out. But to do that, we would have to convince the judge that the police obtained it improperly."

"Which judge we got?"

"I'm not sure. It won't be the same judge from yesterday. The judges in the criminal division work in teams. Judge Haskell is our motions judge. He also sets the trial date. Your case will be assigned to a trial judge about thirty days before the trial."

"Good."

Montante couldn't agree more. Sam Haskell wasn't very popular among the defense bar.

"You find out anything about Isaiah?"

"His family posted bond."

"So he's out, and I'm stuck in here? You gotta talk to him, man. Make him fess up. I didn't do anything."

"Trust me, I'm working on it, Vince."

"His lawyer filed a speedy too?"

"Not as of yet." The public defender put off telling his client that Isaiah's strategy most likely would not be compatible with theirs. "But kid, try not to worry. Let me handle things."

"That's what Isaiah said, and he didn't do jack shit."

"I'm your lawyer. I'm on your side."

"Is Isaiah's lawyer a public defender too?"

The attorney sighed, knowing where the conversation was headed. Year after year, he'd trudged back and forth between the courthouse and the jail defending those no other would. He worked just as hard as any privately retained lawyer, got good results considering the cases sent his way, yet he was defending his competence as frequently as his clients.

"His folks hired a private attorney named Al Knott."

"No, shit." Riley looked impressed for the first time since his attorney arrived. "The word in here is he's real good; used to be a cop himself. Wears cowboy boots and double breasted suits."

"He's a smart ass."

"But you're going to work with him, right?"

"Of course, at the right time."

"That lady, she okay?"

"There's good news and bad news on that front."

"How's that?"

"Good news, she didn't have a heart attack or die, so the most serious charge you're facing is aggravated assault. Bad news, if this case goes to trial, she'll be able to testify."

"Whattaya mean, if this case goes to trial. You're not going to sell me out, make me take a plea, are you?

"Vincent, you're going to have to start trusting me. I'm your lawyer, not the State's attorney."

"The way I hear it, you used to be on their side. Didn't you used to be a prosecutor?"

"Yes, but what matters is I'm your lawyer, now."

"How do I know you won't make me plead out my case. I'm not going to plea, man. No way am I going to agree to serve twenty years. I've had it. As soon as you get my case dismissed, I'm done with it all, foster care, annoying social workers, everything."

"Vincent, I'm not one of those revolving door lawyers. I like defending innocent people, not putting them away. Let's not make any decisions until we know everything about the case."

"You know what you need to know. I told you I didn't do anything to the lady. Never even went inside her house. I'm innocent."

"I believe you, but it's not that simple. They've indicted you under the theory of party to the crime. Under Georgia law, all they have to show is that you intentionally helped Isaiah."

"Okay, say that again – the intent part."

Montante pulled out a raggedy copy of a jury charge on the concept and slowly read the elements of party to a crime. It had come in handy over the years of his defending criminals. They all said they same thing. The State cast a large net and swooped up any one in sight, figuring the jury would sort out who were bad guys and who were not.

"That's it, man, they can't prove intent 'cuz I didn't have the intent to do any of what they've put on me in the indictment."

"You're not listening. The issue is that you intentionally helped Isaiah in the commission of the crimes contained in the indictment by standing outside and keeping watch."

"He told me—

"You don't expect Isaiah to testify that you had no part in this, do you?"

"Hell yeah, Isaiah knows I didn't know what he was doin' in there."

"Vincent, let's be real. Isaiah is trying to save his behind, not yours."

"Man, this is so fucked up!" Riley banged on the window.

"Pipe down over there, or I'll take you back." The jail deputy's muffled voice rang loud and clear on Montante's side of the booth.

"Calm down, son, these are just some of the things we need to think about. Let's wait until I get the discovery – see what the lady says, see if Isaiah has given a statement, and if there are any witnesses."

Riley wanted to be optimistic, but he didn't need to see any discovery. One thing his attorney said was right: he could forget about Isaiah vouching for him. The night they were booked into Atlanta Pre-trial, Isaiah had warned him not to say anything else. Isaiah was mad at him. He was screwed.

"Five minutes!" Montante looked beyond Riley at the guard, acknowledging him.

"Time to wrap things up," Montante said, checking his notes.

"You comin' back to talk some more?"

"Sure. You gotta be patient, though."

"I know, some crap about the wheels of justice...."

FORTY-ONE

"Rotherman is not the squeaky clean prosecutor he wants the public to believe him to be."

The tall, high cheek boned African American woman had long blondish red hair, the kind of full, kissable lips for which many actresses suffer costly collagen injections, real breasts sitting round and high like breast implants and plenty more she wanted to share with the judge that her former lover and baby's daddy was fighting hard to unseat. Until Escobar Secret's last comment, Suzanne was unsure of the reason for the woman's impromptu noontime visit. She had convinced Andi to make an exception and let her back to see the judge. However, Escobar now had a captive audience of one very interested elected official. Suzanne walked over and closed the door to her chambers.

"Meaning what, exactly?" Suzanne knew how to listen and learn a lot, while saying very little.

"Shall I be direct?"

"Please."

"Rotherman fathered my child and won't return my calls," Escobar announced with a pout.

"What are you planning to do about that?"

"I already have."

"Have what?"

"Last week I saw his campaign billboard at the intersection of I-285 and Roswell Road with him standing with his arm around that fat wife of his, the kids and a dog and I decided then and there, I was taking him and his wandering dick to court."

"I see." Suzanne was accustomed to emotional, colorful language from scorned women.

"Teach him to use me and cast me aside liked a used condom. On my day off, I came down here, spent the morning in the Family Law Information Center and by noon, had filed a paternity suit."

"Has he been served?"

"Got the return of service right here. I came back this morning to confirm a hard copy of it was in the file. The Clerk's Office website is pretty awesome by the way."

"Then you must have a court date as well."

"Indeed, I do. When I saw the date, all I could do was laugh."

"I'm not following you."

"We're due in court on Tuesday, November 7th. How hilarious is that! I'm could actually make the bastard acknowledge me and his son on Election Day! Talk about poetic justice."

"I'm not the assigned judge. Because you know I would have to recuse myself and have the case reassigned, even though I am the judge presently presiding over our Family Docket."

"That's why I'm here. Lucky for both of us, the case has been assigned to another judge. I'm here talking to you woman to woman."

"Then, who is the judge, Ms. Secret?"

"Oh, please, call me Escobar. But, to answer your question, some judge named Haskell has the case."

Suzanne inhaled as she mentally processed the shrapnel of the bombshell delivered by Escobar. *Sam Haskell presiding over a paternity hearing involving his golden boy, Chance Rotherman, on Election Day. No way.*

"You should anticipate Rotherman asking for a continuance. And getting one," Suzanne said.

"Yeah, I know. But at least, he won't be able to ignore us forever," Escobar replied, her bronze face suddenly full of self pity.

Suzanne found herself wanting to help yet another single woman who'd found her way into the comfortable black and white chair of choice in front of her desk. While drama seemed to frequent her courtroom and tarnish the public's perception of her as a judge, some of her best work was executed one on one, off of the bench in her chambers.

Why do I keep getting drawn into other people's lives? How is it that these single mothers manage to seek out my advice when I'm the one in need of the advice? Funny how neither Bethany nor Escobar apparently even considered giving up their sons, and yet I, the one who had significantly more materially and came from the intact family unit, gave my son up for adoption.

"Escobar, I appreciate your coming to see me."

"I had no choice. Somebody needs to stop him. Chance Rotherman would be disastrous. He lacks the kind of heart you need to be a judge."

Suzanne slipped up and shot Escobar her "and you slept with him because why again?" look. Many of the parties in the cases Suzanne presided over warranted the same look.

"I know, I know. But I first met him in the gym where we both used to go and he reminded me of a neglected puppy. He confided in me one day after we both finished the circuit in the weight room that his wife had stop putting out and he was about to go out of his mind. You know how men are. I was surprised he was revealing all of this to me, but he did. Over about a two week spell, everything was pretty innocent and then, the next thing I know this law and order man couldn't get enough of me."

Escobar didn't appear to have anywhere to be, but her judicial confidante did. Suzanne was due in court at 1:30.

"Escobar, I'm going to need to cut things off. I need to prepare for my afternoon hearing."

"Sorry, I didn't mean to take your whole lunch hour."

"No problem at all. Again, I appreciate your support..." Suzanne stopped herself. Escobar had only said Rotherman wasn't getting her vote, not that she was.

FORTY-TWO

Suzanne dialed her friend's private line, hoping to catch Judge Fitzgerald before her 9:30 a.m. criminal calendar. The massive arraignments amounted to nothing more than an endless parade of young African American men ill-equipped to handle the consequences of their actions. She'd done her tour of duty prior to transferring onto the Family Docket. Her empathy for the defendant was misplaced. Suzanne's public defender begged her to stop asking the defendants if they had discussed with their families their cases and decision to enter life-altering pleas. *"There's nobody who cares, Judge. Just ...let it be,"* the *defense attorney said in defeat.*

"Becka Fitzgerald." Suzanne's sister-in-black picked up on the first ring.

"Hey, Becka, it's Suzanne. I saw your email. What's up?"

"Love and hate."

"Say that again?"

"I really hate to ask you this with your campaign in full swing, but I know Haskell won't help with this."

"Why do I get the feeling, I shouldn't ask: help with what?"

"Remember the guy I told you I've been chatting with online?"

"You mean the farmer?"

Rebecca had shared with Suzanne that she'd joined an internet dating service and had started communicating with a man who grew gourds in Sedona, Arizona.

"You make him sound like Farmer John, Suzanne. His family has money. His gourd business is more of a hobby."

"Hey, you're a grown woman. I have my own love life to run. Go ahead and ask whatever it is."

"He's invited me to fly out and visit him."

"And I bet you're worried about your furry friend, right? Don't worry about it, I'll find time to run by and feed him while you're out there revving your jets in the red rock."

"That's so sweet of you, but I've found a pet sitter. What I need you to do is cover for me on the outside chance I'm still on trial on the Thursday of the week I'm due to leave."

"What's the date?" Suzanne opened her Outlook calendar.

"October 26th, I'm taking a long weekend. That's my ex's weekend with Kyle."

"I can make that work. That's my last full week of hearings before the final push of the campaign."

"Thank you, Suzanne! I owe you big time. I'd simply die if I had to cancel."

Suzanne laughed, understanding the desperation in her colleague's voice. Her divorced colleague fought hard for primary custody of her thirteen-year old son despite the demands of her job and had very little time for a social life as a result.

"What if you get out there and the man is hairier than a prairie dog?"

"Very funny. After all I went through to get my ex to take Kyle for an extra day, I don't care what he looks like, as long as his parts work."

FORTY-THREE

O liver wanted to target select precincts with a new campaign piece. *"We've marketed you as the judge, it's now time to focus on you the person."* Andi pulled some articles tracking her community involvement since moving to Atlanta: the Links, her church, volunteer work with crack babies at Hughes Spaulding Children's Hospital. Oliver wasn't satisfied. He wanted to include some snippets from her past, growing up. She'd called her mother for her help in pulling together a few photos, awards from her school days, and the like and asked her to overnight whatever she came up with.

Suzanne pulled into the entryway to her condominium complex located in the McGill Glen community of Atlanta, just south of the emerging Midtown business district. The guard's booth was empty. *And how much of my association fees go to pay your salary?* No doubt the security guard was on a cigarette break. She keyed in her security code on the touchpad. Beep, beep, beep. *Damn.* Impatient, she pressed the wrong keys and had to start over. Her mother's email confirmed that the package should be at her door waiting.

"Yes!" Suzanne's favorite parking space right in front of her townhouse was empty. After her workout, she was ready to unwind. Tuesday evenings were reserved for the Always Wanted To Dance Troupe – an eclectic ensemble of late-blooming ingénues Suzanne had pulled together, many of whom had become her good friends and, like her, had always wanted to dance. The troupe was not a group of has-beens clinging to their missed opportunities.

Rather, membership in Suzanne's AWT troupe was all about being bold in the joy of one's now.

Most every Tuesday, shortly after she adjourned court at five-thirty, Suzanne hung up her black robe and the wannabe dancer darted into her inner chamber to change into a colorful leotard and a holey pair of cut-off sweats – the funkier the get-up the better. Suzanne's sister troupe members covered the full spectrum of shapes, sizes and sensibilities. Titles and day jobs were inconsequential on the old, dusty stage of the McGill Glen Community Art Center. What the women had in common was the desire to haul their behinds up onstage to dance. For the pure hell of it, and to shake loose all misplaced regret.

As she approached her door, Suzanne spotted the large brown square package partially tucked behind the azalea bush right beside the front steps. She kneeled to pick up the box. The mail carrier had done her a favor and left the rest of her mail bundled up and concealed behind it. Suzanne smiled when she saw the box was neatly addressed in her mother's school teacher penmanship.

"Call me as soon as you open it!" Velda Vincent was notorious for her notes and 'veldaisms' as Suzanne and her father fondly called them.

Suzanne opened her door into the dark entryway. An antique, walnut grandfather clock and a Romare Bearden watercolor painting set off the hardwood foyer, giving a tastefully decorated, yet lived in impression to those few persons who crossed Suzanne's threshold.

Once inside, she turned on the lamp in the den, put her briefcase on the desk and sat down in her favorite recliner. Savoring the element of surprise, Suzanne delayed opening the package while she sorted through the other mail. In large part it was the everyday stuff except for an oversized, ivory envelope addressed in gold calligraphy. *Oh goodness, not another 'tis the season holiday wedding.* Attending weddings had become a chore for Suzanne. Most of the people in her age bracket were already married. If single, they intended to remain so, having given up on finding a mate or having divorced the one they had. Thus, typically the invitations she received of late were for weddings of the children of some of her older professional acquaintances.

At thirty-six, it was the only type of social function she usually ended up regretting having attended. Some out of touch biddy would single Suzanne out of the crowd, discount her otherwise impressive professional background and convert her age and marital status, or lack thereof, into glaring personal deficiencies. When the sea of guests parted for the bride's much anticipated flower toss at the last wedding Suzanne attended, she actually made a dash for the bathroom and remained there long past any chance of being swept up with the wave of females vying to catch the bridal bouquet.

Suzanne pulled the card from the inner envelope which read *Honorable Suzanne Vincent and Guest.* The bride was the daughter of one of her fellow club members. This time the decision of whether or not to attend would be an easy one. Suzanne had no guest to accompany her and had never even met the bride. She would do everyone a favor by sending her regrets and a gift from the bride's overpriced wedding registry.

Suzanne put the rest of the mail aside and picked up the parcel from her mother. She ripped off the brown shipping paper. Under the wrapping, taped to the top of the box was a note from her mother: *"So you won't have to fret come the holidays." The holidays, come on, Mother. I've got an election to win, later for the holidays.* Suzanne eased out of her jazz shoes and inched the tight lid off of the box, setting it down by her feet. Inside the box, under several pieces of crumbled, yellowed newspaper was her beloved grandmother's antique Christmas wreath. Suzanne tenderly traced the wreath's intricate, bronze, ornamental holly leaves with her fingers.

Her late grandmother, Momo, held such a special place in her heart. Even as an adult, Suzanne continued to call her by the nickname, pronounced "Mom-mo," she had coined as a toddler. When she first learned to walk, Suzanne's mother would take her to visit her grandmother. She would totter back and forth in the large open area on her grandmother's screened porch between her mother's lap and her grandmother's legs pointing and exclaiming, "Ma. Oh. Ma. Oh." At some point, she started calling her grandmother Momo.

She was her grandmother's girl. Momo's only grandchild. Growing up, she so enjoyed helping her grandmother decorate her house for the holidays, just the two of them. Her maternal grandfather died when she was still a baby and her paternal grandparents lived in Michigan, so most of her Christmas memories were etched at the hand of her mother's mother in California. Every year, on the Friday morning after Thanksgiving, her parents would drop her off at her grandmother's, and their annual holiday weekend ritual would begin. They continued with the tradition throughout her college years, except for that one year – her sophomore year, the one that changed Suzanne's outlook on life forever.

Hanging the antique wreath on her grandmother's front door capped a weekend loaded with baking cookies, tree trimming, wrapping presents, enjoying old family photos and snuggling up together in red flannel footed pajamas on Momo's yellow velvet Queen Anne's couch. Suzanne chuckled remembering the year her eighty-year-old grandmother greeted her at the door wearing her own footed pajamas.

When she was young, she could tell her grandmother anything, often confiding about dreams or worries Suzanne thought her mother was too busy to be bothered with or wouldn't understand. Things like the cartoon stick figure some girls drew of Suzanne making fun of her late-to-bloom breasts, on the wall by the shower in her high school locker room. Those cherished chinwags continued until Momo's untimely death on New Year's Eve the year before.

"Oh, Momo, I'm sorry there wasn't anyone around to help you." Suzanne murmured to herself. She took another look at the wreath. Each year since Christmas 1988, she had drawn on the brightness of their late November visit to offer some balance against the dark funk that took hold of her during the early days of December. Suzanne was so deep in memories of those happy visits that she jumped when the phone rang. She set the box with the wreath down and rose to check the caller ID. Seeing the South Pasadena number, Suzanne picked right up.

"Hi, Mom."

"Screening calls, again, dear?"

"You know it. Hey, Mom, I just got home and opened up the wreath. Thanks so much for sending it to me."

"My, that was a fast delivery. It wasn't damaged was it?"

"No, it's perfect."

"Well, I was going through some of her things and ..."

"Mom, I know, I miss her, too." Suzanne swallowed hard, responding to the raw emotion caught up in her mother's voice. "I can't recall many Thanksgiving weekends that didn't end with my hanging that wreath on her front stoop. When you called, I was remembering the last time I spoke to Momo."

That past Thanksgiving Suzanne had to cut short her traditional weekend spent with her grandmother and return to Atlanta to prepare for a high profile triple homicide trial involving an abortion clinic. Momo had been disappointed yet proud at the same time.

"Remember how she tickled in calling you, Judge Suzy?" her mother asked. "She was so proud of her grandbaby, the judge. I wouldn't be surprised if everyone in heaven knows about Judge Suzy." Suzanne's mother's emotional train was back on track. They talked for a few more minutes, then said goodbye.

Suzanne was on her way upstairs to change when she heard the phone ring. She hesitated only for a moment, before deciding to just let it ring.

FORTY–FOUR

Thirty minutes later, Suzanne was back downstairs, somewhat relaxed by her shower and happy to be in her scruffy bathrobe. Suzanne was ready to unwind after her long day. Before Suzanne started on her makeshift *caprese* salad and glass of chardonnay, she balanced the phone under her chin to check voice mail for the call she had missed. It was her mother calling with an afterthought.

"Dear, I forgot to mention that I put the folder with the old papers you asked for in the box under the newspaper cushioning the wreath. Since you wanted them right away, I didn't bother to sort through them. I just grabbed the file out of one of your boxes in the attic and stuck in the box with the wreath."

Suzanne set her tray aside and lifted the wreath out of the box to retrieve the manila folder. She opened it and flipped through the enclosed papers which included her college acceptance letter from UCLA, some interim grade reports, and an article she wrote in the school paper. Near the bottom of the stack was an unopened envelope addressed to her at her grandparents' address in Detroit. The envelope bore an Atlanta postmark of December 17, 1988. It had been forwarded to her parents' address in California a few weeks later. Suzanne flipped over the envelope, but there was no return address on either side. *Who would be writing me a letter back then?*

Suzanne ripped open the envelope and screamed when she unfolded the letter.

Dear Suzanne,

There's something I think you should know. Yesterday, my husband, Zach, died from injuries he sustained in a terrible car accident. It happened a few days after we returned from Detroit with the baby. I don't think I'm prepared to go through with the adoption. It won't be the same. Please call me as soon as you get this letter. I'm so sorry to involve you, but my attorney suggested under these circumstances you might want to withdraw your surrender.

Sincerely,
Mallory Caine
(404) 292-8356

"Oh, my God! This can't be. Not now, not after eighteen years!"

Why me, why now?

FORTY-FIVE

S uzanne broke the seal on the pint of Wild Turkey her father
gave her for *"those rare times when my little girl needs a little
something extra,"* and poured herself a drink. She hated the bitter
liquor burning its way down her throat into the pit of her stomach,
waiting for the dull calm Beck had promised would slowly kick
in.

Suzanne dialed her mother. Suzanne dispensed with any
pleasantries.

"Mom, why didn't you tell me about the letter."

"What letter?"

"The letter from Mallory Caine."

"You mean the woman who—

"Of course, who else would I be talking about?"

"Suzanne, I have no idea what you're talking about?"

"Did you actually look through the folder you sent me with
the wreath?"

"Not really. When I was emptying the drawers in your old desk
and dresser to make room for the new furniture, I came across
several papers and other things you had saved over the years. I
might have skimmed the first couple of things. Then I decided
not to try to purge since it was your stuff. I basically gathered
everything and put it in the folder. Why, dear?"

"I found a letter addressed to me in Detroit with a December
1988 postmark. It was forwarded to me at home from there."

"Your grandparents must have sent it when they got back to Detroit after their trip to New Orleans for Christmas that year. The envelope hadn't been opened, had it?"

"No."

"I definitely don't remember seeing the envelope."

"You mean recently or eighteen years ago?"

"Well, certainly not when clearing out your desk. I would have mentioned it during our conversation when you were here in June. Now who knows from way back then. What does the letter say?"

"Mom, is it possible that you would've..."

"Is what possible, Suzanne?"

"Never mind. It's just really upsetting that I didn't get her letter in time."

"In time for what, Suzanne?"

"Mom, she didn't go through with it," Suzanne said softly.

"You mean with the adoption?"

"Exactly."

"They seemed very sure at the time. Did she give a reason?"

"Her husband was killed in a car wreck. She said she couldn't go through with it without him."

"Oh, my goodness. How very sad."

For me, you mean, or for her?

"I wanted to talk to you before I do anything."

"Dear, I know how upsetting reading her letter must've been for you. Surely, you know that I would've told you myself had I any inkling."

Suzanne couldn't quite shake the notion that her mother knew more about Mallory's letter than she was letting on.

"Mom, her letter changes everything, don't you agree?"

"Does it really, dear? I understand your disappointment in learning that he isn't where you first placed him. Like you, I thought the Caines were a perfect match for Riley. But nothing is guaranteed, and deep in the fine print of the adoption papers, we contemplated the remote possibility that things wouldn't work out."

Maybe you did, Mother, but I didn't contemplate any of this.

"I know but –

"Suzanne, listen to me. You sound like you're reconsidering your decision to give him up in the first place. It's too late to change your mind. I hate to see you worrying needlessly when no doubt he is being raised by another wonderful family."

"Eliminating doubt – not just reasonable doubt, but all doubt – is precisely what I'm after. Before I can move on with my life, I need to be sure as I can about his. That's the least I can do."

"Dear, you're two weeks away from being re-elected. Get that out of the way before you take this on. I'll take a leave and fly back to help you, if you'd like. Please think this through."

"Mom, I'm going to hang up now. I just thought you should know."

An older, unsteady female voice answered.

"Hello."

"Hello. Can Mallory Caine be reached at this number?" Suzanne asked.

"Who's calling please?"

"Suzanne Vincent."

"I don't know anyone by that name. Our number is unlisted. How did you get this number?"

Concern was mounting on the other end. If she was a telemarketer soliciting a sale instead of a mother trying to complete some unfinished business, she'd have the right answer.

"I'm sorry. I must have the wrong number."

"Ma'am, I'm pretty sure I don't know you. Why are you calling here for Mallory Caine?"

Her questions caught Suzanne off guard. "Ma'am, I'm so sorry to have disturbed you. Kindly disregard my call." She hung up before the woman could say anything else.

Moments later, Suzanne's phone rang.

"Hello."

"This is Mallory Caine Adams returning a call from Suzanne Vincent."

Pull it together, girl. Ready or not, you're on.

"This is Suzanne. I assume you remember me?"

"Hard not to, with your campaign signs everywhere," Mallory said.

"Mallory, I know it's been a very long time since we last spoke, but I just became aware of your letter and –

"What letter? I haven't written you any –

"The letter you wrote me back in 1988... telling me about your husband and ...my son."

"Oh, that letter." Suzanne heard Mallory give out a sigh. "You know, Suzanne, I'm not particularly interested in digging up the past. After Zach died, it took me quite a while to put my world together, but everything is okay now and I'd like to keep it that way. What could we possibly have to talk about now?"

"Your letter was included in a stack of papers my mother sent me. I didn't receive the letter when you first sent it which is why you never heard from me. I thought you deserved to know that."

"I see."

Mallory's tone softened a bit and Suzanne seized the dip in their strained conversation. Suzanne struggled to find the right words. "Mallory, is there somewhere we might we meet tomorrow for a quick cup of coffee?"

There was a long pregnant pause. "I don't drink coffee," she replied.

"Okay, well what about a cup of tea, then – I just need a few minutes of your time," Suzanne said trying to soften her tone as well. People sometimes were put off by the judge's Californian directness and crisp, formal manner of speaking.

"Why don't you just ask me what you want to know, now, over the phone?"

"Are you familiar with the little coffeehouse at the corner of 10th Avenue and Piedmont?" Suzanne asked.

"Perhaps." Mallory Caine was not making things easy. Another extended pause lapsed.

"Let's meet you there tomorrow first thing in the morning."

"Sounds like an order," Mallory retorted.

"No, not at all. I'm sorry if that's how it sounded. You would be doing me a tremendous favor by meeting me. Please say yes, Mallory," Suzanne held her breath as she waited for Mallory's response.

"That's a very busy time of day for me. I have to take my son to school."

"Well, then, how about after you drop him off? I promise I won't keep you long."

Mallory hesitated. "Actually, that's not far from where he attends school. I suppose I can make time for a quick cup."

"Wonderful. What time works for you?"

"Let's say 8:15."

"I'll see you then. Good night." Suzanne hung up, not quite sure what to make of the conversation with the woman she entrusted to raise and love her son on that dreary day in Detroit.

FORTY-SIX

T he popular coffeehouse was crowded already full of people transacting business on cell phones and laptops. She ordered a caramel macchiato and made her way through the aromatic cavern to the last empty table. She sipped her drink slowly and contemplated how to ask Mallory what she needed to know.

Through the window, Suzanne watched the black Lincoln Town Car pull into the parking lot. The driver got out and walked around to open the rear passenger door. There was no question that the emerging slender woman dressed in black was Mallory Caine Adams. *My, my, I guess she did pick up the pieces and move on.* She wore her hair in a stylish short precision cut. Its true artistic design was revealed as the fall breeze rustled through her hair.

Mallory stepped inside and looked through the crowded establishment. Suzanne stood so she could be seen. The woman's dark gray eyes acknowledged the pair of deep brown eyes awaiting her. Both set of eyes had deepened over the years and now were complimented by traces of gray resistant to rinse. The large pear shaped glistening diamond on Mallory's ring finger distinguished the path each woman had traveled since their last meeting.

Suzanne stood, extending her hand. "Thank you, Mallory, for coming. May I get you something?"

"No, thank you. You said this wouldn't take long, didn't you? My car is waiting."

"Well, right, it won't," Suzanne replied. "I just thought you might like something, that's all." *You sure were a whole lot friendlier up in Detroit when you wanted to get your hands on my baby, weren't you?*

"I suppose I have time for a quick cup of green tea with a twist of lime," Mallory said.

"Great. Why don't you have a seat and I'll run get a cup for you."

Suzanne returned with the tea and slid in her seat ready to begin once more with Mallory.

"Thanks." Mallory blew on the tea. "So, Suzanne, when did you relocate to Atlanta?"

"I graduated from law school in 1993 and took a position here with McKinney & Lasley that same year."

"You didn't go to a Georgia law school, did you?"

"No, I graduated from Stanford."

"I'm curious, then, why you moved way across country to practice law."

"I clerked with the firm's San Francisco office during my second summer of law school," Suzanne explained. "They wanted to expand their national presence beyond the office there and the one in New York. I was offered a position as an associate in their new Atlanta office. Since I'd never lived anywhere other than California, I decided to give it a try."

"I remember seeing an article in the Atlanta Times when you were first appointed by that new governor. You're pretty young to be a judge, aren't you?"

Comments about her age normally pushed the judge's button, even though most people meant them as compliments. Judge Vincent's demeanor and persona drastically contrasted with the image most people held of female judges. A Judge Judy she was not. Under different circumstances, Suzanne would have been put off, taking the observation as a challenge to her authority rather than an acknowledgement of her accomplishments. Intuitively, Suzanne knew Mallory was simply trying to make conversation – one she did not particularly want to have.

"I guess I am, by most people's standards," Suzanne replied graciously.

Mallory looked at Suzanne's bare ring finger. "What kind of cases do you hear?"

"Right now, I'm hearing divorce, child custody, support, all kinds of family law cases."

"Don't you worry whether you're making the right decisions in your cases?"

"A lot of mental energy goes into deciding a case. But once my decision is made, I try really hard not to second guess myself."

"Do you do adoptions?" Mallory asked.

"Yes." Suzanne responded.

Mallory hesitated, "You must find those very hard to consider."

In fact, they were among the hardest cases Suzanne had to handle. Most judges loved adoptions. They were typically scheduled first thing in the morning and every one involved typically was happy – a nice contrast to a rape case or wrongful death action. Suzanne found the doting parents, tearful grandparents, special requests to bring in cameras and all of the joy accompanying adoptions rather bittersweet.

"Sort of," Suzanne said, "but they come with the robe."

Mallory glanced at her watch and dispensed with any more questions.

"No more questions," Mallory said. "I was just curious about what it is you do since most of the women I know have husbands and families, rather focusing just on themselves and pursuing careers."

I know she didn't just go there...

"So, what exactly is it that you want to know, Suzanne?"

"I'm not sure where to begin, Mallory. Or why I even want to, but I do. Only last night, did I learn that you wrote me back in 1988, apparently right after you returned to Atlanta. Your letter was included in a stack of old papers forwarded to me from my mother."

"Your parents still live in California?"

"Yes, they do."

"Last night, when I read of your loss, I regretted that we never spoke again." Mallory said nothing, her expressive eyes revealing the kind of hurt hard to forget. "I decided you still deserved a response," Suzanne said quietly.

"Earlier you said you wanted to know how things turned out. Things have a way of working themselves out. I remarried. My husband's been very supportive considering all I'd been through. And raising Rilman has been such a blessing."

Suzanne was not interested in the man who rescued Mallory. All she cared about was her son.

"Rilman is your son, correct?"

"Yes."

I guess she had the right to change his name.

"He's finishing his last year of high school. I can't believe he'll be gone next year. It'll be the first time we've been separated since he came into my life."

"Mallory, I'm happy for you. This is difficult for me to ask, but I have to. Has Rilman ever asked you about me or the circumstances of the adoption?"

"I don't recall mentioning that Rilman was adopted." Mallory's edginess returned.

"You're right, I'm sorry. I just assumed...I guess after reading your letter, I called you in hopes of finding out that you'd gone through with the adoption. Then when you mentioned your Rilman, I jumped to the conclusion that –

"I can't imagine why you'd think that. You read my letter. It was very clear, as I recall."

"You're right, it was."

"Believe me, it wasn't easy, but I had no other choice but to give him up. When I met my Rilman's father, he was raising a child alone. Rilman's mother died in childbirth, and he was just a toddler when his father and I married. I adopted Rilman soon after we married."

"Is there anything you can think of that might help me find my son?"

Mallory paused for a moment. "Oh gosh, that was so long ago..."

"How about the caseworker? Do you remember the caseworker's name?" Suzanne hated the desperation she knew was creeping into her voice.

"I only met her once, for just a few minutes. Yancey was her last name, I think. If I'm not mistaken, her name was Wilma

Yancey. With all of your connections, you should be able to find her through DHR."

"The State? You mean a private adoption agency wasn't involved?"

She felt foolish not knowing more about the most important occurrence in her lifetime. *Mom handled everything. How could I know?*

"No. After Zach and I conferred with an attorney and found out you could surrender the baby directly to us, we decided it would be easier to proceed independently of an adoption agency."

"Where did you take him … afterwards?"

"Our attorney was semi-retired. He was working from home. As I recall, he made arrangements for Mrs. Yancey to meet us there to get the baby. Suzanne, there isn't much else I can tell you."

"I understand. Thank you so much for returning my call."

"Good luck. I hope you find him."

FORTY-SEVEN

The doorbell rang. Suzanne peered through her peephole at her next door neighbor, Tyrone Griffin. *I don't think I can pull off the friendly neighbor routine right now.* Suzanne didn't want to, but couldn't help smile. Tyrone's outfit on anyone else would have been downright comical. However, Tyrone's gold crushed velvet jogging suit and matching corduroy Kangol cap were typical of his wardrobe made up of loud warm-ups and dated plaid three piece suits. Not a soul could convince the guy he wasn't every woman's heart throb. He was all about where he'd just been and where he was heading next. There was nothing dull about the guy, inside or out. She partially opened the door to the intoxicating smell of heavily splashed Old Spice aftershave.

"Hey, Tyrone. What's up? I'm ready for today to be gone, I'm headed to bed."

"Sunshine, the night's just begun. I knew you'd want one of these hot off the press." Tyrone handed her a flier through the narrow opening. "I did it. Got my story in print. Think you might invite over some of those foxy friends of yours to meet me and buy my book?"

"Sure, I'll check my calendar and let you know, okay?"

"You know what, Sunshine? That can wait. You look like you could use some of Tyrone's tender loving care."

"I just need to crash, that's all."

"Are you sure? Cuz, honey, you know I'd be happy to come in and keep you some company."

Suzanne almost gave in. Ever since she had moved in, despite trying to get her to go out with him, Tyrone had always been considerate and friendly. No loud music. No drama. No late night visitors coming and going.

"Yes, I'm sure."

"You need to stop mistreating that man of yours."

"What are you talking about, Tyrone?"

"His name was John, as I recall."

"Okay."

"I bet you sent him away, not making enough money or one of those other reasons you women use when you don't want to commit."

"Tyrone, my relationship with John is really none of your business. However, we haven't broken up, if that's what you're insinuating." *At least, I think we're still together.* "You haven't seen John lately because he's been out in Southern California working on a special assignment." *Why am I telling Tyrone this?*

"When will he be back?"

"I'm not sure."

Tyrone smiled that tired player smile of his.

"Well, take it from me, don't let too much time go by or you might lose that love connection," Tyrone said. "Talk to him every day and fly out there as often as you can."

"Sounds like you've had a taste of a long distance relationship."

"You got that right, and it didn't taste sweet for long. If you need a real man to warm up your toes, you got my number, Sunshine."

Tyrone left Suzanne behind closed doors with his advice and advances and her all-consuming fear of losing everything to find her son. *Do I have the right to seek out the truth? Am I really prepared to find out what happened to him? How does a birth mother go about introducing herself to the child she's given up?*

Had she called, John, of course, would've listened. Alone in her den, she needed another woman to confide in, an estrogen laced pair of ears willing to let Suzanne talk for however long she needed to. A tall order considering Suzanne had guarded the birth as a family secret for eighteen years.

Suzanne was good at listening, offering advice, solving other people's problems. When it came to her own worries or problems, she was woefully inept. Since her move from the West Coast, she largely had lost touch with her small circle of girlfriends collected over the years and been too busy to replace them. Tammy was the only person outside of her family who knew about the pregnancy. Once Tyrone got the hint and said goodbye, Suzanne kept her promise and called Tammy, ready to talk, but no one answered. She'd lost contact with her good friend from law school, Noelle Wise, not long after the woman decided to give up mergers and acquisitions to raise her triplets. Cacey was on a cruise with her sister, Candace. And her beloved grandmother was dead.

Suzanne slipped the letter back into the aged envelope and dropped it inside her briefcase. Momo had always told her, "*You're in trouble if you misplace your heart. Dig as deep as you need to, look wherever you have to, do whatever it takes, just make sure you find it.*" Suzanne had no clue where to look for the piece of her heart Riley carried away with him. There was one place where being lost didn't matter. Suzanne freshened her bourbon and headed downstairs for a wild conversation, the kind you can only have when left alone with a set of black and white keys.

FORTY-EIGHT

The young blonde assistant district attorney flipped through her black trial notebook. She'd spent the entire weekend putting it together. This would be her first time trying a case in first chair. She had no intentions of it being her last. Her list of voir dire questions for the prospective jurors, witness lists complete with names, addresses and phone numbers, the detective's file, outlines of her direct examinations, her opening statement and a draft of her closing argument all were there. She closed the notebook and placed it into the banker's box on the conference table, along with a worn copy of *Daniel's on Criminal Law,* exhibit stickers, markers, a laser pointer and box of tissue for the victim. Mary Faith Tucker was due in court in fifteen minutes.

"Looks like a trial getting ready to happen," Rotherman said, standing in her office doorway, watching her organize her work product.

"That's the plan." She was surprised to see him. Campaigning had kept him scarce around the office lately. "You remember your first trial."

"Yep. Sure do. A street walker insisted on having her day in court. I prepared the file just like it was a murder case."

"I thought your leave started today."

"Not till later in the week. What time are you due in court?"

"In about fifteen minutes." She handed him a copy of her voir dire questions. "Anything else you think I should ask?"

"No, those look pretty good, I'm impressed." Rotherman returned them. "Don't shoot the messenger, but I'm afraid there's been a slight change in the line-up."

"In what way?"

"I'm going to be with you for the case –

"Actually, that's great. I could use the support."

"— in first chair."

"Oh, no! Not after I stayed close to midnight every night last week and worked the entire weekend. That's the problem with this office. The top brass suffers from micromanagerialitis. This is so wrong."

Rotherman could only tolerate so much from the feisty prosecutor.

"Feel better? If you're finished, there are a few things I need to go over with you before we report for trial."

"Of course," she said. "I'm sure you could care less about the injustice of this office."

"Have you confirmed that the victim will be able to testify live?"

"Negative. My investigator is down at Grady Memorial as we speak. We're hoping she'll be released this morning and available to testify tomorrow."

"Let me know as soon as you hear."

"Certainly."

"Any priors on the defendant?"

"None. His record is squeaky clean."

"Too bad you blew the Jackson-Denno hearing. The police work hard, out there risking their lives. They don't need rookie prosecutors getting the evidence tossed."

"I did no such thing. You and I discussed the facts, and you agreed it was a close call."

"Bottom line, you lost the motion to suppress. Now the jury won't get to hear Riley's admission.

"What about the co-defendant?"

"What about him?"

"Have you heard back from his lawyer regarding our offer?"

"No, he's seemed okay with letting the Riley kid take the hit."

"As I understand it, the police now suspect Banks as being involved in a couple of other home invasions, with elderly victims in the neighborhood."

"Yes, the detective mentioned that when I was going over his file with him."

"That's precisely why I have to step in here. We have to make sure we get a conviction. There's a chance Riley will help us go after Banks, once convicted. You know how it works. If he cooperates, we can recommend a lenient sentence."

"Rotherman, we don't have time for this right now. Court is about to begin."

"Okay, you're right. Tell you what, you do the opening, I'll close. We'll talk about the witnesses later. You can help me pick the jury."

She rolled her eyes. "Great, another morning's worth of jury selection to add to my resume."

FORTY-NINE

S uzanne wiped her moist hands on her pants and took
Mallory's missive out of her purse. The public image she'd
painstakingly pieced together since she arrived in Atlanta was
at stake. She needed her therapist's perspective on her choices,
including pulling out of the race.

"Dr. Peters, last night, I found this letter mixed in with some
other papers in a box from my mother. It's not very long. Would
you mind reading it?" Suzanne asked.

"Why don't you just tell me what it says? Better yet, share
with me how it relates to what is really bothering you," Dr. Peters
suggested. The therapist took off her glasses and leaned back in
her chair.

"The letter is from the adoptive mother."

"The woman who adopted your son?"

"Yes. She wrote me shortly after I surrendered Riley to tell
me that her husband was killed in an accident and she did not go
through with the adoption. When I read the letter last night, I
called her."

"That must have been a difficult call to make."

"Much to my dismay, she confirmed that she didn't adopt
Riley."

Dr. Peters gazed intently across her desk at Suzanne. "How
did you happen to select this couple to adopt your son?"

"We met them through my grandparents' church in Detroit. My
grandparents' minister, Rev. Douglass, had grown up in Atlanta.
His best friend pastored a church in Atlanta where Mallory and
Zachary Caine were members. One day in early October, Rev.

Douglass asked if we would be interested in meeting a young couple who were looking for a child to adopt. He said he'd met them on a visit to Atlanta to help his friend preach a revival."

"Mallory and her husband flew up from Atlanta to Detroit one weekend toward the end of October and my grandparents, the Caines, Rev. Douglass and I met in his church study on one Sunday afternoon after service. He arranged for my parents to participate long distance by using his speaker phone. Even three thousand miles away my mom took charge of the meeting, firing away with her questions. I wasn't sure how to tell for sure, but I liked Mallory and thought she would be the kind of mother I wanted to be some day – confident, responsible and loving."

"Things don't always turn out the way we plan for them to, do they?"

"Do you think it makes sense to try to find him now?" Suzanne asked.

"That's for you to decide. I can't answer that for you," Dr. Peters said. "However, if you go looking you must be prepared to deal with whatever you find."

"I know. This isn't a good time—

"Would any time be a good time for such news?"

"No."

"Does it bother you that someone you've never met is raising your son?"

"Yes, that's a large part of it. I need to be sure that he's okay. Mallory Caine couldn't tell me much of anything other than she turned my son over to a DHR caseworker named Wilma Yancey. He could be just about anywhere with anybody."

The therapist wrote down the caseworker's name.

"Were you able to find out when she surrendered him to the State?" Dr. Peters asked.

"From what she said, I gathered he must have been about two weeks old at the time, so probably somewhere around the 16th of December, 1988."

"If you'd like, I'll be happy to make a few discrete phone calls and see what I can find out about the caseworker. But you'd need to take it from there," Dr. Peters said. Suzanne lit up, hearing her offer. "Be patient, this could be a slow process. But, I'm here to help. If I find out anything, I'll let you know."

FIFTY

Suzanne's private line rang shortly before noon Thursday afternoon.

"Suzanne, it's Dr. Peters, I've got some information for you," Dr. Peters said. "Wilma Yancey is no longer with DHR. It seems Ms. Yancey retired some time back."

"Well, I guess we knew finding her after all this time would be a long shot," Suzanne said in a low voice. Unknowingly, she had banked on a break-through meeting with Wilma Yancey.

"Yes, we did. But, as it turns out, I was able to get another lead on Riley."

"You were?" Suzanne grabbed her notepad.

"The person you need to speak with is Esther Ingram."

"Is that Riley's adoptive mother?"

"No, Suzanne, she's the Director of the Fairburn Campus of the Georgia Youth Residential Center."

The judge's optimism caved when Dr. Peters mentioned the facility. Not long ago, she had read a depressing, extensive week-long series of newspaper articles in the *Atlanta Journal Constitution* about the staggering number of children who are raised by the State.

"What's the connection?" Suzanne braced for the rest of the story.

The psychologist paused, as if trying to weave an answer, one word at a time. "Honestly, I'm not sure. DHR records show him living there as of 1992—

"But that's fourteen years ago."

"Suzanne, didn't you commit not to rush to any conclusions? Right now, this is all we have to go on. At least there's a beginning point from which to move forward."

"Have you spoken to Esther Ingram?"

"No, but here is her contact information."

Suzanne wrote down the woman's name and number, then thanked Dr. Peters and quickly hung up before picking up the phone again to dial.

Dr. Peter's news changed everything. For the moment, if not forever. *Riley, one of Georgia's hundreds of thousands of forgotten foster kids?* Suzanne's mission no longer was fueled by her maternal curiosity. She had no choice except to make room in her life to assume whatever responsibility a mother has for an almost eighteen year old young man.

"Andi," Suzanne called from her back office.

"Yes, Judge," she said.

"I've no time to explain, but please have Tina cancel my 3:30 hearing today. And also, I need you to call Oliver and tell him to cancel my campaign appearance tonight with the Daughters of the American Revolution. If he asks why, make up something, tell him anything, tell him I'm having female problems and can't stand up straight."

Suzanne didn't get many orders done while waiting until it was time to leave for her newly scheduled appointment. Her concentration was shot. Rebecca Fitzgerald called around 3:00 to tell her she'd sent the jurors home early and she was on her way to the airport. That wasn't all. Rebecca warned Suzanne that Rotherman was the lead prosecutor handling the case.

"How long have they had the case?" Suzanne asked, doing her best to sound cool.

"We picked the jury on Monday. Closings were Wednesday afternoon. They've had the case since this morning. Of course, since I am trying to catch this plane, deliberations are taking longer than expected."

"You think anything in particular might be tripping up the jurors?" Suzanne asked.

"I'm not sure. It might be the defendant's age. He's only 17. I'm sure he reminds a couple of the older women on the jury of their grandbabies. The victim was very sympathetic, yet couldn't make a good identification."

"Becka, if they come back with a verdict tomorrow, what do you want me to do?"

"Remand the defendant to the sheriff, and set the matter down for sentencing on December 6th."

"And if, for some unforeseen reason, they still haven't reached a verdict by lights out tomorrow?"

"As much as I hate to say it, send them home for the weekend, and I'll deal with them on Monday. If that happens, maybe I can get your opponent to cut the kid a deal."

"Fat chance."

"You know he has put on some weight lately, must be all that campaign crow he's been trying to feed folks."

"Cute, Becka. You better get going if you're going to make that plane. Don't worry, I'll handle everything. And Becka—

"Yes?"

"Watch out for those prickly pear margaritas they serve out in the desert. Consume too many, and you'll be dancing under the moonlight in the buff and howling like a cowgirl."

FIFTY-ONE

The boys' home was stuck in the middle of nowhere, a place where visitors were rare. Splashes of crimson, burnt orange and gold broad-faced leaves filled the maple trees surrounding the property, painfully brilliant considering her purpose that late afternoon. She made a mental note to get her campaign sign detail to blanket the stretch with some signs before "Get Out the Vote" Sunday. Loose gravel popped under her tires as Suzanne made her way down the narrow dirt road leading to the entrance. She raised her window to keep out the cloud of red dust rising around the car. As the dust settled, she sat in her car preparing herself for whatever Esther Ingram would tell her. When Suzanne had called earlier, the director readily agreed to meet with her. She had merely to explain that she was a judge from Atlanta in need of the director's assistance. Suzanne seldom flashed her title to gain access. But today she had no other good reason to impose on the woman's time. That is, aside from the admission that she was a mother in search of her son.

Riley was destined for so much more than this.

Suzanne pulled on the glass door. It was locked. She cupped her hand over her eyes to peer inside. A few boys in their early teens were sitting around the television focused intensely on unlocking video game codes and getting the best score. She waited a few more seconds hoping one of them would look up, but no one did leaving her no choice but to knock on the door. One of the boys called out to someone. A plump older woman with two thick plaits neatly tucked in back appeared and opened the door. She was wearing an apron and a hearing aid.

"You must be Judge Vinson," she said. "I'm Esther Ingram. Pleased to meet you. We don't get many judges out our way."

"My pleasure as well, Mrs. Ingram."

The fact that the center was not a recreational hangout, but a long term residence loomed in the air. The grandmotherly director relocked the front door and led Suzanne back to the kitchen where several large aluminum trays filled with peach cobbler were sitting out on the counter.

"I hope you don't mind talking while I finish up here," Mrs. Ingram said. "Baking helps me think when I'm worried. I'm just waiting for the oven to finish heating before I put these in to bake."

"Oh, not at all." Suzanne looked around for somewhere to sit and settled on a metal stool pushed under one of the other counters. Something about Mrs. Ingram reminded the judge of her grandmother. She and Momo had broached many serious topics in the kitchen.

"Excuse me for saying this, but you sure look young to be a judge." The woman began putting the canisters back in their place.

"You know, ma'am, I've heard that a few times."

"I bet you have. Now what's this you needed to drive all the way out here to speak to me about?"

"Mrs. Ingram, I'm here about Riley Vincent."

"Oh, Lord!" Alarm crept into the woman's voice. "Is it bad? I could tell those people didn't care anything about that poor boy. Why should they believe him, much less care? They don't know him like I do. They probably figure if they send him away, that'll be just one less black man to worry about in the future. They're sending him away for good. Is that what you came to tell me?"

"Ma'am, who is they? Where is Riley? Please tell me what's happened to him."

Mrs. Ingram didn't respond. She just kept shaking her head. It was as if she didn't know where to start. The woman opened the oven and slid the trays into the oven. Then she pulled up the hem of the apron to dry her hands, before untying its strings and placing it on the counter.

"Now then, that's done," she said. "Come with me, Judge Vinson, let's go for a little walk and maybe you can help me figure out how all this came to pass."

Suzanne followed her out of the kitchen, her heart racing. She listened intently as the director explained that the facility was home to approximately seventy-five boys who were in the custody of DHR. Sadly for most of the boys, the place was considered a permanent placement. Mrs. Ingram emphasized that foster homes had returned many of them to the YRC. No placements of any kind ever materialized for the rest. The Fairburn campus was originally planned to house youth from the ages of six to ten, but as the need developed over the past few years, more beds were set up.

Standing outside, the director pointed out three, one-story, red, brick buildings on the other side of the basketball court and playground. The boys were assigned to one of the three cottages according to their age. Suzanne's quick glances in some of the windows confirmed that the barrack style rooms were overcrowded, equipped with multiple bunk beds, leaving room only for hooks and small cubbies for boys' basic needs and possessions.

Mrs. Ingram labored as she walked due to swollen ankles. She took her time as she led Suzanne into one of the cottages. They stopped abruptly in front of a curtain. The director pulled the skimpy, madras curtain back to one side so the judge could poke her head in. The cramped area, maybe once a custodian's storage closet, had been converted into living quarters. A neatly made cot, long enough only for a tall child at the most, and a folding chair took up most of the space. Suzanne turned to the director, not knowing what to make of the space bordered by the ugly, cracked, green walls.

"Riley had outgrown us. Most of the boys here are much younger than he is. Until I fixed up this room for him, he had no privacy. We had started talking about his desire to strike out on his own –

"At seventeen?" Suzanne's voice rose.

"Sounds young I know, but one thing we do here, short of anything else, is to help our boys become self-sufficient," Mrs. Ingram said. "YRC life is hard, but it forces them early on to learn what they need to survive. I know it doesn't look like much, but this was the best we could do. Having his own space helped a little. Riley had grown very unhappy here. I couldn't blame him for wanting to leave. He's been in foster care his entire life. Can you imagine what that must be like?"

Suzanne shook her head, trying not to reveal her despair.

"This place met his physical needs, but he wanted more. Riley was ready to prove he's a man. He used to keep to himself at school. Not many friends. Then he started keeping company with a kid named Isaiah Banks. I had a bad feeling about him, but let Riley go on with him."

"Mrs. Ingram, where is Riley?" Suzanne was almost beside herself.

The director shook her head. "My apologies, Judge Vinson. I'm not being very clear, now am I? It's all very upsetting. I feel so helpless. Maybe you can help Riley."

"That's why I'm here. My interest in Riley is very personal. I actually came here hoping to offer Riley the home he deserves."

"What exactly do you mean, Judge Vinson?"

"Mrs. Ingram, I should've corrected you when you first greeted me. My last name is not Vinson. It's actually Vincent, the same as Riley's."

Suzanne looked squarely at the director. Mrs. Ingram studied the judge's face, its oval shape and pecan brown coloring, her serious yet expressive eyes.

"Oh my goodness, don't tell me you're related to . . ."

"Yes... I'm his mother."

Neither woman spoke – both momentarily muted by the judge's acknowledgement. *There now, the truth is out.* Suzanne sat down next to Mrs. Ingram on the narrow bed, ready to take responsibility for her past actions and time lost in the meantime. The judge was not ashamed or embarrassed by her admission. Just concerned that something terrible was going to happen to Riley if she didn't reach him very, very soon.

"Until this afternoon, I had no reason to think he might be here," Suzanne said. "I called you the moment I found out."

The director nodded, the reason for the urgency in the judge's voice over the telephone suddenly clear. "I think it's your eyes. When I first saw you, it was as if we had met before. There's a striking resemblance between the two of you around the eyes."

Suzanne had a desire to explain. "I got pregnant while I was in college. Up until a few days ago, I thought Riley was being raised by the couple my parents and I selected to adopt him way back in 1988."

Mrs. Ingram interjected, "When Wilma brought him here years ago, it was supposed to be a temporary placement. He had been with a foster family and things didn't work out."

"Are you speaking of Wilma Yancey?" Suzanne asked.

"Yes. Now she was from the old school." Mrs. Ingram closed her eyes and smiled. "Wilma was dedicated to her work. She was never too busy for her boys. Funny, I haven't thought about her for years. She put everything she had into trying to find them good homes. Her little warriors, that's what she called them. And Riley, he was no exception. For the first few years, she tried so hard to find an adoptive family or even a long term foster home placement. After that last time, though, nothing else materialized for him."

"Judge Vincent, I'm sure your discovery must be hard for you to accept," Mrs. Ingram said. "There's no point in wallowing over lost time. Don't give up hope, either. You keep praying and one day all of this will be behind the two of you."

"Do you think there's any chance he'll forgive me or am I too late?"

"Riley will give you your answer," Mrs. Ingram said. "The best you can do is love him unconditionally and be patient while he decides what to make of you."

"I suspect that's what you've practiced here with all of the boys steered your way." Suzanne was grateful that for the time Riley had spent at YRC, Mrs. Ingram was there to make his life a just a little kinder.

"Precisely," Mrs. Ingram said.

FIFTY-TWO

M rs. Ingram cleared her throat and slowly began to tell Suzanne the little she knew about the late summer night that Isaiah took Riley with him to visit his grandmother.

"He's been in the South Central County Jail ever since. There was no money to bond him out. The judge assigned him a public defender. His lawyer filed something called a speedy deal. I just can't bear the thought of Riley in that jail. Riley's not a bad boy, he's not a criminal. They're trying the wrong kid. He just doesn't deserve any of this, you know?"

"Yes," Suzanne whispered more to herself, than in response to Mrs. Ingram.

"Out of the blue, Riley's lawyer called me last Friday to tell me his case was being called for trial this week. He said another case pled out and the judge wanted to squeeze in Riley's trial to get it resolved before the end of the month. We're short staffed and there was no way I could be there to attend the whole trial. However, I did manage to get downtown to be there when Riley testified. From what I understand from Riley's lawyer, the issue for the jury will be whether or not they find that Riley had knowledge and acted in a way to make him an accomplice."

"You're saying Riley's on trial this week?" *And I dared to criticize those boys' parents for not being there for them in my very own courtroom.*

"Yes. Well, no. The trial is over. The jury has the case," Mrs. Ingram said. "I'm expecting Riley's lawyer to call me at any minute to let me know when they reach a verdict."

Suzanne looked at her watch. It was already past five. Hopefully, the jury had been excused for the day.

"Mrs. Ingram, what's the judge's name?"

"I'm not good with names. It's a lady judge. I think her name is Fitzpatrick."

Suzanne clutched her stomach, fighting to keep from becoming ill. There were only two female judges on the Atlanta District Court bench, and Becka was out of town confident that her case was in the competent hands of the other one.

"You must mean Judge Rebecca Fitzgerald."

"Yes, yes. That's her name. Can you talk to the judge? Maybe you can talk some sense into somebody's head or pay for the poor lady's damage."

If only it was that easy. The District Attorney called the shots, not the victim's family.

"Mrs. Ingram, I'll think of something."

FIFTY-THREE

"We're set to sail on New Year's Eve, Baby. Call me."
Suzanne seized John's upbeat message to avoid calling
Oliver about her change of plans. He sounded excited. Happy. She
wanted those same feelings. She hit the call back button on her cell
phone. Things with John had improved after spending Father's
Day Eve on her parents' trellised patio. He'd flown back to spend
a couple of weekends with her and joined her at a few campaign
events. Everyone assumed he was her husband and she decided
not to disabuse anyone of their misconception. She went home for
a combined Labor Day/belated birthday visit. She agreed to his
getaway cruise idea at the end of the year, after she was done with
the election and wouldn't have any more distractions.

"Hi, John."

"Get my message?"

"Yes, that's great."

"Don't forget to block out the dates on your calendar. We leave
on Thursday and return on New Years' Day, so you can be back on
the bench bright and early on Tuesday, if you want."

"Okay, I will. I can't now because I'm driving."

"On your way to that town hall meeting you were telling me
about this morning?"

"No, I'm not going. I, uh, had to cancel."

"You said Oliver said it was an important event to make."

"I did, it is, but I can't focus on it right now, something's come
up."

"Baby, what could be more important than your campaign? You only have a few days left to detonate that jerk."

Suzanne laughed, despite her own bombshell. "John?"

"Suzanne, you're breaking up. Hold up for a minute."

She cleared the tree lined driveway and headed toward I-285. "Is this better?" she asked, after waiting a couple of seconds.

"Yes, much. Now tell me what's going on."

Suzanne told John about the call from Dr. Peters, her emotional visit with Esther Ingram and her ethical dilemma.

"John, are you there?" Suzanne asked, her hopes sinking with his long pause.

"Haven't budged."

"I wish you were here."

Frequent flier miles, rollover minutes no longer held their commercial appeal.

"I know you do. Come on now, let's take this one step at a time. Maybe you should hang up and call Oliver, get his opinion about your proceeding to handle the trial."

"You're probably right, but I need to weigh in on my options first. And don't forget, he doesn't know anything about my past. He's due for a two-part conversation."

"You've got to tell him, Suzanne."

"I know and I will. Since the jury hasn't reached a verdict yet, maybe there's a way for me to step in and fix things for Riley." *There's simply got to be a way for me to save him without throwing away my career.*

"How can you do that?"

Suzanne turned silent. "I wish I had the answer."

"At least the campaign is almost over. You've held fast to your campaign pledge to run a clean race."

"Yeah, and lately, even Rotherman has been fairly decent."

"He can afford to be, considering all the trash he's loaded on his website. Have you visited it lately?"

"No, these days, I stick to websites that are uplifting."

"Like "allaboutshoes.com?""

"Exactly."

"Baby, aren't you ready to go on the offensive, now that you're approaching home stretch?"

"We're finishing up our third and final campaign brochure. It's due to drop in about ten days."

"Wouldn't this be a good time to truly slam Rotherman?"

"John, John, John. Sounds like you and Oliver have been talking."

Campaigns make for strange bedfellows. John never graduated from college. He dropped out to take a full-time job to help his parents provide home care for his sister who was bedridden with a debilitating case of Multiple Sclerosis. When she was still at the firm, Oliver repeatedly counseled her that she shouldn't settle for a college drop-out. However, during John's trips back to Atlanta during the campaign, Oliver began to appreciate John's considerable advertising network. Over time, based on their mutual interest in defending Suzanne's honor and position, they'd become more comfortable with each other.

"Yeah, he gave me a call yesterday. The man seems frustrated that you aren't permitting him to be as proactive as he thinks you need to be."

"You're referring to the paternity suit, right? Rotherman's only been sued. Nothing's been determined. Anybody can sue or be sued."

"True, but your opponent isn't anybody. There's a woman, not his wife, who thinks she's carrying his baby."

"As I told Oliver, if the lab test results get back in time, I'll consider making his alleged extramarital conduct an issue."

"Suzanne, I agree with Oliver. The issue is why is the woman making the claim, not can you prove the claim beyond a reasonable doubt."

"John, if I don't want him smearing my name, then I shouldn't smear his."

"Your integrity and laudable ideals won't mean a damn thing to him."

"I personally detest double standards in campaigning, and I suspect my constituents feel the same. But John, let me call you back. For now, Rotherman and his campaign ethics are the least of my worries."

FIFTY-FOUR

First thing Friday morning, Judge Vincent was on the bench in a daze. She listened as intently as she could so she could discern whether or not Gabriella Gomez's opposition to her ex-husband's request for liberal visitation with their ten month old son was reasonable. Having reviewed the file earlier in the week, her judicial gut response was that it was not. But on this particular morning, the judge was happy to provide the mother with the opportunity to prove otherwise. She desperately needed a mental distraction from her agonizing wait for word from the jury deliberating Riley's fate a few floors below her in Rebecca's jury room.

The night before, after she got home from meeting with Mrs. Ingram, she started to call Oliver several times. By eleven o'clock she hadn't conjured up the nerve to call him. Weren't his last words of caution: *"avoid controversy at all costs?"*

When she read Riley's case file which Rebecca had sent up to her office, Suzanne was relieved to find there wasn't much to the State's case against Riley. The State had charged Riley as a party to the crime. In her experience, before juries convicted a defendant, they wanted evidence that he had pointed the gun, done something besides been in the wrong place at the wrong time. Suzanne hoped that Riley's jury would be such a jury and find him not guilty.

Suzanne returned her attention to the Gomez case. The parent-child relationship is all about trust – the parents having confidence in themselves and trusting each other, the child trusting his parents, the parents trusting the child. Sacrifices and compromises by the parent are required when the trust is violated. Even so, incremental visitation makes for a hard sell. A parent anxious to make up for lost time rarely wants to hear about rebuilding trust gradually. Especially if the non-custodial parent perceives that the request for restricted time is a ruse, designed not to ease the child's legitimate fears, but only to appease the mother's bruised ego and unfounded concerns about his parenting skills.

Judge Vincent felt badly for the Gomez's. Citing irreconcilable differences, they divorced shortly before their only son was born the previous February. They faltered in the infancy stages of the divorce proceedings, enjoyed an evening of passion and conceived a child. The attorneys were astute enough not to mention their parties' renewed relations. Had they, jurisdiction would have evaporated and there would've been no final decree.

Once the child was born, they managed things for a short while without court intervention. Mrs. Gomez voluntarily began packing the baby's tote bag for weekend visitation with his father, not long after her six week postpartum clearance. Mr. Gomez provided her with a generous allowance for the child's expenses. For about six months, the parties continued to operate under their informal visitation schedule and the parents were sharing their responsibilities fairly well. When the mother found out about her ex-husband's new girlfriend, Mrs. Gomez reneged on her agreement to permit him unfettered access to their son.

Claiming the baby returned home stressed after spending time with his father, she halted the visitations. She petitioned Judge Vincent to investigate the inadequacies in his parenting skills. Mr. Gomez countered that his ex-wife's action was punitive, had nothing to do with his ability to care for their son, and was in retaliation for his moving on with his social life. He pointed out that had they reconciled, instead of divorcing, his ex-wife would have been begging for his help in caring for their baby.

The more Judge Vincent listened, the more she was inclined to agree with the father. He resented having to defend his ability to care for his son, all because of his ex-wife's insecurities. The mother's rambling courtroom testimony was making Suzanne angry. Left to Mrs. Gomez's subjective evaluation, it was she who was the expert in child rearing, her ex-husband, on the other hand, merely, an apprentice. She was determined to be unhappy, making problems when she really had very little to complain about. Then, all of a sudden, an uncontrollable burning force rose from within Suzanne like hot golden lava erupting from an isolated volcano. The judge's suppressed frustration about her life, her son and all that she'd discovered that week spewed out.

"What's wrong with you, woman." Suzanne knew better, but she kept going. "Here you have a man ready and willing to be a father, and you're bitching about an occasional dirty diaper, a hatless head, and a lost shoe. Grow up, why don't you!"

Sgt. Quarles tried to get Suzanne's attention from the side of the courtroom where he was sitting. She'd said too much, crossed the line, and had kicked her impartiality aside. Mrs. Gomez burst into tears and even Mr. Gomez was shaken by the outburst from the bench.

"My apologies, everyone." Suzanne stood. "We'll take a five minute recess."

Neither the parties nor their stunned attorneys budged. They weren't the ones who needed or called for the break. Suzanne slipped out into the private hallway behind her bench. *What just happened in there? How could I have gone off like that? God, please give me the strength to go on.* She closed her eyes and prayed silently until a sense of calm returned. She reentered the courtroom, took her seat and the hearing resumed. She was horrified at her loss of temper and control, and made herself listen to the evidence – all of it.

A forensic psychologist testified in the mother's case to support her proposed plan for incremental visitation. Judge Vincent was well versed in the subject and really didn't need for the expert to school her on its benefits. However, she was polite, allowing her to proceed with her testimony. Mrs. Gomez's expert had interviewed both parents and recommended that Mr. Gomez be limited to day visitation for a year, beginning with eight hour allotments, once per weekend for the six months, graduating to increments of twelve hours spread over two consecutive days occurring on alternating weekends for the next six months, before unrestricted overnight visitation should begin. A long, drawn out way of saying it was too soon for the father to be trusted with his child.

When the father's attorney cross-examined the psychologist, she conceded that when she interviewed him at his home, she found it to be a perfectly suitable environment for raising the child and that there was nothing other than his absence from the infant's life for the past six months that raised any concerns about his parenting. Mrs. Gomez had failed to show any need for restricting the father's time with his son.

"Having listened carefully to the evidence, I fail to see any basis for restricting Mr. Gomez's time with the child. In fact, I believe some extra parenting time over the upcoming holidays would be appropriate."

"Can she do that?" Mrs. Gomez said, frantically pulling on her attorney's sleeve.

"Shssh!" The attorney was torn between calming down his client and taking notes of Suzanne's ruling. "She's the judge; she can do whatever she thinks is best. We'll talk about this later."

Suzanne could only imagine how Mrs. Gomez's attorney would explain her ruling. The judge was unstable, not to worry, they would appeal.

"Thank you, Judge Vincent, for putting an end to this charade," Mr. Gomez's attorney said. "Shall I prepare a proposed order for your consideration?"

"Yes, I would appreciate that. Please provide opposing counsel an opportunity to review it first, approve it at least as to form."

Suzanne glanced over at Mrs. Gomez who was already standing, stuffing her papers and evidence in her tote bag. She'd lost any chance of the woman being reasonable. In her mind, if it was acceptable for the judge to fly off the handle, she certainly could as well. Ex-husbands certainly could exacerbate one's tendency to be high strung.

"Certainly, Judge. I can have a draft on your desk this afternoon, if you like."

"No, that's not necessary. I won't be able to finalize it today. Next week will be soon enough."

Suzanne was confident that the father possessed the patience he would need during the next several weeks, as he and his son became reacquainted. His broad smile, hearing her decision conveyed his appreciation for the system listening to a dad for a change. She knew he wouldn't betray his son's trust, just as she, given a second chance, would earn and keep Riley's.

FIFTY-FIVE

Invading Judge Fitzgerald's province as the assigned judge was not an option for Suzanne. Her own judicial oath trumped her maternal instincts. A jury had been empanelled to decide what should happen. A court record was being created. Suzanne felt duty bound to uphold the integrity of the process or at least the appearance of such. Upholding her duty didn't make waiting any easier. *What's taking the jury so long?*

"Judge, excuse me," Andi said, shaking her head in amazement. She caught her boss crouched down in the middle of performing her daily lunges, so she waited for her to finish her circle around the office. Andi's idea of exercise was dancing the night away with a dark knight in shining armor. "Do you want me to complete the paperwork for Sgt. Quarles so he can take the jury to lunch?"

The county picked up the tab for the jury's meal if their deliberations took them past lunchtime. Judge Vincent glanced at the porcelain gavel clock on the bookshelf and then back at her judicial assistant who was wearing a chocolate brown leather vest and matching knee high, high-heeled boots.

"No, Andi, not just yet."

It was only eleven, too early to reward the jurors with a free meal.

"Well, I bet if he showed them today's menu, we wouldn't have to worry about them delaying their verdict until after lunch," Andi said, as she turned to go back out to her desk.

It was no surprise that the judge's assistant had previewed the cafeteria's menu for the day. Her plans for lunch typically began before the morning's coffee had finished brewing. Suzanne poured a glass of water from the decanter on her credenza and reached again for Riley's file. Rebecca had stuck an orange note on the front cover asking her to order a pre-sentencing report if the jury returned with a guilty verdict. She flipped through the scanty file, appalled at what little police work had been done – a far cry from the detective work touted on television's crime shows. The only eye witnesses were the victim and Riley. A swift indictment followed and Riley was arrested shortly thereafter.

Unable to gain Riley's release without posting a bond, his attorney filed a demand for a speedy trial in order to push the case to the front of a long line of defendants awaiting some semblance of swift justice. Due to his age, Riley was just old enough to be charged as an adult with felonies in the Atlanta District Court. Indicted for aggravated assault, kidnapping and burglary, if convicted, he could wind up getting more years in prison than he had yet lived. *If only Riley had left Isaiah Bank's sorry behind in the house and caught MARTA home.*

Shortly after noon, Andi buzzed her, "Judge, Quarles just called. Verdict's in."

"Okay, you have the list of folks to call, right?" Judge Vincent asked. They hadn't had a criminal jury trial in a while and she didn't want any legal or procedural errors made on her watch. The last thing Riley needed was his mother causing a mistrial.

"I have it right here," Andi said.

Judge Vincent gave her judicial assistant time to summon the jury clerk, the prosecutor and the public defender to Judge Fitzgerald's third floor courtroom before she gathered her robe and the file, and headed for the judges' private elevator located off of a secured corridor. Only the judges, their staff and senior court personnel were permitted access. It was easy to forget the one way camera located in the remote corner of the elevator. Rumor had it that Chief Judge Haskell was once seen on the camera monitor in a compromising position with his court reporter in the elevator.

Sgt. Quarles was waiting for her by the elevator. Seeing her, he pushed the down button.

"Everything's ready, Judge," Sgt. Quarles said, always looking out for his judge. "Judge, before we begin there's something I think you should know."

"I already know, Quarles. Judge Fitzgerald warned me about Rotherman yesterday."

"Good, I didn't want you to be thrown seeing him in the courtroom. There's something about that guy, I don't trust, Judge. I don't think we've heard the last from him in this campaign."

"You mean something like the calm before the storm?" Suzanne's intuition echoed her sergeant's.

The elevator doors opened, revealing an unexpected occupant, and ending her conversation with Quarles. Suzanne turned on her judicial charm.

"Good afternoon, Rotherman." Suzanne stepped into the small elevator. She didn't recognize the woman standing next to him.

"Judge Vincent, this is my assistant, Mary Faith Tucker."

"Hello, Ms. Tucker, nice to meet you."

"Likewise, Judge Vincent."

Mary Faith was the only person smiling. Suzanne and Rotherman stood side by side in the crowded elevator, arms touching.

"See you at the Chamber of Commerce Forum tonight, Judge?" Rotherman asked.

"Of course, I'll take any opportunity I can get to set my record straight, since you seem hell bent on distorting it. That website of yours is outrageous!" But for her regrettable tongue lashing earlier during the Gomez hearing, Suzanne would have said more.

"Aw, Judge, you know how it is. You're the incumbent. I have to go over the top in order to get any attention on my race. It's nothing personal."

Rotherman forced a nervous laugh. No one else, including Mary Faith found him funny. The elevator came to rest on Judge Fitzgerald's floor.

"Excuse us, Judge Vincent, this is our stop," Mary Faith said. "We've got a verdict before Judge Fitzgerald."

Suzanne stepped aside to let them out first. "Good luck," she said, as they rushed off in the direction of the public entrance to Rebecca's courtroom.

"Think he knows, Judge?"

"He'll know soon enough," she said. "In fact we all will."

FIFTY-SIX

They paused at the back entrance to her colleague's courtroom. Suzanne reached for her deputy's arm to steady herself.

"I feel lightheaded, Quarles."

"Judge, take it easy," he said, ascribing her unusual nervousness to Rotherman. "Why don't you take a moment, while I step inside and make sure the courtroom is ready. My backup should be there." Verdicts had a miraculous way of producing extra deputies otherwise never to be found in the courthouse.

"Thanks. I, I, just need a moment." Quarles left her. Suzanne leaned against the outside wall of the courtroom, closed her eyes and whispered an affirmation she'd borrowed from her mother at the beginning of the campaign. *Today, I will do my best and trust that is enough.* She began humming and temporarily transcended all clouds obscuring her blue sky.

"Excuse me, Judge, we're ready when you are. I explained to the attorneys that Judge Fitzgerald had been called out of town and that you were taking the verdict."

"Thank you Quarles, you seem to think of everything."

"I try." Her sergeant winked at her, and hoped she felt better than she looked.

Quarles ushered her into the dimly lit antechamber. He proceeded into the courtroom where Riley was seated next to his attorney and guarded by Judge Fitzgerald's deputy. *Hold it together. You can do this.* Hearing Sgt. Quarles's booming voice, she stepped up on the bench.

"All rise! The Atlanta District Court is now in session. The Honorable Suzanne Vincent presiding, you may be seated."

FIFTY-SEVEN

"Are the parties ready to receive the jury's verdict?"

"The State is ready, Your Honor," Rotherman said.

"The defense is ready, as well, Your Honor," the stocky, balding public defender, Clyde Montante, advised. He rose and nudged his client that he, too, should be on his feet.

Twice. That's all she'd seen Riley in his entire lifetime. The stark consequences of his life's journey since she held him briefly in her delivery room at Detroit's Hutzel Hospital rested at the foot of the bench. Once more, she'd lost control over his destiny. Before, her mother, Mallory Caine, even Dr. Silas stood poised to determine what was in her son's best interest. Suzanne herself answered that question every day for children and their families: what is in their best interest. On that fateful Friday in October, Suzanne again couldn't exercise absolute control over her son. In the eyes of the law, he was an adult, charged with serious felonies and the jury, not his mother, had the final say. All she could pray was that justice would not be blind, but would see the goodness of her child and that none of this was his fault.

Riley stood, doing his best to keep his county issued slides on his bare feet and keep up his over-sized khaki trousers on loan from the community chest pulled together by the deputies. Proper fitting clothes and accessories such as belts and designer ties were in short supply around the courthouse. Suzanne's dark brown eyes were glued to the adult version of the baby she held close to her breast just once before surrendering him to a young couple whose future had seemed quite certain.

Riley stared cautiously at Suzanne. She studied his face – its angles, teenage blemishes, complexion the color of peanut butter. His frantic eyes were unsettling, yet familiar. His attorney reached up, placing his hand on the young man's lanky shoulder. *That should be my hand reassuring him, not some overworked public defender. Don't let this jury fail him as I have.* As Suzanne found the words necessary to continue the process, her mind raced through the past several days. Her journey had been like a lone car traveling over an unfamiliar, dark stretch of road, narrowly winding through the rural countryside. For what seemed like an eternity Suzanne had pushed on looking for any sign that she was nearing her final destination. Her conversation with Esther Ingram revealed an unforeseen detour in her search for her son. Maybe Riley once lived at the state home for boys, but no more. Her trip was prolonged until this moment when the only force standing in the way of Suzanne and her son was the collective wisdom of the twelve jurors who had deliberated his fate. The courtroom drew silent as everyone waited for her to say something. Suzanne took a deep breath and began. She had no choice but to perform her job as she always did with conviction that somehow the jury would sort through the jumbled facts, apply the law and reach a decision, a verdict that spoke the truth.

"Please bring in the jury," Suzanne told Sgt. Quarles.

One by one, twelve tired citizens trudged into the jury box. The seven women and five men took their seats in no particular order, mostly avoiding the teenager's anxious gaze. Young, old, white, black, even one Asian, the parties had selected a pretty diverse panel. Judge Vincent scanned the jury box, focusing on their hands and spotted the verdict in the hands of a grey haired woman selected by the jury to serve as their foreperson.

"Have you reached a verdict?" Of course, she knew they had, but it was just one of the few things always said both on television and in real life.

Judge Vincent glanced at Vera Applebaum, an older white juror seated at the edge of her chair at the end of the first row, near Rotherman's table.

"Yes, we have, Your Honor," Mrs. Applebaum replied.

The foreperson reached down for her glasses hanging around her neck and put them on, her hands trembling. She stood, shook open the paper dictating Riley's fate.

"Very well, ma'am, please publish your decision," Judge Vincent requested.

"We, the jury, find defendant guilty on all three counts."

Riley collapsed into his chair, dropping his head into his lap. It took all of Suzanne's judicial temperament to ignore her personal turmoil and son's agony to get through the next several minutes. The rotund public defender leaned over to console Riley.

"Is there any further inquiry for the jury?" Judge Vincent asked.

Hoping to invalidate the verdict and identify a faltering juror, Riley's attorney stood, and said, "Yes, we ask that the jury be polled."

The foreperson, exchanged a worried glance with her neighboring jurors. Delila Johnson, the jury clerk, was sitting just below Judge Vincent on the opposite side of the bench to the witness stand. She pushed aside a recalcitrant strand of hair and adjusted her microphone, ready to make the most of her brief moment in the spotlight during the trial. The first eleven jurors revealed no equivocation or reasonable doubt, just jurors ready to go home.

"Ladies and Gentlemen, when I call your name, please stand and answer each of the three questions I ask you," she said, speaking with a heavy South Georgia twang. "Mrs. Applebaum, was that your verdict in the jury room?"

"Yes," replied the foreperson.

"Was it freely and voluntarily made by you?"

"Yes."

"Is it still your verdict?"

"Yes."

"Mr. Baxley...." The jury clerk went through the roster one juror at a time.

"Mrs. Addie Hampton." Everyone waited for the last juror to stand. She was an elderly African American woman, wearing a crocheted marine blue shawl to match her fresh set of blue curls.

"Yes."

"Was that your verdict in the jury room?"

"I think so, she did say guilty on everything, right?"

Delila Johnson looked at Suzanne to make sure she could answer. She'd never had a juror ask her a question before during the polling. Suzanne nodded, unable to speak.

"Yes, ma'am. Now my next question is: was it freely and voluntarily made by you?"

"Yes, I suppose."

"Ma'am you said you suppose. You have to say yes or no."

"Have to? Baby at my age, I don't have to do anything."

Even the victim's family seated behind Rotherman's table chuckled. In any other case, Suzanne would've permitted herself to at least smile. Humor in the courtroom was usually calming.

"Very well, then. Is the verdict still your verdict?"

Rotherman tensed in his chair, with his sidekick, Mary Faith, completely dumbfounded. Montante was whispering to Riley the significance of what was happening. Suzanne froze, waiting for Mrs. Hampton's response.

"Judge, the other judge told us in her instructions that we should not compromise our own judgment simply to be cordial or for the sake of reaching a unanimous verdict. I've been sitting here, waiting my turn, listening to my fellow jurors, and with God as my witness, I cannot in good conscience vote to convict that boy over there. This wasn't his party. So, my answer is no!"

"I understand, ma'am. Your candor is appreciated."

"Sergeant, please take the jurors back to their jury room, while I discuss this with counsel. Ladies and Gentlemen, we'll be with you shortly."

Thank you, Jesus!

Fifty-Eight

All three attorneys were up at the bench, even though such intimate conferences normally occurred only when the jury was seated in the courtroom.

"With all due respect, where is Judge Fitzgerald?" Her opponent demanded.

"My sergeant reported to me that you were both told she'd been called out of town. If that's not sufficient information, you'll need to ask her yourself when she returns."

"How is this going to work?"

"That's the beauty of my years of judicial experience, it comes naturally."

Rotherman turned deep red. Montante played his best poker face. Mary Faith grabbed a strand of hair and began to twist it around her finger, thoroughly enjoying somebody giving her nemesis his due.

"The jury must resume its deliberations. My plan is to excuse them for lunch and tell them to resume their deliberations when they return."

"Maybe the dynamite charge will help, Judge," Montante said.

"Not yet," Suzanne said. "They're not hung; they're just no longer unanimous. Anything else?"

"No," said Rotherman, responding for the trio.

"Good." Suzanne checked the time. "Report back at 12:45."

She excused them, and told Quarles to have his assisting deputy to tell the jurors to suspend their deliberations and to take them to lunch.

Suzanne was done flying solo. She dialed Rebecca's cell phone number. After five rings, Rebecca came on. *Can't take your call right now. Please leave a message.* "Becka, it's Suzanne, hope you're having a blast. Sorry to interrupt things, but please call me. It's urgent." She couldn't blame her colleague for turning off her cell phone. There wasn't much she could do from Sedona. It was Suzanne's problem, not hers, and the true issue wasn't a legal one at that.

FIFTY-NINE

"All rise!"

Quarles pointed to the jury box. Mrs. Hampton led the way, eleven stomachs full of the county cafeteria's culinary best filed in behind her. Since their free lunch, the jury had taken most of the afternoon to deliberate and finally reported they were unable to reach a unanimous verdict. Suzanne patiently waited until all twelve were seated and she had their full attention. The United States Supreme Court had fashioned an unpopular remedy for the quagmire at hand when it decided the 1896 case of *Allen v. United States*. The American Bar Association Standards of Criminal Justice had long since rejected the jury instruction. It was a mouthful. Suzanne began reading the charge, avoiding three pairs of eyes: Rotherman's, the faltering juror's and Riley's.

"Ladies and Gentlemen of the Jury, 'in a large proportion of cases, absolute certainty can't be expected; although the verdict must be the verdict of each individual juror, and not a mere acquiescence in the conclusion of his or her fellow jurors, yet each of you should examine the question submitted with candor and with a proper regard and deference to the opinions of each other; it is your duty to decide this case if you can conscientiously do so; you should listen, with a disposition to be convinced, to each other's arguments; that, if much the larger number were for conviction, a dissenting juror should consider whether his or her doubt is a reasonable one which made no impression upon the minds of so many jurors, equally honest, equally intelligent with himself or herself. If, upon the other hand, the majority is for acquittal or conviction, whatever the case may be, the minority ought to ask themselves whether they might not reasonably doubt the correctness of a judgment which was not concurred in by the majority.'"

The large, wooden door closed with a thud behind the jurors as Sgt. Quarles ushered them back into the jury room to resume their deliberations.

"Any exceptions?"

"The defense objects, Your Honor," Montante said.

"Noted."

SIXTY

It was 8:00 on Friday evening, the incumbent had missed her scheduled campaign appearance two nights in a row and the jury was at an impasse. Reports to Suzanne throughout the afternoon confirmed that not only had Mrs. Hampton not changed her mind, she had convinced one other grandmother to adopt her view of justice. Suzanne dispensed with the statutory water and bread and butter jury provisions, and threw in a couple of cigarette breaks, some fresh air and a late afternoon pizza delivery. She even threatened to send them home for the weekend. The jurors refused to leave, took the breaks, ate all the pizza, but were unable to resolve the deadlock and just a few moments earlier, Vera Applebaum had activated the green light summoning Quarles.

He handed Suzanne the jury's sixth note. The previous five were all marked and in the custody of the court reporter. They had asked her to reread the party to a crime charge, and to clarify the concept of lesser included crimes. She'd discussed the jury's inquiries with the attorneys and told the jurors if they were not satisfied beyond a reasonable doubt that the evidence established all elements of the indicted charges, they could consider the lesser felony of simple assault and criminal trespass. Suzanne wanted to emphasize that the trespass charge was a misdemeanor, but sentence ranges and ultimate punishment were not matters within the province of the jury, just worried mothers. The third note requested more chalk for the blackboard. Suzanne responded to the fourth by telling the jurors not to worry about Isaiah Banks or who would decide his fate. Andi took care of the fifth request: the jurors wanted more coffee.

The courtroom was tense, and full of tired, hungry folks: the victim's family, the attorneys, even Quarles. Suzanne took the bench to address the inevitable.

"Counsel, the jury has not made any progress since the last time we heard from them. They've had the case now for over fifteen hours."

"Your Honor, the defense moves for a mistrial."

"A mistrial, are you kidding? I thought they should've been sent home hours ago. In light of this last note, the State requests that you dismiss them until Monday. They'll come back fresh and our real judge will be back."

As tired as she was, Suzanne thought it best to ignore Rotherman's slight and deal with the crisis before her. "A weekend on their own to think about things might help, or it might broaden the divide among the jury."

"Judge, one of the jurors, I think it's Juror Number Four's eighty-year old mother has heart surgery scheduled in Alabama on Monday," Mr. Montante advised. "We promised him he would be able to go forward with his plans to travel there tomorrow to get her ready."

"You all didn't pick an alternate?"

"We did, Your Honor, but the alternate's little girl got sick on the second day of trial and Judge Fitzgerald released her," Mary Faith said.

Suzanne looked at Rotherman, who was deep in thought. *Worried your verdict is going down the tubes?*

"Under the circumstances, I don't suppose you would agree to release Juror Number Four and go with eleven jurors. Perhaps they'd be willing to give up their Saturday."

"Of course, not," Rotherman said.

"Sorry, Judge, at least there's one thing he and I agree on. I certainly don't want the jurors mad at my client for having to give up part of their weekend. In fact, Judge, at this time, I move for a mistrial."

Rotherman was up on his feet. "The State is vehemently opposed to the Court granting a mistrial. With all due respect,

Judge Vincent, this is not your case and Judge Fitzgerald is the only one who should make that call. The State has invested considerable resources in preparing for this case and these victims deserve closure." He turned behind him, pointing to the elderly woman's family members who were still there.

"And the defense objects to holding the jurors captive any longer. What more do they need to say? They gave it their best shot. There's no point in belaboring this. Hey, we wanted an acquittal, but hung juries happen," Montante said.

Granting the motion was a big deal. Riley couldn't just walk out of the courtroom if Suzanne granted the defense's motion. He would still be held in custody. Rotherman would probably move to increase the bond, if not withdraw it altogether. The State would be entitled to retry him if they so desired. Continuing deliberations until Monday would end Suzanne's involvement in the case as a judge, but not as his mother. She finally had a chance to assume full control over Riley's future. She had no other choice.

SIXTY-ONE

"Thank you, Members of the Jury for the extensive time and close attention you have given this case." *And my son.* "Your foreperson has reported that you still are at an impasse. Do you think additional time will help?" The twelve heads rolled. "Very well, then, I declare a mistrial. On behalf of the Atlanta District Court and in particular, my colleague, Rebecca Fitzgerald, you are excused." Her deputy was facing the jury box, distributing letters for the employers and collecting their notepads, his assistant posted in the rear to keep an eye on the restless spectators. "Sgt. Quarles will escort you…"

All of a sudden, out of the corner of her eye, Suzanne saw trouble unfolding. She stood and yelled across the courtroom, just as a young man, one of the victim's great-grandson's, jumped over the bar into the well, knocked Montante in the head with a steel thermos and grabbed Riley in a chokehold from behind: "LET HIM GO, TAKE YOUR HANDS OFF OF HIM." Shackled in a chair without wheels, Riley sat defenseless.

Quarles turned toward the commotion, radioed for backup and ran toward the defense table. He pulled out his Taser gun and demanded several times that the victim's great grandson drop down to the floor. A loud pop sounded from the gun, sending off a paralyzing electric shock through the young man's body, causing him to fall back and hit his head on the bench behind him.

Suzanne, the prosecutor team and the jurors all watched, frozen in the suspended moment of the courtroom brawl. Quarles handed Riley over to his assisting deputy to remove him from the courtroom. Suzanne heard the handcuffs snapping shut around Riley's wrists despite the noise in the courtroom. EMT's ran in from the rear to attend to Montante and the assailant. Quarles refocused on his judge and the jurors. He frowned seeing that Suzanne was still on the bench and motioned for her to leave at once.

"Ladies and Gentleman, please follow me. We'll see about getting you home to your families," Quarles said, more than ready to end his long day.

Mary Faith started disassembling the prosecution's table. Rotherman simply sat clicking his pen. As Suzanne began to gather her things, Rotherman walked right up to her bench. No leave to approach requested.

"Well, well, well. Don't fool yourself by thinking you're going to get away with this. Thank God, I'm here to make sure you don't trample over another poor victim with your rush to judgment. I'm not done with this. Not by a long shot!"

SIXTY-TWO

"No, Judge Vincent has no comment." Andi rolled her eyes, she detested fielding calls from the press. "No written decision, it just happened. Uh, huh, the case is not over... Despite the mistrial, it's still open... Uh, huh, you know the rules forbid her from discussing her ruling...What did Rotherman say...Uh, huh, ...well you may want to consider your source before running that. We've nothing further to say. Thanks for the heads up." Andi hung up the phone. "She's a snake. I don't trust that woman, not one bit!"

"Leslie Dayo, shall I assume?" Suzanne and Andi were unwinding at Andi's desk in the reception area.

"None other than. She's trying to meet a midnight deadline to get something in tomorrow's paper about the case."

"I didn't see her in the courtroom. Rotherman must have called her the minute he left the courtroom." The sequence of events throughout the day swirled in Suzanne's head.

Andi smiled at her boss. "I wonder why." The judicial assistant was flabbergasted by all her boss had told her.

Sgt. Quarles stormed through the front door.

"Judge, I'm glad you're still here. That cannot happen ever again. You've got to let me take charge of the chaos. We've been over the drill, whenever there is an outbreak in the courtroom, you must leave the bench immediately."

"He's right, Judge. After the March 11 courthouse shootings, I don't know what I'd do if anything happened to you, to any of us, y'all are practically family," Andi said.

"Quarles, I'm sorry. You're right. It won't happen again, I give you my word." Her sergeant nodded, mollified for the time being. "Look I know it's late, but if you both have a few more minutes, there's something I need to tell you. I wish Tina was here but I'll have to fill her in later."

They agreed, despite being anxious to begin the weekend. Suzanne looked at both of her loyal employees. *Will they ever think of me the same?*

"What I'm about to tell you is going to come as a shock. However, it's only fair that I tell you. The defendant on trial before Judge Fitzgerald was booked under an alias." They waited for her to explain why they should care or how this could possibly be shocking news, since both had completed more than their share of duplicate criminal paperwork due to aliases assumed by defendants. "His birth name is Riley Vincent. I gave him up for adoption many years ago, before I moved to Atlanta. This is about as new to me as it is to you. I only found out about him and his case late yesterday afternoon. Quarles, I panicked when I saw that other kid jump the rail and go after Riley."

"I understand," Quarles said. "I probably would've done the same thing, if thatta been my kid."

"Judge, you've been through so much—

Andi was interrupted by the telephone. "Should I answer it?"

"Can you identify who it is?"

"McKinney & Lasley. Oh, perhaps it's Mr. Mason."

"Yes, answer it and ask him to call me back on my cell phone. Then why don't you two go on home, I'll be fine."

"Judge Vincent's chambers,..Yes, Mr. Mason, she's here. She asked that you call her back in her few minutes on her cell phone... Take care now," Andi said.

"Don't stay too late, Judge. I'm going back to my office to finish the jail transport forms, and I'll be back around to walk you out."

"Thanks, Quarles." Suzanne flashed him her 'I'm still the judge, I'm on top of things' smile. "For everything."

"Happy to be of service, Judge."

"Oh, I don't know, Judge, are you sure?" Andi didn't want to leave her, but her boss' revelation had drained what little energy she had left.

"I'm sure." *Definitely not fine.*

Sixty-Three

Suzanne went back to her chambers to take Oliver's call. At least she wouldn't have to look him in the eye. She turned on the small television on her credenza and caught a teaser for the 10:00 Late Evening News. She'd definitely survived the editor's cut. Judge Vincent would be the lead story. Recurring stock footage of her on the bench accompanied a telling trailer: *"Assistant District Attorney cries foul – judge's jockeying jinxes victim's chance for justice."*

Her cell phone rang. It was Oliver.

"Suzanne, you know I don't like surprises! Would you mind telling me what I'm getting ready to hear on the 10 o'clock news?"

Do I have a choice?

"Rebecca Fitzgerald is out of town. A month ago I agreed to take the verdict if her jury was still out when she had to leave."

"Operative words: her jury, your election," Oliver said.

"You said you wanted to know what's going on—

"You're right, go on."

"After extensive deliberations, the jury hung and I declared a mistrial."

"You should've let Fitzgerald do her own dirty work, but what's the hook?"

For me or the thousands of television viewers?

"Rotherman—

"Dammit, I should've known he had his hands in the kiln, stirring up some more crap!"

"He's the prosecutor. He's showboating for the victim. Blaming me instead of acknowledging he didn't have a strong case."

"Tell me about the case."

"Oliver, look the story's about to come on –

"Suzanne, it's not important what they say, you're not going to like their spin, regardless. We know what Rotherman is apt to say. Let's focus on the truth. Break down the case for me. I can't start the damage control until I have all the facts."

"An elderly woman was found gagged and tied up in her bathtub, her home in Palmetto ransacked. The defendant on trial was charged as a party to the crime. The co-defendant is out on bond."

"Why weren't they both on trial?"

"She severed the trials."

"Jesus, you know not to do that, right?"

Five years on the bench, and Oliver was still trying to school his protégé. She ignored the question.

"Why was he tried first?"

"A speedy was running."

"Rotherman was pressing for a conviction to tout during our last week of campaigning."

"And you appeared from the star chamber and snatched the conviction right out of his hands."

"Whose side are you on?"

"Need you ask, Suzanne? Instead of enjoying a late nightcap with my wife, I'm on the phone with you because you're down at the courthouse trying to do everybody's job on top of yours."

"Oliver, there's something you should know, that won't be reported."

"There always is."

"I'm not sure the report will give the defendant's name."

"And if they do?"

"He is being tried under an alias. His real name is Riley Vincent, he's my son."

"Your what? When were you going to tell me you had a son?"

"I was hoping not to have to."

"Suzanne, what are you talking about? You're not the only elected official with a kid in trouble. Remember when we met in my office and I told you –

"Sorry to cut you off, Oliver. I know what you're about to say, but trust me, it's not that simple."

"Well, it sure as hell isn't going to be now, you can count on it."

Sixty-Four

"Good to see you, man! It's been too long," Oliver said, shaking the hand of his Kappa Alpha Psi frat brother. They'd crossed together during their junior year at Morehouse College. "I appreciate you making time to discuss the Riley case."

Oliver rarely conducted business on another man's turf. Folks generally came to him. He knew when to make an exception.

"You look good, dawg," said Rotherman's boss. Prosecuting criminals didn't appear to leave him much time for the gym. "Looks like you've been pumping some iron since I saw you last summer at the Conclave. Or is it that wife you had with you?"

"A little bit of both. She has me on this all protein regimen," Oliver said, ready to start negotiating on behalf of his candidate. "Hope you don't mind me getting right to the point."

"Shoot."

"Your senior assistant isn't playing nice."

"Did you expect anything else?"

"Frankly, I'm a little, let's say, disappointed in his campaign. Exploiting little old ladies to get a few votes, come on, now."

"Oh, you're here to ask me to choke on his leash? He's his own man, dawg."

"Come on, the word on the street is you're not shy about making your wishes known when you want to."

"And what should I be wishing in the Riley case. Your judge threw the case out."

"It wasn't as arbitrary as Rotherman, no doubt, has suggested. Suzanne had her reasons."

"Such as what? Being late for a Friday night date?"

Oliver kept his cool, regretting he hadn't suggested they meet over a gin and tonic instead.

"I'm going to tell you something which nobody in this city knows except Suzanne and me. Once I tell you, and she knows this, her career and reelection will be on the line. Can I trust you, frat?"

"Oliver, you know the strength of the crimson and cream, but I got to tell you I can't compromise the integrity of my office."

"And I wouldn't ask you to. The judge is related to the Riley kid. When the cops booked him, he flipped his names. True last name is Vincent. The name she gave him before she surrendered her parental rights back in college when she had him was Riley Vincent. "

"You're kidding me."

"Do I look like I'm kidding?"

Oliver filled in the details, and left the District Attorney's Office an hour later partially successful. The other part would be up to Rotherman.

SIXTY-FIVE

C ountless protracted rules and process, locks and bars stood in the way of the judge and her son. Suzanne couldn't deny the obvious. She needed help to get to her son. She walked out to Andi's desk in the front of the office.

"Andi, would you make a copy of this for me and then stick the original in interoffice mail to Judge Fitzgerald?" Suzanne handed the report to her judicial assistant, who placed it on top of a mounting "to do" pile. "Right away please!"

"Sorry, judge. Yes, of course." Andi's arched eyebrow raised slightly in response to the judge's harsh tone. She rushed off to make the copy. Suzanne waited at Andi's desk until she brought her the copied report. "Is there anything else?"

"Actually there is. Would you see if you can put your hands on a production order and bring it to me immediately, please?"

Sensing her judge's singular impatience, within minutes Andi located a production order in a neighboring office and brought it back to Suzanne, who was standing, staring out of her window. Andi pulled the door closed behind her recognizing that her judge needed time alone. Suzanne sat down and hurriedly began to fill out the production order to have Riley brought over from the jail.

Listing her name as the requesting judge would raise questions. Judges presiding in the Family Docket rarely had a reason to deal with inmates in person. She paused at the blanks for the date and place of production. Five days a week sheriff deputies ushered long white buses with flashing blue lights under the building producing inmates needed for court appearances. The windows of the buses were painted and covered with protective bars. They resembled motorized cages, filled with hundreds of noisy, frustrated inmates whose fate loomed in the courthouse. Making room for one additional defendant wouldn't be a big deal.

The Sheriff imposed a minimum turn around time of twenty-four hours to process a request that an inmate be brought over from the jail. She pulled up her calendar on the computer behind her. It listed a two o'clock motions calendar for the next afternoon. She quickly blocked out the following morning as personal administrative time on the computer. She didn't want her case manager to seize the time slot and schedule her to preside over someone else's emergency. The judge completed the production order for the next day, Halloween, at 10:00 a.m. in her jury room.

Sergeant Quarles would make it happen, even if her request was a few hours shy of the Sheriff's twenty-four hour rule. Moments later the deputy knocked on the judge's door, responding to Judge Vincent's page.

"Come in," she called out.

"Judge, you paged me?"

"Yes, Sgt. Quarles. Thanks for responding so quickly. Have a seat, there's something I need for you to handle."

"Yes, ma'am," he replied.

Closing the door behind him, he took off his broad rimmed hat, adjusted the bulk of his utility belt and sat in the chair in front of her. She reached over her desk to hand him the production order and gave him a few moments to read it before she began.

"I can't think of any other way for me to get access to him."

"Yes, ma'am."

"Discussions are underway with the DA's office to see how to get his case resolved."

"Will we be handling that?"

"No, it's Judge Fitzgerald's case. She'll take everything from here. However, it is imperative that I speak to him as soon as possible."

The judge started to assure her sergeant that she was not ordering him to do anything unethical, but her pride stopped her. She wasn't in the habit of justifying her directives and besides, she was not doing anything wrong. Furthermore, there was no reason why the deputy would think otherwise.

"Quarles, as you probably can imagine, his present detention complicates things. Other than going out to the jail to speak with him..."

"Would it help if I went out there after court and spoke to him for you?"

"I appreciate your offer, but after all this time, he deserves to find out about me from me. Now, as to the order, I trust it's clear?"

He glanced at it again. "Let's see...um, do you want me inside the jury room? Will his attorney be present? What about the court reporter?"

"No to all three questions."

"Anything else I need to know, Judge?"

She could tell the vagueness of the assignment was not sitting well with her deputy. Typically, Quarles wanted the details. They were critical to his successful execution of any task, he'd told her many times before.

"I don't believe so."

At least not yet, she thought. Quarles had long ago proven, as had all of her staff, that she need not fear their betrayal, professionally or personally. Courtroom proceedings took place with everything out in the open. Everything else amongst them was confidential. Quarles was proud to be the one assigned as her deputy. She had always felt that his particular protectiveness of her was because she was a single woman. For now, though, all she needed him to do was execute her request without raising any questions from the brass and other brown shirts.

Their conversation came to an end. Her deputy stood. The judge knew that she could depend on him to do what she had requested.

"Very well. I'll take this upstairs right away and he'll be seated in the jury room tomorrow morning as you've directed."

"Thank you." He stepped toward the door. "Oh, and Quarles..."

"Yes, Judge?" Her deputy turned to look at Suzanne.

"I'd greatly appreciate your keeping this matter strictly within our office for the time being."

"Understood, ma'am." Her ally pulled the door closed behind him. She picked up the phone to place calls to her parents and John to alert them that she was yet another step closer.

SIXTY-SIX

After a long, late night talk with both of her parents and then with John, Suzanne had laid in bed for what seemed liked hours trying to chart out a course for Riley and her to follow. All three had done their best to sound upbeat about her news, but it was obvious that they were much less optimistic about the sudden turn of events. She finally fell into a restless sleep without deciding on much of anything. When the judge woke up a few hours later to the sound of sheets of rain beating against her window, her entire body ached from fatigue and apprehension. She delayed getting up and getting dressed as long as she could, and dispensed with most of her usual routine for preparing for work. Although normally she would already be at work by eight o'clock, she had asked Quarles to call her at home to confirm once Riley had been brought over from the jail. The buses generally started arriving about 8:15 and the deputies had to take roll of the inmates present and then clear them through the metal detectors before they could be dispersed to the courtrooms expecting them. From that point, it would be another forty-five minutes before her sergeant would be able to bring Riley upstairs into her jury room. She sat in the den, absently flipping channels between the morning news shows awaiting Quarles's call. He called shortly after 9:00.

"Hey, Quarles."

"Good Morning, Judge. A couple of inmates got into a fight in the loading area at the jail, so the buses were late arriving this morning. Our defendant came in on the third bus. We should be upstairs right about 10:00."

"Thanks, I'll see you then."

SIXTY-SEVEN

S gt. Quarles guided Riley behind the interior door leading from the detention cell across the empty courtroom to the jury room, displaying a gentleness he reserved only for those inmates who reminded him of himself growing up in the projects.

"Have a seat, son." Quarles said. "There's someone who wants to speak to you."

Suzanne exited from her private door and crossed the back hall separating her chambers from the jury room. Suzanne knocked twice before opening the door. Quarles sat near the entrance opposite where Riley was sitting, at the far end of the expansive, deliberation table, away from the door. When she entered, Quarles stood.

"Son, this is Judge Vincent. You might remember she declared the mistrial in your case."

The boy looked from the sergeant over to the judge and then back again. He said nothing, no doubt wondering what made him special enough to meet one on one with a judge.

"Judge, I'll be right outside if you need anything."

She slid into Quarles' warm seat. "Thank you, Sergeant Quarles. We'll be fine."

The judge waited for her sergeant to close the door behind him. She turned her full attention to the young man sitting across from her. Her son. *I have him all to myself, after all of this time. Is this truly happening?* Suzanne was startled by how much Riley resembled the boy she fell for in Cancun. Poking through the thin material making up the jail overalls, were impressions made by shoulders resembling those of the teen's father when he, close to Riley's age, had penned her down on the carpet of the hotel room hotel room and entered her roughly and eagerly again and again and again. Suzanne trembled as she thought of the night she lost her virginity. She'd left Keith's room with a fake smile pasted on her face as she tried to forget the burning ache between her legs. Riley's profile was Keith's from his nose turned up ever so slightly down to his chin. Sharp features, not rounded like hers. He looked triumphant for no particular reason.

"I know they woke you up very early this morning so you could make your bus. Andi, my judicial assistant, went to get you something to eat just in case you missed breakfast. Are you hungry?"

Riley shrugged.

"Vincent isn't your real first name, is it?" She instantly regretted the question. The last thing she wanted to do was to make him defensive. *I'm the one who has the explaining to do, not him.* "I'm sure you're wondering why I sent for you," she said as she studied her son's tall lanky frame and his ill-fitting jail attire. Riley shifted in his chair, saying nothing.

Riley didn't blink. Quarles knocked, entering with the food Andi had brought up from the cafeteria. He set the tray containing a plate of scrambled eggs, bacon, clumpy grits, toast and a carton of skimmed milk and orange juice down in front of Riley. After the sergeant left, the teen looked at the food and then back up at Suzanne. She nodded at him, gesturing toward the breakfast.

"Yes, please go ahead and eat, Riley," his mother urged.

Hearing his name, the boy froze, then hunger took over. He pulled the tray toward him and started eating. She let him eat, while she tried to figure out what to say next. He opened the milk carton, took a quick swallow, grimaced and set it back down, before picking up the orange juice, consuming almost all of it with his first swallow.

She couldn't resist smiling. *Yes, this definitely is my son*, she thought, remembering the countless magenta colored skimmed milk containers she herself had discarded into the large gray trash can in the lunch room at Caldwell Avenue Elementary School.

"I don't care for skimmed milk, either," Suzanne said, sounding silly.

Riley's manly munching and gulping grew louder, as if to say "whatever." When he finished, she walked over to his end of the table and sat down in one of the chairs near him.

"I'm glad to meet you, Riley."

Those words drew a response.

"Lady, why do you keep callin' me Riley?"

Suzanne had to blurt it out before she lost her nerve.

"Because I'm your mother."

"My mother? Is this some kind of trick?" He stood and angrily pushed back his chair. As he did so, the teenager's hand accidentally knocked over the carton of milk causing some to splatter on the judge's hand resting on the table. The boy looked Suzanne squarely in the eye. "My mother's dead!"

What in the world was I thinking, springing all of this on him without any warning, trapping him in this miserable jury room and forcing him to listen to what I want him to know. What kind of mother would do that to her innocent child?

Suzanne closed her eyes and breathed in deeply, as she dried the back of her hand on her pant leg. It was too late. She had to finish. Whatever the consequences, she was prepared to handle them.

"Please sit down, and give me a chance to explain."

John had cautioned her to be concise and straightforward to keep the boy's attention. *"Don't try to catch up on his whole lifetime in one conversation. You'll lose him with too much, too soon."* The boy awkwardly folded his thin frame back into his chair as best he could. His movements were impeded by the crippling leg braces concealed under his wrinkled orange jumpsuit.

The distressed judge peered out of the large window facing south. It was still raining. The low hanging, gray-black, nimbus clouds concealed the tops of the buildings normally in view. Atlanta's Turner Field was barely visible. There were so many questions she wanted to ask him. Trivial things such as was he a baseball fan or had he ever been to a professional game. Gut wrenching, hand-wringing matters such as did some well meaning person tell him she was dead or had he come to that conclusion all on his own. *I might not get to ask him anything if he decides he wants nothing to do with me. And who would blame him?*

With a trembling voice, she pressed on, "You were born almost eighteen years ago in Detroit on December 2nd at 12:45 in the afternoon. I know Dec. 2nd is your birthday because I was there bringing you into this world. I was just a little older than you are now."

Suddenly, Suzanne was overcome with emotion. Unprepared for her onslaught of tears, she reached for Riley's used napkin and dabbed at her eyes. Riley sat completely unfazed by his mother's emotion or her disclosure. She had no idea what he was thinking or what to say or do next, so she continued recounting what had happened. He listened with a chilling, stoical indifference.

"I didn't want to give you up, but I was young and not ready to be a mother. So I agreed to allow this young couple who lived here in Atlanta to adopt you. I thought they would make perfect parents for you. After I gave you to them, I returned to my home in California." As she listened to what she was telling him, the entire ordeal sounded much simpler and easier than it in fact had been. She had carried the pain and anguish over the separation for so long that now that the opportunity presented itself for her to convey her true feelings to her son, she felt completely inept and at a total loss for the right words. "Riley, what I didn't know until last week was that the adoption never took place because the man was killed in a car wreck soon after he and his wife returned with you to Georgia."

"Once I found out, I began searching for you. Just a few days ago, I met Mrs. Ingram. I know you've had to go it alone for most of your life, and I wouldn't blame you for hating me. But I'm here now, Riley, and I hope you'll decide it's not too late to give me a chance to be the kind of mother you deserve."

The judge fought hard to conceal the despondency she felt over her son's apathy toward her. She had been foolish to hope for anything else.

"Riley, son, please say something," Suzanne implored as she reached out to touch him. He flinched, pulling his arm away from her.

"Why 'cuz you woke up and realized your time for the mama show is runnin' out, and then you remembered you dropped me a few years back?"

Clearly, it was too soon. Suzanne told herself there would be time later for whatever affection and forgiveness an abandoned son could muster for a repentant mother seeking atonement.

"Riley, I'm so sorry. You must believe me when I say I had no idea. I'm ready to try to make up for some of all that you've missed out on, if you'll let me. I love you, son."

"Are you for real? You don't love me; you don't know anything about me. According to the nightly news, there's nothing to love about us black boys anyway. Showin' up on Halloween frontin' as my mother. Hey Sergeant!" Riley called out to the closed door. He paused before continuing, talking almost to himself, "Have you heard the news? The mystery woman in the black robe who filled in for the real judge turns out to be my mother. I don't believe this shit!"

SIXTY-EIGHT

D r. Peters had predicted Riley's anger and Suzanne knew she'd be the target for his wrath. Riley had earned every bit of his rage, the hard way. If he let her do nothing else for him, she'd do all with her power to make sure he didn't turn eighteen behind bars. A rite of passage both mother and son would rather bypass.

"You're absolutely right. It's bold of me to show up after all of these years asking you to give me another chance. But I'm here asking you to do just that. After your case is finished, you can decide what you want to do about what I've told you. For now, though, you need all the help you can get. Judge Fitzgerald's a fair woman and happens to be a friend of mine."

Riley spoke very low, with his lips barely parted forcing her to lean forward and strain to hear him.

"You willin' to get her to dismiss my case?"

"Unfortunately, it's too late for that. We're probably talking about some type of a plea."

"But I didn't do anything."

"Have you talked to your attorney about entering a plea?"

"Yeah, a while back he told me about the State wantin' me to do time."

"You're gonna make me go back there tonight?" The distress in Riley's voice as he said "there" was almost more than the judge could bear, betraying a vulnerability even he didn't know existed. What seventeen year old boy would?

"Riley, please try to understand…"

"You see, that's just it. There's nothin' to understand. Nobody's ever cared. But hey, don't sweat it. I get it, same-o, same-o. Can I leave now? Where did that guard go?"

His chilly abruptness whipped against her. The judge had envisioned that when they were ready to part, she would have given him some hope for the future. Instead, it was clear all that she had done was agitate her son. Not knowing what else to do, Suzanne pushed an index card bearing her home number across the table toward him.

"I've written my number down on this card. Take it just in case you or your lawyer needs to reach me. I'm working on getting you out. As soon as possible, I promise. Try your best to hang on until then."

As Suzanne studied her son's sullen face, her maternal instinct kept her from promising him anything more. It didn't matter what she wanted. Her son's immediate future was in the hands of Chance Rotherman. The ball was not in her court.

SIXTY-NINE

When Judge Vincent came back into her office, Andi and her case manager, Tina, already had left for lunch, sparing their boss the awkwardness of returning from her absence during the morning with a tear stained face. She pulled off the pink "urgent" message slip Tina had stuck to the back of her chair informing her that the afternoon hearing had been cancelled because the parties had reached a property settlement in their case. Alone in her chambers, Suzanne couldn't shake the haunting, hollowness of Riley's eyes when Sgt. Quarles appeared to take him back to the jail, the feigned bravado masking the brokenness of a young man put off so many times before, that once more hardly registered. It was if she had handcuffed him herself. Suzanne feared that her son didn't perceive that she wanted to protect him. *Am I merely a figurehead of the very system that has failed him for his entire life?* The familiar depression she felt every year around the time of Riley's birthday snuck up on her like a mugger's chokehold.

One of the things Suzanne had discussed at length with John the night before was her sending him back to the jail. She argued that it would be more shocking to Riley for her to show up unannounced at a future hearing in Riley's case. John intimated her decision to reveal herself to Riley before the hearing was selfish and served the boy no purpose. His opinion notwithstanding, she was the parent, the one with the double-edged stake in the outcome. Unable to agree, they eventually changed the subject.

In hindsight, her insistence on plowing ahead with her plan for the morning struck her as arrogant. How could she go home to the simple comforts she took for granted, knowing that her son may not be sleeping on a bed at all and didn't even have a private place to go to the bathroom. As if Riley's sheer knowledge that she was prepared to reenter his life would cloak him with a protective armor from the ills of his temporary residence – the noise, the fights, the filth and uncertainty as to the outcome to play out in Judge Fitzgerald's courtroom.

"Judge, speak with you for a minute?"

Judge Vincent looked up from her desk at Quarles, his face full of concern. "Sure, Quarles," she said.

"I thought you might like some follow-up on this morning's, um, case."

"Yes, of course."

"I got him loaded on the first bus, so he didn't have to wait down in that crowded detention cell all afternoon until the 5 o'clock bus. You know how rough it can get down there with inmates late in the day," Sgt. Quarles said.

"I sure do. Hey, thanks for looking out for him."

Quarles hesitated before turning to leave.

"Is there something else, Quarles?" The judge asked.

"I hope I'm not out of place, but—

"Please, go ahead. What is it?"

"You got to get him out of that jail as soon as you can. He's not safe. There's no telling what somebody in there might do to him if word gets out that he's your kid."

Judge Vincent greatly appreciated her sergeant's foresight. The jail was dangerously overcrowded. Some might even describe it as a state sanctioned ghetto. Tension ran high. Tempers constantly flared. Despite the deputies' efforts at maintaining order, they were alarmingly outnumbered by the inmates and fights, beatings, stabbings, even rapes that took place among the jail population.

"You're right, but how would anybody find out?"

Quarles looked uncomfortable.

"What is it, Quarles? Did something happen in lock-up?"

"I'm not sure, Judge. It wasn't like we were conversating or anything. Like most of these young defendants coming through, he's hard to read. You know they put great effort in appearing blasé, blasé."

"Isn't that the—

"But—

"But what, Quarles?"

"From the expressions of a couple of the defendants who were standing near where I left him in detention, I think maybe they overheard me talking to him."

"Oh, dear," Suzanne replied.

"I'm sorry, Judge, there may be nothing to it. I'll let you get back to work. I know we have that hearing in a little bit—

"Actually, that's gone away. Tina left a message that the case had settled."

"Okay then, Judge. Is there anything else you need me to do?"

"No, you've done plenty. Thanks again for your assistance."

"You bet. Hit me on the hip should anything come up."

SEVENTY

"Hi Mom, I bet you're swamped," Suzanne said when her mother came onto the line. Her mother had returned to work that morning after attending her principals' conference during the first part of the week.

"You can imagine the fires they saved for me to put out. And I will, as quickly as I can, one at a time. But dear, I've been worrying about you all morning. How did it go?"

Suzanne related what took place during her first visit with Riley.

"You sound disappointed. What now?"

"I have to focus on Riley's sentencing tomorrow. Oliver and Riley's attorney are still working on the DA's Office. As you might expect, Rotherman isn't trying to make this easy."

"You said the judge is a friend of yours, right?"

"Yes," Suzanne said.

"Have you spoken to her yet?"

"No and I'm not going to. I don't want to take the chance of things backfiring and Rebecca feeling pressured to sentence Riley more harshly than she would otherwise for the sake of appearing impartial. I think it'll be best if I simply attend the hearing and ask to speak on his behalf."

"Will Rebecca give you a chance to say something before she decides?"

"Of course, she will."

"I thought you told me once judges weren't permitted to testify in cases."

"In many instances, that's true, but this is different. Besides, a defendant's family is always permitted to speak," Suzanne told her mother.

"I understand, but in this case, well, these aren't the normal circumstances."

"More the reason why he needs me to speak up for him, don't you think? I mean, if I don't, who will?"

"What will you say, dear, you hardly know anything about him."

"I know enough – he doesn't belong in prison."

"Meaning what exactly?"

"Meaning, I'm going to ask Rebecca to probate his sentence, releasing him to me."

"Surely you aren't thinking about taking him into your home. That may not be safe."

"Riley's my son – your grandson – for God's sake!"

"He's also a stranger, Suzanne. Getting to know the boy is one thing, taking him into your home right away is something else."

"Mom, there's no time for that. His sentencing is tomorrow." *And I have a campaign that's going down the toilet.*

"I know, honey, but maybe he should be returning to YRC. You could visit with him there."

"How can you suggest such a thing?" *You made me give him up once. If I hadn't listened to you then, maybe we wouldn't be having this conversation. Whether you agree or not, I'm going to do what I know to be the right thing.*

"Please don't get upset."

"Mom, I'm not upset, but I need you to support me, not try to convince me not to go through with it. Kids his age – hundreds of them – consider walking out on foster care every day. It took a lot of courage for him to leave the home in August. I know it'll be difficult, but now that I've found him, he belongs with me in his own home, not some state institution."

"Are you really prepared for everyone to know about this?"

Hearing her mother, she was dismayed. In 1988, she had no choice except to defer to her judgment. Now, she was ready to stand her ground.

"Mom, I thought you said you understood and would support—

"Suzanne, this isn't about me, this is about your going public in your workplace with something we decided it would be best to keep strictly confidential. Aren't these hearings typically covered by that legal rag you've told me about?"

"Riley's case isn't sensational, so I doubt the press will be there."

"You're missing the point, once you open your mouth, you are the story," Mrs. Vincent said. "Don't forget you're also planning a campaign. Your personal business will be all over your workplace.... "

"Then so be it. And if somebody has the gall to make Riley a campaign issue, let them bring it on! The reality is I have a son – a freshly convicted felon – and he's in trouble. Am I looking forward to the courthouse rumor mill spinning my story? Of course not. But, I don't see that I've much choice, do you?"

"No, I guess not."

"This is the situation he's got himself into. I'm his mother. He needs help. I'm not going to turn my back on him again."

"Dear, you didn't then and I know you won't now. All I'm saying is that you need to be cautious, think this through."

"I've thought about nothing else since I read that presentencing report."

"Do you want me to fly in for the hearing?"

"No, I need to go this round by myself," Suzanne said, lowering her voice.

"All right dear, I need to hang up now. Let's talk again this evening. Be strong. I love you for being you and admire what you're taking on. Really, I do."

SEVENTY-ONE

S uzanne's phone rang early the next morning. It was four a.m. She reached over the side of the bed to retrieve the phone.

"Hello," she answered, not fully awake.

An automated voice dispensed the message, "Vince Riley is calling collect. Will you accept?"

"Yes, please put him through." Alarmed, she waited a moment before speaking to be sure a live voice was on the other end. "Riley, is something –

"He can't come to the phone right now." Raucous laughter broke out in the background.

"Who is this?" she demanded, straining in the dark to decipher the caller ID.

"An equal opportunity enforcer."

"Would you please stop playing around and get to the point?"

"So how do it feel, bein' the one beggin' fo' mercy, lady?" The caller joined in with the background laughter. "Riley asked me to call and give you a message."

"I'm listening," she said as she held her breath.

"He might not make it to court today."

"And, why not?"

"'Cuz we haters snuff out Mamas' boys the same way we do pedifreaks. Jail's an equal opportunity experience."

The dial tone resonated in her ear.

Wide awake, Suzanne hung up the phone. She dumped the contents of her purse out on the bed and searched for the card

Sgt. Quarles had given her with the jail phone number written on it. It took ten rings before the jail switchboard answered.

"This is Judge Suzanne Vincent calling from Atlanta District Court. I need to speak to someone in charge, right away, please. I need someone to check on Inmate Vincent Riley, Bunk No. 803056."

She told the operator about her phone call. The operator put her on hold, then came back on with a promise that the watch commander would report back within 30 minutes. A half a hour later, no one had called her back. Her second call was intercepted by a recording telling callers to call back between the hours of 9:00 a.m. and 5:00 p.m. She slammed the phone receiver down. Justice felt quite differently when on the receiving end.

Left with nothing to do except get dressed, Suzanne took care in selecting her outfit. Uninterrupted black was safe – judicial, maternal and conservative, all sound bites she could live with should Oliver's prediction of the presence of plenty of press prove correct. Suzanne's case manager, Tina, had checked the docket and confirmed that Rebecca had signed a Rule 22 order request from a variety of media hounds, including the scorned, but heavily read *Courthouse Review*. The phone rang one final time as she was closing the clasp on her pearls.

"Who is it?" Suzanne didn't even bother to check the caller ID.

"Judge, you sound on edge," Andi said. "This is a big morning for you. I was calling to pray with you before you head out."

Her judicial assistant was such a dear. Suzanne had become more faithful with her religion over the time they had worked together in the courthouse. Andi's spirituality touched all who came across her path. Never too ardent or self-righteous, just a good Christian lady trying to do unto others as she'd want them to do for her.

"How thoughtful, Andi. I've been up since about four."

"I thought you were going to take something to help you get a good night's sleep."

"I did and I was sleeping until the phone rang."

She told Andi about the call from the jail. The judicial assistant lifted a prayer for Riley and her boss, asking God to make way for a better place for the mother and son. Andi's judge closed her eyes, as she listened to the woman's sultry voice and blocked out the beep of another call trying to snatch away her brief moment of peace.

"Judge, everything is going to turn out fine. You're not doing anything but what the Bible teaches us: to take care of the widows and the orphans. Love covers a multitude of sins, yours, mine, even Rotherman's. Just impart your best, Judge. Impart your best."

SEVENTY-TWO

L ater that morning, Judge Vincent pulled her car into the judges' underground, courthouse parking lot. To avoid running into the other judges, she broke with routine and walked out through the exit to enter the courthouse from the public entrance on the ground floor with the legions of mothers, grandmothers and uncles there that day to see about their boys. After the hearing, she planned to exit the same way, having promised her staff she wouldn't come up to her office. Without her black robe, away from her courtroom, she was but another anonymous face in the crowd of strangers. She waited for the elevator at the front of the pack near a young man donning a throwback jersey and matching warm-ups, a baseball cap turned sideways and a set of shining gold teeth with a playboy bunny etched in his left incisor. He gawked at her.

"Yo, mama, nice suit," he said as genuinely as he knew how, flashing his best smile. "I like keepin' my lady lookin' good. Where can I pick up one like that?"

Are you for real? "Sorry, I can't remember," she mumbled, moving away from him as she stepped into the elevator.

Lawyers and their clients were milling about. None of the attorneys looked up as she stepped out of the elevator and approached the crowd. Last minute note taking, witness prepping and firming up payment of legal fees commanded their full attention. Suzanne spotted Oliver leaning against the corridor rail talking on his cell phone. He waved and made his way through the human thicket.

"Couldn't sleep?"

"Not a wink." *Such tact, Oliver.* "So what are the terms?"

"Blind plea. Rotherman will recommend a lengthy prison term. You can make your appeal along the lines of our original plea offer."

"Riley's attorney is okay with all of this?"

"Don't worry about him. I talked with him at length and he's more than satisfied. He headed directly over to the jail to talk to Riley as soon as he and I hung up from talking yesterday late afternoon."

"Oliver, I don't know how to thank you."

"Suzanne, there's one condition that I suspect Haskell is leaning on Rotherman to demand."

"Do you think Rebecca will go for it?"

"Not demand of Rebecca, demand from you," Oliver said.

Everything comes with a price. "Rotherman? I thought you were dealing with the District Attorney directly."

"I was, but he said he owes Rotherman the right to have the final say. He credits Rotherman with his own election to the office and pretty much lets him have his run of the office and his cases."

"What's the condition?"

"Your resignation."

"You've got to be kidding me, Oliver. And you agreed to that? Don't I get any say in this?"

"Of course, I didn't agree. That's simply his condition and since he'll get to make his recommendation first, I wanted you to be ready with a strong response. Here take a look at what I've prepared."

Suzanne was so angry she could barely read the statement he'd outlined for her. She stopped when she saw the reference to Escobar Secret's paternity suit against Rotherman.

"Oliver, I thought we agreed—

"We didn't agree, I've let it go until now. When you walk up to that podium, your career and professional reputation will be on the line. I refuse to let you throw everything away because you're hell-bent on playing Judge Goody Two Shoes!"

"Oliver, I just don't know. What time is it?"

He pulled out his gold pocket watch and checked the time.
"9:45."

"I'll be back in ten minutes. I can't breathe, can't think. I just,
I just have to get away. Go on in and save me a seat."

"Okay, I'll be sitting midway on the left side of the courtroom.
Let's hope today it'll be the defendant's side of justice."

Suzanne pushed her way through the crowd toward the
judges' corridor, drowning out the reporters' questions. *"Is it
true, Judge Vincent? Is the defendant on trial really your son? Has
Rotherman...Anything, can you tell us anything at all..."*

She pulled open the heavy door leading into Judge Fitzgerald's
courtroom from the outside corridor. Everyone had filtered inside.
Court was about to begin. Riley's case was first on a final plea
calendar – most defendants' last chance to negotiate a plea with
the prosecutor. She entered from the rear and slid onto the bench
next to Oliver with a few minutes to spare. Rotherman and Mary
Faith were seated at the State's table.

At first she didn't see Riley's public defender, which concerned
her. A critical stage of the process, the sentencing wouldn't
proceed without the attorney. Indigent defendants were in no
short supply. Court appointed lawyers typically had an unwieldy
caseload.   Their presence often was required in multiple
courtrooms simultaneously. In addition to a raise in salary, a pair
of rollerblades would make their job a whole lot easier. When
attorney conflicts arose preventing a hearing from proceeding, the
judge had no choice but to continue the case. All Judge Vincent
could do was hope that Riley's case was on the top of his lawyer's
scheduled court appearances that day.

For Suzanne, her shift from active participant to passive
observer of the courtroom activity and its nuances was surreal.
She imagined it was something similar to the lead actor attending
a play performed by the understudy. The court personnel's
innocuous, idle chatter and muffled laughter seemed too casual,
even flippant, as they went about readying the courtroom and
themselves for another day's work. They knew the rules, what

mood their judge was in, and the likely outcome of the cases appearing on the calendar. Judge Vincent now could empathize with the uncertainty, worry and interminable waiting befalling onlookers and family members held at bay by the railing running across the middle of the courtroom.

Just then, Judge Vincent heard the lock turn on the door concealing the adjacent detention area. The public defender, Clyde Montante, came out first, shaking his head, followed by Riley and the deputy assigned to guard him. She gasped when Riley turned around – the entire left side of her son's face was a swollen mass of dark red, the eye practically shut and his lip split.

His attorney tapped him on the arm to alert him that court was beginning. Hearing the bailiff wrap in Judge Fitzgerald, Riley turned forward to give the presiding judge his full attention. The prissy court reporter sat up in her chair, straightening the black lace doily covering her shapely legs.

"Are the parties ready to proceed with sentencing in the case, *State v. Vincent Riley*, Indictment No. 04CR091258?" Judge Fitzgerald asked.

"Yes, Your Honor. Yes, Your Honor," both attorneys responded in parrot-like succession.

"Very well—

"Judge Fitzgerald, excuse me for interrupting, but I need to address my client's condition here before anything else. When I arrived this morning to meet with him, this is how I found him." Riley's attorney motioned toward him with open hands. "This is outrageous. Stand up, son, so the judge can see your face."

Judge Fitzgerald looked at Riley as he stood slowly, then she glanced over his head acknowledging Judge Vincent, for the first time, seated in the audience three rows behind the defense table. Surprised to see her colleague, the judge briefly nodded to her, before refocusing on the morning's complication. It was clear that no one had alerted her to the situation prior to her coming into the courtroom. She summoned one of the deputies up to the bench, and then quietly dispatched him to get some answers.

The public defender continued, "I should've been notified immediately when this first happened. All the deputy in the back could tell me was that some inmates jumped my client last night."

It was too late, but Suzanne recognized that if she had listened to John and delayed her meeting with Riley, her son wouldn't have been harmed on her account. Even Sgt. Quarles had alerted her to the possibility. *Why couldn't I have waited?*

"Mr. Montante, I share your concern." Indeed, Judge Fitzgerald appeared quite upset. "I've sent Deputy Runyon to get a complete report on what took place, which I will pass on to you and to Mr. Rotherman. Whoever did this will be dealt with properly. In the meantime, has your client received the medical attention he needs?"

"He told me he's been to the infirmary, that's about it. Not being a doctor, I can't say what he needs."

"Very well then, counsel."

Judge Vincent sighed, recognizing the annoyance in the presiding judge voice.

"All I'm asking is if the two of you are prepared to proceed with sentencing at this time."

Judge Vincent held her breath. She didn't want a continuance. Whatever sentence her friend imposed or medical treatment Riley needed, she would help her son deal with it.

The public defender peered over at his client before responding, "Yes, Your Honor, we wish to go forward."

"The State's ready. Our victim is present and as far as we are concerned, time is of the essence," Rotherman said.

SEVENTY-THREE

"Counsel, did you both receive a copy of the pre-sentencing investigation report?"

The two attorneys nodded. Riley had entered his plea of guilty and now it was time to persuade Judge Fitzgerald as to the appropriate sentence. Because the plea was tendered as a blind plea, he had admitted his guilt on the record without first knowing what sentence he would receive. Blind pleas were risky business but both sides and Suzanne were counting on the judge to see the case as they did.

"Mr. Rotherman, does the State have any victim impact testimony to present?" the judge asked.

Rotherman took his time approaching the podium, fully intending to maximize the free publicity one week before the election.

"Your Honor, I'd like you to hear from our victim's grandson, Terrell Finley."

"That'll be fine. Please have him come up."

Rotherman turned around to motion to his victim's advocate to wheel the young man up to the podium. His head was wrapped with a black shiny do-rag and he was wearing dark glasses. The advocate stretched the microphone downward so he could speak. He turned around and glared at Riley before beginning.

"Mr. Finley, are those prescription eyeglasses? Because if they're not, please remove them so I can see you as you're speaking," Rebecca said.

"Judge, Mr. Finley was shot in the eye and leg, which is why he's in a wheelchair," Rotherman said. He left out that the grandson had gotten caught up in an exchange of gunfire over a bad drug buy in a languishing section of Atlanta known as Mechanicsville. The State has to take its victims as it finds them. "If you wouldn't mind him keeping his shades on, he's blind. His family is hoping the blindness is only temporary."

"Oh, my goodness. Yes, of course," she said.

"Mr. Finley, please proceed when you're ready."

"My grandy is all I got, me and my four brothers. I jus' wish Ida been there to take 'em out myself. Give 'em what he's got comin'. 'Cuz if he or his associate come near my grandy again, no tellin' what I might do. I swear."

"Thank you for speaking on behalf of your grandmother. I hope you enjoy a complete recovery, young man." Rebecca nodded to the victim's advocate to wheel him back to the audience. "Anything else, Mr. Rotherman?" Fully in his element and anticipating all to come, he pushed back his chair and stood longer than was necessary for any purpose, other than grandstanding.

"The PSI does not address some additional information which has come to the State's attention since it was prepared regarding the defendant's family history. As you would expect, we've shared the information with the defense, and if this hearing proceeds as I anticipate, you will hear shortly from the defendant's mother. My recommendation takes into account all of the facts and has not been compromised by the defendant's newly discovered political connections. He should be treated no differently than any other convicted felon. Indeed, it is our eighty-five year old victim and others like her we need to be concerned about, not some sob story conjured up by a defendant who's conspired to commit such serious crimes as these.

"We need to teach him a lesson now, while we have his attention. If we don't, I promise you, he'll be back and the next time he may decide to enter someone's home himself, armed, rather than post as the lookout outside. We're lucky that this poor woman had the strength and fortitude to pull through that horrible night. If she hadn't Mr. Riley and his co-defendant would be facing murder charges and a mandatory life sentence or worse."

"The State requests that you sentence him concurrently to serve twenty years to do fifteen on the aggravated assault, the balance probated, a straight fifteen on the kidnapping, and suspend the twelve months on the criminal trespass, require him to pay restitution for the victim's medical bills and damaged property. Thank you, Your Honor."

Mr. Montante stood aside to let him pass.

"Your Honor, my interest is simple – justice for my client. Contrary to what Mr. Rotherman wants all of us to believe, my client is not a career criminal in the making. This is his first brush with the law. The State has never budged on its demand that Vincent serve time in this case. As you saw, there wasn't much to the State's case. It was completely circumstantial evidence and not much of that. This is another case of the three wrongs; the wrong place, the wrong company and the wrong decision to be there with the co-defendant. Actually, there's a fourth wrong, the biggest one of them all – Chance Rotherman. Mr. Rotherman should be ashamed of himself for over trying this case. The real criminal is on bond, and my innocent client is left to hold the bag and fend off hardened thugs in the South Central County Jail."

"Mr. Montante, let's stay on track."

"You're right, judge. And I apologize, I truly do, but somehow this all just doesn't seem fair. My client qualifies to be sentenced as a first offender. I'm asking you to give him the chance to keep his record clear of this felony conviction. The State's recommendation is excessive. The three months he's already been locked up and last night's beating are lesson enough."

The lawyers had done their jobs. Judge Vincent was ready to begin hers. She stood up in the audience.

"Your Honor, before you pass sentence, if I may address the Court regarding this case." Judge Vincent waited to be invited to the podium. The attorneys exchanged a knowing glance.

"Certainly, Judge, please come forward."

The deputy closest to the defense table held the gate open for Judge Vincent as she approached the microphone. She longed to touch her son's shoulder as she passed him. Hearing the silent shutters clicking away anyway, she held back and focused on trying to convince her colleague – her friend, another mother – to do the right thing under the totality of circumstances. No one knew, not even Oliver, what she would say. Her voice trembling, Suzanne began.

"Thank you for permitting me to speak. My presence before you this morning has absolutely nothing to do with my re-election campaign or my manipulating the criminal justice system. I respect victims' rights and my heart goes out to this victim and her family. My grandmother was brutally assaulted in her home last December so the alleged facts of this case hit home with me. I have done nothing to interfere with the State's prosecution of this defendant or any other defendant. Furthermore, I've intentionally refrained from attempting in any way to influence this honorable court's judgment. Like any other family member would and should do, I waited until this moment to make an appeal on behalf of the defendant."

A roar funneled through the packed courtroom.

"Our system has failed this defendant and so have I. The only thing Mr. Rotherman has done in this case with which I totally agree is to insist that everything occur out in the open. Despite his personal and political motives for my making this disclosure in public and his inviting the press to cover today's proceeding, I wouldn't have wanted it any other way." Suzanne paused to look back at Riley sitting next to his attorney. "The public is entitled to know that I am the defendant's mother. I am here on his behalf, as I would hope any parent would be at such a critical time. My grandmother used to tell me, 'Love covers a multitude of sins.' Whatever my son has done, I love him nonetheless and can assure the Court that you will never have him before you again as a defendant."

"Likewise, I hope and pray that he will come to love me and forgive me for all that has transpired during our time apart. I made a decision when I was not much older than the young man before you, Judge Fitzgerald, and as a result, forfeited the opportunity to raise the defendant. I'm here now. *Please don't let me be too late.* Please give him a second chance."

Judge Vincent paused to allow her colleague to absorb her plea for mercy.

"Your Honor, for the record, the defense does not oppose a probated sentence," Riley's attorney volunteered, eager to close in on the manna tossed his client's way.

"Noted, Counsel," Judge Fitzgerald said absently.

Suzanne began to conclude. "The State also correctly points out that the report fails to identify anyone who could monitor him to make sure he successfully completes a probated sentence. Judge Fitzgerald, I'm asking you to grant him a probated sentence with whatever conditions you believe his circumstances warrant and to remand him to my supervision."

She returned to her seat next to Oliver and awaited Rebecca's sentence.

"Young man, please rise," Judge Fitzgerald began. Riley and his attorney both stood. Suzanne held her breath as Rebecca spoke. "Your participation in criminal activity must have consequences. This poor woman has the right to live in her home without fear for her safety. Your actions have robbed her of that peace of mind. Based on the facts of this case, I am sentencing you to ten years of probation to serve concurrently on both counts, the first year to be intensive probation. You will meet with a probation officer shortly who will explain all of the conditions. You may be seated."

Suzanne grabbed Oliver's hand and squeezed it tightly. After eighteen years of regret and wondering she finally would be bringing her son home.

The prosecutor stood, ready to continue the duel. "Your Honor, if you'd indulge me for just a moment longer, please."

Judge Fitzgerald held up one finger.

"Thank you, Your Honor. I promise I'll be brief."

"As you know this case was being presented to you as a blind plea. Before I made you aware of the State's final condition, I wanted to see if Judge Vincent had decided to do the right thing. It appears that she continues to be preoccupied with what's in her own best interest under the guise of what's supposedly in her son's best interest, rather than the public she was appointed to serve. The reason the press is here is because of the overwhelming public interest in this matter. This case is bigger than the Vincent household. The overriding principle is the integrity of our criminal justice system –

"You got that right," an unidentified person shouted out.

"Justice for the rich ain't look nothin' like justice for the poor," another heckler said, joining in the unrest.

"Order in the Court!" Rebecca's deputy commanded

"As I was saying, the only appropriate thing for Judge Vincent to do is to withdraw from the race for her re-election and tender her letter of resignation. Perhaps that way she can give her full attention to supervision of the defendant and provide a space on this bench for someone prepared to make dispensing justice his or her priority."

"Mr. Rotherman, how dare you interject politics into my courtroom!"

"Forgive me, Your Honor, please take no offense. I realize that you have no authority to impose such a condition. I am merely extending Judge Vincent the professional courtesy of advance notice that I intend to ask the public to impose such a condition come Election Day."

The prosecutor turned from the podium, looking quite satisfied. He nodded to the chief judge sitting in the very last row before taking his seat, posing for the audience already beside itself. Whispering, nudging, muffled dictating, reporters' pens scribbling the latest in Rotherman v. Vincent all began at once. For everyone in the courtroom except Suzanne, Riley Vincent was an afterthought – the bane of his existence for as long as he could remember.

"Order in the Court, O-R-D-E-R- I-N-C-O-U-R-T."

SEVENTY-FOUR

Everyone filed into Judge Fitzgerald's office after Rebecca – Suzanne, Riley, Deputy Runyon, Montante, and the trial clerk. Rotherman was about to piss in his pants over the public spectacle he'd engineered. The court reporter trailed behind everyone, struggling to keep up while carrying her stenographer machine and the roll of transcription tape unwinding out of the spool onto the carpet.

Crowded around Judge Fitzgerald's oval conference table, the closed post hearing began. Unlike Judge Vincent's highly decorated office three floors above, Judge Fitzgerald focused most of her creative energies at home camouflaging the empty spaces where marital property had been equitably divided and sent on with her ex-husband. Her chamber walls were barren and the minimal art work displayed was uninspired.

Her mother had finally convinced Suzanne to disclose only the essential facts on the record. There were surprisingly few. The judge matter-of-factly explained that Riley Vincent was the defendant's birth name, Vince Riley an alias used upon his arrest and that she and Riley were separated at birth. Arrangements had been made for his adoption, but unbeknownst to her it didn't take place and she had only recently located him. The bottom line was that she was prepared to take him into her home at this time. Suzanne knew the route she took to reclaim a second chance with Riley might ultimately cost her the election and even her judicial career. But she did what she felt she had to do.

The attorneys declined to ask her any questions or say anything else. For the time being, only Rotherman was unwilling to let Suzanne off the hook so easily and ignore the more pertinent question of why she proceeded to preside over the case in Rebecca's absence once she had made her discovery. Rotherman was ready to get back to campaigning where he fully intended to make Suzanne answer the question on everyone's mind. The others, including Judge Fitzgerald, were anxious to be done. Even more so, Rebecca Fitzgerald wanted one-on-one time with Suzanne. Once arrangements were made for him to meet with a probation officer, the prosecutor asked to be excused and left. Further need for the other attorney was less clear.

"Judge Fitzgerald, shall I wait with Vincent, I mean, Riley, until he's completed probation intake?" Mr. Montante asked.

Judge Fitzgerald deferred to her colleague, not sure what to tell the attorney. Judge Vincent smiled at him.

"Mr. Montante, I'm sure you have other courtrooms holding for your report. Thank you for all that you've done for Riley." Judge Vincent was not completely sure he had done all that much, or that there was much he, in fact, could have done, but she felt it important that he understood she fully appreciated his standing by her son's side throughout the ordeal. "I think I can take things from here."

"Well, if you're sure, Judge," the attorney replied. "I'd like to speak to Riley privately, though, for a moment, if that's okay with you."

"Of course," Judge Vincent said.

Judge Fitzgerald instructed her deputy to go ahead with Riley and Mr. Montante to a nearby consultation room so the attorney could speak to his client and she could have a few words with her colleague before the probation officer arrived. Once the three left, Rebecca spoke first.

"If only you'd told me, we could've done things – well, differently," Judge Fitzgerald said softly.

"I don't know, Rebecca, somehow, maybe because I found out very late in the process, it just didn't seem right for me to ask," Suzanne said. "And I certainly didn't want to make things awkward between you and the DA's Office."

"I can't begin to fathom the magnitude of your discovery and all that you're going through. Hopefully, I don't even need to say this, but if there's anything and I do mean anything I can do—

Suzanne nodded at Rebecca in appreciation. She was too full to find the right words.

"Actually, there's one thing. In light of what happened last night, I don't want him mixed in with the others on that bus. Even though I know he has to go back to the jail one final time to be processed out, I just couldn't bear the thought of someone attacking him again," Judge Vincent's voice broke.

"We should be able to address that. I'll just ask my deputy to call upstairs and request access to one of their cars to take him back," Judge Fitzgerald said.

"That would be great. In fact, Rebecca, do you mind if I ask my sergeant to come down and relieve your deputy. That way I can keep tabs on Riley more directly."

"Not at all. Why don't you call him now and get him to radio Deputy Runyon when he's on his way."

Judge Fitzgerald repositioned the conference phone on the table so her friend could dial upstairs. Suzanne made the call and hung up.

"Thank you so much, Rebecca. Your presence alone made this much easier. Can you imagine all of this occurring on Sam Haskell's clock?"

"Now that's a scary notion," Judge Fitzgerald said.

They both laughed. Sam Haskell was pompous, chauvinistic, a real good ole boy, for whom tolerating educated women was an occupational hazard. Female lawyers loathed appearing before him. Some flatly refused. The pantyhose brigade – his nickname for Rebecca and Suzanne – were hoping he would take an early retirement.

"Good luck, Suzanne." Rebecca came around the table, to give her a parting hug. "You know where to find him, right?"

"I'm happy to finally be able to say, yes, I do."

SEVENTY-FIVE

Q uarles and Riley were seated, talking when the long haired probation officer and Suzanne arrived, simultaneously. She followed him into the room, not recognizing the husky man. His goatee and neatly braided ponytail, the tight squeeze into the short sleeved shirt and dated wide tie she would have remembered. He likewise gave no indication of being a voter or reader of the *Courthouse Review*. Before saying anything to anyone, he sat down at the table and read over the copy of the sentencing sheet Quarles handed him. Rebecca had probated his entire sentence. Ten years on both felony counts, with the first year intensive. Suzanne had mixed feelings about the sentence. She was relieved that he would be released to her custody immediately, but felt the length of the probation was excessive. They waited for him to begin.

"Do you go by Vince or Vincent?"

"Whatever."

"Okay then, whatever, my name is Bobby Battle. I'm here to do your probation intake. After today, you'll be assigned a field officer to supervise you."

"Yes, sir," Riley replied.

"Son, have you ever heard the expression "trouble's easy to get in, hard to get out?" Mr. Battle asked.

"No, sir."

"Contrary to the word on the street, your P.O. is your friend. If you listen carefully to what I'm about to go over here, you'll avoid trouble, and this little chapter in your book will be over. It's all about being disciplined. You see this braid of mine?" He lifted his ponytail, caught up in making his point, "Every day, as soon as I step out of bed, I undo it and re-braid again, the same exact way – discipline."

"Yes, sir."

Mr. Battle interrupted his own spiel, "Now, who's this with you?"

Riley didn't respond immediately. He looked at Quarles, then at Suzanne. "Uh, she's a long lost relative trippin' off of some biological guilt."

The probation officer ignored the teen's hostility. He couldn't place the woman even though she looked familiar. Something was amiss between the kid and the lady, but he was too busy to inquire. The defendant had a parent with him. That was enough for Battle.

"Good to meet you, ma'am. I'm glad you're here," he said. "I could stand to see more interested family members, sure would make my job easier."

"You won't have to worry about him, Mr. Battle," Suzanne responded as she locked eyes with Riley.

The probation officer went over the sentence with Riley, and then collected some personal data from him. Riley responded confidently until Mr. Battle asked for his address. When the boy glanced over at Suzanne unsure what to say, the man raised an eyebrow and pulled on his goatee but said nothing. She hurried to fill in the gap with her address and to explain that Riley was not living there prior to his detention.

The P.O. asked Riley several questions designed to assess his predictable success for completing the probation without incident. Riley listened as he explained the conditions accompanying his freedom, emphasizing the zero tolerance for drugs, firearms or alcohol. The boy's eyes widened ever so slightly at the man's mention of the 7 p.m. curfew for his first six months of regained freedom.

Mr. Battle concluded by handing Riley an appointment card to report to the field office in a week. Picking up his clipboard, the probation officer shook both of their hands, nodded to the sergeant, and left them to figure out the rest.

SEVENTY-SIX

The county jail, a massive structure of red brick towers bordered by treacherous coils of barbed razor wire, sat atop a hill in a depressed section of northwest Atlanta, not much further than a handcuff's throw from the courthouse. Suzanne had only been there once before when she took a tour of the facility during her new judge orientation. The deafening noise made by the inmates, their defeated faces, and the overall dismal environs all had a lasting impact. But the heavy security door slamming shut behind her, segregating those inside from everything else, made the greatest impression. She remembered being surprised five years ago, at the end of the tour, by the relief that swept through her when the heavy door reopened, ending her brief detention.

Quarles estimated it would take at least an hour to process Riley's release once they arrived back at the jail, so she took her time driving there.

"You've disgraced this court for the last time, Suzanne, and I intend to make sure the Governor and the Judicial Qualifying Commission are aware of it." Haskell had cornered her in the judges' parking lot after the hearing. *"If the voters dummy up on us and reelect you, be warned that you will not be returning after the first of the year to business as usual!"*

"Meaning what exactly," she'd asked.

"You don't belong on the Family Docket. Our constituents and the county's families deserve much better than attention grabbers like you. This isn't some court television show, this is real life and you're everything but judicial."

"You do whatever you think you need to do, and I'll do likewise."

"Perhaps you'd do better conducting probation revocations at the jail. You'll have my final decision in writing after I confer with our executive committee."

"Changing my rotation will change nothing. I'm not going anywhere, anytime soon. You best get used to the idea that I am a parent. Now if you'll excuse me, I need to go pick up my son."

"Well, you run on now and pick up your boy," Haskell said, as if she was picking up her son from basketball practice after school, rather than from the South Central County Jail, where he'd been locked up on felony charges for the past three months, after being confined within the Georgia foster care system for the past eighteen years.

Within minutes and a change in the zip code, the commercial landscape had devolved into one where burglar bars, graffiti and predatory for-sale signs were rampant. Suzanne passed some church workers standing outside of their cars which were parked on a concrete slab in a weed-infested, vacant lot, handing out sandwiches to a group of men crowding around.

Up the street, a street vendor was set up under a large white canopy hustling everyday needs and pre-holiday bargains. She drove past slowly, looking in her rear view mirror at the counterfeit jerseys and jogging suits flapping on the display clothesline. *Who would buy their clothes on a street corner.* Thinking again, she turned around, and went back and bought a pair of oversized gray sweats just in case Riley didn't have anything warm to put on.

Rehab centers and bail bonding businesses soon appeared, lining the street at the bottom of the hill where the jail was located. An obese woman dressed in a floral printed duster and pink, high-top house shoes was walking ahead just before the driveway leading to the parking lot. Suzanne paused to let the woman cross in front of her. But the woman had other plans, and stopped alongside the car, knocking on Suzanne's passenger window.

The woman motioned to Suzanne to lower it. She complied. The woman leaned down on her door to make eye contact, her large bosom blocking most of the view and her meaty fingers leaving smudge marks on the car's finish.

"Chile, I'm so tired. Could I get you to give me a lift up the hill?"

Suzanne sighed. "Sure, ma'am," she replied.

Suzanne unlocked the door and took the filmy blue, plastic bag containing the sweats from the empty seat beside her, stuffing it behind her seat to make room for the woman. The lady dumped herself into the car, backside first, leaning over on Suzanne in order to swing around and close the door.

"I don't do seat belts. They hurt my breasts," the woman announced. Looking over at Suzanne's chest, the woman laughed, "Guess you don't have that problem, Chile, now do you?"

Suzanne grimaced, hearing the bottom of her car scrape the cement driveway as she let off the break to head up the hill.

The woman grunted. "My grandbaby used to work on fancy cars like this one. He was on his way out of the hood. I'll be glad when they let my boy go. Yours been in long?"

"No, not too long. Here we are," she said, pulling up to the curb a few feet back from the Sheriff's guard line, ready to unload her chatty passenger.

"Aren't you coming in?" the woman asked.

"Yes, in a minute. I'm going to park first and then try to collect my thoughts," Suzanne said.

The woman uttered another grunt, shifting her load to get out. "Chile, I do understand. These boys can wear you down."

SEVENTY-SEVEN

S he pulled into a parking space, easily visible from the entrance. Suzanne glanced at the clock on her dashboard. She would have to wait for at least another thirty minutes or so. Several women – mothers, girlfriends, aunties – came and went as she waited in the car. A boisterous group of women – cutting up as if they had just left a party – stood across the lot, waiting for the MARTA bus. Two other women and a crying child were sitting on a bench outside of the front door, his mother shaking a box of animal crackers to distract him. After awhile, the little boy settled down, pressing his face against the glass to peer through the lobby window – perhaps wondering why until that very moment the only men coming out through the revolving door wore uniforms.

The minute Riley came through the door and stepped off the curb, Suzanne was out of her car. As she suspected, he was wearing only the tee shirt and shorts he had on when arrested. She was happy to see him in his street clothes, albeit ill-suited for the blustery December day. She held back her hugs and pecks on the cheek she had stored up during all the years when she had no child to fuss over. John had warned her not to embarrass the teenager with any public display of affection. She offered him the blue bag instead.

"It's pretty cold today. I picked these up, thinking you might want something warmer on."

Riley took the bag and peeked inside as they stood beside her car. "'Preciate it," he grunted, pulling out the hooded top and putting it on over his shirt.

"That should feel better," she said, shivering as the cold cut through her coat. "Hey, Riley, why don't we go ahead and get inside the car."

She put his bag in the trunk. Inside, she smiled, watching him bend his long lanky frame into her little car. There was barely an inch clearance above his head and his bent knees were almost as high as the door handle. No one, not even John, had ever seemed as uncomfortable as Riley did in her car.

"Uh, nice ride," he mumbled, his deep voice barely audible.

"Thanks. This car has been fun, but looks like we'll need to get something larger. Maybe you can help me pick something else out."

"Are we anywhere near Fairburn?"

"Not really. How come?" Her heart stopped.

"Forget it," he muttered.

"We're going to get through this, okay?"

Abandoning John's counsel, she reached over and touched him lightly on his arm before starting the car. Riley slumped down in his seat and minutes later, he dozed off. Suzanne headed toward Fairburn. She decided a brief visit would be reassuring to the teen. He slept until she reached the YRC's driveway and the loose gravel noisily popped up against the car.

"Riley, wake up," she said softly.

He sat up in his seat. His eyes brightened as the youth residential center came into view – the only place he knew to call home. Riley peered over at her, his hand on the door handle, uncertain why she had brought him back.

"I felt bad an' all, you know, I left without tellin' Miz Ingram and the other kids goodbye. They're like family, you know what I'm sayin'?"

"They'll be thrilled to see you. Take your time, son. I'm in no hurry. Hey, why don't you take your sweats out of the trunk and slip them on while you're inside."

John and her parents both were waiting to hear how things went. As she waited in the car, Suzanne called them with brief accounts of the morning's events. She confirmed that Riley finally was where he belonged, with her. Inside, Riley endured some hugs and lecturing from Mrs. Ingram. The director asked him what he wanted to do and he admitted that he didn't know. She reminded him that he had been ready for a change from life at YRC and told him that maybe giving his mother's home a try would be just the change he was looking for. They both knew that Suzanne Vincent was the only viable option Riley Vincent had at the present. He gathered the few belongings he had left behind in August, said goodbye to some of the older boys who, like him, had lived at the center for longer than anyone wanted to admit and walked out with the older woman to Suzanne's car.

It was time to try something new and Riley squeezed back into the car, holding an envelope Mrs. Ingram had given him. The residential director laughed as she watched the teen scrunched up in the car.

"Be careful what you feed that boy or else you'll have to cut a hole in your roof," Mrs. Ingram said.

"You're right. I'm hoping Riley will help me pick out something a little more practical very soon. I'm sorry we didn't call first, Mrs. Ingram, but, well –

"Oh, no, don't you fret. Seeing this boy again has made my day. He's welcome anytime. You both are. Now, Riley, don't you forget to give your mama that envelope. It has all your important papers in there."

"Yes, ma'am," he replied, sounding more upbeat than Suzanne recalled ever hearing him. From the judge's assessment of Riley's demeanor, the drive several miles down to Fairburn, while out of the way, had been time well invested.

"Well, I better get back inside." Esther Ingram patted Suzanne's arm. "Call me if I can help in anyway. Good luck, my dear. Bye now, Riley. Be sure to mind your mama."

SEVENTY-EIGHT

S oothing smooth jazz filled the car. She offered Riley a chance
to choose a different radio station. He shook his head, showing
no interest. The eclectic peaks and spires of the downtown
Atlanta skyline emerged above the hilly terrain of the sprawling
metropolis. She slowed down as the late afternoon traffic began
to back up on the expressway. They passed the So So Def Jam
billboard welcoming travelers to the ATL – the hip, younger set's
nickname for Atlanta. Suzanne resisted her natural tendency to
fill their still space with idle talk and opted to let Riley simply
be. Not sure what Riley liked to eat, Suzanne decided on a self
serve eatery in her neighborhood which specialized in hot plates
piled plentifully with home cooking, baskets of cinnamon rolls
and mason jars filled with peach lemonade. Mentally, she kept a
running log of the preferences and dislikes she didn't know about
him that other mothers would take for granted regarding their
children: favorite foods, taste in music, clothing and shoe sizes,
how to get him to say more than two or three words at a time.

Moving through the food line, he chose fried chicken, macaroni
and cheese and mashed potatoes. His missing green vegetables
were all on her tray. They carried their food to a freshly wiped,
still moist vinyl covered table. A blond pigtailed waitress, her
pink arms vibrant with blue and red tattoos, brought their jars
of lemonade and the coveted basket of freshly baked sweet rolls.
After they gave the girl their trays, Suzanne closed her eyes to
bless the food. Another item for her list: religion.

She ate a little, talking mostly. He devoured everything and said very little. By the time they finished eating, she had told him about her family, growing up in Southern California, moving to Atlanta. She described her neighborhood, McGill Glen, the low hanging trees, the park and high school not far away. He surprised her when he broke his silence.

"What am I supposed to call you?"

His question deserved a well thought out answer. She wished she had one.

"Why don't we see over the next few days, what feels right, okay?"

"Yeah, okay. You stay by yourself?"

Suzanne nodded.

"I'm not married, if that's what you're getting at."

"Oh, you look like you'd be married. You know, like Bernie Mac's wife."

"I hope to be, one day," she said, wondering if Riley and John would get along.

"You want you some more?"

"Some more what, Riley?"

"Kids."

"You know, I haven't thought about that. Right now, all I'm concerned about is you. In fact, we need to get you a few clothes and pick up some groceries. Are you up for making a couple of stops before we head home?"

Riley responded with another shrug.

SEVENTY-NINE

Indeed, Riley was quite capable of making choices. His ability to be decisive surfaced in the Urban Orbit clothing store. She told him the types of things he should look for, how much he could spend, how much time he had to spend it and sent him off to tackle the shelves and racks filled with denim, shoes and other teen inspired items. As he made his selections, Suzanne roamed through the store on her own, looking at labels, turning tags, flipping through hangers, now having a reason to pay closer attention to the popular styles and curious coordinates she had seen kids wearing.

He proved to be her father's kind of shopper – quick, focused and under budget. Riley, carefully balancing his load, found her browsing in the women's section. She held up a pair of jeans with two ripped knees in front of her.

"I might get a pair of these for myself. What do you think?"

His horrified expression said it all. Flashing him a grin, she refolded the jeans and placed them back onto the neat pile of shelved denim.

"Don't worry, I'm just kidding. This is definitely not my store. Show me what you found."

He stood next to her, holding the sizeable pile of clothing, as she quickly perused what he had gathered. He had exactly one of every item they had discussed. She helped him carry the size 14 shoe box and clothes over to the check-out counter, sending him back to get a pair of khaki slacks, and a couple more shirts. The bagging clerk, who must have been about Riley's age, began preparing the items for the cashier to ring up. He commented to Suzanne, while she waited for Riley to return with the last items, "Your son's cleaning up. Sure wish you were my mother."

Suzanne smiled at the clerk. *I'd give the world to have Riley feel the same way.*

EIGHTY

Suzanne turned the key, pushed her front door open and flicked on the light in the entryway.

"Welcome home, son," she said, standing aside so he could enter. Riley slowly crossed the threshold. The warmth of the room wrapped around them. The kitchen was located just inside the entrance, on the right. She placed the grocery bags she was carrying on the table and gestured to him to do the same with his Urban Orbit bags. Anxious to show him around, she quickly put the milk, bacon and eggs in the refrigerator, leaving the remaining groceries to unpack later. They lingered in the small kitchen, while she instructed him on a sundry of details; things she figured a teenage boy would need to know like how to work the security alarm, where she hid the spare door key or which kitchen cabinet contained the glasses or the cereal. He followed her, silently, a few steps behind, out of the kitchen past the antique grandfather clock in the hallway as she led him from one unfamiliar room to the next showing him far too much.

Upstairs, she showed him her bedroom done in champagne and cantaloupe pastels, with the French doors opening to a private terrace with a rare view of the Atlanta skyline facing northwest and a master Jacuzzi bath. He watched and listened as she opened and closed the doors to the linen closet and the laundry room.

When they reached the second bedroom, Suzanne held back, letting Riley go in alone. From the doorway, she watched as he slowly moved about, sizing up his new abode and the furnishings – the nightstand and lamp, the chest of drawers, television, and the shuttered bay window. But out of everything in his new room, it was the bed that finally extracted a verbal reaction from the teen.

Suzanne heard his whistle but didn't react. In contrast to the narrow twin cot Mrs. Ingram had showed her, the queen size white oak sleigh bed was massive. It was neatly covered with the patchwork quilt made by Suzanne's Grandma Vincent and generously stacked with the three layers of pillows Suzanne had purchased in an effort to replicate the bedding she had seen on display in the bedding section of the local department store.

A room rarely used except for the closet where Suzanne hung her out-of-season wardrobe, she regretted now never having ventured beyond the bed with her decorating. But when she saw her son pause at the entrance to the private bathroom, his reflection in the mirror captured the room's true allure: its peacefulness.

"Riley, it's getting late. I'm going to leave you to settle in. Don't forget to go downstairs and get your bags. If you need anything, I'll be in my room. Good night."

"Nite," he replied.

A lopsided exchange, perhaps, but Suzanne claimed it as a beginning.

EIGHTY-ONE

The next morning, Suzanne woke up early, ready to begin their first full day together. The house was still, but she felt his presence just the same. Wrapped up in an old chenille throw, she tiptoed, barefooted, down the hall to check on him. She paused outside of Riley's room. His door was closed. There was no sign of his stirring, no rush to be awake, just faint snoring coming from inside. Oliver told her to take the morning, but she would have to be available for an important forum that afternoon. Her campaign had lost its rhythm and they only had a few days to try to salvage her bid.

Back in her room, the last remnants of nightfall lingered outside her window. She hadn't yet heard the pre-dawn thump of her copy of the *Atlanta Journal Constitution* cast against the pavement, but she cracked her shutters anyway, peeping out in hopes of finding the sleeved newspaper resting in its normal spot. The walkway was empty. She forced herself to get back in bed, pulling up the covers around her, as far as they would stay. At least until the paper arrived, she would concentrate on warming up her feet and compiling a to-do list. She kept her list short. Two things, though, she wanted to address first thing. She needed to rent a van for campaign canvassing. A larger vehicle would also accommodate Riley's long legs. Then there was enrolling him in school. Ralph McGill High School, one of the city's top schools, was just a few blocks away from where she lived. For more than a half century, civic leaders, business owners, ordinary folk, their children and grandchildren, had filed through the large red metal doors of the high school to obtain their secondary education. Named for one of Atlanta's own – a newspaper publisher during the pre-Civil Rights Era known for his outspoken criticism of bigotry and segregation in the South – the white brick building still provided its students with a quality education. The kind that drove up the asking prices for the remaining historic homes throughout her neighborhood and caused mamas and daddies, unable to afford one, to rouse their sleepy teenagers before sun-up to catch the bus to Suzanne's part of town.

When she purchased her condo, being single with no children, she appreciated learning about Ralph McGill High School's academic rating, but was more interested in the neighborhood's other amenities. Suzanne had learned a great deal about the school from her neighbor whose fourteen year old daughter attended the magnet school. The school had an international baccalaureate emphasis, a well organized PTA and a partnership with the Atlanta Police Department's Weed and Seed program to make sure education was not just on the teacher's minds, but a priority for all of the school's students as well.

Now, the high school – its curriculum tracks, extracurricular activities, student/teacher ratio – was of keen interest to her. Even though her mother had schooled her on standard procedure for mid-semester secondary school transfers, she made a note to go online to determine the intricacies of the Atlanta Public School's enrollment process. The envelope from Mrs. Ingram appeared to include everything needed for registration – his birth certificate, immunization records, test scores, an end of the year report for his last completed year, the eleventh grade. His grades were above average. Encouraged by them, she hoped, with a concerted push, he might still be able to graduate the following spring.

The one thing Mrs. Ingram's envelope didn't contain was documentation excusing Riley's absence from school for the past three months. Suzanne sat up in bed, rocking gently, hugging her legs. She thought hard, trying to conjure up a credible reason for his nonattendance. Nothing, other than the truth, came to mind. She sighed, reflecting on how different her son's senior year would be from what it might have been if she had found out about him sooner, or if Mallory had gone through with his adoption.

Suzanne slid out of bed, determined to try to make amends for some of his loss. It was time to end the regrets, time to get dressed, time to do the mother thing and make her son some breakfast.

EIGHTY-TWO

Pulling into the school parking lot, Suzanne told Riley she thought it would be best for him to let her answer the questions. She wanted the process to go as smoothly as possible. They climbed the steps leading into the old building, following the signs to the office of the School Registrar. Bertha Mae Bumpers didn't look pleased to see Suzanne and Riley appear, unannounced, at her gray metal desk. Based on the Vincents' address, the school was legally required to accept him. Like it or not, the registrar would have to make time to assign him a locker, issue some books, and make up a class schedule. Suzanne knew that, but she also sensed their exchange with the unpleasant, stern-faced woman would be pivotal in her son's placement in the school. So she stood there, patiently enduring the rudeness of the dumpy woman with the pink lipstick and matching chipped fingernails. Bertha Mae Bumpers was an excellent candidate for one of Oprah's makeover shows.

Unlike most parents, Suzanne chose not to go make a big deal in advance of her desire to register her son. She wanted to get through the process with as little fanfare as she could. The registrar made it clear their showing up without notice was bad form, especially just a few days before winter break.

"You aren't aware that making an appointment to register is customary this late in the year?" Ms. Bumpers asked.

Suzanne apologized, indicating that when she called, nobody mentioned the need for an appointment. The woman sighed, shaking her head. She took the documents from Suzanne, wetting the bottom of each document with her moist finger as she flipped through the pages. Ms. Bumpers set aside the paperwork, and frowned at Riley, who was slouched down in a chair next to the office water cooler.

"Looks like he's been in a fight recently. You know, ma'am, we're really too busy here to deal with discipline problems, perhaps the Open Campus would be more appropriate for your son," she said, leaning back in her chair, her arms crossed.

"My son is not a discipline problem. He just had a little mishap playing ball with his friends," Suzanne replied, determined not to let the woman's accusatory tone or looks upset her.

"Hm-hmmm."

Ms. Bumpers clearly didn't believe Riley got his bruises in a friendly competition, which was her problem, not Suzanne's. She just wanted the registrar to do her job and waited for her to give her one of the blank registration forms on her desk.

Hoping to avoid answering any awkward questions out loud, Suzanne offered to complete the form herself, "I'll be happy to fill that out, if you'd like."

"No need, I've been doing this for years. Parents always mess them up and I have to retype them, that's why I like to ask you the questions, then type out your answers." Ms. Bumpers replied, loading the form into her typewriter.

"You're his mother, I assume," she asked.

"Yes, that's correct." Suzanne said, glossing over the fact that while she was Riley's biological mother, technically, she no longer was his legal parent due to her surrender of parental rights after his birth. *Another detail I need to attend to as soon as possible.*

"Should the other parent be listed?" Riley perked up, hearing the question.

"No, that won't necessary under the circumstances." Suzanne said no more, planning to tell Riley the truth later.

"I see. What is your reason for this late registration?"

Suzanne had prepared for this question, "A mid-semester move." She turned her head toward Riley, and winked at him. The wink was not returned.

She spent the next twenty minutes, negotiating with Ms. Bumpers over which classes Riley should be enrolled in. Ms.

Bumpers expressed her skepticism that with only one week of classes left before the winter break and three weeks remaining before end of semester exams at the end of January, Riley would be able to pass the exams. She suggested Riley be placed back in the eleventh grade. Suzanne thought that was outrageous and argued repeating the year would be a waste of time, insisting that he should be given the chance to keep his place in the class of 2007. They compromised with the decision to place Riley in a number of combination classes consisting of 11th and 12th graders and agreed that his exam scores would determine whether he finished the school year as a junior or senior.

Suzanne realized afterwards she should have consulted with Riley before committing him to such an ambitious plan. But it had all happened so quickly. Then Ms. Bumpers caught her completely off guard.

"I believe I have all I need from you, Ms. Vincent. We're about to start fourth period. If you'll excuse us I need to show Riley to his class," she said.

"Yes, of course," was all she could say. She rummaged in her purse to give Riley some lunch money. All she had in her purse were two singles and a $10.00 bill. Suzanne gave her son the ten dollar bill. "Riley, I'll pick you up in front after school."

"I'll walk," he mumbled, slinging his black book bag over his shoulder.

"Uh, are you sure you know the way?"

Everything is happening too fast.

"Yeah," he said.

"What time does school let out?" she asked Ms. Bumpers.

"Three o'clock," the registrar replied.

"Then I guess I'll see you at home, Riley. Son, please come straight home."

He nodded, just as the bell rang, and Ms. Bumpers whisked him out of the office, leaving Suzanne behind.

EIGHTY-THREE

Driving home, Suzanne tried her best not to worry about Riley. Toward the end, everything became so rushed. From the looks of the kids pushing and shoving in the hallway as she was leaving, the student body at McGill High appeared to include a little of everything. Riley would fit in. It was not a matter of trust. *He's seventeen years old, fully capable of fending for himself, not some forlorn kindergartner facing his first day of school.* But nonetheless, their sudden separation left Suzanne unsettled. Once again, someone had snatched him out of sight without getting her permission.

She drove past a group of women with young children playing on the playscape in McGill Glen Park up the street from her complex. *So what do stay-at-home mothers do while their teenage children are at school?* There were no undone chores to speak of. Her cleaning lady had just come for the monthly cleaning. Riley had washed the dishes, leaving little for her to do around the house to pass the time. The judge detested the soaps and daytime talk shows, and she was too hyper to try to work on the files she had packed in her briefcase for her week away from the courthouse.

Suzanne didn't do much other than piddle around the house until it was time to look out for Riley. She waited for him in the den since he didn't have a key. He arrived about 3:45, his book bag full of books.

"Hey, how did it go?" she asked, closing the front door behind him. They were standing in the entryway, right at the entrance to the kitchen.

"Alright," he said, looking around as if to decide where to set his books down.

"Just set them in the den for now. Would you like me to fix you a snack?"

"I guess," he replied.

She went into the refrigerator to pull out a container of tuna salad, and begin to make a sandwich. He pulled out a chair and sat down at the table. Suzanne reached over and turned on the little portable television on the kitchen counter. She decided to give him a chance to strike up a conversation. By the time she placed the sandwich in front of him, and set a bag of chips and a soft drink on the table, he still hadn't said anything.

She sat down across from him. "I know you have a lot of catching up to do, but before you get started, I have to make a brief campaign appearance this afternoon. I'd love some company, want to go with me? What do you say?"

"No, thanks," was all he said.

"Oh, are you sure? Well, maybe it would be boring to you." She tried not to show her disappointment over his disinterest.

"Yeah, I need to get goin' on my homework." He reached above the refrigerator to put the chips away, tossed his empty can in the recycling bin in the utility closet she had shown him the night before, and took his plate over to the sink to rinse it off.

"Okay, then. Spread out wherever you like, here at the table, or in the den. I shouldn't be too long."

She went into the den to get her briefcase and coat. Suzanne could hear the sound of his television coming through the ceiling overhead. She was less surprised that he had gone up to his room without saying goodbye, than by his book bag left behind. *Oh well.* She stepped out into the frigid afternoon to find a few more votes.

EIGHTY-FOUR

"Judge Vincent, thank you so much for participating. It's such an honor to finally meet you in person."

Suzanne shook the hand of the eager young lawyer in charge of the political action committee of the host organization, the Georgia Association of Black Women Attorneys.

"Oh, thank you. It's nice to be appearing before such a friendly audience."

Oliver wasn't convinced that their precious time would be best spent at the GABWA forum. *You already have their votes. We need to work on the ones on the other side of town.* Her district was almost seventy miles long and extended north and south of the city of Atlanta and the Chattahoochee River.

"We'll be starting shortly. Can I get you anything?"

"I'm fine, thanks." Suzanne smiled at the pretty woman, dressed fashionably in the season's hot colors of gray and eggplant. "Shall I just take a seat near the front of the sanctuary?"

"Yes, I'll be in as soon as your, uh, opponent arrives. His office called and said he's running slightly behind."

"Will the judicial candidates be speaking first?"

"No, we're going to hear from the County Commission races and then your race, ma'am."

Am I already a ma'am? You're a ma'am, a mother, a judge barely hanging onto her robe. Suzanne entered the newly renovated sanctuary of the First Congregational Church, taking in the scent of the mahogany pews and the tall, narrow stained glass windows on both sides of the church, depicting scenes from the church's beginning as a worshipping place for freed slaves and Northern white missionaries.

She took a seat on the front row and looked around. Several people had gathered. Oliver would be pleased with the size and diversity of the crowd. Suzanne overlooked the attractive woman dressed expensively in a black knit pantsuit with dark gray eyes and a trace of silver highlighting her stylish short bob, seated with a teenage boy off to the right. Shortly after seven o'clock, several candidates Suzanne recognized from other campaign functions stepped up and took their seats at the tables.

Another GABWA member approached the podium, welcomed the audience and guest moderator, a weekend news broadcaster, and got the forum underway. Suzanne appreciated not having to go first. By the time they were ready for her race, she was completely relaxed and ready to answer questions. Done with playing nice girl, she decided to completely ignore Rotherman and his campaign rhetoric that evening, as well as for the rest of the campaign. He didn't know that she knew the one thing he didn't want her to know.

"As with the previous race, after I briefly introduce you, we would like the candidates running for judge to briefly state their platforms. Seated before you is Judge Suzanne Vincent, the incumbent for Post 7 on the Atlanta District Court. She's no stranger to GABWA. We've held monthly meetings in her courtroom and she has spearheaded our very successful judicial clerkship job fair. Judge, won't you tell us briefly why voters should re-elect you?"

"Thank you, Cicely. First, allow me to acknowledge the tremendous work this bar association is doing in our community. I'm proud to be a member and to have GABWA members practicing in my court." In a few short months, Suzanne had become a polished politician, capable of turning questions on their head and to her advantage. "Now to answer your very important question, I'm running for re-election because my professional experience, judicial temperament and extensive community service make me the best person for the job. Next Tuesday, I ask you to vote for me and ask your friends and relatives to do the same."

"Thank you, Judge Vincent."

"There's one more reason why I'm the person who should continue to serve in this post."

Chance Rotherman tried to interrupt, "Isn't her time up?" His flushed face almost matched the red buttons sported by his lone two supporters who were seated in the front row, dead center.

The young lawyer ignored Rotherman. "Of course, Judge, please continue." She glared at Chance. "We will make sure Mr. Rotherman gets equal time when it is his turn."

"I chose to serve on the Family Docket of the Atlanta District Court because of my unique life experiences." Suzanne saw the two Rotherman supporters exchange a glance. She continued, "I was raised by two parents who loved me and each other unconditionally. As some of you may have heard by now, I recently have been reunited with the son I had when still in college and gave up for adoption. Things did not work out for him as planned and now it is my responsibility to be the parent I now am able to be and he deserves, regardless of what may be the consequences. I hope that groups like GABWA will help me diffuse the perception my opponent wishes to create, that I do not take my job seriously, that I do not ascribe to family values like he does. I visited his website before coming here this afternoon to see if he had updated it to include his third child."

"What the hell—

Rotherman was on his feet headed for the podium.

"I'm done, Mr. Rotherman. As a matter of professional courtesy, allow me to introduce my opponent. Ladies and Gentlemen, also running for this seat is Chance Rotherman. Mr. Rotherman is a Senior Assistant District Attorney for the Atlanta District Court. Everyone is anxious to know about your new baby and how his mother, Ms. Secret, was forced to file suit against you last week to get you to legitimize him and start paying child support. You did realize that judges must pay child support like everyone else, right?"

Rotherman was speechless. He'd underestimated the power and bond of the GABWA sisterhood. He tried to recover by telling a joke, but no one laughed, not even Mallory Caine, who Suzanne had noticed when speaking. Oliver Mason stood up in the rear and pulled out a Cuban cigar. He headed outside to wait for Suzanne to congratulate her on her performance.

As she was leaving, Mallory reached out into the aisle and touched Suzanne's hand. "Judge Vincent, I'd like you to meet my son, Rilman Adams. We attend church here and since he's thinking about becoming a lawyer one day, I brought him out for a taste of politics."

"Nice to meet you, young man. Your mother and I knew each other, long ago, when we weren't much older than you are now, I suppose."

"You've been through a lot during this campaign, and I just wanted you to know that you have at least one vote."

"Your confidence means a lot, Mallory. It's great to see you. Good night."

EIGHTY-FIVE

Attending the welcoming forum and running into Mallory Caine lifted Suzanne's spirits considerably. She'd hated not being able to spend the evening at home alone with Riley, but he didn't want to come with her and missing another campaign event was out of the question. Riley didn't answer when she called to let him know that she was on the way home. The entire house was pitch-black when she got there.

"Riley," Suzanne called, opening the front door. She turned the light on in the den hoping to find a note on the desk, but none was there. Nor did he leave a note in the kitchen. Upstairs in his room, she opened up the closet, checked in the bathroom, and pulled out his chest drawers. Nothing appeared out of the ordinary, everything was still there. Everything, except Riley.

In her room, she took off her jacket, and sat down on her bed, trying to decide what to do, how long to wait before she had true cause to worry. Less than two hours ago, she left him up in his room, watching TV. Now all she could think of was him wandering around somewhere out there, on the dark unfamiliar streets running away from her. A single mother's panic set in.

Suzanne picked up the phone to dial John, willing to consider his perspective. John, she knew, would see things differently, free from her emotion and guilt.

"And hello to you, too, beautiful," he answered. "Did you two have a good day? What did you decide about the school thing?"

The night before, when he called to check up on her, they talked about her plans for the next few days. *Go easy, Suzanne. Get past the election. A few more missed school days won't be the end of the boy's world.* When they hung up, she still was equivocating about whether to enroll Riley in the morning or wait until after the election.

"John, I got him enrolled and he attended classes today. But we need to talk about that later. There's a problem. I just got home from the forum and he's gone. No note, nothing. Do you think I should call the police?"

"Not so fast, baby. Tell me what's going on. Last night, didn't you say you were going to take him with you? I warned you that you were trying to do too much all at once."

Suzanne took a deep breath, reminding herself that she called him, not the other way around. They were back to talking regularly since her visit home for Father's Day. Lately, most of the conversations centered around Riley. There was no doubt in her mind that John loved her and was doing his best to be supportive. They had never shared their views about childrearing before all this came up with Riley. She valued his input, but sometimes his strong opinions were hard to take.

"Riley didn't want to attend the forum. I didn't have any choice except to leave him at the house. Missing another campaign event was out of the question, John."

"Was he upset when you left?" he asked.

"That's a big part of the problem. He says so little when we're together. I don't know what he's feeling or thinking."

"Does he have a key?"

"Not unless he took the spare key from the hook in the utility closet downstairs. Hold on, I'm going to go see." Suzanne placed the phone on the bed, to run downstairs to check the hook. The key was still there. She picked up the phone in the kitchen, out of breath, "He didn't take the key," she said.

"Baby, I know this is tough, but you've got to be patient with him. All of this change is a helluva lot for him to deal with. Wherever he is, he's processing things in his own way."

"He can do all the processing he wants, and take as much time as he needs to do it, upstairs in his room. I just want him home where it's safe."

"This isn't about what you want anymore, Suzanne. You wanted your son back, you've got him. But you've got to face the fact that he's survived life for what – this side of eighteen years? It's going to take more than twenty-four hours on your turf for him to feel safe or at home."

"So what do you think I should do, just sit here and wait to see if he comes back?"

"I can tell from your voice that you think I'm being heartless–

She forced a laugh, "Well not quite, but..."

"Baby, all I'm saying is, exhale. He hasn't been gone that long. There's no reason to conclude his ducking out is anything other than restlessness. Give him a couple more hours. It won't take him much longer to realize that he doesn't have anywhere else to go. He'll be back."

EIGHTY-SIX

When Suzanne called to report to John that Riley had missed his 7 p.m. curfew, she was on the verge of tears. John even sounded concerned. They decided to give the teen a final thirty minutes to show up before calling the police. It was not simply a matter of seeking aid from the police. As a recently sentenced first offender released on probation, Riley's AWOL placed his future liberty at stake. He could be re-sentenced to thirty plus years for any infraction.

After she hung up from John, Suzanne walked over to her Zen garden on the bookshelf in the den. She picked up the small rake and shifted through the sand, smoothing the granules around the center stone which years before she had placed in the center of the shallow box to represent Riley. The other four stones she had added since the first: one for her parents, another for her career, the third added after she and John had been dating for about a year and then the fourth stone which encompassed everything else in her life. As she groomed the garden, Suzanne tried to calm down. *Please bring him home soon, God,* she whispered. Bethany Lovejoy came to Suzanne's mind for a split second. *If Bethany is committed to fighting for her little boy and doing for him with so little, I promise I will do what you'd want me to for Riley, if given the chance.*

She jumped when her phone rang. Her hopes, though, quickly plummeted upon discerning that the low voice she longed to hear was not Riley on the other end calling her to come get him. Instead, Suzanne recognized the voice to be that of the friendly, elderly guard posted on night duty at the front gated entrance to her complex.

"Judge Suzanne," he began. When she was first appointed to the bench, the guard and the judge had agreed that he would call her "Judge Suzanne." She wanted him to continue to call her Suzanne, as he had since she first moved in. But, he was of the old school, where good manners required that one's title be acknowledged, especially if the person with the title lived where you worked. "I got a young man with me here at the front gate —

Suzanne interrupted the man, "Freddie, do you have Riley there with you?"

"Hold on, Judge, you know I can't always hear so good and these young people today, mumble so. Let me check...Yes, ma'am, you're right, he says his name is Riley. Anyhow, like I was saying, he claims he is staying with you and forgot his key. Are you expecting him?"

"Yes, yes." *What an understatement,* Suzanne murmured under her breath. "Please let him through. And Freddie, thank you!" Suzanne said.

She quickly dialed John, who was waiting in his office for an update, and told him the good news. They spoke briefly and then hung up. Suzanne didn't give Riley a chance to knock. The moment he appeared on the stoop, she swung open the door. He brushed past her, his new jacket reeking of cigarette smoke.

"Where have you been?" Suzanne asked, looking up at him.

Riley shrugged. "Out," he said. He picked up his book bag and started up the stairs.

"Hold on, son. That's not good enough. Out where, Riley?"

He turned around. "I was jus' checkin' out the neighborhood. Caught up with some niggas over at the park, played some ball, went to see if I could catch you a few votes, no big deal, okay?"

Suzanne cringed at his use of the "N" word. But his street language was the least of her concerns at that moment.

"No, it's not okay. I don't expect you to stay cooped up in the house 24/7, but I would appreciate your leaving me a note. You didn't even take the key. I was worried sick about you," Suzanne said. "Especially after you told me you needed to stay home to do your homework."

"I did it already," Riley said.

"All of it?" Suzanne asked.

"I'm fixin' to finish it –

"Riley meet me in the den. Now! And take off your jacket and hang it up in the utility room, so that smelly smoke can air out." Suzanne looked at him sharply, then turned leaving Riley standing in the hallway.

EIGHTY-SEVEN

"Have a seat, son," Suzanne moved aside the fringed throw pillow resting next to where she was sitting on the couch and patted the seat cushion with her left hand. Riley sat down, his fingers tapping on his long legs spread eagle.

"If this is going to work, you and I must learn how to communicate. This virtual monologue I've been carrying on since I picked you up at the jail yesterday is getting a little old, Riley. If you feel like a lot is being thrown at you, all at one time, well, believe it or not, I feel the same way. Four weeks ago, I never would have thought I would be sitting in this den with my son. Four weeks ago, I assumed, as I have for the past eighteen years, that you were living a happy life with the Caines. Oh, I often wondered what you were doing, especially around this time of year, with your birthday and all. But the possibility that I, not Mallory Caine, would get to enjoy, along with you, the excitement of your senior year of high school, and help you select a college to attend or take pictures of you on the night of your senior prom. I just never...."

As her voice broke, Riley stopped tapping his fingers and glanced at his mother. She breathed a hard sigh, willing herself to remain composed enough to get through with what she wanted to say.

"You need to give me some clue as to what's going on inside of that head of yours," Suzanne said, returning to a more regular breathing and an even tone of voice. "I guess what I'm trying to say, perhaps not so well, is that I would like us to back up just a tad so you can tell me about your life before last Thursday. I know things have been tough for you growing up, and I understand if you're angry with me, but I'm hoping that somehow you'll find it in your heart to let me try to be the mother you never had. After you get to know me and trust me, I hope you'll come to regard me as your mother and meet me halfway on the road toward forging a mother/son relationship."

"Riley, this next point is key. I know there are many parents who are separated from their children for an extended period of time, maybe, had their kids too early and through a lack of responsibility or maturity they shirk their duties and rely on someone else – a grandparent or aunt or even the state – to raise their kids. Then, when all of the work is done and the kids are nearly grown or else, or when it is more convenient for the absent parent, they resurface in their kids' lives and want their kids to get over the missed birthdays, graduations and childhood illnesses with a snap of their fingers and instead smother them with hugs and kisses and gratitude because they showed up at all. That's not what has happened to you and me. Yes, I'm knocking at your door just when you're ready to step out into the world, asking you to hold up and come back inside with me. But it's only so we can regroup and plan a course of action that's in your best interest. I would love for you to make my home yours until you're ready to set out on your own. Mrs. Ingram told me what you and she were discussing right before you left YRC. While I can't, and certainly don't blame you for wanting to be on your own – what young man doesn't – I'm hoping you'll feel comfortable living here with me and decide to do so, especially as you contemplate finishing high school and maybe going to college."

"Son, I want nothing but the best for you. Riley, if only I had known about Mallory Caine's decision twelve years ago, when I first moved to Atlanta, I would have stepped in then and brought you home."

She thought of the pride in Mallory's voice when she spoke of helping her son fill out his college applications. *Riley, hang with me. We can get to that point too.* Like many teenagers, Riley had an uncanny way of appearing not to be listening, but hearing every word. Suzanne paused to catch her breath and clear her head, which was pounding.

Riley broke in, "Where's my old man?"

My God, how should I tell him about Keith. There was so, so much the boy didn't know and had a right to be told. His knowledge of his family tree was barren. She possessed the leaves of pertinent facts and personal information. As she formulated how to respond, Suzanne could hear John as clearly as if he were sitting across from them in the recliner. *Be direct. Keep it short and simple, or you'll lose him in the rhetoric.* She had bristled at John's use of the word, rhetoric. After all she always chose her words carefully – an art crafted early in her career as a medical malpractice defense attorney. Each and every word propounded by her during depositions, posed while cross examining witnesses challenging the integrity and professional competence of the physicians who made up her client roster, closing arguments made before juries, and now her judicial opinions, was measured and intentionally selected to convey her point.

But now, up close and in the middle of this slice of life, sitting next to her precious son, Suzanne knew John was right and Riley deserved a simple, direct, concise answer to his question about his father.

"Riley, your father's name was Keith Grayson. He played football for UCLA, where I also attended. We took an African-American Studies class together during the fall semester, 1987. I was a freshman and he was a junior. We really didn't meet, though, until the following semester, during a spring break trip to Cancun, Mexico."

Suzanne spared Riley the details of his parents' moonlit dinner on the beach which led up to the midnight tryst which resulted in his not so immaculate conception. Nor did the boy deserve at that moment to be further burdened with the details of what happened between Keith and her after spring break. There was nothing to gain from forcing the young man to weigh in on the implications of Keith's cavalier disregard for his mother and his own stake in her pregnancy. It was enough that for almost eighteen years, Suzanne herself had carried the pain of her aborted May 1988 visit to the seedy clinic with the torn, blue curtain. Riley had endured his own life long hurt and she knew in that instant that she would spend the next eighteen years and beyond, if necessary, trying to ease her son's pain.

"You were born during my sophomore year of college. Riley, coincidentally, when I flew out to California a few months ago for a weekend with my parents, your grandparents, Velda and Beckham Vincent, I ran into my college roommate, Tammy Dillard. I hadn't seen or spoken to her since 1988. She told me that her husband and your father remained very close friends after college until last year, Riley, when your father was....killed...."

Her announcement sent Riley over the edge. He cowered over from the waist and started rocking, and then, uttered a low, guttural moan – like that of a sick animal – it rose up from the space between Riley's bowed head and the floor. Tears rushed down Suzanne's own face as she reached across the back of her son's trembling frame and pulled him closer. For the present, she had told him all he could bear. She might not know why he was crying or for whom. He showed no emotion when she disclosed herself to him, so she was startled by his reaction that evening. Under different circumstances she might even have resented tears she would have preferred be shed for her rather than for a man who abandoned her. Intuitively, she knew the best thing she could give him was a silent space within which to weep. What was important was that her son still was able to feel and release his emotions despite all that he had grown up without. And so, the two of them sat in the den side by side in the dark until neither had any tears left.

EIGHTY-EIGHT

After about thirty minutes, Suzanne reached over to turn on the Tiffany lamp next to the couch where they were sitting. In the light, she turned to look at her son. He was staring straight ahead. She resisted the ridiculous yet intuitive urge to offer him something to eat.

"Just so you know, I didn't do anything to that lady," Riley said, turning to look at her.

"I believe you," Suzanne said softly.

The teen finally began to talk. What Riley told Suzanne convinced her that their reunion was nothing short of a miracle. He told her about his friendship of sorts with Isaiah. The other boy always had lots of unexplained cash on him and most often was headed toward trouble. One night Isaiah invited him to chill over at his aunt's house where he said his aunt would cook for them and let them play video games all night. After Riley convinced Mrs. Ingram to allow him to stay over at Isaiah's aunt's house and made arrangements to meet his friend at Greenbriar Mall, Isaiah admitted he had lied and there was no such aunt. He had run away from home and wanted someone to hang out with him while he worked up the courage to return home. Riley stunned his mother as he described how the two boys had slept that night among a group of homeless people in a make shift encampment erected under the graffitied overpasses of one of the area's oldest freeways, 166, still called Lakewood Freeway by those who grew up in Atlanta instead of its new name, the Arthur Langford Freeway.

"The thought of you sleeping on the cement foundation under the expressway....You were so exposed to everything out there," Suzanne said.

"Jail was worse," Riley said. "Nobody can be trusted and there's no privacy."

Riley shared how on the day he and Isaiah were arrested they had met up mid-afternoon at the Palmetto Community Recreation Center where Riley watched Isaiah blow more dollar bills shooting dice with a group of boys on the floor of the men's locker room than Riley had spent in his entire lifetime, much less gamble away. Broke and humiliated, Isaiah was forced to pull out of the game. He mentioned that his grandmother lived not far away and was a soft touch for giving him spending money. Riley agreed to walk over to her house with his friend so he could get some more cash. When she didn't answer the door Isaiah explained his grandmother must not be home and he was going to enter through a back window. He asked Riley to stand guard out front.

"I'm so sorry. I'm so sorry about everything you've had to deal with, all that you've missed," Suzanne said.

"Don't sweat it. After a while, you learn to stop wishin' for stuff," he said, "and just accept what is."

"I'm going to try to make up for that. Come next Tuesday and this campaign will finally be over, and I promise you, I will give you my undivided attention. We'll have a great Thanksgiving, your birthday, Christmas, all of it."

"Uh – I'm not into Christmas."

"Why do you say that, Riley?"

"You don't want to know."

"Yes, I do."

"I got lucky when I turned seven. I got a placement right before Halloween. Ms. Yancey told me if I was extra good, she might be able to convince the family to keep me. Maybe even adopt me, at least that was what I was hopin'. I remember being so excited 'cuz I'd never went trick-o-treatin' before, but I didn't get to go 'cuz the lady said it was the Devil's holiday. I still pray every night for the kids still at YRC. There's nothing worse than wantin' a family. After a while I could tell my foster mother didn't like me all that much. She had two little kids of her own and I think I got on her nerves or somethin'. She made me stay in my room a lot, 'less she needed me to do for her. On Christmas Eve, she asked me to help her put their Christmas tree together. I had to stand on a chair to reach the higher branches. I lost my balance and fell into the tree. The whole thing fell over, and the top of the tree fell down on an open box of glass balls. She got so mad at me. She was screaming about how stupid I was and that I had broken her best balls. I had to stay in my room until late the next day when Ms. Yancey came to take me back to YRC. I missed opening up the gifts, Christmas dinner, everything. Ever since then, Christmas and the tree thang sort of creep me out, you know what I'm sayin'?"

Riley's revelations had caused his mother to lose what little appetite she had. Suzanne had eaten very little all day. She was too nervous and excited to focus on eating. She looked at him. *Will this work? Will Riley be able to fit into this way of life? How will I ever be able to make amends for abandoning him?*

"Listening to you, I know I won't be able to erase the bad times, the sad memories you may have of things growing up. That's not what a good parent should try to do. We all are who we are because of our experiences. Our job is to take what we've been handed and become better because of it. We can't do anything about our time apart except try to make the most of what lies ahead of us. Riley, do you understand what I'm trying to say to you?"

All she got in response was another "Whatever, lady" shrug. *Time to vary the landscape.*

"I'm hungry," Suzanne lied, knowing Riley had to be hungry even though he probably wouldn't admit it. "Let's go into the kitchen and see what we can throw together."

EIGHTY-NINE

Suzanne Vincent's Election Day arrived right on time with frost in the air, a house full of hungry men and a newspaper bearing more bad news. The frigid weather was the least of her concerns. John had surprised her the day before by pulling up to her door with her parents in a taxi straight from the airport. *"John is such a dear, he called us Saturday night and said he'd purchased three tickets and could we please come," Velda Vincent told her daughter when they had a private moment together.* They'd agreed her mother would stay at home until Riley got home from school, while John and her father would take turns driving around with Suzanne in her campaign van.

Living alone, Suzanne rarely cooked full meals, and never breakfast. Weekdays, she was rushing to work or a meeting. Weekends, well, she didn't see the point of messing up the kitchen when she could take her paper and walk up to the neighborhood coffeehouse and leisurely enjoy a caramel macchiato and a carrot zucchini bran muffin.

Everyone was still asleep giving Suzanne time to think while she cooked breakfast. She prepared more than enough – homemade biscuits, turkey bacon, scrambled eggs, cheese grits – trying to eliminate problems by starting with her family's appetite. She looked up as her mother come down the stairs.

"Hey, Mom. Did you sleep well?"

"I did. Your father and I felt bad, booting Riley out of his bed, so soon."

"Mom, don't fret. I'm so happy you're here. We're all having to make adjustments."

"Don't try to do too much, Suzanne. Why, Honey, what's wrong?"

Suzanne couldn't hold it together any longer. "Come here, you, let it out – all of it." Her mother held her close as she released. "Things are going to work out; you just have to believe that."

"I think you were right," Suzanne wailed. "I'm going to lose everything, the judgeship, Riley, John, all of it – what did I do to deserve this!"

"Not John, Sweetheart. He's a keeper, no matter now difficult you might make it for him. And Riley seems like a nice kid. Much more … normal than I'd expected."

"I just need to get past tonight. Once the election is over, I'm going to take the rest of the year off."

"At least until after Thanksgiving. That's a great idea. Do you want me to stay?"

"No, Mom. It's wonderful having you and Dad here, but I need one on one time with Riley. We need to get to know each other and decide what's next." Suzanne got up and wiped her nose.

"Judge Suzy, you have an election to go win. Why don't you go get dressed and I'll finish up here."

"Thanks, Mom."

"You don't need to thank me. I wanted to be here with you, even before we knew about Riley, but you didn't invite us. That's why I was delighted when John took matters into his own hands."

"Mom, you never need an invitation. I didn't want to impose, that's all. I think I will sneak upstairs and get dressed. Love you." Suzanne gave her mother another squeeze, before looking over at the stove.

"Don't worry, I won't ruin your breakfast. I know there are two handsome men upstairs you're trying to impress. Is the key to the front door still in the utility closet?"

"Yep, it is."

"They should be down soon. What's wrong, Mom?"

Velda was sitting looking out of the breakfast alcove. The morning's paper was folded on the table next to her.

"Dear, I simply don't know how you handle being an elected official."

"I didn't get it, did I? Here, let me see what it says."

Her mother handed her the paper. Suzanne was devastated. Her interview with the Editorial Board of the *Atlanta Journal Constitution* had gone well, she thought. But since then she'd found her son, declared a mistrial in his case and gone public about their relationship at his sentencing hearing. She'd misjudged the public's willingness to empathize with her situation. Everywhere Rotherman went, he called for her resignation. A full page ad in the *Atlanta Journal Constitution* appeared the day before listing "Mothers Supporting Rotherman." Desiree Wainwright's and Gladys Fury's names were at the top of the list.

"Despite her relative youth and lack of family and criminal law experience, Judge Suzanne Vincent's judicial career held such promise when Governor Miriam Moss appointed her almost five years ago. No doubt, the governor is as disappointed as the rest of us. However, the very reason for the November 7th election is to give the voters the right to choose who will sit in judgment on this community. We say that person no longer should be the incumbent. Although he has no judicial experience, his interview with us established that he has plenty of common sense and his exercise of prosecutorial discretion should serve him well on the bench. We recommend that you vote for Chance Rotherman."

Velda waited for her daughter to finish reading the journalistic assassination.

"If Atlanta is anything like Los Angeles, voters typically go for the incumbent when it comes to judicial races."

"Mom, let's hope you're right."

NINETY

By early afternoon, Suzanne broke away from the frenzy of her campaign and swung by the office. Her dad offered to take Riley to get a much needed hair cut while she returned some calls.

"He's a good kid, Suzanne. I'm not sure you're going to crack his nut as quickly as you had hoped, but over time things will happen. For now, more than anything he needs a strong concerned male role model in his life. How about if I send your mother back home and I stay another week or so to help you with the transition?"

"Really, Dad? What about the club?"

"Your phone works, doesn't it? I haven't taken more than a long weekend in years. Beside that, Luther owes me for the extra time I gave him when his kid was born. He can run things for a few days. I think you two need me more here than they do there."

Andi looked up from a busy desk full of telephone messages, courier packages and half-opened mail.

"What in the world are you doing here?"

"I know, I know, but Andi, this was the only place I could count on not running into Rotherman. If I have to fake nice one more time, I'll die."

"Turns out, it's a good thing you're a workaholic. You've got a stack of messages stuck on your chair."

"You saw today's —

"I did. It'll be old news tomorrow, Judge."

"Yeah, I guess you have a point."

"Judge, I transferred a message that came in on the main line over the weekend. Be sure to listen to it before you leave. And Judge, don't worry, God has a plan for you. All you have to do is follow his lead."

"Thanks, Andi. Lord knows I'm trying not to second guess his plan. That's the main reason I have such a hard time getting John up on the dance floor. I'm not good at the following the lead."

Suzanne escaped into her chambers and shut the door. She played her voicemail.

"Judge Vincent, I'm not sure you'll remember me, you got so many cases. This is Bethany Lovejoy. I never thanked you for the money. You're the only one it could've been from, I figured. If it's not too late, I'd like to help out with your campaign to say thanks."

No sane candidate turns away campaign volunteers. Suzanne jotted down the girl's number and called her volunteer coordinator to go pick her up. The last shift of poll watchers and precinct campaigners was gathering at her headquarters at 3 p.m. to rally with their candidate and get last minute instructions from Oliver.

"Hey, Judge Vincent."

"Hi Bethany, you're looking well."

Bethany Lovejoy had let her hair grow out, the cut from her boss's ring on her cheek had healed completely and she was glowing.

"Things are coming along. Thanks to you and Mr. Nelson, I've got my certificate and a job in this public dental clinic downtown. I even got a boyfriend, now. He's a commercial truck driver."

"Oh, that's wonderful. I knew you could do it, Bethany. I'm so proud of you!"

"Wanna see a picture of Dami? He's getting so big."

"What a cutie! It was sweet of you to call and offer to help us today."

"When I save up enough money and Dami gets to be a little older, I was thinking of maybe going to Georgia State and then to law school. You think I might be able to do that?"

"Absolutely. That would be wonderful. Speaking of the little guy, where is he?"

"She's taking care of him for me."

"She, as in Mrs. Wainwright?"

"Yes, ma'am. I didn't tell her what I had to do, cuz she'd probably be busy then. She's funny like that, you know?"

Boy, do I.

NINETY-ONE

T he rollercoaster ups and downs of Election Day had Suzanne literally sick to her stomach. Unlike her volunteers, she hadn't eaten and the fatigue of the long, stressful day was setting in. Stuck between a shouting match involving her loyal campaign workers and Rotherman's last minute say-anything-to-earn-a-few-bucks-recruits, in the parking lot of a school in Southwest Atlanta, proved to be the last conceivable straw.

"D-I-T-C-H V-I-N-C-E-N-T, R-O-T-H-E-R-M-A-N I-S W-O-R-T-H A

C-H-A-N-C-E!"

"V-I-N-C-E-N-T V-I-N-C-E-N-T!" Dana hollered back.

"Bitch, you better get the hell out of my way," commanded Rotherman's campaign worker. "This is my spot. Who you think you are coming up here at the last minute waving your ghetto sign in my face?"

"Who you calling a bitch?" Dana looked ready to punch the competition out. Suzanne motioned to Dana to walk away, pick another spot. The last thing she needed was a fist fight. Voters would be turned off easily by such nonsense.

A WSB-TV news truck pulled into the parking lot and a reporter named Mark Winne jumped out. Suzanne turned the other way, hoping to avoid an interview. The station was famous for its breaking stories and Suzanne was not in the mood to be its latest break. He began interviewing voters on their way in and out of the precinct. Winne stopped to speak with one of her volunteers, who proudly pointed in her direction. *Two more hours and the polls will be closed.*

"Judge Vincent, Mark Winne," the senior reporter called from across the lawn. "Have a word with you?"

"Of course."

Suzanne politely waited for him. As he approached her, she noticed how much younger he looked in person than on television. Winne extended his hand.

"Care to make any comment about your opponent's press conference?"

"Which one are you referring to?"

"He does like press conferences, doesn't he? Did you know he held one at four this afternoon right out front of the courthouse?"

"No. I don't suppose he had anything new to say, did he, Mr. Winne?"

"He formally called for your resignation, citing a number of situations which he termed, uh, let me get my notes here, uh, scandalous was the word."

The veteran reporter stuck his writing pad back into his jacket pocket.

"Mr. Winne, are you familiar with the legal phrase: *res ipsa loquitir.*"

"Sure thing, that's the tort principle meaning the thing speaks for itself."

"Bingo. Let's go off the record for just a moment."

"As you wish, Your Honor."

"Mr. Winne, I'm about as far removed from being scandalous as Chance Rotherman is from being a black woman trapped in a white man's body."

"Off the record, you say?"

"Here's a real news tip straight from the courthouse: Recently an exotic dancer named Escobar Secret came to see me. She's listed in the telephone directory should you want to confirm what I'm about to tell you. She dances at Headlamps, that adult establishment owned by Chief Judge Sam Haskell's cousin. About two weeks ago, Ms. Secret filed a paternity action against Chance Rotherman in Atlanta District Court. In addition to the two children featured on Mr. Rotherman's website, according to DNA testing he now has a two month old son who he has not acknowledged. The case has been assigned to Haskell and the first hearing was supposed to be held today, but conveniently has been continued until sometime next month. You will not find the case file containing all of the juicy details in the Clerk's Office because the file is now sealed. I assume Rotherman approached Haskell ex parte and asked him to keep all of this off of the radar screen until he gets through the election."

"Got it – I wish all of my sources were as clear and to the point, Judge."

"And I wish I was on the bench listening to a case."

"That's what makes life interesting, Judge, the unpredictability factor. Good luck, Judge Vincent!"

"Thanks."

"Where's the victory party going to be?"

"McKinney & Lasley, 49th Floor of the Crickman Consortium Building at 14th and Peachtree, 8 o'clock. We'd love to have you stop by."

"Maybe, I will. Right now, I need to try to get this story on the 6 o'clock News."

Ninety-Two

"I never should have applied, Oliver. Nobody could've convinced me the day I sat in your office and you told me that the partnership had voted to invite me to join the firm that I wouldn't be spending my entire career with McKinney & Lasley. It was all I'd wanted ever since being a summer associate. And look what I did. Threw it all away and for what?"

"Don't waste time with regrets, Suzanne. The numbers don't look good, but you have nothing to be sorry about or ashamed of. You're a dynamite candidate. You're attractive, articulate and you have integrity. Most importantly, you're one hell of a judge and a much better person than I. And you slammed Rotherman at the GABWA forum. I was so proud of you."

"Rotherman wouldn't let up. I had to do something. You were right, though, I waited too long to respond."

"It would be nice if politics could be won by playing fair. That isn't reality. However, Judge, we need to get you back to your supporters. There are a lot of people here tonight. At the very least, please enjoy yourself. You've worked hard during the campaign. Go downstairs and eat some shrimp. You can even have a drink. The reception is my gift, so don't worry about us overrunning our campaign budget."

"Oliver, how generous. I won't be ever able to thank you enough for guiding me through the campaign, and for just being my friend."

"It's been my pleasure. No matter what happens, don't change. You're a classy lady about to find out what it's like to try to juggle your career with family responsibilities. I'd never thought I'd get the opportunity to be a father. With our baby on the way, I'm ready to pull up a bit and make time for what's really important – family."

"Me too, Oliver, me too."

"I'm going to run downtown to the Tabulation Room, where they compute and canvass the returns. We'll talk again in about an hour. Let's not give up, it's way too early. The Southside precincts are always the slowest to report. Now show me that California sunshine smile of yours." Suzanne grinned, feeling better after her chat with Oliver. "If the voters fall for Rotherman's road show, then they don't deserve you and will get what they vote for. But I think we'll pull through."

Suzanne, with John at her side, spent the next couple of hours personally thanking everyone who'd come out for the evening and periodically checking on her mother who was content to sit at a table and take in the exquisite surroundings and lively crowd. She'd asked her father to stay at home with Riley. Shortly after ten, Oliver pulled Suzanne aside. One look at him and she knew.

"Suzanne, it's very close. 50.8 per cent to our 49.2 per cent. It doesn't look like we're going to be able to pull it off." She gasped. "I think you better go ahead and address the crowd. It's getting late. Allow for some wiggle room; tell them things may look different in the morning."

With John and her mother, her staff, Bethany, Oliver and so many others watching and clapping, Judge Suzanne Vincent conceded the race. It was the hardest two minute speech of her career. She got through it, just like she got through the dark days of December 1988, the past eighteen years of wondering about the son she reluctantly gave up for adoption and the twists and dips of the past year. When finished, she excused herself to make the phone call every incumbent dreads having to make.

"Chance, this is Suzanne Vincent."

"To what do I owe this call?"

"I called to congratulate you. Our tabulators are telling us you've won. We'll speak a little later regarding the....uh, transition."

"You have more fight in you than I'd expected."

EPILOGUE

Suzanne lit one final candle and dimmed the overhead lighting in her bathroom leaving just a trace of artificial light. Relaxing music was playing softly in the background and a glass of chardonnay was waiting for her on the ledge surrounding the porcelain tub. She took a long sip of the wine before wrapping her hair and tying it down tightly with a scarf. Suzanne moaned as she slid down into the hot, bubble bath. The aromatic, sweet scent from the candles surrounding the bathtub filled the room. For several minutes Suzanne lay still in the warm water with her eyes closed as her knotted shoulders and lower back muscles began to relax and the stress from her long day temporarily departed. Her mother had told her when she and Riley had flown out for Thanksgiving that in order to be able to take care of others, she needed to take care of herself.

Even after her bath she was still too wound up to fall asleep. Suzanne picked up a book and settled in her rocker. Not long thereafter she heard the floor creak. Riley was standing in her doorway. Suzanne smiled and pulled together the top of her velour robe.

"Uh, you busy?" Riley asked, his low monotone voice barely audible.

"No, not at all," Suzanne replied. "I wasn't ready to go to sleep, so I decided to do a little reading." She folded the book sleeve over the first few pages and closed the book, setting it aside on the antique trunk next to her chair. "Come on in, what's up?"

"There's, uh, somethin' I wanna show you," Riley said, shoving his hands down in his pockets.

"Okay," Suzanne waited, unsure what he wanted her to do.

"Can you come downstairs?"

"Sure."

Suzanne followed Riley down the stairs. As they neared the bottom steps, she breathed in the smell of fresh pine. Out of the corner of her eye, she caught a stream of flickering light. Riley turned left walking through the dining room to the living room and stopped abruptly behind the love seat facing the balcony window.

Suzanne stepped around Riley's tall frame to see what he was referring to. She took a long gaze across the living room to where their Christmas tree stood. Riley had found the perfect spot for the tiffany angel and had planted it in the small garden of delicate branches at the very top of the illuminated evergreen. Suzanne smiled, looking up at her son, himself almost as tall as the tree.

His efforts as a seven year old boy to please his foster mother were misjudged. And other bumps and bruises followed him as he made his way home. Having endured a long, lonely, difficult eighteen-year journey, Riley was not an impressionable child anymore. The lanky teen with the dark brown eyes and pecan brown skin broke through his angst over holiday hype and boldly risked another effort at bringing joy to a mother – this time his own flesh and blood.

"I figured you couldn't reach it, that's why you left it in the box."

"I couldn't do it. John is usually here to do it. I was going to ask him to put it up when he comes for dinner tomorrow."

"Uh, you got this funny look on your face right now."

"It's called being surprised, son."

"Yeah, I've seen you look that way before."

"Oh, when?"

"Remember when Mr. Mason called and made me wake you up late on election night?"

"Yes, I do."

"When you were talking to him on the telephone that night, you had the same look on your face then."

"I simply couldn't believe it when he told me that the final count showed that I had been reelected after all. That was outright shock, Riley. But you know what?"

"No, what?"

"No matter how wonderful that news was, nothing has brought me as much joy as finding you."

Suzanne's pleasure at his gesture was evident in her beaming face. Yet, deep in his mother's expressive eyes, Riley discerned her impatient pleas for something more. She yearned for his forgiveness and acceptance. It was too soon for Riley's response or commitment. There were no guarantees, and both of them knew that far too well. Mother and son were each at a better place. For the time being, that was enough.

ABOUT THE AUTHOR

G ail Tusan Washington has over twenty years of judicial service, including serving as a guest justice on the Georgia Supreme Court. Presently, she presides in the Family Division of the Superior Court of Fulton County. Previously, she served on the State Court of Fulton County and the City Court of Atlanta. She has lectured nationally and taught judges in Russia and the Philippines. Currently, she is a member of the faculty of the National Judicial College.

She has served as a member on the Georgia Commission on Family Violence, the Georgia Commission on Child Support and served as Chair of the Georgia's Supreme Court Commission on Continuing Lawyer Competency. She has served in leadership capacity on the boards of the Atlanta Legal Aid Society, Camp Fire USA Georgia, Georgia Association of Black Women Attorneys, Judicial Sections of the Atlanta and Gate City Bar Associations, Legal Clinic for the Homeless, Buckhead Cascade City Chapter,

The Links, Incorporated, National Conference of Christians and Jews and the YWCA of Greater Atlanta.

Her numerous awards include the Peace and Justice Service Award bestowed by the Martin Luther King Jr. Center for Nonviolent Social Change, and being recognized as one of Georgia's Most Influential Women (Top 50) and the YWCA's Academy of Women Achievers.

She has served as a "Judicial Expert" on the *Montel Williams Show,* helped create the Atlanta cable television show, Legally Speaking, and has appeared as WSB Channel 2's Noonday Show *"Legal Expert."*

Gail lives in Atlanta with her husband, Carl, and their four children, Ashley, Shannon, Lauren and Colin.

Learn more at www.gailtusanwashington.com.

Printed in the United States
104513LV00003B/127/A

9 781434 350206